Praise for Lil

"Darkly compelling, fascinatingly unique. Lilith Saintcrow offers a breathtaking, fantastic ride."

—*NYT* bestselling author Gena Showalter

"In the *Watchers* series, Saintcrow writes stories that are almost always nonstop action from beginning to end. Her women are kick-ass strong, her men ruggedly handsome and dedicated to the women they serve. It isn't a bad combination at all."

—*CJReading*

"I read *Dark Watcher* with growing delight. As chapter followed chapter, I never quite knew what was around the corner."

—*eBook Reviews*

". . . a one-of-a-kind author."

—*Romantic Times magazine* on To Hell and Back

"The story will keep you on the edge of your seat. . . ."

—*KD Did It Edits* on *The Demon's Librarian*

Of Dante Valentine . . .

"Dark fantasy has a new heroine . . ."

—*SFX* magazine

"Saintcrow snares readers with an amazing alternate reality that is gritty, hip and dangerously mesmerizing."

—*Romantic Times* magazine

"She's a brave, charismatic protagonist with a smart mouth and a suicidal streak. What's not to love?"

—*Publishers Weekly*

Books by Lilith Saintcrow

The Watchers

Dark Watcher

Storm Watcher

Fire Watcher

Cloud Watcher

Mindhealer

Finder

Sons of Ymre

The Sons of Ymre: Erik

Other Titles

The Society

The Demon's Librarian

Sons of Ymre

Erik

by

Lilith Saintcrow

IMAJINN

ImaJinn Books

Sons of Ymre

Erik

by

Lilith Saintcrow

IMAJINN

ImaJinn Books

IMAJINN

ImaJinn Books
PO BOX 300921
Memphis, TN 38130
Print ISBN: 978-1-61026-172-2

ImaJinn Books is an Imprint of BelleBooks, Inc.

Published in the United States of America.

ImaJinn Books was founded by Linda Kichline.

We at ImaJinn Books enjoy hearing from readers. Visit our websites
ImaJinnBooks.com
BelleBooks.com
BellBridgeBooks.com

10 9 8 7 6 5 4 3 2 1

Cover design: Debra Dixon
Interior design: Hank Smith
Photo/Art credits:
Man (manipulated)© Aleksandr Zamuruev | Dreamstime.com
Banner © Jaguarwoman Designs

:Lysd:01:

Dedication

To Brenda Chin, for just going with it.

Part One: The Potential

Bad Date

IT WAS THE LAST bad date she would ever have, but Liv Stellack didn't know it at the time. If she had, she probably wouldn't have allowed it to go on so long.

Or she might have decided to stick with it, considering the after-party.

As it was, though, the guy had a strike against him as soon as they sat down and he sent the hostess off for drinks. It was a Friday, just after Thanksgiving, and Liv had left the office early, but she was already wishing she'd stayed home.

"I prefer to order for myself," she said, gazing levelly over her menu. "And I don't like white wine."

The Hobson was downtown, its restaurant heavy with leather booths, expensive light fixtures, and whiskey tastings on the weekends. It had sounded like a great idea except for the cigar bar, but that section was well behind glass double doors and only the faintest tinge of smoke crept into the dining area.

"Really?" Neal—his last name was forgettable, but at least he'd put it in his online handle instead of choosing something stupid—gave her what he probably thought was a very charming grin. Nice shoulders, good suit, his dark hair a little long on the top and mussed artistically just the slightest bit, he ticked all the boxes. He'd held the front door for her too, that preferred first move of chauvinists and gentlemen the world over. Even his chat game was on-point—they'd texted, pretty agreeably, for about a week now. "I thought all girls liked white wine."

"Not this one." She attempted a smile, deciding she'd give him one last chance. Maybe he was just nervous; even an attorney used to verbal sparring could be tongue-tied or anxiety-rude outside the courtroom. "What are you having?" Maybe if she got him distracted about his *own* decisions he'd leave her alone to make hers.

"Steak. You want the farmer's salad; it's good for you."

I'd prefer the lemon chicken, thanks. She leaned back in her chair, examining him. Well, he'd *seemed* nice over chat, but you could never tell until they got right in front of you. "I said I'd order for myself, Neal."

"Women's lib." He grinned, showing expensively capped teeth probably whitened once or twice a year. "Speaking of which, I'm glad you didn't dress up. You don't need it."

Well, this particular grey dress had a decent neckline and long sleeves to keep her from freezing to death; that was the same reason she'd worn tights and her beloved grey pashmina. She'd even put her hair up to balance out the rest of the ensemble.

The words even stung for a bare moment before she realized the technique—the bastard was negging her, for God's sake.

As if she didn't get enough of that at work. "Thanks." She decided a taste of semi-insult could be good for the gander, too. "I'm glad you didn't dress up either. We can be slobs together."

His jaw loosened; he stared at her over the table for a few moments, blue eyes narrowed. A woman under thirty might have mistaken that look for interest. "Uh. Yeah, I guess."

Well, now she knew. Liv was batting zero once more. *You have to try, at least*, her friends said. She'd agreed, grudgingly, once Mika pointed out a four-year dry spell after the man who had been Liv's college steady took a surprise solo vacation to Cancun and popped the question to someone else entirely was long enough.

She'd gone along with the great roulette spin of online dating because her buddies meant well, especially Mika. But her bestie was a perpetual optimist, even when it came to men. Usually it balanced out Liv's caution nicely.

When it misfired, though, it was a doozy.

The whole thing was depressing, but not nearly as bad as actually dating this guy would be—and now she was old enough to know *that*, too. Maybe their text sessions hadn't been as nice as she'd thought; he always brought the conversation around to himself, but men were just like that. It was the cost of doing business, so to speak.

I should have ordered some DVDs. Or a new vibrator. Anything but this. "So, do you come here often?" What was the earliest graceful exit she could make? Maybe she'd have to suffer through an entire meal. Was it acceptable to ghost him after drinks?

And if it wasn't acceptable, did she care?

"No, actually. First time." The little double-blink he gave at the end of the sentence said he was lying; even a lowly paralegal could tell as much. "The, uh, the reviews are great. So where do you wanna go after dinner?"

After dinner was never part of the deal, sir. "I haven't decided yet," she said, diplomatically enough. He'd probably been lying about taking art history classes in the evenings, too.

"It's a Friday." The charming smile had returned, smooth and seamless. "We should go clubbing. You like that?"

I love dancing. But not with this guy, she was thinking. Besides, clubs were sonic assaults full of date-rape drugs and pushy men, and she'd been glad to leave them behind halfway through college. "Maybe," she hedged, just as help arrived from an unexpected quarter.

As in, the waitress saved her. "Here we are." A sprite in black and white, with a dyed-black pixie cut and a set, professional smile, the young woman held a pad of probably unnecessary paper with a pen poised at just the right angle. She rattled off the specials with the ease of long practice. "Would you like some appetizers?"

Neal didn't even ask, rattling right into ordering steak for himself and "the farmer's salad for the lady," with a wink and an ingratiating grin. Liv set her jaw and answered the waitress's inquiring glance with the merest fraction of a shrug.

"Excuse me," she said, barely waiting for Neal to finish talking—he wanted to order dessert as well, for God's sake, and thought port would go nicely with it. "Where's your restroom?"

"Oh, the regular one's being cleaned." The pixie nodded sagely, pointing down a short hall ending in a pair of swinging doors. "It's this way; I'll show you."

"Thanks." If Liv could get up before the waitress left, Neal would be forced to sit here and wait, since he had arrogated the right and duty of ordering. Social judo wasn't just for the predators in the room. "Excuse me, Neal. I just need to check my lipstick. Won't take but a moment."

"Okay." Neal reached for his wineglass, settling back in his chair with an indulgent gesture. It clearly never crossed his mind to wonder why his date hadn't brought a coat, just the pashmina—and why she was still wearing said shawl inside.

"I'll show you," the waitress repeated. Her nametag read *Fiona*, and she looked every inch of it. Her hips moved with an aggressive switch that was part youthful exuberance and all business; Liv hid a smile.

Past the swinging door with its round portholes was a short hall, clearly not meant for customers since the floor was bare, polished concrete. Fiona beckoned her through, and as soon as it swung closed she was all business. "Go all the way down and to the left; there's the stairwell. If you go right just outside the door, the alley will take you to

Sixteenth. You want me to call you a cab?"

"Nah, I've got it, thanks," Liv muttered. Bostwick's was only a block or two north of here, and she could hide in the smoking section if Jada or Lou were on duty. Either of them would find this hilarious and pour her a shot to take the edge off; college buddies laboring under the same student loan debt and depressed hiring market were a fantastic resource. "You must see a lot of these."

"At least he didn't put anything in your drink," Fiona said cheerfully. "We had another one of *those* last week. I hope she presses charges."

I guess this guy just didn't have time. "Me too. Thank you." Liv dug for the cash she'd intended as a rideshare tip and pressed it into the woman's hand. "Put that order in before he realizes I'm gone."

"You know it." A laugh, a wink, and Fiona was gone, the swinging door giving a tired wheeze on its hinges.

The stairwell exit did indeed give onto an alley, and it even appeared fairly clean—at least, she hoped it was. Early winter dusk had crawled over the city, and it just might have been too cold to smell anything rotting. It was, however, dark as sin, and she set off for the gleam of passing headlights and shimmering streetlamps to her right. A hum of traffic whispered down the alley's throat, and she shivered as she wrapped her pashmina and yanked pins free of her chignon. Her hair would keep her neck warm.

Halfway through, she heard a clatter. She glanced uneasily to her left—the alley grew another leg there, and voices floated past the bend. Probably another kitchen; the Hobson wasn't the only restaurant in the Wellington Building or the Haze Mutual skyscraper next door.

Liv turned hard right; once she was out of the circle of incandescent light from the fixture over the Hobson's stairwell door she had to blink hard, her eyes adjusting with reticence. She'd read somewhere it took about twenty minutes to really get your night vision on.

Pretty soon she'd be home with a pint of ice cream and her phone, bringing everyone up to date on the current fiasco. It would make great self-deprecating fodder to trot out the next time anyone started making *let's set Livvie up* noises. Especially Mika, who had made it her personal quest to bring Liv to a more perfect union, so to speak.

I just want to see you happy, Mika would chirp. Well, that was a noble cause, but Liv was beginning to think spinsterhood was the golden path to that hallowed state of being.

For one thing, it meant you didn't have to share a bed *or* clean up anything other than your own bathroom mess.

"And to think," Liv murmured as she picked her way cautiously down the alley, "they have a whole separate exit for girls to escape before drinks." It was a good story, one she could deploy over mimosas at Sunday brunch, and she grinned with satisfaction. The minor business of blocking Neal's number—and ritualistically swearing off dating apps—could wait until she was home in her pajamas, too.

The only fly in the ointment was her heels, definitely not meant for this type of urban rambling. She kept to what seemed the driest portion of pavement, and wished she was home already. This was a killer outfit, and she wasn't even that cold since the striped tights were insulated, but she should have worn boots.

No, she wasn't shivering, but she *was* unsettled. And who wouldn't be, sashaying down a downtown alley after dark?

It was a very *long* alley, too. Thankfully, her footsteps didn't echo against the brick walls; still, she wondered how long it would take for Neal to come looking for her. Assuming he could be torn away from his goddamn white wine.

Who drank that stuff, especially with bourbon around? Liv shivered, snuggling her chin into the pashmina. A thin thread of anxiety wormed through her chest, banishing any amusement at the prospect of telling her crew about this failed date.

Later, she would wonder if somehow, some dormant part of her had known.

As it was, when the light of Sixteenth Street dimmed ahead, Liv's chin came up and she froze, caught between one step and the next. There was a sound like a rubber tire ripping from its wheel and a sudden wave of nauseating stench so bad she almost reeled. It hit the back of her throat like a Jagerbomb and she gagged, catching her balance and standing, stock-still, trembling in her pretty grey suede heels.

What the hell? Gooseflesh poured down her back.

"*Civilian*!" someone yelled; something hit her from the side. One of her shoes went flying, and so did she—right into the Wellington Building's ample, brick-buttressed ass.

A brief, starry jolt of pain, like hitting a rock and soaring over the handlebars of her beloved Huffy Pink Princess when she was eleven. She hadn't broken anything or even chipped a tooth, both common side effects of bike wrecks she was glad to have avoided later, but she *had* come back to consciousness lying face down and stunned on a grassy verge, her bike's wheels spinning lazily as it lay on its side, a beached sea creature.

Liv surfaced only briefly, hearing a deep, throbbing growl and another shout, a clattering and that awful smell swallowing her once more.

It was undoubtedly a mercy, for the shadowbeast would have eaten her whole.

Born That Way

"DUMBASS." JAKE stamped on the shadowbeast's skull again, was rewarded with a splattering crunch. His blond hair glowed in a random reflection of streetlight; the rest of the alley was beginning to fill up with reflected lumens now that the beast wasn't exhaling foulness, masking while it hunted. "Erik? How we doing?"

How do you think? It was useless to reply with sarcasm; such things bounced right off his little brother. Erik hissed an exhale, probing his shredded shoulder with careful fingertips. The thing had attempted to shake him like a ragdoll, not caring that a Son's blood would be poisonous to it. They usually weren't so willing to stay and fight.

It must have been extraordinarily hungry, or found high-value prey.

Erik had expected the prey to be something else from the underside, but it wasn't. Instead, a fucking civilian had waltzed right across the thing's path. Which was odd.

Or at least, that's all he thought before the entire world changed between one breath and the next. He sank into a crouch, clutching his shoulder, driving his fingers in deeper to test the pain. Yeah, it hurt, and he was in for more if the thing was venomous. His veins would burn for the next six hours while he metabolized. He was ready to wipe the civilian's memory and make sure it got home safe before his eyes adapted again and his shoulder gave another flare. *Ow. Son of a . . . wait. Wait just a goddamn minute.*

The pain receded and a strange tingling warmth took its place, working in through the wound. Erik's mouth fell open, and he stared for a few moments before bringing his jaw back up with a snap. "Uh, Jake?"

His Younger Brother was busy stamping on the thing's malformed head again, muttering obscenities. Jake's blood was up, and that was a bad sign.

He was getting touchier and touchier out on patrol these days. They both were, and Erik thought it likely the voices in Jake's head were intensifying.

Just like the persistent soft whisper inside his own. Erik clamped his fingers on his shoulder again, hoping for a burst of steadying agony. It hurt, yeah—but the pain was rapidly fading. He blinked, and his heart—if a Son of Ymre could be said to have anything other than a metronome cardiac muscle ticking off the slow slide into insanity—did something like a triple backflip before settling into its usual postcombat *thunkadunk.* "What the *shit*?" he muttered.

A woman. Nice grey wool dress, knee-length, long-sleeved, a ballerina neckline. A pretty grey cashmere pashmina, well-loved and dry-cleaned, knocked almost clean off her. One of her feet was bare—or at least, covered only by those striped tights, a strange choice but the verticals made her legs look like they went on forever. She had a mop of wavy darkish hair, strands moving under a cold breeze from the alley mouth.

Where the hell had she come from? They'd driven the shadowbeast in here because it was off the main drag and nicely deserted.

"What the fuck?" Jake had stopped stamping, and drifted up on his brother's nine o'clock. He peered over Erik's shoulder. "Is it dead?"

You'd better hope not. "Uh, nope. Still breathing." Erik sighed. "How you feeling?" It had been a busy night so far, all sorts of underside bastards coming out to play in the rain and the long winter dark.

And this explained why.

"What? Like I just got the shit kicked out of me all the way from here to. . ." Jake trailed off. "Huh."

"Yeah." Erik exhaled softly as his shoulder finished healing. The flesh twitched, closing itself and expelling toxins in a thin dribble soaking into layers of cloth—thermal shirt, body armor, hoodie, leather jacket for even more bulk and a first wall of protection. The venom would eat through everything but the leather and Kevlar. Thin threads of acrid steam rose as it kept consuming, but it was a lot less virulent now. Another soft burst of warmth was teasing it away, drawing the steam out to vanish harmlessly into the night. "It's her."

"You have *got* to be shitting me." Jake pushed against his shoulder, peering at the crumpled form. "Seriously?"

"I am seriously not shitting you." Erik's pulse was down out of the redline, but he still felt a little woozy. It had to be shock added to the poison—sure, shock, and not at all the idea that one of them—or the shadowbeast—could have easily battered this small, fragile creature beyond repair, and *that* would have been extremely bad luck. More tingling warmth spread from his shoulder, creeping through his bloodstream. "You don't feel that?"

"Oh, I feel it all right." Jake sounded grim. He crouched too, a lazy, supple motion, and ran his hands through his hair. A slight crackle of spent power cleaned muck and sweat away; his little brother liked to wash off between battles. "You go first then, I guess."

"What?" Erik never bothered to clean up before getting home. Why get rid of the filth when there was more waiting just around the corner? Getting scraped and dry at the end of the night was the one ritual he *liked.*

"I'll keep watch." Jake shifted a fraction, bumped his shoulder. It was a rough, welcome reminder of affection. "You go ahead, seal her up."

Oh. Erik shook his head slightly. "I'm not going to."

"What, you think *I* should, first?" Younger Brother's laugh didn't quite echo down the alley, but it was close. "Didn't think you were the sharing type."

No, you idiot. I'm not, but that's not the point. "I'm not going to rape her, Jake."

"It's not rape." He sounded baffled that Erik would even suggest such a thing; the inoculation a *lirai* could provide against the god's voice required deep physical closeness and intent from one or both parties, not necessarily desire or even affection. "It's a *lirai.*" As if he had just verified for himself that the woman was, indeed, one of the Dreamers in living flesh.

No wonder the underside had been out to play. Even as mere potentials untriggered by the Flame, *lirai* were good snacks for a wide variety of things. "She's knocked out." And that was Erik's fault—he'd hit her hard enough to break delicate human bones. "Besides, apparently anyone could come down here at any moment; it's a regular old freeway. We'll take her home."

"Oh, you want to make points with Father?" Jake snorted. "That'll be nice. I'm sure he'll be touched."

"No, goddammit." Erik gave his little brother a long, considering sidelong glance. "I can't believe you think I'd actually do that in an alley."

"It's not rape, *goddammit.*" Jake mimicked his tone, right down to the slight pause after *god.* "It's a *lirai*, it's insurance, and you're closer to the edge than I am. That's all I meant. Besides, sooner or later . . ."

Sooner or later she'd have to choose a seal, yeah. More than one, if she was powerful enough, or if losing her protectors to the underside bothered her. "Then she'll decide, and she'll be conscious for it." *Not to mention consenting.*

"You're gonna regret that." Jake didn't need to say more. What woman—let alone a *lirai*—would choose Erik, with his blond, easy little brother around? "I'm just sayin'."

"Yeah, well." Erik rocked a little, keeping his muscles nice and warm in case some-damn-thing *else* happened. "See if you can find her shoe, huh?"

"Oh, my lady's *shoe* has gone missing?" Jake didn't quite roll his eyes, but it was close. "The tragedy."

"She's got to vanish without a trace." There were no cameras high on the brick walls, but he still checked. The one over a restaurant's back door, before the alley made a hard ninety-degree turn and went past a kitchen in the bottom of the skyscraper next door, was pointed down to catch whoever was exiting, that was all. Maybe she was taking a shortcut? Or she'd gotten lost?

Yet another thing that didn't matter. Outside the range of that electronic eye, the brothers and their new treasure were safe enough.

"You knocked her right out of her heels." Jake found that funny. At least, he laughed, like a good Younger Brother providing amusement and hijinks to help an elder hold on. "Man, you are something else."

"Born that way," Erik muttered. He eased forward, taking in what he could of the woman. That dark hair was in a real tangle. He wondered if she was pretty. Not like it mattered much, once she'd been given to the Flame she'd be well-nigh irresistible. "Lucky lady, huh? Gonna wake up like Sleeping Beauty and get everything she ever wanted."

Nothing was too good for a *lirai*. The fact that the vast mass of humanity was unconscious of the debt everything on this spinning rock owed to the Dreamers just meant those who *did* know had to pay double.

Or more.

"I'm sure she's real grateful." Jake obviously couldn't help himself. He kept laughing, and fished a grey suede heel out of a pile of damp black plastic garbage bags on the other side of the alley. "God *damn*, man, right out of her shoes. It's meant to be. A modern fairytale."

"You're an asshole," Erik said, but not very loudly. He brushed aside some of her hair, wondering what she did for a living. Was she meeting someone? The silky strands clung to his fingers, and he was suddenly very aware that he was painted in underside sludge, blood, and various other things. What the fuck was she doing in a rancid alley after dark?

What mattered was getting her to the temple before she woke up. Once she was inside those walls and Father was alerted, things could take their natural course.

He spread his hand over her shoulder and let a little tingle of power slip across the gap and into her. If he hadn't already known she was *lirai*, it would have been confirmed by even a cursory touch. The radiation effect crawled up his arm, narcotic honey, and there didn't seem to be any internal injuries. It was a moment's work to get the *lirai* over his shoulder. He'd have to go slowly, but Jake would watch his six and engage any hostiles. A nice early evening jog across rooftops, with a bouncing, deadweight burden.

At least she wasn't throwing up, or screaming. Small mercies—the only kind a Son ever got.

*

THE GREY STONE bulk of the Islington frontier temple was easily reached if they paralleled the freeway, and they were back too early for a finished patrol. Which meant lean iron-haired Ignatius met them in the great hall, his hands behind his back as he paused on the main staircase, right on the landing where the two separate flights met like a pair of stately, dusty, red-carpeted rivers. A bust of Pallas Athena glowed, staring over his head with the set look of a *lirai* listening to the Flame.

"Father." Erik halted, snapped to attention—or at least, as well as he could with an unconscious woman over his shoulder. Jake gave a crisp salute, no doubt his own little joke. "We found a *lirai*."

Ignatius did not move for several moments. Beneath the dusty black of his cassock lingered body armor and one or two little surprises; the lone Father of a frontier temple often stayed at home ready for a call from higher up, but that did not mean he was unready.

Ever.

"Yep, just happened across her in an alley," Jake added. "What are the chances, huh? Erik knocked her right out of her *shoes*."

"She was in the way," Erik muttered, and wished he could elbow his Younger Brother.

Father didn't like chatter.

Ignatius's pale eyes—very similar to Jake's, though all three of them were orphans—narrowed slightly. "And is she sealed?" he inquired, in his driest, most passionless tone.

That took the wind out of Jake, but probably not for long. "Nosir," he said. "Erik said to bring her home."

If there was a punishment involved in that particular judgment call,

Erik wouldn't have wanted his Younger to suffer it anyway. Still, it rankled a bit. "No internal injuries, sir, but she came across a shadow-beast. Looked like a leaper; it had a pelt and non-venomous claws but its bite was otherwise. It stood its ground."

"Ah." Ignatius nodded. "Very good, then." He descended the rest of the stairs, his step soundless despite heavy boots. "And you are certain she is of the Dreamers?"

"Yes, sir." *Come on over and take a look*, was what Erik wanted to say, but that was a little past the line of obedience and good sense. Jake could probably say it, but then again, a little brother could say anything.

It was the perk of his position. Probably the only one, just like making the call when they were on their thankless grinding patrols was Erik's.

Ignatius halted only once, glancing quizzically at Erik, who realized what he wanted.

"Hey, Jake." He shifted a little but didn't want to let her slide free. Little brother got the girl off his shoulder, and that was when Erik finally saw the *lirai*'s face. She lolled, not so much deadweight now, her hair falling free in a long sheaf of tangled waves and outright curls. The humidity probably had something to do with that.

Strong nose, good cheekbones, her underlip a little fuller than the top one, charcoal eyebrows and long eyelashes. Vivid bruising crawled up her face, those lashes were fluttering as she tried to regain consciousness, and Erik was once more aware of how filthy he was. Her pashmina was never going to be the same, but at least it had kept her a little warmer.

Ignatius's narrow hand hovered over her closed eyes. The great ring on his left third finger glinted, a scintillant of the Flame trapped by a Dreamer's will in heavy, glassy hematite. A signet, a gift from another *lirai*, one with plenty of seals and a suite of their own, sending a Father out to cleanse the night. "Be at peace, Dreamer," he said, softly, and the woman was deadweight again. "There lieth a blessing."

"So it is," Erik murmured; Jake's ritual response came a half-second later, overtaking Erik's and finishing first, too. As usual.

"We will need to make arrangements." Ignatius glanced at Erik. "Take her to the smaller *liraim*. Jacob, come with me."

"Yessir." Jake unloaded her into Erik's arms with a wink. "Gonna make our Snow White nice and comfortable. Maybe she'll sing to the birds when she wakes up."

"Unlikely." But Father's mouth twitched slightly, as if he found the image amusing. Which meant Jake was doing his job. "Good work, lads.

We might survive this yet."

That'd be nice. Satellite temples had much higher casualty rates, since they didn't have a *lirai* or two inside to remind the Sons what they were fighting for. This city was too large for a mere trio to keep clean of garden-variety predators and the Mad God's faithful monsters.

Erik *still* couldn't salute, but Ignatius didn't expect him to, for once. Instead, the closest thing to a real parent Jake and Erik now had set off to the left, heading for his study, and Jake made a face before following, his boots leaving dark streaks on the foyer's slate tile. Father wasn't going to be happy about that, but Erik wasn't going to try to ameliorate that shit as an Elder Brother should. Not right now.

Instead, he looked at the woman's slack, bruised face. She was going to have a hard time with this, snatched from a relatively normal life and thrust into an entirely new, nightmarish world.

The fact that her new protectors would be able to at least visit a bigger temple for the first time in decades was beside the point, and the squeamish gratefulness Erik was doing his best not to feel at the prospect, was yet another sign that he wasn't a good person.

Then again, the good didn't survive the Mad God's mark or the Sons' training. You had to be a bastard to fight the nightmares of the underside.

"Don't worry," he muttered, though she couldn't possibly hear him. "Let's get you a little more comfortable, *lirai.* I'll take care of your face. Must hurt."

He knew, miserably, that she was going to hate him. Why bother fighting that particular losing battle?

Still, as he carried her up the stairs—thanking all the gods for enhanced musculature granted by the alien god whispering at the bottom of every Son's brain, because hauling around an adult's deadweight was no joke—he exhaled harshly, and a slight tingle of cleaning-sorcery crested over them both.

Being a Son had some benefits.

The power, not so incidentally, would add to the healing he'd poured into her body earlier to make sure she didn't have any critical injuries.

By the time he reached the second floor, the bruising on her face and ribs was going down. He could *feel* it, high-pitched waves of physical misery growing blunt and faraway. She'd still feel like shit when she woke up, but nothing was broken and she wouldn't have any visible hematomas.

Just the aches.

She was going to hate all of them except for maybe Jake, and after she was delivered safely to a bigger temple Erik would no doubt be reassigned to another satellite, fighting yet another series of losing battles until he died with his guts torn out in some filthy hole or alley like the one they'd found her in.

Still, another Dreamer would help hold back the tide. Maybe Ignatius's higher-ups would even grant their trio a break or two for finding their first potential. *Finally*, after all this time.

The woman's breathing was soft, scarcely detectable even with heightened senses, but her pulse was strong and sure. Whatever she'd been born as, she was *lirai* now, and once burnished by the Flame, her very presence would mute the Mad God's persistent cajoling whisper even more. Not to mention providing waves of incandescent force for Sons to beat back the monsters, expanding safe zones and making their long-ago victory fractionally deeper.

Just not total. But every potential rescued and Flame-triggered bought them a little more time.

And every Son, from the Fathers to the youngest, was well aware that was well worth fighting for.

Even if they were all damned.

Get to Work

UGH. AT FIRST LIV thought she simply had a massive, truly world-ending hangover. Which wasn't entirely out of the question after a bad date, but still, it . . . bothered her a bit. She didn't remember meeting the girls, or even getting home and putting out a Friday night drinking call. God as her witness, she'd intended to stop only for a couple consolatory shots and a cup of coffee at Bostwick's if one of her friends was there, before going home and diving into a carton of ice cream. How had she been talked into anything else?

God knew Mika could talk her into just about anything, though, as the date with a douchebag she'd met online proved beyond a doubt.

Liv's eyes were almost crusted shut, and her nose tickled, as if she was coming down with a cold. Great. Or, wait.

It was dust. She was smelling dust.

The second shock was rubbing at her eyes, opening them, and finding herself in a white cotton nightgown that wasn't hers, between threadbare but once very high-quality cotton sateen sheets that weren't hers, either. And, to top it all off, the bed, while being, of course, a total stranger as well, had the gall to be a curlicued wrought-iron thing straight off a Hammer movie set.

It was a nice enough room, if your taste ran to *not antique, just fucking old.* Thin misty winter sunlight poured through mullioned windows with panes of thick, wavy glass; there was a wardrobe that looked big enough to hold a couple Narnias, and there was an actual *vanity*, one Mae West would have called too restrained but secretly coveted, if only for the faded red velvet bench and beeswax-polished drawers.

Liv rubbed at her eyes again. *What. The ever-loving. Fuck.*

For the first time since college, she was just barely awake in a bedroom she didn't recognize at *all.* There was a bookshelf holding a bunch of dark, ancient spines frowning over a big leather easy chair, exactly the thing you'd want in front of a window on a rainy day. You could curl up in it and listen to the rain while napping or pretending to read; you could actually absorb a romance novel or do a bit of studying, too, if you had some hot chocolate or a good cup of tea.

That was a nice thought, and ordinarily she would have liked it a lot. But she ached all over, so badly she couldn't tell just *what* had happened to her, and she not only didn't recognize this place, it smelled like it hadn't been used for a while. Even the comforter was musty, though everything was painfully clean. Even the rugs on the hardwood—Persian if she ever saw one, or *really* good fakes—were worn down in patches that shouted *someone's actually used me.*

Two doors. Three if you counted the closet, pulled ajar so she could see a few desultory wooden hangers on a thick dark rod. The other slightly open door held a brighter gleam off tile and porcelain—a bathroom, probably.

That was good.

It was the third door that bothered her the most. The big, thick, heavy one that was probably the only way in or out unless you wanted to defenestrate. It was firmly closed, and she didn't like that.

Liv didn't like that at *all.*

First things first, though. She managed to get her legs free of the covers and shuffled barefoot for the bathroom, smoothing the sleeveless cotton nightgown with her palms. It wasn't dirty, but it wasn't hers, and it was way too long. She had to bunch up a good portion of the skirt to keep from tripping, for God's sake.

On the way there, she glanced out one of the wavering-glass windows, and *that* was bad news too. It was a long way down to old, winter-naked trees edging what looked like a university quad. Stone walls held ranks of other windows just like hers, and she stared for a few moments, trying to figure out how high up she was. At least three stories.

Great.

It could be fine. There could be a perfectly rational explanation for this. *Pee first, then assess the rest of the situation.*

The bathroom was relatively updated compared to the bedroom. At least, the plumbing looked reliable, even if the cast-iron tub could hold two of her along with the scrubbed-at rust stain dripping from the faucet—the handles were wheels, their spokes thick and polished satin-smooth. The water ran clear in the sink, though; the toilet was one of those chain-flush numbers, also running clear.

The next step was to try the door that had to lead to a hall. The knob was cut glass, gleaming and warm; she twisted it and was rewarded with a click. At first she tugged before noticing it wasn't usual—it swung *out*; she shook her head and pushed.

Nothing. Maybe it was blocked. She pushed harder.

Of course, if it opened out, the hinges would be in the hall so she couldn't get to them, and she wouldn't be able to hide behind it and brain someone when they brought her food.

If they brought her food.

Liv stood very still for a few moments. *Think, goddammit. Think very carefully.*

All she remembered was the alley, a hideous, overpowering smell, and then . . . something had hit her, right? It was definitely a kidnapping. Maybe they'd used chloroform? Maybe Neal had followed her?

It didn't matter, she told the panic beginning to squirrel-scratch behind her breastbone. Mika had probably already called the cops by now, since Liv definitely hadn't been home. All she had to do was survive long enough for them to find her. If Neal was behind this, he wasn't very bright. She'd forwarded his pic and profile link to at least two people *besides* Mika.

But if he wasn't stupid, if he'd planned for as much, well . . .

Either way, she needed to get moving. There was no sign of her clothes or her purse. It was idiotic, but her missing shoes irritated her almost past belief.

She'd loved those grey suede heels. Now she was probably never going to wear them again.

Liv put her back to the door and closed her eyes, listening. Nothing. It was absolutely silent except for a faint, ghostly dripping from the bathroom faucet. She couldn't tell from the window if the rest of the place was in disrepair; a place this size had to need landscapers and cleaning staff, right? It looked almost like a school.

Great. I'm trapped in Suburbia College. They take all your blood out and put in tofu instead.

A thin, pale laugh fell out of her mouth. It sounded good, like she was amused at the damn situation instead of fighting off steadily rising terror.

She didn't want to, but she opened her eyes. The water worked, did the power? There was an old-fashioned toggle switch by the door; she pushed it and was rewarded with golden glow, faint in the daytime but still very welcome, from a curlicued, glass-dripping overhead fixture.

So somebody paid the electric bill here, which meant there was a paper trail. Great news, but it didn't help her now.

This will be an amazing story to tell the girls once it's over. Right?

"Right," she muttered, and her gaze snagged on the half-open closet door again. No use—she couldn't get the clothes rod down without something to unscrew the ancient, disc-shaped holder. "So there I was, trapped in the fucking suburbs."

There was another rod in the empty, cedar-smelling wardrobe that could be lifted out. It was a good inch-plus dowel, nice and heavy since particle board wasn't a thing when that furniture had been made.

It would probably make short work of the window. Then she'd have to figure out a way down to the ground. The tree branches looked sharp—and very far away.

"So there I was . . ." Nah, she couldn't open like that. It would be too unbelievable. "Once upon a time, yours truly . . ." Oh, that was a good one. She'd start with that.

Liv prowled the room one more time, looking for more supplies, muttering bits of the story under her breath.

Then she got to work.

No Harm

FATHER AND JAKE were late returning, but he didn't mind. When they finally showed he was deep in shadow at the end of the hall, and didn't step free until Ignatius nodded.

You learned not to move until necessary, as a Son. Erik saluted, then stood at ease. "She's stopped breaking things." He pitched the words low and soft, even though the door at the far end glowed with a unidirectional baffle. Nothing outside would penetrate the small suite with its infinitely precious, infinitely fragile occupant. "But not swearing," he offered judiciously, just in case Ignatius wanted a full report.

"Modern women. She will hate one of us." Ignatius shook his head. "Easiest if it's me."

"If she was sealed—" Jake began.

"Your brother was right to refrain," Father continued, inflexibly, almost as if their younger hadn't spoken. "We follow the times, my sons. They do not follow us. Come."

Jake glanced at Erik, his eyebrows raised, and looked about one short second away from saying some bullshit Father would not find appropriate at all. Erik shook his head slightly, just the tiniest fraction.

Ignatius paused, his black-clad back to both his Sons. There was a painful, glass-crunching clatter from the smaller *liraim*—she was trying the windows, again. Hopefully she hadn't noticed how the damage sealed itself up, slowly but thoroughly.

Or maybe she had, and that was what triggered the steadily increasing volume of her cursing. Also, hopefully she hadn't managed to rip any of the glass free. Erik almost winced—Ignatius didn't like bad language.

But she was *lirai*. She could say whatever she liked, and do almost anything except escape her protectors. The trick would be showing her the new shape of the world in a way that didn't end up with her getting . . . well, even more terrified than she already was.

Ignatius paused before the door. The baffle folded aside, spent energy sinking into stone walls, wooden floor, the fabric of the door itself.

Ymre—not his name, but you never wanted to say *that* out loud—had granted his chosen hands great dominion over the underside, and their physicality was supposed to give him a foothold. Now, of course, they had the best of both worlds, physical *being* and invisible power. The mark on Erik's wrist gave a sharp twinge under the leather band used to hide its more . . . unappetizing movements, and Jake stiffened slightly.

He felt it too. If there was any chance they were mistaken, it was gone now. Not that Erik *could* be wrong about something like this, but still, it was comforting to know he hadn't kidnapped a civilian.

Well, *lirai* were all civilians to begin with, but still.

Ignatius turned the knob and swept the door open into the hall. Erik moved for entry but Jake, disregarding the protocol they'd followed a thousand times before, got through before him.

As a result, he was the one to get attacked first.

The girl had a great deal of time to work up some emotional pressure, and that was dangerous. It was a good thing she was merely a potential instead of fully awakened, or the blast of uncoordinated power might have given Jake some trouble.

As it was, Younger Brother caught the weapon as it descended—looked like she'd torn the clothes rod out of the wardrobe, smart girl—and twisted it free with almost no effort. If she'd been anything other than a *lirai,* he would have moved reflexively in to gut her; for a moment, Erik's skin was cold and loose. He almost, *almost* twitched a knife free and sank it in his little brother's back.

Shit. The protectiveness was natural; unforgiving iron training hammered it home. The first priority in any situation was to keep a Dreamer safe.

Everything else was a distant second.

"Hi," Jake said, letting the rod drop. It clattered against hardwood floor, and she backed up barefoot. She'd torn the nightgown at about knee level, presumably for freedom of movement, and the room looked like a bomb had hit it. A loose fabric coil lay near one of the windows—strips torn from the sheets, braided together and knotted at intervals.

She'd been busy. The windows were all cracked, some of the metal mullions bent, and it looked like she'd tried to take apart the bedstead too.

Huh.

"Careful." Erik couldn't help saying it. "Glass on the floor."

She looked at him directly the first time, and he found out her eyes were dark blue. "Three of you." Her voice shook, but her chin lifted and her hands were fists. "Great."

"We mean you no harm," Ignatius said, spreading his hands; his signet glittered. She barely glanced at him, all her attention taken up with Jake, who moved in on her with spooky, darting speed.

Don't, you idiot. Erik winced as she stumbled back, her heels hitting hardwood with hurtful, bruising sounds. His left wrist burned—if he was feeling it, how much more was Ignatius? Age meant experience, experience meant power, and all three responded to *lirai* with exponential sensitivity.

She was heading right for scattered arcs of broken glass. There were even marks on the inside of some of the slivers worked free of the uprights.

Wet smears, crimson as the throbbing not-tattoo on Erik's wrist.

"Miss Stellack." Ignatius's tone said he was used to being obeyed, but Erik didn't think the *lirai* cared. "We do not wish to harm you in any way."

"But you'll do it if I don't cooperate, right? That's how these things work." She was backing for the bathroom. Not a bad choice.

"Father." Erik heard his own voice, soft and exact. Funny, it didn't match the tension gathering in him. "She's bleeding."

"Just relax," Jake said. "Just relax, sweetie."

That was the wrong thing to say. Her eyes narrowed and she bolted sideways over a glittering arc of broken window. The bigger pieces were twitching, trying to gather enough ambient energy to fly home, and her heel landed squarely on one.

Erik didn't even know he was moving. One moment he was a coiled spring behind Father, right where he should be. The next, his arms were full of spitting, scratching, screaming wildcat, and she gave him a good open-handed slap across one cheek—more because she was flailing than from any real intent, but it snapped his head aside and he had to work to control the reflex that would have answered such a blow from anyone, any*thing* else.

"Easy," he muttered. "*Easy* there, ma'am. Easy."

Looked like this girl didn't *do* easy. She might have taken a self-defense course or two, but her slight weight and wild motion were both all but helpless against a trained Son of Ymre, one who had taken the touch of the Flame on the corrupting mark of the god's will and not turned away despite the agony.

Still, he tried to be as gentle as possible. And it was . . . pleasant, to be this close to a potential.

Very pleasant indeed. She was throwing out a lot of energy. Tiny champagne bubbles slipped over his skin, following the meridians. The mark was whittling itself deeper on his left wrist, too. "Easy," he muttered into her hair, and took a deep lungful.

That might have been a mistake. The scent poured down his throat, filled his skull. She hadn't showered, and the glossy waves were full of concentrated woman-smell right at her crown. There was the burnt tinge of anger as well, and underneath it, the yellowish tang of outright terror.

Stay focused. "Easy," he said again. "Sh, shhh."

She kept fighting, but her struggles were running out of steam. No wonder, she hadn't even been fed yet.

"Erik?" A mild inquiry from Father.

He concentrated, and the coppery tang of her blood vanished under a roil of heavy incense-laden power. The slices on her fingers, and the bigger one on her heel, closed seamlessly. *That's better.* "Sir?"

"Very good." Ignatius stood right where he had been, a straight blade of a man with a shock of iron-colored hair, his uncollared cassock neatly hemmed a little shorter than a priest's for freedom of movement.

That made two compliments since they'd brought the *lirai* home, which was not at *all* normal. Still, surviving long enough to become a Father meant knowing when to buck tradition and habit, or so he always said.

"Miss Stellack," Ignatius continued, "we mean you absolutely no harm. You may not believe us, but it is the truth."

"Oh yeah. Sure." She drew the last word out and went limp, hanging in Erik's arms. "You just kidnap people for fun, huh? That it?"

"You have not been kidnapped, Miss Stellack. You have been placed under guard. There is a difference. You are very important, and—"

"If you're wanting a ransom, you're barking up the wrong tree. Nobody will pay for me, and if you rape me you'd better use a condom because I'm herpes-adjacent." She surged against Erik's hold again—he had one arm across her waist, the other across her shoulders, and it probably wasn't good that he wanted to bury his face in her hair again and just breathe that fascinating scent in over and over until he had it memorized. "You let me go and I won't tell the cops a thing. It's the best offer you'll get."

What? Erik met Ignatius's gaze, and he could swear the flinty old man looked . . . amused?

"I like her," Jake said, with his most ingratiating grin. "Girl's got spunk."

"Fuck you," she spat. "And you too, you fucking *priest.* Aren't you fucking *ashamed* of yourself?"

Erik was doing a lot of wincing internally today. That sort of language was not acceptable in a Son. At least, not in front of Ignatius.

"Every day." Father's slight smile did not alter, nor did his own dark eyes flare with wet huntglow—the diseased light granted to a mad god's chosen, repurposed in service to the Dreamers—or spatters of corpselight. An observant witness would note he wore no collar, just the cassock—but she probably wasn't thinking clearly right now. Adrenaline was only a friend in some situations. "It comes with the territory. Erik, take her to the larger *liraim.* Jake, you'll clean up here."

"Yessir." Erik didn't move just yet, though. He wanted to be sure Ignatius didn't have another order. Or he wanted to draw out being this close to a potential, even by a few seconds. He couldn't tell, and that was dangerous.

"Man, he gets all the fun." Jake straightened, and his most charming smile was aimed at the *lirai* hanging in Erik's grasp. "Honestly, lady, we're not going to hurt you. Promise."

"Promise your mother," she snapped.

Ignatius nodded, which made it official—Erik had to move. His first step called up a fresh spate of struggles, but she was getting tired. He could have cut off her air temporarily, just enough to get her to calm down. While no doubt the most efficient way of solving the problem, it would just create a hundred more.

So he carried her, still wildly kicking, for the door. She stopped when she couldn't see Ignatius, but the way she froze told him she was braced for unpleasantness. It didn't take a genius to figure out what kind, either.

"It's all right," he found himself saying. "Nice and easy, ma'am. We're not gonna hurt you."

"Fuck you," she snapped again, and tried to bite him. She got exactly nowhere, and Erik's face felt funny. He had to work to keep his expression neutral, instead of grinning like a fool.

It didn't matter—she was *lirai*—but he already liked her.

Strategy

THREE SO FAR: the old guy, the blond with the white-capped smile, and the dark-haired brick shithouse who now hauled her into a suite instead of a room—more hardwood, heavy paneling over stone walls, antique throw rugs which had seen a lot of hard use, another heavy wardrobe and a bedstead of pale ashwood instead of wrought iron glimpsed through an interior door. That was bad, but maybe she could break off a chunk of it and batter her way to freedom.

Motivation makes miracles, as Mom always said. And oh God, Liv didn't want to think about her mother right now.

"Bathroom's through there," he said, swinging around so she could see yet another half-ajar door on the other side of the bedroom entrance, a bright, clean, cheery slice of tile glowing through. "The windows won't let you out, so don't try it again. You gonna go crazy if I let go of you?"

"I'm not crazy." Her ribs heaved. She'd been silent the whole trip, looking for a way out; no dice, he didn't even put her down. *Be smart, Liv.* "Why did you kidnap me?"

"Like Father said, you're under guard. That's all." He was a solid mass of muscle and very warm. It felt like he could snap her in half, and if he tried, she was going to fight some more. Sink her nails in to get skin underneath, so when they dumped her body, she would have DNA evidence trapped there—

"Don't fade out now, ma'am."

That's the last thing on my mind, asshole. But she went still, breathing as deeply as she could. He hauled her around like she weighed nothing, which meant she had to get creative.

At least she'd been right about the door. It opened up into the hall so she couldn't get behind it, and now she knew that standing nearby and braining whoever came through wasn't a winning strategy.

Not unless she could find a better weapon. How many of these rooms did they *have*?

She still hurt all over, too. And all she was wearing was the goddamn nightgown. Her rope was in the other room, too, and a fat lot of good it did her since the window glass was some fucking bullshit.

How badly was she bleeding? At least that was evidence. They could clean, but a black light would show blood, right? It was a fine time to wish she'd actually read forensic research instead of just watching police procedurals to laugh at the mess they made of courtroom technique.

The guy was talking again. "Okay. This is how it's gonna go. I'm gonna set you on the bed, and—"

She erupted into wild motion again, achieved nothing. Again.

"Okay, okay." He hauled her up, somehow avoiding her kicking. "Not the bed. Look, you . . ." He paused when she went limp again, lowered her slowly. "Tell me where you feel safe, and I'll turn you loose there. Okay?"

"Outside." It was worth a try. "That's where I'd feel safe."

Hopefully he'd cracked a smile, a chink in his armor, but he sure didn't sound like it. "Come on, ma'am."

"You just doing your job here?" It was only partly sarcasm— whatever he said would give her a clue. A psych degree was good for something, even if it was near useless during after-graduation job searches. Getting the paralegal gig at Maddox, Baker, & Kinnock had been a lucky break, and she *liked* the work. She was even good at it, and the office picked up the tab for her continuing education. She was just a few credits away from qualifying for actual paralegal accreditation, too, which would give her a raise.

"Sort of." He set her gingerly on her toes, but no further. He was *really* warm, and now she realized her feet were numb.

It was a mercy, if she had stepped on broken glass. It was probably only sheer adrenaline keeping her from feeling it. *Think. Okay, he's split off from the other two. Make an ally.* "You don't seem like the kidnapping type, kid." That was a complete lie—evidence had him as *very much* the kidnapping type, but still.

"Kid?" He sounded baffled, but his arms didn't soften in the least. "Oh, yeah. I look young, don't I." His voice rumbled against her back. Wasn't he tired, holding her up like this? She could barely breathe. At least his beefy forearm wasn't pressing on her throat.

Hopefully you didn't just give him a complex, Liv. "I'm thirty-five, everyone looks young to me."

"Thirty-five. That's just a baby." He even, God damn him, sounded amused.

Well, if he felt like he was in charge he'd relax, and then she could get the drop on him. Or so she hoped. "That's awful kind of you." She tried not to sound condescending, and maybe succeeded. So, they didn't know much about her. She was probably a target of opportunity.

"Must be hard for you to breathe like this." A mild observation, nothing more. "Where should I set you, ma'am?"

"Bathroom," she decided. If she could get on the other side of *that* door, she could at least buy some time to think. "Listen, you're not with Neal, right? No. You're too smart to be with Neal."

"That your boyfriend? Reason I ask is, you were dressed real nice." He lifted her and took a few strides, her feet dangling helplessly. "You'd've had to wash your scarf, though."

It's cashmere, you dolt. "It's dry clean only." If they made a habit of dry cleaning their victims' clothes, they were going to get caught sooner or later. She devoutly hoped they were that stupid. "You could give it back. It would be awful nice of you."

"Considering the situation?" He stopped. "Now, I'm going to put you down. I'm leaving the hall door open because it doesn't matter, I'll catch you. You can try as many times as you want. I won't hurt you, but you're not leaving. Sooner we get that down, the better."

Is this part of your game? Guys like this had a script. You played along, you stayed alive—at least, up to a point. "If you're not going to hurt me . . ." *Come on. Give me a little more to work with.*

"You're safer than you've ever been your whole life, ma'am." His weight shifted slightly, and he set her gingerly down, turning her back to the bathroom door. He moved her like she was a doll, and that was scary.

She expected pain, but all she felt was cold. Nothing seemed wrong with her heel, but she didn't dare look away from the man.

Dark hair, dark eyes, about her age, and built like a firetruck. At least he wasn't dressed up like the priest, and he didn't have the cocky, smarmy smile of the blond guy. He looked jockish, good-natured but essentially dumb, but for all she knew he could be the motivating personality in this little *folie à trois.* And beyond him, at mirage distance on the other side of the sitting room with its table, chairs, settee, and empty bookshelf, the open door to the hall. She didn't know the layout and he hadn't taken her down any stairs, but if she could just get *out* . . .

"What's your name?" *Don't break eye contact. Humanize yourself.* "I'm Livvie." Nobody called her that unless they wanted to get her goat; it was either Liv or Olivia—or Ms. Stellack, if they were nasty.

God, her brain just kept jumping around with inconsequentials. *Focus, Liv.*

"That's pretty." He considered her a moment. "I'm Erik."

At least he didn't go for a handshake. "Erik . . .?" Would he give her a last name, one she could take to the cops if she got loose? She tried a smile, the placating expression every woman learned early. *Don't look at the door. Don't.*

"You can try it," he said, almost kindly. "Go ahead. Break for the door. It might even be easier."

So if I run, he'll do something. All right. "What if I just stand here?"

"We can talk." He glanced down. "Or, you know, I can leave you to get dressed. Your toes are blue."

Of course he was trying to throw her off her game. Still, she took a half-step back, unable to stop the movement. "Dressed?"

"Clothes on the bed. Father took care of that."

Oh, that's great. The need to look at the hall door was almost physical, a sharp mounting urge—and, embarrassingly, she had to pee like a racehorse again. All the water she'd gulped from the bathroom faucet midway through destroying the other bedroom was attempting to escape, and was none too choosy about its exit. She swallowed bile. Her mouth tasted monstrously foul. "I'll be sure to thank him." *Right between the eyes.* "Look, Erik, you don't have to do this. I won't tell anyone."

"Divide and conquer. You're really smart." He nodded, once, a crisp military motion. "And you're probably terrified right now, but listen to me. You're safe. Nothing will hurt you here."

Bullshit. She lifted her hands—and stopped, staring at them.

The thin slices on her fingers—and the big one on her palm—were gone. The blood was still there, slicking her fingers and going tacky-wet in the folds, but underneath, her skin was whole. Unmarked.

There wasn't even a pink line or two to show where the edges had scraped or gone in.

"That's impossible," she whispered, and realized she'd taken her eyes off him.

"See?" He regarded her steadily. "Nothing here will hurt you, Livvie. Least of all me." He even leaned forward slightly, like he was going to try to touch her.

Something in the water. Has to be. Shit. She retreated as fast as she could, slamming the bathroom door and throwing its ancient lock with sweating, scrabbling fingers. There was nothing else *to* do, and though her foot with its mask of drying blood slipped a little on hardwood and tile, there was no sign of a wound.

Liv huddled on the commode for a long time, shaking, watching the white-painted door.

She wasn't quite out of ideas yet, but it was close.

Lack of Faith

JAKE HAD BEEN busy, of course. He liked gathering intel, and had set up the screen-and-laptop array in one of the smaller temple cells years ago, updating it religiously. "Olivia Stellack." An electronic glow bathed him; their *lirai*'s face looked gravely down from the screen. It was her driver's license photo, and managed to make her look plain. It was probably the only thing that could. "Born in Los Angeles, her mama was a single hairdresser. Thirty-two—"

Erik shifted in his office chair. He hated the damn things; they felt too spindly to support any real weight. "She said thirty-five." Once, this had been a monk's or a Son's bedroom; nowadays, the cells stood mostly empty. Only three men in residence, when the place could hold at least thirty.

Sometimes Erik thought they'd been forgotten out here. At least Ignatius filed reports and arranged for gear drops and other shipments; sometimes he even mentioned directives from higher up. It was a Father's job to take care of all that, just like it was Erik's and Jake's job to run patrols and try to keep at least some sections of the city clear of underside predators.

"Did she?" Father's eyebrow raised slightly. He would draw his own conclusions. "Proceed."

"Paralegal for Maddox, Baker, & Kinnock ever since graduating college. Four-year psych degree, paid mostly in cash as she worked her way through. Looks like our *lirai*'s got a naughty side—she stripped for tuition." Jake's blond eyebrows wiggled slightly.

"Nothing wrong with that," Erik muttered. Everyone had to make a living, and women most of all. Imagining her in skimpy clothing was pleasant, but imagining other men's gazes crawling over her was . . .

Well. He didn't like it, but then again, it wasn't any of his business.

"Looks like she was saving up to go back to school, too. Or for something. Anyway, address is a shitty apartment on the west side, but she's got a tight-knit social circle. Last contact before we ran across her was an internet date."

"Let me guess," Erik said. "Neal." *No, you're too smart to be with Neal.* It made sense that she'd play the situation that way. She was looking for some control, any control—and an escape route.

When Erik considered it from her point of view, he was surprised she wasn't still screaming.

"Give the man a prize!" Jake's laugh cut itself short, seeing the look on Father's face, and he clicked to the next slide. A blond man smiled down at them, a bright summer beach behind him and a look of such patent self-satisfaction on his face Erik longed to find and punch the expression into oblivion. "Neal Allen Penn, suspected in two date rapes and probably about to commit a third but our girl ghosted him at the table. If not for the camera over the restaurant's back door, the cops would still be sweating him."

"Unfortunate," Father said. Now their potential would become a statistic, one of the many people who vanished each year. The cops—or any other regular human organization—would never find her again, and any family or friends would grieve and move on.

Considering the alternative, it was a mercy. Plenty of the missing simply met with natural bad luck or plain old human homicide, and some of them were even found. But a significant proportion were taken by the underside, and the old chestnut *a fate worse than death* was horrifyingly apt for those.

"Not necessarily. It becomes a random encounter, and we know how hard those are to solve." Jake, curse him, was looking like he enjoyed this. "Anyway, I'm still building her profile. The cops are involved early because our girl's smart, she had check-in times agreed with her friends."

"Very wise of her." Father pressed his fingertips together, settling back in his chair. "And her effects?"

"I cloned everything personal on her phone for profile-building, then incinerated it and her purse too." Jake recited just like a good little brother, ticking off chapter and verse on his blunt, strong fingers. "The clothes she was wearing went right after. I wouldn't have minded keeping the panties."

"This is a *lirai* you're speaking of, Jake." Father frowned.

Erik watched the screen. Now she had no money, no keys, no ID, no phone, not even the clothes she'd been wearing. Erik had piled the purchases on the larger *liraim*'s bed, hoping Father had her sizes right. Once she met the Flame she'd be effectively hobbled by a Dreamer's sensitivity, needing a Son or two around to mute the harsh edges; they just had to keep her contained until then.

"Sorry, sir." Jake even managed to look chastened for a second. An inset on the screen was the live feed from the larger *liraim*. The girl was at the window—at least she'd gotten dressed, jeans and a black T-shirt—gazing at the quad and its overgrown gardens below. Was she hoping to see someone she could flag down?

After the Flame, she would have everything her heart desired, except freedom from the Sons. That would probably be the only thing she'd want, though. And why did the thought make him . . . uneasy?

Even if she didn't trigger the first time, they'd keep returning her to the Flame until it took. *Lirai* could handle successive bathings; it was what made them Dreamers. It didn't even hurt them, really.

It only burned corruption.

The god-mark on his wrist was raw and aching. If Father's was acting up, he made no sign, but Jake grimaced slightly and scrubbed the leather cuff on his left wrist against his side once as he turned back to the laptop, a slight habitual movement.

"She's bound to be hungry," Erik said. "What should I bring her?"

"Taking point on this one, huh?" Jake caught Father's glance and sighed, spreading his hands. "Sorry. I just . . . I never thought this would happen."

"I find your lack of faith disturbing," Father murmured.

Erik had to work to keep a straight face; it was a safe bet Ignatius hadn't seen that movie. He probably remembered when silent films were all the rage.

Jake's mouth twitched, and he tapped at the keys again. "So, the diet app on her phone's got meals logged for months. She flirted with vegan around last New Year's, but she's been an omnivore since Fourth of July. Breakfast's usually Greek yogurt and blueberries."

"A healthful choice." Ignatius's dry tone could have been approval or irony. "Did you stock the kitchen accordingly?"

"Yessir." Jake restrained himself from rolling his eyes with a visible, almost physical effort. "Delivery was yesterday while you were doing the clothes, Father."

"I do not doubt your ability, my son." As always, Ignatius knew when to praise their temperamental younger. "I am merely being thorough."

"Yes, Father." Jake gazed at the laptop. "That's about it. Everything else is details. We should probably take her some breakfast."

"Erik will. Show me everything else."

"He got to take her to the larger *liraim*." Jake obviously thought this wasn't fair.

"And he is the one who will take her breakfast," Father answered, inflexible. "I understand your eagerness. Now proceed."

Erik pushed his chair back, slowly, giving Father plenty of time to add more—or to change his mind. Unfortunately, it didn't look like the old man was going to. "Sir?"

"Yes, Erik?"

"When do we take her to the Flame?" *That* was the only thing he was worried about. Traveling with her was going to be a real joy unless she was sedated, which called up a whole host of other concerns.

"I consulted with Central this morning. The prevailing feeling is that it would be unwise until we have more daylight for traveling." Father pressed his fingertips together, his nails turning pale from the pressure. "That will give us time to make her stable and at least slightly cooperative. That, Erik, is your task."

Great. From the swift startlement on Jake's face, Erik was willing to bet Younger Brother hadn't figured out that his elder sibling was going to end up being the one she'd feel betrayed by. Now that he realized it, of course, Jake would be all sunshine and daisies.

"Yessir," Erik said, and pushed himself upright.

The thought of a potential's natural disgust didn't hurt as much as he expected. No, it hurt *worse*, but that was the price of being a Son of Ymre. He saluted and left the room as Jake started going over the details.

Looked like Father knew Younger Brother was the top contender for her first seal. It didn't help that Erik had, dismally, suspected as much from the start too.

Guilty, Not Mad

SHE HAD BARELY enough time to bolt for the bathroom when the hall door gave a theatrical creak. Liv was entirely sure they had a way of getting in if they really wanted to, so for the time being, hiding seemed like the best option. That left her standing in sock feet on cold tile, hyperventilating and staring at heavy, white-painted wood. Footsteps creaked through the room; there wasn't the sound of the hall door closing.

It's a trap. Don't.

The footsteps paced slowly, deliberately, into the bedroom; it had to be the broad-shouldered, dark-haired one. Liv eased the bathroom door open, her fingers on the lock just in case. The hall door stood open, and she thought she could almost feel a draft from that direction.

He told you he'd do this. It's part of their little game; the others are probably waiting in the hall.

But maybe, just maybe the big guy wasn't quite hip to the program the priest and the smarmy blond were running? Maybe he was giving her a way out but couldn't say as much? Were the walls bugged?

Focus. She measured the distance. It was creepy enough that the ashwood bed had been piled with bags and boxes—jeans, sweats, T-shirts, underclothes, all in black, white, or grey. There were even two sets of cotton pajamas, both dove-grey. No shoes, but an array of black and grey socks.

The funny thing was, they were expensive. Nobody had gone into a box store for these. And everything fit, even the big fluffy white bathrobe. The tags had been removed and everything was washed, but she couldn't identify the fabric softener. It smelled high-end, though.

There was no *way* she was wearing those panties. Who knew what these guys had done with them?

Come on, Liv. Try it. Remember what that cop said? "No matter what, fight like hell." Easy for that particular law enforcement conference presenter to say, he'd been two-fifty if he was an ounce and nobody had ever catcalled *him*. Still, the classes to keep her paralegal job, not to mention qualify for certification, were paying off in spades now.

She was moving before she was quite aware, throwing open the door and pitching forward. Her feet slapped hardwood; she skidded, recovered, hurled herself across faded, worn rugs—

And was dragged back, an iron bar around her waist and a scream welling from her diaphragm.

"I told you," he said when she ran out of breath, his warm exhale touching her ear. "Every time, beautiful."

Jesus Christ, where did he come from? Even if he'd been waiting in the bedroom, how in the *hell* had he caught her?

She'd barely taken six steps. Liv thrashed, screamed, kicked, tried to elbow him, tried to bite. He kept saying *calm down,* and didn't react even when her elbow found something she hoped was tender and his breath huffed out.

"I told you," he repeated. "It's all right. See? Not gonna hurt you, calm down."

She went limp again, staring at that traitorous door and the hall beyond, a window across the hall letting in a sword of pale-grey sunlight. Heavy, threadbare red velvet curtains flanked said window, and the parquet was absolutely spotless. "Let go, goddamn you, *let me go,*" she raved, but it made no difference.

He just waited until she sagged in defeat, still staring at the hallway.

"Better." He even sounded *soothing,* for God's sake. "Now, you can try that again, as many times as you want. It's only natural. We understand."

Understand, hell. She willed the hallway to move closer, willed the earth to open up and swallow this entire fucking place, willed her brain to think of a way out of this.

"Potential's waking up," he muttered. "Okay. Good. You want some breakfast?"

What the fuck? Her stomach cramped. "Let me go," she said again, hopelessly.

"Not gonna happen, beautiful." But his arms loosened. "You can try it again, or you can have something to eat and I'll answer your questions. Or both. I've got time." He set her on her toes, and she pitched forward again. He let go, and she made it a grand total of two steps before he caught her once more. This time he carried her into the bedroom, and she began fighting again until he stopped near a small, wooden table—too heavy to lift, too solidly constructed to take apart and smash the windows, she'd already tried—with two also-heavy wooden chairs. There was a family-sized container of Trader Jay's honey Greek yogurt and a carton of blueberries, along with a bottle of mineral water, arranged neatly on a white linen placemat.

What the fuck? The world came to a screeching halt. It had to be a coincidence.

"That's what you like, right?" He even sounded a little wistful. Eager to please, maybe. "You want some coffee? We didn't know if you're coffee or tea, or one of those decaf people."

I'd rather have withdrawal headaches than ask you for anything. She stared at the familiar, cheery yellow yogurt container. Had they been *watching* her? Dear God. She wasn't interesting enough to be stalked, not that it mattered. Stalking was about power. Control. At least, all the literature said so, and she'd heard all the stories.

Every single awful, murderous one. "Oh Jesus," she whispered. "I don't even know you. I don't know any of you. Just let me go."

"If you sit down and eat, we can talk. I'll tell you everything you want to know, all right?"

It was an attempt to get her to collude in her own imprisonment, but there were nutrients in the yogurt and she needed all of them if she was going to avoid brainwashing. Sleep deprivation, infantilization, and lack of protein—the holy trinity of brainwashing, let alone Stockholm syndrome.

Liv didn't intend to play along. "What did you put in the water?"

"The water? Uh, it's municipal. Nothing but chlorine and fluoride. Why?"

"Bullshit."

"There's nothing in the water, beautiful. Nothing in the food either."

From what she could see, the yogurt container was unopened. It might even be safe. There was silverware—a fork, two spoons, and *silver* was definitely the word. They looked heavy, too, and absolutely antique. No knife, but she could use the fork, right? If she could steal it, or a spoon—

"Put me down."

Much to her surprise, he immediately did. When she staggered at finding herself on her feet again, he steadied her. She flinched away; his hand fell to his side as she put the table between them. He had his back to the bedroom door, and getting past him would be a chore and a half unless she could somehow stick the heavy silver fork in a vital area.

"You can try," he said again, gently. "I don't bleed easy, *lirai*."

"My name's not Larry." Her throat was dry; the blueberries looked wonderfully tempting. Her stomach growled.

"*Lirai.* It's a . . . look, this'll go better if you sit down. And eat. You'll pass out if you don't. You can't fight without fuel."

It didn't help that he was probably right. Liv eyed the yogurt. "I thought you wanted me compliant."

He shrugged. *Either way*, that little movement said, and she studied him from boots to the top of his short dark hair. There was a stubborn curl to it, and something in the cut said military, which was bad news. Failed service types were a dime a dozen in Serial Killer Land.

Great.

"There's nothing in the water," he repeated. "And you don't know it yet, but we're keeping you safe."

From what? Neal? Oh, my God. "From what?"

A muscle flicked in his cheek. "Sit down and eat, and I'll tell you."

She dropped into the chair, wincing as her muscles protested and glaring at him through her tangled hair.

"All right." He folded his arms, legs slightly apart, a variation of parade rest. "So, there's not an easy way to say this, but—"

"*You* sit down." She wondered if he'd comply.

"Yes ma'am." Much to her surprise, he did—but gingerly, like he expected the chair to break. It didn't so much as creak, though she vengefully wished for a leg to snap and spill him onto the nice hardwood floor. "Go on, eat."

"Not until you tell me why you kidnapped me." How far could she push? Was it better to play along for a little bit? She could scramble out of her own chair and bolt for the door again. Maybe she could toss the water bottle at him, slow him down for a second or two?

"It's not kidnapping. We put you under guard, like Father said." He obviously meant the guy in the black high-collared coat; if these guys were looking for a Catholic girl, they were barking *way* up the wrong tree. Gramma Poe had been a Baptist and Mom a Unitarian Universalist—*a fancy name for hippie*, she'd always joked.

It hurt to think of her mother, as usual. Which just made Liv angrier. "Fuck off with that bullshit. Why did you *kidnap* me?"

He paused, visibly shuffling through what to say. How many times had they kidnapped someone? They were far too practiced for her to be the first. How many rooms were in this place?

Too many. Nausea squeezed inside her ribs with rubber fingers, pushing a thin thread of acid up to the back of her throat.

Finally, he spoke, each word slow and very clearly enunciated. "You have very vivid dreams. You remember them more than normal people, too. You've dreamed about a door."

Of all the things she would have expected a kidnapper to say, that was the absolute last. Her stomach turned over, hard. "Everyone has dreams."

"Stone sides, stone top, one step in front. The step's slippery with something; it gleams. The door's painted yellow, and it has a bright red splash on it, right in the middle. The red makes you sick to look at, but when you do, it looks less like splatter and more like writing."

He's guessing. He can't possibly . . . Liv couldn't quite finish the sentence, even inside her own head.

"The thing behind the yellow door," he continued quietly, "is going to come out any moment, and you know it. But you can't move."

"Who the fuck *are* you?" she whispered. He'd just described one of her recurring nightmares; how was that even *possible*?

She'd never told anyone about that particular dream. Not even her mother.

"Your protector." He moved, very slowly, probably trying not to spook her. It was no use—she was already plenty spooked. He undid the leather cuff on his left wrist, peeling it free with a grimace. "The mark, okay? On the door. Looks like this, doesn't it." It wasn't a question.

He turned his wrist up, and there, pressed into the vulnerable, paler underside, a bright-red splotch moved against olive skin.

Right over the veins.

Liv grabbed at the table. Her throat shrank to a pinhole, bile crawling up its sides, and she stared at the thin red twisted symbol. It didn't look like a tattoo.

No, it was more like a brand, something pressed against skin and burning, *burrowing* its way inward. The color was wrong, too. No tattoo artist in the world could get that bright oversaturated crimson.

Something in the water. Has to be. Or a gas? Maybe a patch or something while he was holding me? It was impossible, it was im-fucking-*possible*, and she held onto the table as if it could keep the earth from sliding further sideways. "You're insane," she whispered. "You're a criminal, and you're insane."

"I'm guilty, sure. Everyone who wears the mark is. But I'm not mad. Not yet, at least." He glanced at his wrist, tilting his head a little, examining the not-tattoo. It pulsed, sickeningly, and she was suddenly very glad she wasn't trying to eat, even if she could smell the blueberries—tart and sweet at once, full of delicious coolness. "I'm gonna cover this up. You don't want to eat with it looking at you." Now his dark gaze was on her. His eyes were somewhere between hazel and brown, and very . . . still.

A thin, placid surface over something deep and black.

It was a relief to have the mark covered up. She suspected the feeling was short-lived, however. "What did you put in it?" Liv studied the yogurt container. It appeared unopened, but you could slip a syringe point through foil, right? And blueberries—she didn't know how you could drug blueberries, but these guys probably had it figured out. Where did they get the money for all this? They didn't seem like squatters, and the heating bill for this place was probably sky-high.

"Nobody spat in the berries, if that's what you're asking." He finished buckling the cuff and laid his hands flat on the table, regarding her with that strange, distant look. "I left the yogurt unopened so you'd know it isn't drugged. Neither is the water, but I can get you sealed bottles if you want."

"I want to go home." Her chin jutted out, what Gramma Poe would have called *sulling up*. As in, *don't you sull up, little girl, I don't hold with that.*

God, if she could just channel her redoubtable grandmother long enough, she might get out of this in one piece.

"You *are* home." Patient and even, as if talking to a tantrum-prone child. "We're protecting you."

"Bullshit." She gripped the edge of the table, her fingers bloodless, aching.

"How do I know about your dreams, Livvie? Answer me that."

That was the problem. She'd even gone for a psych degree to try and figure out if she was crazy, or just . . . imaginative, like Gramma sometimes said.

Liv fixed the dark-haired man with her mother's patented Hairdresser Glare, the one that warned clients, overbearing attorneys, or prospective boyfriends they had Gone Too Far. "You don't know fuck-all about my dreams," she lied. "Fuck you, fuck your breakfast, and fuck your funky-ass tattoo."

She pushed her chair back, rose with as much dignity as she could muster, and stalked for the bathroom. She didn't try running for the open hall door again.

Maybe that was why he left, closing and locking it with a sound like a tiny bone snapping.

Dangerously Smart

"HOW DID BREAKFAST go?" Jake's grin suggested he suspected, but youngers had to pester. It was in their nature. "You milady's favorite yet?"

"I'm supposed to betray her to the Flame." Erik folded his arms, his back to the wall. The *liraim* door to his left almost glowed with the force of its trapped inhabitant, or maybe it just seemed so because he was exquisitely conscious of every small sound reaching the protective muffling. "What do you think?"

"Can't betray what doesn't trust you." Little brother sobered quickly, at least, and shoved a hand back through his bright hair. "Father says it's time to teach her caution."

"Great." Erik sighed. "I told her as much as I could. Don't think she believed me."

"But she's a Dreamer." Jake had apparently forgotten every *lirai* started out unconscious of the underside. "It's all over her."

"She's also a traumatized civilian." One who was holding up under the strain of what she considered a kidnapping for unknown purposes pretty damn well, in fact. "She doesn't remember the shadowbeast. Probably never even saw it."

"Well, it certainly saw her. Wouldn't kill the girl to show a little gratitude." Jake tipped his head from side to side, readying for action. He rolled his right shoulder, too, testing range-of-motion. "So, you wanna break her out, or should I?"

"She's gonna hate me anyway," Erik said, and to his relief, he didn't sound hopeless, just flat and informative. "You go ahead."

"Spread the bad luck around, huh?"

Erik suppressed a frown. "You never know, she just might think you're a hero."

"Ain't I just." Jake turned to the baffle over the *liraim* door. "Wanna sprawl out?"

Yeah. Guess so. Erik folded himself down into a puddle on the floor, limbs loose and head turned as if he'd been hit from behind. The invisible baffle folded aside, the mark on his wrist burning, and he shut his eyes, letting his mouth fall slack.

Jake wasn't making any particular attempt to be silent, but he was still much quieter than most mortals. Quiet enough to surprise her, at least—he heard a muffled cry, a clanging, and a crash. Sounded like she'd thrown a bedside lamp at him.

Erik had to banish a smile. He was finding out he liked this girl. Oh, she was *lirai*, which meant she was far above such things as a Son's personal feelings, and she had so much potential it about popped your eyes out of their sockets to stand near her and feel the pressure wave. But still, he *liked* her.

He hadn't expected that. He hadn't expected any of this, just a long slow slide into madness. He hadn't seen a potential, let alone a *lirai*, in years.

Not since his own excruciating, terrifying brush with the Flame. The touch of that fire gave a Son enough strength to stave off the worst of the Mad God's whispering inside his skull, but it took a Dreamer's presence to keep the noise contained. Best of all was being chosen as a seal, of course.

Erik had long ago made his peace with the fact that any *lirai* would have far better options than his own brick-dumb self. It didn't even sting anymore.

Not much, at least.

Jake's job didn't take very long; maybe she didn't need much convincing. "—to the front gate," Erik's little brother said, softly. "Then you're on your own." Was he holding her the way Erik had?

The thought sent a blood-red lightning bolt through him, and he had to force himself to go limp again.

"I'm used to being on my own." She had a nice voice. Husky, with an edge of faint sweet rasp that made a man think of all *sorts* of interesting things.

"Aren't we all." Jake sounded well and truly amused, not the facsimile of bared-teeth grimace that passed for it in a satellite temple most days. "This way, then, and keep quiet."

"If this is one of those weird psychological games, I'm going to stab you."

"It'll make the first time I've been stabbed by a fork."

A fork? Oh, yeah. She hadn't eaten her lunch, either. *Must be starving.*

"Might not the last," she muttered darkly, and the sounds of movement drew closer.

Erik knew the instant she stepped over him in sock feet, holding her breath as if she expected him to erupt into motion. The mark on his wrist gave another heatless pang, burrowing inward, and he kept his breathing virtually imperceptible. They were at the end of the hall when she whispered again. "You couldn't have brought me some shoes?"

"Look, babe, I'm getting you out of here," Jake whispered back. "You want to complain, I can put you right back."

Erik flowed to his feet, not bothering to brush at his coat or pants. He ghosted after them, soft and steady, hearing her pulse. Jake's was kept controlled and muffled, of course, but hers was a wild beacon. Erik could almost *taste* the hope flowing through her, a rich dark river singing in time with her pounding heart.

It was a cold night, but that didn't stop her from following Jake through the quad, stepping carefully. Younger Brother didn't pause to help her over the overgrown patches, or put a hand out to brace her when she stumbled. Erik almost gave the whole game away, almost twitched forward to catch her, but remembered himself just in time and stayed quiet, just at the periphery of Jake's sensing-range.

She landed hard on her knees, let out a breathless curse that would have scorched pavement into breaking if it hadn't already been cracked, and scrambled after Jake's retreating steps. Her steps landed with soft damp sounds—sounded like she'd put more than one pair of wool tubes on her little feet.

Smart girl. *Dangerously* smart.

The large, ornate wrought-iron gate stood ajar, a sure sign that Father did indeed know about this night's little excursion. Not that Erik doubted . . . but the other duty of an Elder Brother was to watch for inconsistencies and tiny tells, just as a Father or a Younger Brother would be weighing his own behavior, searching for signs of inconstancy or slippage.

Or treachery.

"This is as far as I go," Jake said softly. "Just follow the road, ma'am."

The indistinct shadow that was their *lirai* stepped through the iron gate quickly, as if afraid Jake would change his mind. "Thank you."

The catch in the words put a rock in Erik's own throat. *Don't,* he wanted to say. *They're out there, beautiful, and you're fragile.* It was a moment's work to reach the top of the stone wall and drop down soundlessly on the other side, moving through the undergrowth like a ghost.

"Anytime." Jake made a small shooing motion. "Go on, now. Be careful."

She turned and bolted, each footstep jolting in Erik's own body. The mark on his wrist flamed, warning him.

Of course Father knew. It was Ignatius's job—the most difficult one of the night—to bring a shadowbeast close if one wasn't already prowling the edges of the temple, sensing a Dreamer inside heavily reinforced walls and defenses. Erik paralleled the road, moving with the ease of long habit and enhanced agility.

He knew the exact moment one of the foul things noticed her.

There were at least three converging on the road. Either Father wanted to test Erik's skill—unlikely, if there was even the slightest chance a *lirai* could be harmed—or he'd been occupied in whittling down a crowd of shadowbeasts to a manageable number.

Erik's hands burned, dropping to his knifehilts. She wasn't going very fast. Oh, she was running, all right, probably flat-out.

But it was barely walking speed for a Son of Ymre, and practically standing still for the nightmare creature that reared in front of her, its eyes dripping crimson and its claws whistling as they clove thick, freezing night air.

Psychological Games

EACH STEP SMACKED her aching feet, jolted in her knees, slammed into her hips, and shook the rest of her for good measure. Liv had successfully escaped, and each gulp of cold night air tasted bubble- alcoholic like sweet champagne. She didn't care that her feet would be ribbons by the time she reached anywhere likely to have a phone she could use to call for help, that hypothermia was a factor, or that the other two men might find out the blond guy had let her go.

You want to get out of here? I'm only gonna ask once.

No, the only thing Liv Stellack cared about was that she'd gotten free, she was *outside*, and she flung herself away from the wrought-iron gate at full speed. It wasn't so much being kidnapped, though God knew that was enough to make anyone run.

No, it was the persistent nagging dread, spurred by the bright, oversaturated crimson of the mark on the dark-haired man's wrist. That was the final straw. And his describing one of her goddamn recurring dreams—it had to be a common one, right? Had to be.

Anxiety, bad food choices, you name it, everyone had nightmares about nasty doors and the bad things that happened when you opened them. Everyone got déjà vu from their nighttime brain-walks; Liv's vivid, quasi-lucid ones were just a sign she had an active imagination and a good memory.

Most days, she had herself convinced there was nothing wrong with her sanity or her sleep. But kidnapping had a way of making you doubt things, or so she'd discovered.

If she just ran fast enough, she'd escape this nightmare too. It was uncannily like one which had tormented her ever since college—a black night, her feet sodden-slapping, her breath tearing in her throat . . .

. . . and a sudden looming bulk of something utterly *wrong* rising from the ground like a mushroom after a hard rain.

Liv skidded, saved from falling onto her ass only by a sideways leap threatening to throw her into a tangle of thorny vines alongside the single-lane road. The thing hulked its shoulders and thrust its ungainly head forward, crimson eyes dripping with nasty rheum.

A gurgling, pointless scream rose from her throat as the wind of the thing's claws passing over her head ruffled her tangled, dirty hair. That faint breeze convinced her the thing was real, not just a fevered hallucination, and she scrabbled back crabwise, erasing skin on her palms, her heels thumping uselessly, as the thing loomed over her. Its next strike wouldn't miss; she knew it as surely as she knew her own name and the hard surfaces of her own teeth as her tongue was caught between them.

Liv dropped flat on her back, a jarring silvery jolt. A metal tang of blood from her abused tongue filled her throat and the attacking thing was darkness itself, its stench burrowing into her nose.

"*Stay down!*" An indistinct shape hurtled past her, twin bright metal gleams disappearing as they were driven into the monster's hide. It roared, the blast stripping her hair back and slathering her bare skin with a reek so foul she knew, miserably, she wouldn't feel clean again for a long, long while.

Maybe forever.

A pale, leprous light bloomed from somewhere, running wetly along the beast's every muscle-curve. Its chest was too big for its tiny back legs, but the thing could stand, drawing itself up, and up, and *up* in a horribly liquid movement. One ungainly arm flashed out, but the dark-haired guy dropped under the strike with clean, blurring grace. He uncoiled, driving forward, and the metal glitters were curved, wicked-looking knives. They slashed, and the thing howled, striking out again.

Get up. Run, while it's occupied. Come on, Liv. You know how this goes.

And that was the whole problem, wasn't it? She did know how it went, because she'd dreamed this same thing over and over. The thing would come for her, batting a dancing, spinning gleam out of the way, and its maw would yawn wide, inward-pointing rows of sharp serrated teeth dripping with that sticky red fluid, then the jaws would snap shut with her in them, and—

"*Stay down!*" he yelled again, as if he could hear her thinking about moving, and one of his knives sank to the crossguard in the thing's side. It threw its head back and howled, its hide running with that pale diseased light; Erik yanked the blade free and coiled himself. He leapt, and there must have been a trampoline or some Superman-powered muscles in his legs, because he went higher than he had any right to, twisting gracefully to avoid another swipe of those terrible glassy claws.

The thing howled once more, but one boot hit its shoulder, his other knee jammed under its chin, and he drove both daggers into its glowing, murderous eyes with a short, grunting sound of effort.

Liv gulped back another scream, scrambling again with stinging hands and scooting back on her bottom. Cold dampness worked through her jeans; she was going to have a huge soaked patch on her ass but that was unimportant.

The monster dropped like a pile of insensate meat, with a cartoonish *thud* that might have been funny if it hadn't smelled so ungodly awful. Liv's mouth worked aimlessly, and she kept scrambling, trying desperately to retreat and not managing it very well.

Erik turned, and that pale light was all over him. His eyes were dark but still burned, with starlike blue glitters, live coals set in a thin-lipped face, and he launched himself straight at her.

Good Prey

OF COURSE IT couldn't be simple, or easy. She was doing great, she was staying down just like he told her instead of rabbit-running, but now it was apparent Father's whittling down of the shadowbeasts drawn to the small flame of a potential-triggered Dreamer hadn't been quite as successful as either of them hoped.

The big beast was bad enough, but it was the mass of slithering to the left which concerned Erik most.

He unfolded over her in a leap, gaining what speed he could, and hit the nest of writhing, rearing heads with a crunch that would have snapped every bone in a normal man's body. Seeing the *cthulhuth*'s heart was easy—all the tentacles led back to a common point.

Stabbing said nexus, however, was another story. It was a mercy the thing quickly lost interest in a Dreamer when a bigger threat appeared, and that it was already wounded.

It was a further mercy that a powerful, invisible pulse from their potential dizzied it, and Erik was able to slide both knives in to their hilts, one foot flicking up to knock a tentacle aside that might otherwise curl too close to her further down the line. Tearing the creature's heartknot free with a half-grunting sound of effort, he landed, deceleration slamming through him, and whirled to check.

Nothing. Just trees, thorny vines laced with invisible protections and all-too-visible, smoking ichor, the broad grey back of the driveway.

And *her*, half-sprawled on cold concrete, her hair a wild mass and her eyes as big as a frightened child's. Deadly pale, fever spots high on her cheeks, their new *lirai* vibrated with terror, a heady exhalation of musk and copper scraping pleasantly across his nerves. The mark in his wrist burned, gulping at fresh fuel, sensing the fragility of good prey.

Just like the things that still lurked in the dark, ready and waiting. He was one of them, even if the Flame had freed him of the Mad God's service, and it wouldn't do to forget it.

So he just stood, boots solid on concrete, ready for the next attack. The remainder of the beasts would be cautious now, circling.

And the girl, her potential awake and much more active even if she hadn't been scoured clean by the Flame yet, would feel them.

A normal person's habit of rationalization was strong enough to overcome even direct proof, and even though potentials could sense far more than the average headblind nine-to-fiver, they still had the very human habit of ignoring what they didn't want to see. Something unignorable was called for, just to drive home the fact that outside was dangerous and the Sons meant protection.

She made a tiny, sobbing noise. Ichor dripped from Erik's blades. He hadn't needed anything other than the knives, thank the Dreamers, and the more evidence he left right in front of her face, clearly visible in the corpselight he held steady, the better.

"You . . ." She sounded like she'd been punched. The flash of red rage pushing through him at the thought of anyone striking this particular *lirai* tightened his skin and lifted his lip with a snarl. "Oh my God." She probably thought she was screaming, but it was merely a shocked whisper.

He turned his head slightly, not enough to catch her in peripheral vision though he longed to, but enough to let her know he was waiting for orders. Soon she'd understand that posture and wouldn't leave one of her guards without guidance for long.

Of course, by then Erik would be back on duty in some other satellite, maybe even part of a different trio, depending on how badly he fucked this up. She'd probably want to keep Jake but get rid of him and Ignatius, and he didn't blame her one bit.

It took a short while for her to realize she was still alive, and she recovered more quickly than most, slight noises telling him she was pushing herself upright. Probably trembling, too, if the fearful little sips and gasps for breath were any indication.

"Is . . . is it gone?" she whispered finally, and he allowed himself a moment of believing she might almost understand.

"These are." The growl was in his throat, and he still sounded close to murder. At least he was completely as advertised, and she'd figure that out sooner or later. "The others aren't."

"You mean there's *more*?" Amazingly, the last word broke on a pale, shaky little laugh. It was the kind of sound a woman made before she passed out or underwent a complete psychotic break, and he wondered which way she'd jump.

She wasn't retreating for the iron gate and the safety of the temple, though. A girl with mettle.

"Plenty more." He really shouldn't be talking to her. He should just let events speak as they would. *You're safe,* he longed to say. *I'm here.*

But that wouldn't get him anything but kicked in the teeth, so he shut up.

"Planned this." Very softly. "You guys got together and . . . An object lesson. Right?"

She was too smart by half. Erik kept his mouth shut and stayed where he was, though the underbrush was alive with thin sliding sounds. Crackling. Tiny creaks.

Amazingly, he also heard a soft, padding footstep. Then another, and the warmth of a Dreamer approaching fell on his back. Sunshine, on a cloudy day.

Wasn't that a song? And why was he thinking of that when there were shadowbeasts drawing closer? What was she doing, hiding behind him?

Good instincts, though she didn't know it. Maybe she was planning on stabbing him with a fork.

She stepped even closer. "All right." The words broke in the middle on a not-quite-sob. "What do we do now?"

We, little girl? But that was a good sign. "Don't suppose you'd like to go back inside."

"I'm thinking about it." A long shuddering exhale, soft and ragged. "I, uh . . . what are *you* going to do?"

Smart *and* brave. Wasn't she just the whole package. "Wait for you to make up your mind." He wanted to add *I've got all night*, but they really didn't. The longer she was out here, the higher the risk, even with Jake lurking atop the wall ready to reinforce and Father in the dark wilderness, attempting to deter or outright slay most approaching predators.

"I'm really not feeling all that capable of handling this situation correctly," Liv informed him, primly. It would have sounded better if she wasn't shaking so hard her teeth chattered. It took her two tries to get the entire sentence out.

His mouth opened, despite his brain issuing strict prohibitions against the very act. "I'm surprised you haven't passed out."

"Me too." A tiny, pale whisper, barely audible even to his enhance senses. "These things. What are they?"

That's the right question. Good girl. "Shadowbeasts. Nightmares." His throat was extremely dry. "You've seen them before."

"Not while awake." The admission, probably wrenched out of her by shock alone, was *also* surprising, even if he'd suspected. "I've seen this, uh, before. But in my dream, you died."

Ah. "Dreamers often have—" he said, but she made another soft, distressed noise and crumpled.

He almost dropped his knives whirling to catch her before she hit the ground. In fact, he was a lot slower than he liked, and she almost hit concrete. He had her in his arms and was over the wall again in a hot second, the protections a warm weight briefly stroking his entire body, given fresh strength by a potential's nearness.

Erik didn't like how everything had gone silent—underbrush, animals, and even the wind. "Jake?"

"Right here, oh master of discretion." A theatrically sepulchral laugh drifted from the top of the wall even though little brother was all but invisible, his bright hair blurred with hunting camouflage. "She screamed."

"Not after the thing was dead."

Jake hated losing a bet even more than he hated spidery, greasy *ukkar*-trawlers. "She still screamed."

"You still owe me five bucks." Erik cradled the *lirai*, the mark on his wrist sated with bloodlust but still avid and tender-throbbing at her nearness. "Oh, and . . ."

"And what?"

"She has possible-dreams." Erik tried not to sound too satisfied. The amount of potential this woman exuded even before being dipped in the Flame was unsettling; it was maybe how she'd stayed alive, basic precognition moving her one step in front of the underside's predators before allowing her to cross paths with Sons. But still. . . . "You owe me *ten*."

Jake swore, good-naturedly, and fell into rearguard position as his Elder Brother carried their *lirai* toward the temple.

Erik told the persistent unease sharpening under his breastbone to settle down. There was no reason to be this jumpy, not when they'd won a round.

Or at least, they'd kept her from being eaten. When she woke up, there would still be hell to pay.

Deconstructing

ONE SECOND LIV was doing pretty all right, considering the situation, and even thinking of a wisecrack. Then, *boom*, synaptic overload, the world clicked off like a giant light switch. The next thing she knew, she was horizontal instead of vertical, still in jeans and the same black T-shirt but with fresh socks, and alone on a familiar-unfamiliar bed.

Oh Jesus. The thought that she might have had a complete psychotic break and this was an asylum with a particularly liberal attitude toward treatment—especially pharmacological—was super comforting.

Or it would have been, if the several pairs of wet, filthy socks she'd had on yesterday—or whenever it was—weren't at the foot of the bed, gravel caught in their outer layers. Her ass hurt, her back ached, and her palms were abraded, but the injuries felt days old instead of fresh. All that she could have explained away, one way or another.

But the socks. Mud. Twigs. Tiny pebbles. She stared at them for far too long before realizing both her bladder *and* her stomach were incredibly unhappy. Fortunately, one problem was way more critical than the other, and after it was attended to in the bathroom's clean white-tiled glare, her stomach settled with a thump. A healthy dose of cold water to her face felt incredibly helpful, but she stopped, hunched and dripping over the gleaming porcelain sink.

It walloped her again, the sheer grinning, slavering *unreality* of what she'd seen. The memory drove a short, strangled sound out of her, and she wandered into the bedroom without bothering to dry her face. Stopped, staring at the bed.

More specifically, at the socks.

If it was a psychological fake-out, it was a damn good one. Touch of genius, really, right up there with the blond guy springing her from the room.

Thump-thump.

Liv whirled, almost toppling in her haste, and froze, staring at the doorway. A few lone drops kissed her shoulders; her hair was a wild mess. The sound came from the suite's other room, but she didn't quite think her legs were up to carrying her that far.

For one lunatic moment she wondered if they would consider putting a lock on *her* side of the door. The funny thing was, in this state of mind, she'd absolutely, one hundred percent use it.

Thump-thump. There it was again. Someone knocking.

But you can't . . . come . . . in! The ancient pop song blared inside her head, and she managed to croak, "Okay . . ." It was barely a whisper, but there was the faint sound of the door opening, and the woozy certainty that this was the beginning of yet another vivid, overwhelming nightmare swamped her hard and fast. The world wavered, an underwater undulation.

"Oh, shit." The blond guy appeared in the bedroom doorway, and she stared uncomprehendingly at him. "Father? *Father!*"

"I told you, she's deconstructing." The dark-haired guy shouldered past him and bore down on her.

Liv flung up a hand, fingers spread. A hot flush ran through her, scalp to toes, and the dark-haired guy stopped dead, leaning forward as if into a heavy wind.

"You're in a type of shock," he said quietly, his gaze locked with hers. Oddly, that soothed her. He'd fought those things off last night. Moving in ways no human should be able to, and with a pair of wicked curved knives that were definitely not for chopping onions. Still, he was able to keep the monsters at bay, and that was good enough right now. "It's all right. It's normal, and you're gonna be fine. You just have to adjust."

Oh, sure. I'll adjust. To those . . . those things . . .

The worst thing wasn't suspecting that she was crazy, or that the world held secret, hidden terrors. It wasn't even seeing one of those terrors with its shape so subtly, appallingly *wrong*, either.

No, the worst thing was those fucking socks. She could have ignored everything else, if the goddamn socks hadn't been just sitting there, smug in their sock-ness, in their plain, modest assertion that yes, the terrors existed, and yes, Liv Stellack had been dreaming about them her entire life.

"Acute psychological distress." The lean, iron-haired older man in his long black cassock appeared behind the blond. With all three of them in here, the room was awfully small, and she wanted to back up, get away; there wasn't enough air. "Jake, go into the hall."

The blond's eyebrows headed for his hairline. "Father?"

"Go." The old man waited until Jake had retreated with one last long glace at Liv, who stood and trembled, fighting for air. "Erik?"

"Yessir." The brunet guy didn't look away. He seemed to be willing her to stay cool, to keep herself together.

Oh, God, I'm trying. Liv's hands opened and closed, convulsively. There was a little more space since the blond was gone. If the old guy would just back off too, she could probably handle it.

Or at least, handle something. Did this mean all her other dreams were real too? Or just the gruesome, monster-laced ones? How about the other dreams, seeing a fall of light or a particular view and running across the very same thing a week to a few months later, the déjà vu pouring through her alternately scorching and icy?

How about *those*, friends and neighbors?

"I will be in the outer room." The older guy inclined slightly in her direction, a small bow like an uncertain butler. Did priests have butlers? "Be gentle."

"Of course." Erik still didn't look away. "We'll just hang out for a little bit, take it easy."

The idea that there was such a thing as *taking it easy* when there were tentacled horrors with giant bleeding suckers and strange hulking quadrupeds with hellfire eyes, tentacles, and coats made of shifting glass walking around, walloped her again. Erik took another step forward.

"Shhhh," he said, in that same strange, gentle murmur. "It's okay. It's just you and me, Dreamer. Take your time, all right? You're safe, you're not crazy. Okay? I'm gonna be right here with you." He spread his hands, raising his arms a little, like he was talking to a terrorist or robber during a standoff. "Just keep your eyes on me, beautiful."

"You're . . . monster hunters?" she managed, tentatively. *Please tell me this makes some kind of sense.* "Right?"

"Right." A slight, approving nod. With only him in the room a lot of the air returned, and the iron band around her ribs eased up. "Good. You're doing great."

"There's not enough air," she whimpered, hating herself for the stupidity, not to mention weakness.

"The air's coming back," he answered promptly, and that made a mad kind of sense. Enough that she whooped in a gigantic breath, and he gave that little nod again, as if she'd accomplished something just grand. "See? So yes, monsters are real and we're monster hunters; that's a good way to put it. We rely on people like you. *Lirai.* Dreamers."

Who's Larry? Lar-ai? Liv tried to think, got exactly nowhere, fastened on the most bizarrely logical part of the whole deal. "So . . . I'm a monster hunter too?" *Should I put that on a resume?*

"Oh, beautiful, you're so much more." Erik shook his head slightly, and his faint smile was a co-conspirator's now, encouraging, as if they shared a secret. "You've seen all the movies, right? This is the part where you have a little trouble with the idea, and I calm you down, then I ask you to trust me. This is exactly that part, Livvie."

Oh, God, don't call me that. The annoyance was a wonderful bracer, like a shot of tequila after a bad breakup. "I don't think I want the training montage," she managed, and was rewarded by the intensifying of that slight smile. He had a face like a sheer cliff, but if you looked closely, there were flickers of expression.

Here she was staring at a guy she didn't know, who had kidnapped her and saved her from a giant tentacle squidbeast and some kind of supersized alien werewolf. There wasn't any sort of rulebook or manual for this. She couldn't even find a legal definition, despite all the reams of court documents she'd read, depositions she'd proofed, or official letters she'd written.

"I don't think I would either." And, strangely, Erik sounded like he'd actually considered the notion and made a serious decision. "Now, the best thing for you would be something to eat, and something warm to drink. Just to let your body know the sabertooth tiger's gone now, all right? Right now you're still in fight-or-flight."

"Are there?" Her throat was a sandpaper wasteland, but *fight-or-flight* made sense. She couldn't do either at the moment, so she was vapor-locking, like Mika when faced with the prospect of snakes. "Sabertooth tigers, I mean?"

"Haven't seen one yet." *But,* his tone said, *I don't rule it out.*

Oddly enough, his simple matter-of-factness helped. The room opened up again, her lungs filled once more, and Liv was suddenly aware that she was sweating, every muscle either trembling or gone numb. She wanted to sit down very, very badly, but not on the bed.

Not where those socks were.

"All right." All intransigence drained away, and she took a step forward. Another, and reached out blindly.

Erik's hands clasped hers. His grasp was solid, warm, and undeniably human.

Liv let out a dry, barking sob, caught her breath, and stared at his almost-expressionless face. He waited, holding her hands in his hard, warm palms like it was no big deal. The touch steadied her, and she wanted to get away from the bed and the goddamn socks.

"Can we go in the other room?" she whispered. A scream boiled in her throat; she denied it.

"One step at a time." He even backed up with eerie grace, holding her gaze the entire way.

Behaving Admirably

"YOU MAY THINK of us as a priestly order, Miss Stellack." Father kept his tone deliberately neutral, and much softer than Erik had ever heard the old man speak before. "We are sworn to certain ideals, and to the protection and defense of the *lirai*." He paused, his gaze steadily and studiously sunk in a mug of black coffee he would probably not even sip. "The Dreamers."

"Like . . . a secret society?" Huge-eyed, she huddled in the largest chair in the room, clutching at a similar heavy white mug holding a tolerable hazelnut latte. Jake used too much syrup for Erik's taste, but maybe she enjoyed that.

"Exactly." Ignatius tried a smile, except it was more like a grimace than an expression of amusement. "We are the Sons of Ymre."

"Okay." Amazingly, a ghost of a smile touched her pale lips. She was almost transparent, but Erik had never thought a civilian would hold up this well after facing down two nightmare-beasts at once. "Sounds like a biker gang."

"Ah. Well." Father cleared his throat. "*Ymre* is a nonsense word, because we do not speak *his* name aloud."

"His . . . name?" A line appeared between her eyebrows, and she glanced at Erik as if seeking confirmation. "Like, your founder or something?"

It wasn't a bad assumption, but Erik's stomach still made an unhappy motion. He dropped his gaze, staring at the mug in her slim, pretty hands.

Her nails were bitten all the way down.

"In a way." Ignatius didn't flinch. "He is a god, of course, a terrible one. He almost had the entire world, but we betrayed him. So he cursed us."

At least she didn't shut down at the mention of gods. "Cursed you?"

"Yes." Father tapped at the cuff on his left wrist with one bloodless fingertip. "You have seen Erik's, I believe. Would you like to see mine?"

"Uh, no thanks." The wheels were visibly turning inside her head. Disheveled, ashen, her hair a wildly curling mop, she was still . . . well, Erik was glad Father had suggested they wrap a blue woolen blanket around her shoulders, and also glad the *liraim* was well heated.

She just looked so damn *small.* The Dreamers were power incarnate—but not physically. For endurance, speed, and sheer mayhem, you wanted a Son.

"So when you say *a god* and *he had the world*, what exactly do you mean?" Their potential squeezed the mug, her knuckles whitening a little, and glanced again at Erik, who tried to look encouraging. His own plain latte was rapidly cooling and he had no desire to taste it, but he took a sip anyway to remind her that he was human.

Or whatever passed for *human* once you received your mark. Before the great betrayal, the red glyph burned into a Son's flesh was a sign of being chosen. Nowadays, it was just the penultimate step. Then a *lirai* sealed the wound and stopped the corruption from spreading. The agony of burning was a relief from the god's attention. Or at least, it had been for Erik.

Even with the training, sometimes a heart stopped or sanity broke under the double assault.

"All creatures dream." Ignatius chose his words with slow, finicky care. His dark eyes lit with a strange gleam, as usual when he had to give The Speech. He'd been closeted in the comms room all morning, probably arguing with Control over moving their potential. "Dreaming is, in fact, an entire world in and of itself. A whole ecosystem, and there are predators within it. Think of *him* as one of the biggest, a creature quite beyond human understanding but nevertheless capable of granting, at its whim, certain favors upon those who bring it . . . offerings."

"Right. Okay." Their potential absorbed this, her big dark eyes blinking slowly. "An actual god? Like, as in, Zeus or Yahweh or . . ."

"A cruel and horrific god, yes. One far worse than anything human beings could create, one they were all too ready to worship." Ignatius's shaven lip curled, and he suppressed the grimace with what had to be a painful effort. "The offerings *he* liked best, of course, were humans with a certain capacity for sensitivity, a certain talent for what you might almost call magic. We call them the *lirai*."

"Larry. Okay." She mangled the word, glanced again at Erik, and he took another sip. Just for appearance's sake.

The fact that his chest got tight when she looked in his direction, only easing when she seemed to find some comfort there, was beside the point.

"The Sons were once priests and servants of Ymre." Ignatius passed over centuries of terrible history in a single sentence, then distilled a war humanity barely remembered into another. "But we betrayed him, and he cursed us."

"Cursed. Okay. And the larry—the *lirai*—" She caught herself, checking her pronunciation. Her fingers twitched, and she looked at the table as if surprised to find it empty except for Ignatius's mug. "Do they break this, uh, the curse?"

Father glanced at Jake, who perked immediately, lowering his own cup of hot cocoa. "No, of course not." Younger Brother's usual good humor was muted, at least. Jake, like Erik, had never explained this to a potential before. They should be taking notes on Ignatius's delivery. "He's a *god*. But we decided to do something good anyway."

Father's attention settled on Erik, who found the next part of the catechism without much trouble. "We waged war upon our own kind," he said, heavily. How long had they been attempting to hold back the tide in this city, only finding *one* potential? The emphasis they gave to this sort of thing in training seemed inefficient, but then again, Erik's lot wasn't to question why. His job was just to keep Jake and Ignatius stable, and now ensure their potential's survival. "Humanity was *this close* to dying out completely, because once he'd eaten them, he was going to start on us. Some of us realized as much, almost too late." Good old human self-interest had once more saved the day.

"We fought, and won." Father took up the thread again, apparently satisfied with his boys' recital. "Barely, and because of the *lirai*. We owe them everything."

"Okay." A nervous shake of her dark curls, normalcy attempting to reassert itself. Another sliding, sipping little glance at Erik, and he hoped her reasonable human fear of the monsters outside wasn't going to whiplash anger in his direction. "All right. Whew. This is a lot to take in."

"Quite understandable." Ignatius was trying to sound soothing, but even to Erik the flat, emotionless tone was a little jarring. "You're still not completely ready for the truth, Miss Stellack, but you are behaving admirably."

She inclined her head, a queenly movement. "Thank you. I've forgotten your name."

"Ignatius, Miss Stellack. Please, do not hesitate to use it." Even in dry schoolteacher mode, the old man had some smooth manners. Erik tried not to catch Jake's significant look and failed. Younger Brother was trying to keep the smirk down, and not doing too well. "I will repeat, we do not mean you any harm. The boys came across you during a standard city-cleansing operation."

"City cleansing?" At least she didn't ask *what boys?* with an eyebrow-quirk. That would have been embarrassing, and Erik had enough on his mind already.

"Suffice to say the Mad God is merely the largest predator in the ecosystem of the real, half-real, and dream." Now Ignatius was back on firmer ground; lecturing was a Father's native state. "Other things prey upon humanity, or intersect with us. The Sons are somewhat of a . . . police force, if you will."

"Monster hunters." She was doing a lot of nervous glancing at Erik. Did she think he was going to flip the table or something? Naturally her unease would fasten on him. He was a safe target for her reaction, whatever it was going to be. "Right?"

A direct question, and she was staring right at him, eyebrows up and her lips slightly parted. Erik had to answer. "Right."

"Okay. All right." Another little shake of her head, trying to get all the ideas to settle. "So, you're going to teach me to hunt monsters? I'm gonna have a funny mark too?"

"Good heavens, no." Ignatius managed to look shocked but not quite disapproving. Even *he* wouldn't dare criticize a Dreamer, though he more than once waxed irritated with Control's orders. *They have no idea what the front lines are like, my boys.* "There is no corruption in you, Miss Stellack. Suffice to say you are a source of power, and we are amplifiers. You make our work exponentially easier and more effective."

It didn't seem possible for her to shrink even further into the chair, but she somehow managed. "Like a battery?"

"Like an electric guitar," Jake piped up. "You sing a song, we turn up the volume to eleven, monsters go *poof.*"

"Great." Liv freed a hand long enough to rub at her temple. "This is all really interesting, guys, but I think I want some time to process. Alone." Her gaze darted to Erik again, as if asking permission, but he was already rising. So was Father, and a moment later Jake caught the telegram and hurriedly straightened, blinking, holding his mug cautiously.

"Of course." Ignatius performed a very correct little half-bow. "Shall we bring you some lunch?"

"I'm okay. I, uh . . ." She was still looking at Erik, who tried to hunch, as small and nonthreatening as possible. It wasn't going to work; he was built to much heavier specifications than Jake, but still . . . he wanted to try. "Look, can you stay for a second? Just you."

"Of course," he mumbled, and set his mug down on the heavy antique table, pushing his chair in and settling at parade rest. Jake followed Father out, casting a single indecipherable glance over his shoulder.

"I don't mean to be rude," their potential said, in a breathless rush. Her knuckles paled again; if she had a Son's strength, she might shatter heavy ceramic just by clutching. "I just . . . Can I ask you for something?"

"Of course," he repeated. She was probably going to tell him she hated him and never wanted to see his face again. Her anger had to fasten somewhere, a perfectly normal reaction to getting a peek under the skin of the waking world.

"The socks. On my bed." Her throat moved as she swallowed, and the pulse there was a hummingbird's wings. "Can you . . . I don't want them there." Half shamefaced, half determined, she searched his expression, her dark eyes very wide.

Is that it? "I'll take care of it. Right now, if you want." Was it a test of his willingness, or was she fixating on socks to get her through the interaction?

It didn't matter. The important thing was that she'd made a request he could answer. A good way to build trust, and—oh, hell, he *wanted* to help her.

He longed to get that breathless, terrified look off her face.

"Please?" After all that, she was still polite. She watched him, but for the first time, not like he was a danger to be kept in view, but as if she . . .

That didn't matter either. If it made her happy, or even took a little of that devouring, paralyzing fear away, he'd break down the whole bed and cart it out piece by piece. He'd even do it with a smile and a whistle. "You don't even have to ask," he said. "Just tell me, *lirai*, and it's done."

Lesser Evil

AFTER THE OLD guy—Ignatius—brought her a half-ream of unlined paper and a collection of pens, there was only the sound of sleet hitting the window and her own breathing as well as the small creaks and crackles of an old structure settling on its bones as the weather changed.

The loose sheets were heavy, cream-colored, and obviously expensive; the pens were a fresh package of high-end black gel numbers. She'd have loved them for work, especially if they came in different colors.

Color coding would have helped immensely. Legal research was easier when you could glance at a page and see concepts highlighted in different shades. She tried to think of this as a deposition, or a case needing to be built.

If all this bullshit was a kidnapping or some kind of con job, it was so intricate and seamless she couldn't find a way out. If it was a hallucination, likewise. Was it reality if you couldn't find a hole in it?

The problem was, though, there were plenty of cracks in the situation. She just didn't like what was grinning at her through them—something old, rancid, and terrifying even if it was completely unbelievable.

But she'd *seen* the monsters, and not while sleeping—in Technicolor-vivid 4K while conscious, or at least during what was passing for awake at the moment.

First things first, Liv. Get systematic. She drew a long line down the center of one sheet, but she couldn't quite figure out what to label either side. Lies and truth? Well, they could be lying to her about a whole lot.

On the other hand, she had never told anyone about the yellow door in the dream. Not a therapist, not Gramma, not even Mom.

And that was another terrible thing, wasn't it? Mom and the closed doors locked from the inside, every window closed as well, with the safety dowels still in place. Liv remembered measuring and cutting the wooden cylinders when they moved into the tiny house, but it hadn't done any good. *Unless the attacker came in through the chimney,* the detective had said meditatively, scratching at the side of his neck.

Liv, hugging herself so she didn't break and fly apart, had simply stared at him from the stairwell, uncomprehending. They thought she was in shock, and who wouldn't be finding their mother's body in itty-bitty pieces all over the living room?

Don't think about that, Liv. For Christ's sake.

Mom knew she had nightmares. *Ever since you were little*, she'd say, and would bring warm milk in one of her crazy-colored, hand-painted mugs. *Here, sweetie. It's all right.*

Oh, her mother would sort this *right* out; if she didn't, Gramma would. They were both gone, and it was too goddamn painful to think about so Liv stared at the paper, the pen moving almost of its own accord. Spirals and hearts were her usual doodles, only now the spirals reminded her of rubbery, bleeding tentacles. She tried lightning zigzags, but that reminded her of the strange glow outlining the creature and the way Erik *moved.*

"Oh, hell," she muttered, and turned the sheet over. Now another blank page confronted her.

The little things were giving her the most trouble—her kidnappers' utter stillness when they weren't accomplishing some task or another, unnatural in fidget-prone human beings. The curved knives, blades shining with their own sickly, pale glow. The leather cuffs all three of them wore, and knowing what they covered. The mark on the dark-haired guy's wrist.

That crimson, twisting glyph and its vivid pulsing, the way it made her stomach churn.

Erik. She wrote the name, then the old guy's. *Ignatius*. Who was the blond, again? He looked a little like Neal. Maybe it was only the self-satisfaction lurking around the set of his mouth; she was usually much better with names than this. The attorneys all knew the Stellack girl had a mind like a steel trap.

They'd probably replaced her by now. Would the partners want to investigate a missing paralegal?

Listing things was supposed to help her make some sense of all this. There didn't seem much sense to be found.

God, she wished Mika was here. Anyone, really, but Mika would have been best; despite appearing flighty as fuck and butterfly-unreliable, she was ferociously organized underneath. *Camouflage*, she would occasionally laugh. *They don't ask me to do shit if they think I'm a brainless bimbo.*

Well, what would her best friend say? *You and your lists. Look, what does your gut tell you?*

Liv pulled out a fresh piece of paper. Maybe, instead of listing whether or not she believed this shit, she should take a different tack.

First, I want my phone back. She bent over the table like a schoolgirl, ignoring her complaining stomach. She wanted to eat, sure—but she *needed* the sliding, squirrely sensation behind her breastbone to go away. Needed to find some way, *any* way, to make all of this seem somehow reasonable instead of a horrifying madness she was trapped in.

How would she be able to tell if it was a hallucination? Even the sleet outside, a fine thin drizzle that looked like it would intensify as the afternoon wore on, was just as it should be. She couldn't see the huge, scroll-festooned front gate from this window, but she was still on the third floor. The trees and winter-sleeping garden below hadn't changed—or would she be able to tell if they had?

Biting her lip slightly, Liv began to write.

"IT'S NOT THAT difficult to understand." She tried not to scowl at her latte—double coconut, just to see if they had it. She was *definitely* sulling up; Gramma Poe would have waved a gnarled finger at her. "I want my phone back, and my purse. That'll go a long way towards making me believe you."

"The first thing you would do is attempt to contact your friends or family." The old guy glanced at the blond, who had brought the coffee and a tray of high-end pastries. There was no receipt or paper sleeves to show where he'd bought them; it was par for the course. "That cannot be allowed."

"So I really am a prisoner." She dared him to disagree, fixing him with Mom's Hairdresser Stare.

Unfortunately, it didn't seem to make a dent. "It's better for your loved ones to grieve you than for them to come to the attention of the unclean. These protocols are in place for your protection, Miss Stellack, and for the protection of those you care for."

"Isn't that convenient." On the surface, it was a reasonable enough policy. If she thought about this like a lunatic version of the Witness Protection Program, would it get any easier to handle? "Isn't that just *peachy*. So the threat of these imaginary things is supposed to keep me isolated and—"

"You are under no obligation to believe me, Miss Stellack." Ignatius folded his dry, callused hands. He didn't even glance at her list of demands, though the blond was peering over the top of his own blank white paper cup at them. "In any case, your cell phone and your purse have both been incinerated. There is nothing left of either."

Well, great, you son of a bitch, thanks. They weren't giving her a lot to go on. She opened her mouth to protest again—for all the good she suspected it would do—but he beat her to the punch, so to speak.

"Much of the rest, we will be more than happy to provide." How did he know, if he wasn't even looking? But Ignatius continued, briskly. "For example, footwear—since you will not be leaving the temple just yet, it seemed unnecessary. You have not listed your preference, simply *shoes.* How many pairs, and of what type?"

Temple. Okay, old-fashioned, but so's he. "So I get shoes, that's great." She couldn't help herself, the sarcasm just slipped out. "You burned my phone?"

"And your clothes, and your purse," the blond piped up, regarding her steadily. Where was Erik? She liked him better than either of these assholes, but then again, they could be manipulating her into considering him a refuge. Sleep-deprived, hungry, and walloped with unfamiliarities, she was probably vulnerable.

Probably? No, Liv felt extra super-duper vulnerable. She looked away, at the painfully clean fireplace; it stood to reason they didn't want to give her a match or two, not to mention firewood. Sleet rustled, sweeping the walls. It would have been nice to have a fire and a good book or two.

"Great." The word trembled. *That's just great, Liv. Show them you're scared.*

"I know it seems harsh, at this point." Ignatius wore a very faint smile, like a senior partner watching a junior attorney dig a hole during a deposition. "But the rules are there for good reasons, *lirai.* Your safety is our primary goal, then, and only then, your comfort."

"Order of operations," she muttered, and set the stupid latte down. She didn't even like coconut. There were two *pains au chocolat* on the tray, and they looked good—but how could she trust the food?

"It's very natural for you to be doubting any evidence we could provide." The old guy was utterly imperturbable. "Even that of your own senses. You are attempting to force this situation to obey the rules of the daytime world. It will not, and you'll have a great deal of difficulty for some time yet."

The daytime world. "Shoes and some decent shampoo." She glanced at her list, just now noticing how jagged and uneven her penmanship was. Her hands just wouldn't stop shaking. "And a laptop, because—"

He shook his iron-grey head, a precise little motion not daring to ruffle even a single hair. "You will use it to attempt contact. We cannot risk your safety, or a civilian's."

Civilian. What a telling little word—it was the way cops talked. You were on one side of the line or the other, with no straddling or, God forbid, time-sharing. "You aren't acting like the good guys here, you know."

"Who told you we were?" The blond obviously thought she was a rude little bitch; she longed to return the favor with interest. "All we are is the lesser evil, ma'am."

"What's your name again?" *So I know what to call you when I stick a pin in a voodoo doll.*

Of course, if monsters, mad gods, and superhuman monster hunters were real, it might even work. Maybe she could add *voodoo doll* to the list?

"Jake, ma'am." He even gave her a cheeky little wink, very sure of himself. "Short for Jacob, but as long as it's not *late for dinner*—"

You get more irritating the more I hear you talk, kid. "So you're not the good guys. At least you admit it."

"We could discuss the nature of *good* quite philosophically, if you were inclined." Ignatius gave the blond a quelling glance, a brief odd light folding over his eyes before fleeing and returning them to human darkness. "But Jacob is quite correct. We are indeed a much lesser evil, Miss Stellack. And though we might be sorry for it, the fact gives us a latitude of action necessary for defending what we must from *him* and other creatures."

Latitude of action is a pretty fancy way of saying you're well aware said actions are inexcusable, young man. Doing her famous Granny Goose impression wasn't going to get her anywhere, though. And she was starving.

If they'd drugged the pastries, she'd find out. The plates were whisper-thin porcelain, a few of them holding tiny hand-painted forget-me-nots. Neither of them made a move while she took a *pain au chocolat* and glanced nervously at the door to the hall.

It was open. The dark-haired guy was probably right outside. They'd arranged the whole "almost get eaten by monsters" to drive home the point that escape was, if not impossible, then going to be very difficult.

Now that she knew what was waiting outside.

Despite being mass produced, the pastry was still tasty as all get out. The blond watched her while she chewed, maybe trying to be encouraging. And, impossibly, as soon as she swallowed the first dose of simple carbs and oven-fried butter, everything suddenly seemed much more manageable.

"Keep talking," she said, grimly. "Go down the list, and tell me what you *will* do. Then I'll write another one."

Ignatius studied her for a few moments, and his thin lips curved the slightest fraction. He absolutely reminded her of an old criminal prosecutor, aware of every human foible and just waiting for roadkill to ruffle his feathers over.

"Yes, *lirai*," he said, as if it was a formal response, and used a single fingertip to bring her list closer to his slice of the table. "We will do what we can."

Room Service

THE KITCHEN—wide, airy, and with its granite countertops ruthlessly scrubbed—was their usual pre-patrol meeting point, though Ignatius would probably have preferred them to use the armory. "Real cute." Jake shook his head, shrugging into his coat. "Puts *cell phone* and *ID* at the top of every list. Stubborn girl."

"That'll serve her well when she faces the Flame." Ordinarily Erik would be preparing for patrol with him, but instead, Ignatius was going to take point tonight. It was Father's first time on patrol in a while; Erik's job tonight was to be on call for the *lirai*, who had spent the afternoon making progressively longer lists of things for her protectors to fetch and carry. Some, like shoes, were reasonable enough. Others, however. . . . "She wants houseplants? Father didn't tell her we're going to travel?"

"Control wants more daylight before we do, though. You'd think they'd want her locked up in an active temple by now, but . . ." Jake tested his knives, spun them, and slid them back into their homes, then popped his jacket collar. Grunts always complained about higher-ups having no idea what the front lines were enduring; it was a very human quality. Probably the only one a Son had left. "I think she's just being difficult."

Taking all the identifiable packing off luxury purchases was going to be a chore, but it was better than slogging through muck and killing the unclean. He didn't envy Jake that at all. "Well, her entire life's been turned upside down."

"Shoulda sealed her first thing," Jake muttered, as if that would have done any good in this situation. He shook his head, settling his coat afresh over a couple layers plus the weapons rig. "Easier to make her see reason, but no, you had to be all noble. Anyway, Father's bringing his sword."

That was news. "Sounds serious." Of course, a *lirai* at a frontline, almost forgotten temple—even just a potential—wouldn't go unnoticed. The non-sentient—or even just semi-sentient—would gather, and the smarter unclean would be planning.

"It sounds overprepared." Jake was a big believer in improv.

Ignatius's feelings on preparation closely mirrored Erik's own, and Erik further thought improv wasn't any goddamn use without planning providing a foundation. "Well, we *are* Boy Scouts. After a fashion."

"Bite your tongue, bro." Jake blinked and grinned, an amused echo of the orphan boy he had been so long ago, arriving at Nightshade's dormitories for initial training. "I haven't helped a little old lady across the street in decades."

"Well, you've got tonight." Erik's hands tingled with the urge to check his own weapons, probably the equivalent of a nervous tic. "Go get started."

Jake laughed, sketched a small salute, and left. Erik finished with the tray—even a sprig of fresh rosemary in a tiny fluted vase, in case the chicken needed more seasoning—and was surprised into immobility, suddenly wishing he was doing patrol prep instead. It wasn't that he underestimated Ignatius, or Jake, but . . . he just would have felt better if he was out killing unclean instead of held in the house, waiting for the *lirai* to get another whim or the shadowbeasts to chance the temple's passive defenses.

He felt the change as Father and Younger Brother left, like a weather front moving through. Erik's head cocked; he stared at his reflection in the wide bay window over the triple sinks. Keeping the place updated was fun; he liked construction work. Maybe after they took their potential to the Flame, they could come back. Or settle in a temple closer to other *lirai*-held territory, expanding the clear zones.

Wouldn't *that* be nice. Finding even a single potential opened up the world for a Son. It wasn't just the prospect of a Dreamer liking you enough to seal up and shut off the Mad God's constant whisper; an active temple with access to the Flame meant you could catch glimpses of *lirai* and get a little peace, the need for constant painful second-guessing of your own motives and thoughts ameliorated by proximity to their deep, soft power.

Balancing the tray on one hand while he knocked was like a coordination test in training. He could even make it a game, so steady water in the carafe didn't ripple. Erik listened intently, hoping she wasn't going to come at him with part of the bedstead.

They'd barely finished repairing the smaller *liraim*.

"Come in, I guess." A reluctant mutter on the other side of the baffle, and from the sound of it, she was near the window. The door swung wide, and there she was, arms crossed, staring at him.

Black sweater, a wide ballerina neckline slipping to show the curve of one pretty shoulder, her hair a wild mass of half-combed tangles, shadows under her dark eyes, and a pair of combat boots bought just that morning laced up so tightly they probably hurt peeking from under her jeans' hems, their precious *lirai* regarded him mistrustfully. The table was scattered with paper both flat and wadded, scribbled on and blank, and plain white boxes were piled on her bed.

The lady had certainly kept them hopping.

"Oh." Her hands dropped to her sides. Did she actually look relieved? "It's you."

"Yes ma'am." He barely knew where to look, or where to set the tray. "Dinner. Lemon rosemary chicken, pilaf, Californian *chenin blanc*. Father thought you might like it, but if you don't I can—"

"I order my own drinks." But a faint smile touched her soft, chapped lips, and she hurried to clear the table. "Sorry, let me just . . . okay, there. I didn't expect room service."

"You think we'd leave you to starve?" The instant it was out of his mouth, he regretted the question. There probably wasn't much she *didn't* think them capable of at the moment.

"To make me amenable? Maybe." She eyed him sidelong, a flicker of those big dark eyes. "I wouldn't put it past him. The old guy."

So her irritation was settling on Ignatius. He was going to lose *that* bet; Erik had been sure she'd hate his own clumsy guts. "Father's just . . ." He checked the heat-bubble over the plate, keeping the dish at optimum temperature. Everything was pretty artistically arranged, if he did say so himself. "Well, he's set in his ways, and he has to argue with Control all the time to get us equipment." Not that she needed to know about budget battles, or that she'd fallen into the hands of frontline grunts unable to provide even a fraction of a *lirai*'s due. "He doesn't want to lose you. You're important."

"If you say so." Her chin jutted a little; she laid paper and pens on her crowded bed, carefully not turning her back to him. "Where's yours?"

Sleet swept the window, a soft restless stroking. It was a miserable night outside even with a Son's ability to turn aside freezing, falling water. Durability and weather tolerance was sometimes a curse. "What?"

She didn't roll her big dark eyes, but it was probably close. "Where's your dinner?"

"I . . . um." Erik went over the tray again. Plate, bread plate, bread basket, cutlery, water tumbler, water carafe, wineglass, wine bottle sweating tiny clear drops—everything was there. Then the full meaning struck home. "Oh. I don't need one."

"I'll feel rude, eating in front of you."

That was a surprise. He would have thought she was past being polite. "I . . . suppose I could get another wineglass? Or just use the tumbler, or—there's your bedside glass, I can bring you a fresh one after—"

"You don't eat?" Her distress was almost visible, pinging around the room in high-pitched waves, a sonar of misery. "Or you just don't eat with me?"

Now wasn't the time to tell her exactly what a Son of Ymre subsisted on. Food was fine if you couldn't get the usual stuff, though. "It didn't occur to me that you'd want company." Erik fought the urge to stand at attention. It didn't seem like she'd find it at all comforting. "Especially mine."

"That's fair." She glanced at the plate, a shy doe eyeing a meadow. "You don't have to, I guess."

"A *lirai*'s invitation is an honor." It wasn't quite an Ignatius impression, but it was close, and Erik had the satisfaction of seeing another of those tiny, fleeting smiles. "Come on, eat. You've got to stay strong."

"If you want to brainwash me, there needs to be less protein." Another faint vertical line had begun between her winged eyebrows, and she didn't take the chair he pulled out for her. Instead, she settled in the one Erik had used a few hours ago, and regarded him with some trepidation. "You know that, right?"

Was that what she was afraid of? "I'll let Father know." Erik bent—slow, no sharp angles or twitches, just as if he were stalking a motion-sensitive beast like an *iraich* or a siphoner—and took the plate, arranging it in front of her. He was trying not to loom, but he had to lean close to get the wineglass settled, the way he'd seen waiters in better restaurants perform the trick. "In the meantime, you should really eat something."

"Father?" She sat bolt upright, almost quivering, and though the glow of potential through her was soothing, it had an edge of rasping almost-fear. "Is he your dad?"

God, no. Erik all but shuddered. The few faint impressions remaining of his earthly chromosome donor weren't as bad as training or the night battles, but they still sent a shiver down his spine. He'd been outright glad to go to the orphanage; he'd never asked, but Jacob probably felt the same. "More like a sponsor, I guess."

"Have you ever met any others like you? Or like me? *Lirai?*" She handled the word tolerably well.

"Yeah, back in Europe." He sank into the chair across from her, painfully slow. "There's lots of us, though. We're just soldiers. Potentials—you know, people with the ability to become *lirai*—are a lot rarer." All the statistics he'd heard were in the neighborhood of one in around a thousand civilians, and plenty didn't survive adolescence. The only thing the shadowbeasts liked better than snacking on defenseless potentials was getting close to full-blown Dreamers. But the latter had the Sons, not to mention the Flame's, protection. She didn't need to know what kinds of odds she'd bucked at the moment, though, so he searched for something else to say. "We're frontliners, didn't get sent stateside until training was finished. We took this satellite territory to keep the fringes clear. Closest active temple is . . . oh, probably Stanfeld." Ignatius would know.

True to form, she seized on that little piece of intel. "And where are we right now?"

You're pumping me for information, beautiful. That's okay. He couldn't blame her, and it made no difference anyway. "A little north of Longpoint."

"Good neighborhood." She touched her plate with a fingertip. Fragrant steam lifted as the heat-bubble folded aside, sensing the end of its usefulness. "I'm sure the schools are nice."

Easy access to prime hunting grounds. Ignatius was always talking about how they should have some backup, *any* backup, occasionally even muttering about how Control expected miracles without parting with any funding to provide them.

"I wouldn't know." Erik sat just as straight and tense as their potential, waiting for her to change her mind.

"So, Erik." She poured with a facility that showed a bit of food service in her past but gave him the wineglass *and* the wine, confining herself to water. "Do you have a last name?"

"No ma'am." *Not any I'm willing to claim.* He'd even have to think and count on his fingers a bit to figure out exactly how old he was; he was fairly sure any kin he had was plowed under by war or poverty by now.

"Family?" she persisted.

He could answer that easily enough, chapter and verse. "The Sons are my family, ma'am."

"It's not *ma'am.*" A mild flare of irritation, but at least she was regarding the plate as if it contained something remotely edible instead of offal. Progress was being made. "It's Liv."

"Not Livvie?" *Button your mouth, Erik.*

"You can try *Ms. Stellack*." She picked up her heavy silver fork, and her shy glance was more mischievous than he might have thought her capable of. "But not *Miss* like the old guy says. Where did you find that fossil?"

He found me. Erik could still remember standing at the end of his dorm bed, his hair freshly cropped and the mark burning on his wrist, while Ignatius paused, eyeing him. *Lirai* had first pick of trainees, of course, but Fathers going out to the front lines came right after, and it was good to be found acceptable for once. "Somewhere in a sediment bed, I guess. How's the rice?"

"All right." Did she look, of all things, hopeful? "You want some?"

"Not very hungry." He took a slice of the bread, telling himself it was just to remind her he was mostly human and not as big a threat as the unclean. It wasn't bad, for mass-produced baked goods masquerading as restaurant quality. In an active temple instead of a fringe one, there would be a chef or three and a kitchen kept humming at every hour to provide anything a *lirai* might take it into their head to consume. "Thank you."

That seemed to soothe a little of her anxiety, and Erik might have congratulated himself on finally handling her the right way if several tiny nails hadn't scraped featherlight over his skin, tightening the sleeve that kept muscle, bone, and blood neatly packed. A man was just a sausage, when all was said and done.

"Excuse me," he said, politely enough, and left her with her fork in midair, closing the *liraim*'s door as softly as possible.

It was a *leng*-spider, a crafty hunter. Still, it obviously didn't expect a Son to fall upon its unprotected back as it worked at breaking the eastern curtain of defenses. Such a thing was easily dispatched, and with the wet and cold sluiced off him, Erik returned to find the barely touched tray still on the table, food rapidly cooling since the heat-shell had been broken. The *lirai* had hidden in the bathroom the entire time, her pulse entirely too high, thudding in his own ears.

He wanted to knock on the door and ask if she was all right, but what purpose would that serve? So he just took the tray and retreated, trying not to hear that frantic heart-pounding and wishing he knew what to say—if anything—to make her a little less afraid.

All Right Ever Again

THE BED WAS soft, at least, and the sheets smelled of that same expensive fabric softener as the clothes. The blankets and comforter weren't heavy enough, but the suite was relentlessly warm so it wasn't a problem. It was even pleasant, she admitted, to be curled up in comfort while a thin freezing rain needled the windows.

If she hadn't been kidnapped by funky monster hunters, she might have been enjoying herself immensely. As it was, the only control she had in this situation was making lists of things for them to fetch; as a coping mechanism, it kind of sucked.

As soon as she had a handle on one aspect of this bullshit, something else came along and she lost her grip. The latest thing was dinner—oh, the rice was all right, she supposed, but the bottom dropping out of her stomach just before Erik's expression changed and he excused himself hadn't been optimal for further consumption of foodstuffs.

What was even worse was how she could literally *feel* him retreating through the house, and the sudden sense of being almost alone as she rattled at the locked door had turned everything inside her to quaking mush. Not only that, but her head hurt, swift lancing pains retreating all at once a few minutes before he came back.

It didn't take much in the brain department to figure out he'd probably driven off another . . . well, another monster. That same strange instinct, like the fine hairs rising all over her body when the barometric pressure changed, showed up when Jake and Ignatius had returned near three in the morning too.

Which was why she was tossing and turning despite the exhaustion.

We are a lesser evil. Nice of them to admit it out loud, but still.

The whole thing was ridiculous, especially the idea that she wouldn't trust her own senses. Sure, they could have drugged her—but what drug in existence would give her *precisely* that kind of hallucination without any other side effects?

The portion of her psych degree spent going over pharmacology was coming in handy now. Even recreational substance use in college was. Unfortunately, though, paralegal experience only worked when there was a court willing to take on a malefactor or two.

Liv had also spent some time listing, in two columns, *what if it's true* and *what if it's not.* The implications of either were unpleasant, but honestly . . . it didn't make sense for them to spend all this time or effort, not to mention cash, if all they wanted was a pliant captive for rape or control.

The biggest weight on the scale was, of course, the dreams.

Liv moved restlessly again, punching a pillow—allergy-free down substitute, or so the tags said—into submission and wishing she could slide a bare foot from the blankets' stifling embrace. It was the only real way to cool off if you needed to, but the strange, childlike idea that there might be something waiting in the darkness to close cold bony fingers over her ankle was too strong to permit such a move.

It didn't help that she sensed one or another of the guys outside the suite's door. They probably slept in shifts. Monster hunters needed rest, too.

Take a deep breath, Liv. Think this through.

If it weren't for her vivid nightmares, the goddamn constant ever-loving *dreams*, she'd be able to chalk all this up to kidnapping with an as-yet-unknown endgame, and be on her guard.

But Erik *knew.* She had never, ever described the one with the yellow door to anyone, not even her mother.

Liv winced. Thinking about Mom was not good this late at night. Or early in the morning, whatever. Even Mika only knew Liv's dad had gone in a car accident and her mother had passed some time afterward, not . . . the rest of it.

Unless he came in through the chimney, the detective had said, and Liv wanted to scream. It would probably be intensely therapeutic to wail into the pillows, except one of the men might knock at the door and want to know if she was that most absurd of things, *all right.*

Nothing was going to be all right ever again.

She turned again, this time onto her back, arms and legs starfish-spread. It was a nice bed, the kind you could eat breakfast in before reading a transcript on a lazy weekend morning. Plenty of room, and the mattress, like Baby Bear's, was *just* right. Plus her eyelids were so heavy.

Oh, the dreams. They showed her terrible things, and part of the reason she'd chosen a psych degree was to figure out why nightmares and déjà vu mixed so frequently inside her head. A few times, the terrible things *had* actually happened, and the swimming feeling that she'd seen it all before was enough to make her doubt her own sanity.

Finding out she maybe hadn't been at the mercy of faltering neurons wasn't even remotely comforting.

A sudden swift falling sensation swallowed her, and she jolted back into wakefulness. That was the thing about dreams—you *had* to rest or go insane, and the evanescent bastards lay in wait for you just beyond the door of conscious thought, grinning with yellow, blood-grimed teeth.

Sleep-deprivation psychosis was looking more and more appealing all the time.

The Mad God, they said. *A nonsense word, because we don't mention* his *name*. Funny, when they mentioned the guy, the stress on *he* or *him* made it perfectly clear who they meant—and wasn't that thought-provoking too, that super-fast, super-strong monster hunters had something they wouldn't even name hanging around?

Yeah. It provoked a whole lot of thoughts, not to mention feelings.

The first few faint tinges of grey were blooming at the window's edges when she finally dropped off, curled on her side, her breathing deepening. After a long motionless time, her eyelids began to flutter, and her lips twitched.

She dreamed of a dark well, curved and cyclopean blocks of stone fitted together without mortar into a vaulted ceiling receding as she fell into a dark throat. Strange variegated fire coruscated in rainbow ropes up the sides, and she knew, with the sudden startled certainty of dreams, that it would hurt very much when it touched her—*if* it reached her before she hit the bottom of the well, ramming against stone with the force of an exploding star.

Daylight strengthened; a faint, formless mutter slipped from Liv's lips, and she drifted deeper into slumber.

Safe Than Sorry

THE SALLE—ONCE a small refectory—was long and high, its walls pierced by high narrow windows, soupy winter sunshine highlighting golden motes of falling dust. The floor, stone blocks carefully mortared together, had been washed almost daily for years, but nothing could remove the faint odor of institutional cooking and the sharpish odor of men crammed shoulder to shoulder on hard wooden benches, hunched over their bowls.

Racks of weapons stood at prescribed distances—but nothing modern. The salle was where a Son trained with edge, bludgeon, and chain, not with bullet or bolt.

"Good night?" Erik held the satin-polished iron bar level, his back straight, and waited for his Younger Brother to lose patience as he inevitably did.

"Exciting." Jake's hair glowed under buzzing fluorescents and thin grey winter light. His eyes hooded and he moved in, his own stave blurring and bending fractionally as velocity and gravity both clawed at it.

The noise was immediate smithy-clattering slipslither music punctuated by soft exhales when a blow landed exactly where planned. Erik played it safe, holding defense against Jake's battering. Younger Brothers often had an edge in speed, but as Father said, age and treachery were more than enough to meet youth and skill.

"Everyone wants a piece," Jake continued, backing up a few steps and regarding him. "We were on the jump all night long. Here?"

"The same." Erik hoped the *lirai* hadn't felt the gathering predators too much; every time he returned to the baffle outside her door, everything behind it was silent except for the thunder of her pulse. "Looks like everyone knows we got lucky."

He wanted to add *what the fuck is Control thinking*, but the person making decisions about bringing a potential in would be a fully trained *lirai*; Control was just passing along the news.

"Can't hide it." Jake's smile was a snarl. He smelled of rain even after a shower and less-physical cleanup, and the deep unsteady fume of rage hung on him, too.

Younger Brother with the fury, Elder Brother past anger and holding out against insanity, a Father who had mastered both, that was the way of the Sons. At least, as far as the Mad God's whispering could be mastered, without a *lirai*'s presence—or a seal, for those truly lucky bastards who managed to earn a Dreamer's trust—to hold it at bay.

Erik moved, then, breaking his steady defense pattern for a short, brutal flurry. They were both breathing in great deep swells by the time he retreated again, and Jake's gaze had taken on a hard seamless glitter.

"Thought you were supposed to be *fast*," Erik taunted.

"Thought you were supposed to be smart," Jake spat, and threw himself at his tormentor.

Iron was fun, but you had to keep its shear tolerances in mind or you'd end up with shards and nothing else. Erik batted aside a flurry of testing blows, knowing his own slight smile would irritate Jake all the more.

"Temper, temper," he crooned, and had the distinct satisfaction of seeing an opening in his little brother's pattern. Erik's stave leapt, and it was a good thing it was blunt instead of edged. Even so, and at minimal strength, the strike tossed Jake half the salle, and Younger Brother landed hard but balanced, feet barely touching before flashing in a complicated pattern to bleed momentum.

"Asshole." But Jake was slowly learning to throttle the anger. Maybe he'd make elder status soon, heading out to another trio, and another younger would move in to keep Ignatius and Erik cheerful. "So? Did you?"

Are you still on that? "Did I what?"

"You didn't." Jake *tch-tch*'d, like Father when more-than-usually disappointed.

Erik shook his head, his pulse barely rising above somnolence. He remembered being in a Younger Brother's shoes, the scratching impatience, the deep welling ferocity. Once the discomfort was gone the insanity began to rise, the god whispering in your blood with the papery sound of a thousand blinking eyelashes against damp silk. "Not gonna, Jake."

"Better safe than sorry." The mulish set to his younger's mouth meant he knew he was wrong, but he wasn't going to back down just yet.

Beating sense into your junior was a time-honored Sons tradition.

"Exactly." It wouldn't do any good to explain—once Jake got an idea he was like a terrier, shaking it until nothing remained but a rag. Still,

Erik tried anyway. "We're gonna be with her a while."

"The sooner one of us seals her, the sooner we can—"

"What, fuck up our only chance with a *lirai*?" Some of Erik's weariness probably leached into the words. "She ends up hating us and we'll be back out on rotation, maybe with a different Father."

"So?" Jake's chin set even further, and with his long nose, he looked more like a petulant teenager than a full-fledged Son. At least he knew better than to bring this up with Father, or so Erik hoped. "Change'll do us good."

"Don't try it." Erik didn't like giving the ultimatum—it was the quickest way to make Jake decide to risk what he was warned against—but what else could be done? "The last thing she needs is more trauma."

"It's not like it won't happen anyway, sooner or later." Sweat had begun on Jake's forehead, a slight healthy glow. The chiming of metal on metal was almost soothing; he batted a stray strike contemptuously away. "And I'd be *respectful*."

"Sealing a *lirai* without consent isn't respect, Jake." Why did they need to have this conversation more than once? Was Younger Brother working himself up to something unwise? "Come on."

"She'd get over it." Jake's smile was a masterpiece of fetching fecklessness. "They always do."

"Uh-huh." There were songs about a *lirai* sealed against their will, and they were all plaintive. "Would *you*?"

"Shit, man . . ." Jake bashed aside both the question and Erik's next blow. "She's got it easy. Just sit up there while we're bleeding."

"Remember what your first nights in dorm were like?" Erik tapped a halfhearted return-strike aside. "Or your first live-fire run? Now imagine not knowing what the hell was going on." *And not having a weapon handy to fight with.* A Dreamer's concentration of numinous force was instinctive, even if it blinded them while utilized. A Son, picking it up and channeling, became several orders of magnitude more deadly to the Mad God's other followers, not to mention garden-variety predators.

The point seemed to get through to his little brother, though Jake's lower lip pooched out a bit. He was giving ground, slowly but surely, the iron staves just barely kissing before springing apart. An onlooker might have thought they were dancing. "We've explained everything."

"And you think that's good enough?" Erik's pulse dropped, a sure sign that he was taking this more seriously. *Why?* He moved in, a flurry beating little brother back, and back, and back.

"We're *Sons*." Like Jake would say *water's wet* or *it's winter*. "It should fucking well be."

It gave Erik the opening he needed, and his stave blurred in a complicated pattern to distract the eye before he kicked and sent Jake flying. The sudden silence after clash-chiming steelplay was alive with echoes.

The end of Erik's stave, round and polished, lingered under Jake's chin. "It takes time," he said, almost kindly. The anger was the last thing to go before simple endurance became the watchword, waiting for the whispers to finally drive you closer to *him*.

The only thing standing in the way of that slow, agonizing slide was a *lirai*. He couldn't quite blame a younger for just wanting the whispers to stop.

"You're just like Father." Jake's cheeks were scarlet. They should be; he'd been taken by a sucker move. "A fucking coward."

He didn't really mean it, but still, it almost stung. Erik found his mouth curving, a cruel grimace almost passing for a smile. "Yeah, but I'm the coward who knocked you on your ass."

Jake almost surged up, but Erik's stave didn't move, and he kept his Younger Brother there long enough to make the point before retreating with a light fencer's shuffle, weight and weapon balanced at every moment.

"Shit." Jake wiped at his bleeding mouth. He also winced, a little theatrically; for all that it granted much greater endurance, the mark didn't halt pain. "Sorry, Erik."

"Not necessary." And it wasn't. You became an elder when you could forgive the petty shit; Erik had the idea it might take a while for his companion. "Just glad one of us can still feel, you know. Anger."

"Yeah." Jake rose, a single graceful motion. "Wanna switch to knives?"

Not today, little man. And especially not after he'd won one; Jake got mean when he lost.

"Nah." Erik stepped back, clearing his weapon to assure himself of free play, a movement so habitual, it was now instinctive. "I gotta report to Father."

"Great. I'll take Her Majesty breakfast." Even that prospect didn't cheer Jake up much. "She better not give me another list."

"If she does, you'll smile and be happy to have it." It was a risk, but Erik decided to turn his back while he racked his stave. The skin between his shoulder blades roughened.

"I guess." Jake didn't move. Was he watching; did he understand the message?

"Cheer up, little brother." The words threatened to stick in his throat. "I'm giving her to the Flame; you'll be the one she likes after that. It'll be easy."

In other words, *don't be selfish, wait your turn.* If Erik had just learned that lesson he might not have become a Son; the trainers and winnowers went through orphanages looking for barely controlled powder kegs with the requisite mental—and moral—flexibility on a regular basis.

An utter bastard survived the training better, even if they were sometimes lost when the mark was first applied.

"Silver linings." Jake still hadn't moved, and he sounded thoughtful, now.

Erik did him the further courtesy of not looking back before palming the door to the locker room open. Trust was rare, even among your brothers.

So was respect.

Mad God

ONCE THE SUN was up Liv could sleep, but damp, ghost-pale morning brought breakfast, delivered on a covered tray by the blond one. He rapped at the bedroom door, and she could even distinguish *his* knock from the other guy's.

Erik tapped politely. The blond guy all but rattled the blockage off its hinges.

"Ma'am?" Even through the heavy wood, he *sounded* like a douchebag. Liv considered turning over and clamping a pillow to her head, but the thought that one or more of them might break in and drag her to the table brought her out of the warm safe nest in a rush. At least he didn't jiggle the doorknob, but she was already up, and when she peered cautiously out of the bedroom the blond was all the way at the suite door, his hands crossed loosely in front of him and his hair glowing under weak pearly daylight.

He was grinning, too. Almost ear to ear.

"There she is." His smile didn't alter; it looked painted on. "Not gonna bite you, *lirai.* It's Jake, short for Jacob."

I don't think I care. She took her time from behind the door, studying him. Checking the emotional weather of her captors was a survival measure, but she didn't have to like it.

He looked altogether too satisfied with himself, but not irritated. "I can leave, if you want to eat alone. Didn't know what you wanted in the latte this time, so it's plain."

The fact that he'd made the right choice, even by accident, was infuriating. Still, Liv took stock. She had grey pajamas and black socks, thankfully clean and dry—where the brown-haired guy had put the others she didn't want to guess, and hoped it had been an incinerator—but she didn't have a weapon, or anything that could pass for one.

Short-for-Jacob didn't look like he was going to leave, so she coughed slightly, working the sleep out of her throat. It felt like something dry and scaly had scraped down her esophagus, and wasn't *that* a terrible mental image? "This isn't the part where you offer to let me escape again, is it?"

"Nope." Jake stilled, the uncanny immobility he shared with the other two men. It was disconcerting, seeing them pause while the rest of the world continued. Like a bad special effect—or a terrifyingly good one. "I'd say sorry about that, but I'm not."

At least he admitted it.

Liv leaned against the small slice of opened door, bracing it in case he got ideas. Her stomach cramped, right on the verge of an embarrassing rumble.

"But we had to make the point without you getting hurt, and that was the only way to do it," Jake continued, soothingly, nice and reasonable. "Father was out thinning the ranks of the unclean, Erik was defending you, and I was midrange. Standard."

Standard, he said. How many times had he done this? "How often do you do this sort of thing? Kidnap *lirai*?"

"You're the first potential I've ever seen outside of training, ma'am. Haven't seen a real true *lirai* for about thirty years or so."

What, you were in diapers then? But if she could believe in giant tentacled horrors, why not a little bit of eternal youth?

The worst part wasn't the nightmare beasts or even her own unruly, terrifying dreams. It was that she was beginning to accept a lot of outlandish bullshit as natural and possibly inevitable. "Thirty years?"

"Probably thirty-two. What year is it?"

For the love of . . . "I don't know unless I look at my phone," she hedged. If he was a sexist asshole, he might even believe it.

"Nice try." His smile didn't alter, but a shade of genuine warmth crept into its curve, like he was pleased at a good move in a sports match. "Yeah, thirty-two years. Time gets funny when you get your mark."

The thought of that violent crimson tattoo was enough to kill her appetite. Or it should have been, but she was flat-out *starving*. "Does it keep you young?"

"Sort of. We don't really age, part of *his* dominion over flesh." There was no doubt who he meant, the loathing in the single syllable was all but bubbling-toxic. "You want me to leave you with your breakfast, ma'am? It'll stay hot until you get to it."

Isn't that useful. "Is that magic?"

"Sort of." He didn't relax, but his gaze slid away to the window, came back with a smooth arc that reminded her of a security camera. "Father would call it *an application of natural laws mankind has only begun to codify*."

It sounded like a direct quote; Jake obviously had a gift for mimicry. It was the old guy's even, controlled, robotic delivery right down to the breathing. A tiny laugh snuck past Liv's lips, a happy little thief.

"And she has a sense of humor, too." Jake's grin widened, less a grimace and more true amusement. "The total package, ladies and gentlemen."

Liv let the door swing open a little further. The covered tray beckoned, and if it held a new heart-stopping surprise, she was going to see if she *could* stab him with a fork. She might not be able to hurt these guys, but her training as a monster hunter had to start somewhere, right?

Always assuming that was what they had in mind. But if they didn't, what use was she? "I'll come out," she said, finally. "If you answer a question."

"You don't have to bargain, *lirai*." That sobered him up; the grin faded by degrees, and his sandy eyebrows drew together. "Just ask, I'll answer as best I can. Always."

Awful nice of you, but I don't think you're trustworthy. They paid a lot of lip service to being polite, but of course, she'd been *kidnapped*. "When do I start training?" She took a deep breath. "To hunt those things, the monsters."

Jake made a restless movement, like a horse smelling fire. "Any sane person wouldn't want to."

Well, she couldn't argue, but still. It was just like wheedling a favor or some paperwork out of a particularly cranky court clerk. "I've been kidnapped by a trio of monster hunters. Sanity might be a drawback in this particular situation."

"Well, technically we're straight predators instead of monster hunters, but good point." He rubbed at his gold-stubbled chin with blunt, callused fingertips. "As for training, you won't need it; *lirai* are instinctively deadly. All you need is the Flame, and that's not here."

The Flame. Okay. "Where is it?"

"Any temple with an active *lirai* will have access to it. We just take you to one of your own kind, and then . . ." He spread his hands, a helpless movement but still a relief from that uncanny stillness. "Well, would you believe me if I said you have to see it first?"

I might not have a week or two ago. She didn't even know what *day* it was. "Maybe." Grudging acceptance colored the word; Liv pushed the bedroom door a little further open. "So, Jake. You got a last name?"

"Nope. Won't be passing anything on." The grin was back, but an uneasy shadow moved in his dark gaze. Electric light was kind to him, bringing out all the gold in his hair, lightening his eyes a bit. If she saw him in a bar she might look twice; he had the kind of relaxed magnetism that caught the eye, and his shoulders were nicely broad. "Besides, I was an orphan. Nobody wanted me. Well, except the Sons."

Is that how you got here? She made a mental note to brood on the implications of that tiny nugget of information, and opened the door a little further. Erik had said basically the same thing. "I'm sorry."

"About what?" Now he sounded honestly puzzled.

She could make conversation, empathize, and maybe find a chink in his armor all at once. "It's never nice to feel unwanted."

"That psych degree of yours must be getting a workout." But Jake didn't sound sarcastic. Just thoughtful.

"It's useful." She hesitated a little more, but a thin thread of coffee-smell reached her. Her stomach was about to tear itself free and go running after victuals caveman-style soon. "How long do you guys live, then?" *I can't believe I'm asking this.*

"Long time." He tilted his head, giving the question his entire consideration. "Unless we die in combat or go 'round the bend. Bet they haven't told you that bit yet, huh?"

Liv just stared at him. *Obviously* she hadn't heard about this, but saying so would only give him another reason to mock her.

This guy probably did a lot of mocking.

"Well, then." He made a short, arrested motion, settling his shoulders. It was a relief to see him actually move; their habitual stillness was goddamn uncanny. "Storytime with Jacob, little *lirai.* You gonna come out?"

When he put it that way, she didn't think she wanted to. "You going to behave if I do?"

"Absolutely." Now his perfect white teeth gleamed at her. "Like the good little boy I once was."

"Were you?" *I don't think you were. You have narcissism written all over you, and underlined as well.*

"Right down to my toenails, ma'am." He didn't move as she edged into the rest of the suite, though his eyelids lowered a fraction. He didn't try to shrink like Erik; this guy had probably never thought about how his sheer size would make someone else feel. "So, let's say you have the qualities necessary to become a Son of Ymre."

"Which are?" It was on the tip of her tongue to say *like kidnapping?* Which probably wouldn't go over very well.

Like a lead balloon, Mom would have said. It hurt to think of her mother, as always, and Liv didn't have her usual distractions around to anaesthetize. No phone, no friends, no job—they were probably climbing the walls at the office right now. Sal Kinnock often said missing a good paralegal was like missing his hands.

Someone else was going to have to miss his groping pinches, though. Liv was trying not to feel relieved about *that*, too, and failing miserably.

Jake ticked off qualities on his callused fingers. "Stubbornness, intelligence, and a certain . . . flexibility." He halted, obviously wanting her to ask another question.

So, he liked performing for an audience. Liv took a few steps toward the table. "Physical, mental, or moral?"

"Yes." The way his grin intensified said he was pleased, teaching the little lady some of his tricks.

Even with superhuman abilities and loaded with weapons, men were all the same. Liv lifted the tray's big silver cover. Pancakes—looked like whole wheat—and strawberries. Milk. A blushing, absolutely ripe peach, neatly sliced, a tall white paper latte cup. "Great."

"That's not even the fun part." Jake probably didn't like sharing her attention with breakfast, which was right where she wanted him.

So she threw him another question, just like a bone. "What's the fun part?"

"Along with being able to survive shit that would kill a superhero? The creeping insanity." He paused, examining her expression. A puppy or toddler, checking to make sure someone was observing so they could be certain of their own reality. "It's the god, you see. *He's* nuts, and does his best to drive us off the deep end, too."

"A mad god?" *There isn't anything in the DSM about that one.* Even if she could believe the tentacle-horror she'd seen with her own eyes, a god was something else—or maybe it was just her good old-fashioned American agnosticism talking. "So . . ."

"Well, mad or obeying the dictates of an inhuman intelligence, what's the diff? Anyway, if we go off the rails, *he* can reach through us." Jake warmed to his work, losing his faint professor's sneer. He was a lot handsomer without it; Mika would have liked his easy manner but not his disdain. Her old roommate Sandra would have snapped this guy up in a hurry, putting him through his paces and coming back with a full report before leaving him in the dust the instant he stopped performing. "The unhinged were always his chosen prophets, before."

"Great." Her stomach closed, tight as a fist. Still, Liv settled herself gingerly at the small table and reached for the latte. How many more euphemisms for mental disorders would this guy come up with? "So . . . is it a cumulative effect?" In other words, was she going to have to worry about one of them snapping and doing something nasty to her?

Dealing with men always revolved around that question.

"Sort of. The only real inoculation's a *lirai*; even a potential's presence mutes the whispers some." Jake folded his hands behind his back, settling into what was probably called parade rest. Erik often stood that way, too. "Seal a Dreamer up, though, and you—"

Okay, hold on a second. "Hang on." A thin icy drizzle slapped at the window, borne on a cold breeze. Looked like the storms had moved in for real. She certainly wasn't missing the indignities of her morning commute, to be honest. "Seal?" *I don't like the sound of that.*

"You should ask Ignatius about that part." Jake's posture changed, and he spread his hands—but slowly, carefully; maybe he'd just realized the relative difference in their sizes. Or maybe he'd said too much. "He wouldn't like me making a mess of explaining."

"I'll do that." She rescued a pen and a scrap of plain paper from the clutter of last night's festivities, scrawled a note. *Ignatius: Seal?* "You want some of this? I can't eat it all myself."

"You think it's poisoned?"

"No." *Not anymore.* "I'm being polite, but if you don't want any, just say so."

"Oh." He scratched at the side of his neck, and for just a moment there was a vulnerable flash of the kid he must have been, however long ago. "Really? Okay. Sure."

Oh, Liv, you can't really believe all this bullshit. The trouble was, she was sort of starting to. "So I'm just a potential, I'm not really a *lirai* yet." Liv sniffed gingerly at the latte—it was, indeed, blessedly plain—and took a long almost-scorching swallow, then picked up the heavy antique butter knife. "I'm gonna cut this in half and we can share. So you guys live for a long time. Do you ever die of old age?"

"Nope." He watched her division of fluffy, golden-brown cakes, and his gaze kept stuttering to her face, patent disbelief making him look even younger.

"Because you stay young?"

"Because it's a violent life. Statistics aren't on our side." Jake paced across mellow hardwood, his footsteps only making a token noise every now and again. He dropped into one of the chairs opposite her with that same eerie quiet. "And because if one of us goes around the bend, his brother—or his Father, or his sons—have to hunt him down and kill him. They know him best, so they can hunt him quickest."

Well. There goes my appetite. The butter knife shook, so she laid it carefully down. "Is that so," she managed, picking up her latte again. The pancakes could wait for a second. Coffee slopped inside a trembling paper cup.

"It's all right," Jake said, almost kindly. "You won't go insane. *Lirai* are immune."

Not comforting, kid. Funny, the longer Liv spent talking to this guy, the older she felt. "That's nice."

"And I'm too young to go dark, plus Erik would hang me up like a side of beef if I did. So don't worry."

"What about if Erik . . .?" She didn't want to ask. And the old guy, did that mean he was more at risk of this nebulous insanity too?

What if all three of them decided she was too much trouble, or . . . God, it was a hall of mirrors. Even absolute proof of monsters seen with her own damn eyes wasn't helping.

"Coffee first," Jake said, and there was no levity remaining on his fair blond face. "Then worry about sanity."

It was good advice, but she still didn't like it. So she took another burning gulp and studied his face. "You still want some of my pancakes?"

"Maybe just a bit." But he smiled, and just maybe she'd gotten through to at least one of her captors.

It was a start. "We're going to have to share the plate." She worked to keep her tone businesslike. "But I'm not sharing my coffee."

Understatement

"FATHER?" ERIK finished shaking droplets from his dark hair, hissing slightly through his teeth to smoke the moisture into invisibility. You could keep the rain from touching you, but other spatters and stray droplets wormed their way in during winter, when everything was a grey aching mess.

At least, this far north it was.

"Ah, yes. Afternoon shift." Ignatius considered the plate; on it, a wrapped vegetarian bagel sandwich sat, neatly cut in half and surrounded by an arc of plain potato crisps, misshapen gold coins. "She had a good appetite this morning. Perhaps she'll want tea."

"Maybe." Erik glanced across the kitchen. One long counter held plain white boxes—everything from outside had to be examined and re-wrapped, not only to keep their *lirai* insulated from reminders of lost freedom but also to make sure no thin thread of ill intent wormed its way into the temple. Looked like Father had been busy shopping. He was an inveterate internet bargain hunter. "Who's taking it in?"

"You may have the honor; Jake took her breakfast. I will visit the lady at dinner; I am told she has questions about her new status." Ignatius's frown was not quite magisterial, merely distracted. There were distinct smudges under his dark eyes, and he moved stiffly. A froth of parsley stood in a well-scrubbed water glass to his right; he selected a sprig and arranged it carefully.

"Restaurant quality." Erik couldn't help but smile, sobering when Ignatius glanced in his direction. Still, the old man looked pleased.

"It's a good thing, to remind oneself of the . . . oh, the aesthetics of food." Father's fingertips flicked, and a preservation folded over the plate. The tray's domed silver cover stood ready at a precise angle, its surface showing an upside-down version of the kitchen and two men, distorted into monstrous shapes. "It sounds snobbish, doesn't it. In any case, it helps to have something novel to focus on, or to anticipate a small pleasure."

"Yeah." But you had to be careful, too *much* novelty and your moorings started to slip. It was a tricky balance; the god had as many whispers as there were dreams, and they were all shapechangers. Erik almost wanted to ask *how are you holding up*, but Ignatius might be offended at the implications, no matter how well-meaning the inquiry. "So, it's a little active out there."

"Active." Ignatius did not raise an eyebrow, but it was probably close.

"Yes, sir." Erik had long ago fallen into Father's habit of understatement. The bleak humor in such a practice suited him. "Any word from Control?"

"Not in the last day or so." Ignatius paused, examining his elder son closely. "It's . . . worrisome, Erik."

Erik's back ached and his shoulder bore a ring of fresh, savage purple-red bruising. It would fade quickly, but fighting without backup was a good way to get an overload of cumulative damage, not to mention run a greater risk of sliding off the rails.

Keeping the god out of your head during a fight robbed a Son of concentration needed to stay alive. "They still want to wait for more daylight?" It boggled the mind, but they were just a frontier temple. Even moving the relatively few miles to Rochester—not Stanfeld, as he'd thought—was fraught with danger.

"Apparently." Ignatius's gaze met his fully, and Erik was sure his own discomfort—and suspicion—was plainly visible.

"Great," he said, and watched Ignatius cover the tray. The sorcery under the large silver dome would keep everything fresh, crisp or soft, and at optimal temperature.

God—any god—forbid a *lirai* should have to nibble soggy bread. Or get food poisoning.

Ignatius gave him another sideways look, one too worried to be properly amused. "My thoughts exactly. I shall continue the attempt, but it may become necessary to leave rather quickly."

That was concerning, too. They could hold their temple almost indefinitely, but their potential in her pretty rooms needed the inoculation of the Flame sooner rather than later. Her dreams would intensify now that she was exposed to active sorcery, and while the god's madness wouldn't brush her, contamination or other illness could very well sneak through.

"I'll keep my go-bag packed," Erik muttered, picking up the tray.

"Do that," Ignatius said, equably, and glided for the sink to begin washing up.

"COME ON IN." The *lirai* was at the windows, inspecting a grey afternoon—the sleet was trying mightily to snow, but unless it warmed a few notches, tiny ice-freighted particles would keep spatter-rattling disconsolately at glass and stone. She turned, studying him somberly, and maybe Jake had said something right at breakfast, because she looked . . .

Well, she looked reasonably relaxed. Her wide dark eyes still held shadows and the bruised half-moons of sleeplessness under them were pronounced, but her mouth tilted up at the corners and she didn't hug herself *or* flinch when he set the tray down.

"Oh, hey. It's you." She even sounded pleased. Well, she was probably lonely, with her world turned upside down and confined to a frontline temple's substandard *liraim*. "I was expecting the old guy."

"Father will visit you at dinner, he said." He hurried to add more, in case she didn't get that they were on call for her and not the other way 'round. "Unless you want me to summon him now."

"God, no." Her shudder looked only half theatrical. "Where's Jake?"

Did she prefer Younger Brother already? It was only to be expected. "He's on guard outside the temple, but I can get him in if—"

"Nope." A quick, graceful shake of her pretty head, honeydark hair rippling and bouncing as she moved. "I was just curious. Unless you'd like to escape?"

Was she asking if he found *her* company upsetting? Wonders never ceased. Then again, she was probably searching for any habit, routine, or certainty she could grasp. It occurred to Erik that she might like a television, though a laptop was entirely out of the question.

At least, for now. "No ma'am. Was outside all morning."

"Shopping?" Bright, polite interest lit her eyes, and it wasn't fair. She was a Dreamer, of course, and the power and scale of their gifts shone through them, especially after the Flame's burnishing.

Even without it, she was gorgeous, and he was just a big dumb brute. *Killing the beasts, beautiful. They're weak in the light, but the chance to get a mouthful of you is powerful motivation.* One he could, after all, relate to. "Not precisely."

She waited, crossing her arms defensively after all, cupping sharp elbows in soft palms.

"It's winter," he said, finally. "When the sunshine's weak, some of the shadowbeasts can come out to play. If there's something they want badly enough."

"Meaning me." Her chin rose slightly, she studied him from top to toe, and suddenly there wasn't enough air in the room. Strangely enough, though, she didn't seem to be having any trouble breathing, not like her shock-laced gasping the other night.

"Meaning you." What else could he say? At least he didn't sound like a squeaky preteen babbling incoherently at the prettiest creature on earth.

Or at least he hoped he didn't.

"But they didn't know about me before you guys found me?"

She was a smart cookie, all right. "You probably avoided the worst of them with low-level precognition." It was just barely possible, he supposed, and the thought of what could have happened to an unprotected potential—to *this* unprotected woman—threatened to turn his guts into an ice-lake. "Maybe you want to talk about this after lunch?"

"Think it'll ruin my appetite?" A shadow of pained amusement filled those pretty dark eyes.

Erik forced his throat to work, his tone to stay level and flat. "Don't want to take the chance."

"I don't think my appetite could get worse. But if it makes you upset—"

"No ma'am." She thought *he'd* get upset? It was an exotic idea, almost laughable, and he dropped his chin, staring at the hardwood floor and the antique, threadbare throw rugs so she wouldn't see the stupid smile threatening to twitch his lips. "Just want you to be comfortable."

"Awful nice of you." She lifted the silver cover and stared at the bagel sandwich like it had personally offended her. "You want some potato chips?"

"I wouldn't say no." Not to a token bite or two, at least.

"Why do you repackage everything?" Their potential settled gingerly in her seat, refusing to look up at him. "Is it really that bad if I know exactly where this place is?"

Ah. Still thinking like a kidnap victim. "It's not that. It's a protective measure, so nothing can hitch a ride into the *liraim*."

"Hitch a ride?"

Having a civilian to instruct was an exotic experience. "Like an ill-wishing, or a telltale, or a seeker. The unclean have a thousand ways to try to reach the *lirai*, and even a potential in an active temple's got to be careful. You don't know enough yet, so we'll be careful for you." *Before and after you do, beautiful.*

"Okay." She took another peek at the bagel, as if she expected it to grow teeth and lunge for her. "So it's like . . . washing everything before you wear it because of the finishing chemicals used on textiles?"

"Pretty much." He would never have been able to put it so elegantly.

"Okay." She eyed him sidelong as he lowered himself slowly into the seat least likely to crowd her, and gave him half of the sandwich. "We'll share."

If you only knew who you were breaking bread with. His eyes prickled; he took a deep breath. "Yes ma'am," he muttered.

"It's not *ma'am*, it's Liv." She set herself to dividing the crisps into two roughly even piles, and Erik realized he was going to have to eat his half of the damn sandwich, red bell pepper notwithstanding.

He hated the vegetable's grassy taste with a passion, but a *lirai*'s gift was too important to be wasted.

Ever.

Sneakers, Stranglers

THEY KEPT SAYING *you're not a prisoner*, but Jake still trailed behind her as she left the suite. He didn't look too happy about it, either—that easy smile of his had shifted just a few millimeters into a polite grimace.

Liv didn't care. She was too glad to be seeing something, *anything* other than the same four walls. Or did each room count as a discrete number of vertical surfaces? Bedroom, bathroom, the big outer room of the suite—that made twelve walls total.

You knew you really were a prisoner when you started counting like that. Today, she was going to find out the exact dimensions of her cell in the time-honored fashion of choosing a direction and going until one of them grabbed her.

She'd only picked Jake because he was shorter than the old guy and leaner than Erik. Neither of *those* two would let her out of the suite, even if she asked nicely and batted her eyelashes.

Mika was better at that particular skill, but Liv wasn't a slouch by any stretch. If she ever got back to her real life, she was going to have to give Mika a full rundown on using one's wiles to escape, and she didn't want to be embarrassed when she did. This guy, with his lingering appreciative glances, was both a good target and an asshole.

But a useful one, if she could get him pried away from the other two. At least, that's what Liv was hoping. As it was, she set off down the parquet-floored hall like she had somewhere to be, grateful for the brand-new, tightly laced Nikes cradling her feet.

If today went well, she might even get to use them. She examined the red velvet drapes, wondering who cleaned them. Did they have magic for that, too?

Jake drifted behind her, eerily quiet but always within easy reach. "Where you going?"

"Exploring." *Weren't you listening?* Liv's mood was too sunny to be dinged, and besides, she had to start sweetening him up if she expected anything good to happen. "We should have packed snacks. And a rope."

"A rope?" Now he sounded dubious.

"Didn't you read Tolkien?" She glanced over her shoulder, gauging the distance. No use, he was still too close. "Sam's always going on about rope until the elves—"

"Don't read much, ma'am." It didn't sound like he missed it, either. "But you don't want to mess around with elves."

Now there was an interesting statement. "Are they real?"

"Depends on your definition, really." Once he got started, he warmed to the theme like anyone talking about their actual avocation instead of just their job. "Like the stragglers, they creep under the surface of the world. Little grey things. Most of the time, when people think they've been abducted by UFOs it's the stragglers. But sometimes it's the stranglers, and *those* never let go of their research subjects."

Liv slowed, eyeing him sidelong. Maybe he was having her on, but the memory of her filthy socks laid neatly at the end of the bed—silent, incontrovertible witnesses—just wouldn't go away. "You're saying UFOs aren't real, but elves are?"

"I'm saying the legends come from somewhere." His stride lengthened; now he paced next to her, a sleek golden cat. He was so damn *quiet*, it was unnerving. Nobody with boots that heavy should be able to drift so cloud-silent. "The world's a lot different than civilians think."

Well, there was an objection to that, and she reached the end of the hallway, glancing both ways while she made it. "*I'm* a civilian." The passage to the right was disconcertingly dark at its end, so she turned that way to see if he'd stop her.

Jake didn't. He just fell into step beside her again as she started off. "Not anymore. Not completely, anyway."

"Thanks. You really know how to compliment a girl." *You are a living font,* Ignatius had intoned solemnly during last night's dinner, *of a force the uninitiated might call magic.*

Liv suppressed a shiver. The black sweater was cashmere, nice and warm, and the jeans fit like a dream. Well, if they'd brought her in knocked-out, they'd had plenty of time to get her measurements.

She wondered which one of them had performed that little duty.

"There are songs about *lirai.*" Jake's smile was armor-clad now, a social mask. "We could sing you a few."

Maybe I could make you dress up in straw hats and striped shirts. "You're one short of a barbershop quartet." The darkness at the end of the hall was only relative. There was a staircase heading down, but Jake was somehow in front of her, looking into the well.

He also turned, his heels a scant inch from the edge of the first step, and folded his arms over his broad chest as if daring her to push him and run. "We come in threes. Father, Elder, Younger."

"Sounds awkward." *Which one of you's the top*, she wanted to ask, but decided he wouldn't get it. Or he would, and he'd consider it an invitation instead of sarcasm.

As it was, he just regarded her narrowly, making it quite clear they'd reached the limit of her cell in this particular direction. "It's meant to provide complete consensus, and to make sure we watch each other. *He*'s always whispering, little girl."

"Your mad god." She drew out the last two words, wishing she had Mika's dead-on drawl sharp as a razor. What was Mika thinking now? Were her friends putting up flyers for Liv, with a grainy selfie harvested from her now-silent social media feeds? *Missing, please call.*

Did anyone even notice she was gone?

That was a terrible thought—that she'd just dropped out of sight, and after a few days' worth of confusion, the world would close over her absence and continue as usual while she was trapped here. Who would clean out her condo? God, she hadn't done laundry or *anything* before she left, either. Thinking of her entire life on display to whoever had to go in to clear that overpriced though terribly conveniently located few rooms for the next occupant made her skin crawl with hot embarrassment.

"*A* mad god. Not mine." Jake, suddenly sober, straightened and dropped his hands. Now there was a dangerous glimmer in his blue gaze, and if he was this serious all the time, she'd like him a lot better. "Never mine."

"But you have the . . ." Her brain refused to serve up the right word for it. Tattoo? No, it didn't look like it was inked, more . . . branded, pressed into the flesh with hot metal. Which was another disturbing thing she never wanted to think about ever again. "The thing, on your wrist. Right?"

"Well, yeah. It's the only way to get strong enough to not-die the first time you play with a shadowbeast. But it comes with the whispers, and those are damn awful." He hunched, casting a guilty glance past her at the brightly lit hallway. "Shouldn't talk about it, really, but I guess it's okay. You're *lirai*, after all."

"Just a potential, though, right?" At least she had that much down. Ignatius kept patiently repeating things, but they refused to stick in her head.

The fact that he was boring and terrifying in equal measure probably had something to do with it.

"That's like saying a Ferrari's just a car." Jake shook his head. "You really want to go to the kitchen? That's what's down there, by the way."

"Sure." *Maybe I could get my hands on a knife. Or a pan.* Liv tried to look extremely interested in cookware and food preparation. "Never been called a Ferrari before."

"Well, they're blind out there." He made a dismissive little movement, consigning the entire outside world to a heap. "And if you're thinking of getting to the knives and stabbing me, we can try it. I like knifeplay."

It was her turn to retreat, knowing a threat when she heard one. "So you're the young one in the trio?" *Baby boy of the band?* Liv had always gone for the less conventionally attractive guys, figuring she wouldn't have a chance with the pretty boys—especially since they so often turned out nasty. Now she was trying to remember the name of the manufactured pop group they'd all been gaga over in middle school.

She couldn't quite put her finger on it. Maybe her memory was getting patchy with all the jolts; maybe it was a sign of incipient Stockholm syndrome.

God, she hoped not.

"Yeah." Jake rolled his shoulders, a loose easy movement, muscle twitching under cotton T-shirt and his black canvas jacket with heavy plates sewn in. Probably Kevlar, she could see the outlines of the stuff when he moved the right way. "My antics are supposed to help the other two hold on. Funny thing, though, I've been feeling a lot less antic-y lately."

Is that a good or a bad thing? Liv decided not to ask, chose a less obvious question, and backed up two steps, then another. "Because of me?"

"Sort of." He took a single step forward, away from the stairs, and it was official. He was *herding* her. "I never thought we'd find a potential. It's like finding out Santa Claus is real."

Now there was a chilling thought. "Is he?"

"If he is, you don't want to meet him." Jake considered her for a few moments, his golden head cocked and his mouth turning down at the corners, a long assessing look before he straightened and smiled, the mask in place again. "You want to see some cool shi—I mean, you want to see something cool?"

If I say no, will you pick me up and put me back in my cell? Well, what did she have to lose?

Liv almost winced. Thinking that was a sure way to invite the situation to get worse—if that was even possible at this juncture. "Sure."

Of course, it might be possible anyway with those nightmare *things* around, and she did her best not to consider the notion as she followed Jake, his head up and his steps deliberately short, back toward the glow of electric light.

Losing Battles

HE SURFACED FROM the deadly doze passing for sleep once a Son reached Elder Brother status, greasy sweat slicking his skin, settling in every crease. For a few moments, staring at the vaulted stone ceiling, he didn't know where or even *who* he was, the dream sliding away in eggshell fragments to drop on hard floor polished to satin sheen by God alone knew how many footsteps.

Erik stayed very still, listening. Sometimes you could catch the tail end of a whisper, so you knew where the attack came from. Not that it mattered—the next would arrive from a different direction, or not, according to where the Mad God thought your weakness might best be approached. It was a constant, losing battle, besieged inside a treacherously weak piece of meat—of course, that was humanity even before the Mad God ever got involved, too.

A Son had much better weaponry than a civilian or the unclean, but using it meant vulnerability to the fucking whispers.

His dark eyes half-lidded, Erik held himself perfectly still. Sometimes it was a waking dream, taking advantage of a man's relief. Thinking you were safely escaped from sleep's ever-shifting country, vigilance might slip a fraction, and then it was all over.

The walls, bare and grey, looked just the same as they always did. His cot was the same; so was the functional nightstand with its tensor lamp, knives, and gun set at precise angles, the weapons rack across the room, the ancient, severe wooden wardrobe holding spare clothes and whatever gear wasn't stored in the armory. Everything as it should be, with no warping at the edges or air of secret wriggling satisfaction.

All right, he was awake. His ears tingled; he was straining, listening for the far-off murmur of the *liraim* and its precious, fragile inhabitant. Of course even a Son couldn't hear it from this end of the temple, but it didn't do any harm to think about, did it?

Except it would. Longing could provide an opening, just as inattention could. The urge to find some reason to tiptoe to the *liraim*'s door, to peer in, to maybe ask her if she wanted anything was all but overwhelming, and Erik exhaled hard, rolling out of bed, stretching lithely and scratching his soles on chill, slick stone.

It was no use to punish yourself when you recognized an attack. The god could use fanaticism as well as laziness. The middle way was safest, but then you risked turning into an ineffective milquetoast.

A losing game all the way around, but then, everything was.

The bathroom was just as small and chilly as the bedroom—a functional washbasin, a painfully clean commode, a scrap of cataract-clouded mirror over the sink. He examined himself; not too bloodshot, not too haggard, needing only a splash of cold water and a round of monotone cursing before he could get back to business.

And what kind of business is that? You heard Father, you're going to betray her to the Flame. She's going to hate you, and you'll deserve it.

"Father won't give me anything I can't handle," he muttered, and twisted the cold faucet with maybe a touch more force than necessary. It was old-fashioned robust metal and could handle a little abuse.

Not like the *lirai*. Of course she'd be more pleased with Jake. He had the temperament women liked.

His closed his eyes, wet fingers curled over the edge of the sink's flower-cup. If he exerted a little more force he could leave marks in the tough ceramic, and if he made a sudden wrenching movement he could tear the entire thing away from the wall. Water would spray, he'd have to snap a word or two of sorcery to get it to seal off, and repair would take an hour or so.

It was always easier to destroy.

Let that be a lesson, Ignatius would say. If the old man was worried about Control's reluctance to move their potential, that meant Erik should be flat-out alarmed. A full *lirai* should be in charge of the whole operation, eager to bring Liv to safety in an active temple.

But a *lirai* often only knew what the Sons told them. If a control liaison had turned . . .

There was no good way to finish a thought like that. The world was full of losing battles; the entire thing was a rigged game.

And despair was just as much a trap as anything else. A soft, subtle slithering filled his skull. Erik's eyes flew open; he stared unseeing at the mirror, his mouth agape.

"Oh, no you don't," he said finally. The words echoed oddly against stone walls, and he grabbed the towel, swiped his face once, and hurried to get dressed.

He could amble past the *liraim*'s door. It helped keep the whispers at bay.

He could even tell himself it was a necessary measure, and hope it was the truth.

A Peg or Two

A LONG DARK echoing room sprang into full life when Jake flipped a switch and fluorescent bars buzzed into life. Three stalls reached halfway across one short end of the rectangle, and the far wall shimmered strangely. At first, she thought it was heat, like the ripples above concrete on a summer day, but it didn't *behave* the way those mirages did.

She stared, trying to figure it out, and her eyes ached as if she'd been reading in the dark.

"Our own private shooting range." Did Jake sound anxious? He pointed at a series of cabinets behind the stalls and ranged along the back wall; through reinforced chicken wire embedded in glass doors she could see brutally efficient shapes, oiled metal gleaming. "Fully equipped and automated. Pretty neat, huh?"

"Wow." Now she could see the pulleys from each stall, just right for clipping a paper target to. The shimmer over the back wall—was that to take care of ricochets? Of course, if they could fight off those *things* and keep food warm without microwaves, magical bullet protection wasn't that much of a stretch.

There were plastic bins for spent and ready-to-use ammunition, and two sets of orange ear protectors were neatly hung in each booth. It smelled like oil, male excitement, and burning metal, a tang she supposed was gunfire.

Any cop she'd ever dealt with, not to mention a good proportion of the male attorneys, would love this.

"You don't like it?" Yes, Jake was definitely anxious. It did good things for him, got rid of the veneer of toxic confidence. Mika would have said *gotta take him down a peg or two, until he's reasonable.*

God, she missed her bestie. She'd have some damn idea of how to handle this that wasn't screaming or trying to pry a window open every time they left her alone for more than a few minutes.

Liv half-spun and put on her most ingratiating smile, the one she used on clients who just *had* to see Sal Kinnock without an appointment. "Can you teach me how to shoot?"

"What?" He looked like she'd just addressed him in some weird language only a handful of scholars could decipher, and cast a nervous glance at the cabinets as well. They were padlocked, but if she could just get him to open one, they might be in business. "Why?"

Even if the cupboards stayed locked, Liv could probably figure something out. It would be easier if this guy would help, though. There was another door between the glass-fronted cabinets, heavy dark metal, and it looked locked too. Maybe that was where they kept the big stuff—rocket launchers? Grenades? "Because if I'm going to hunt monsters, I'm going to need it."

"Oh, man." He found that very funny. At least, he laughed, and the sound echoed off hard edges, bare-swept floor, and scarred walls. "You won't need a *gun*, Miz Stellack. You've got something deadlier. Or at least, you will, when you meet the Flame."

"Who's the Flame?" She was getting tired of cryptic answers that didn't really give any new information. It would be great to get her hands on some artillery, if she didn't blow her own foolish self up with it. "Is it another superhero monster hunter like you, or . . .?"

Jake's face fell. "I really shouldn't say anything." He shifted uneasily, his bootsole squeaking against a mat in one of the booths, the kind grocery checkers stood on to relieve back pain during long shifts. "Come on, let's get you back to the *liraim*."

Oh, no you don't. "Can't I just hold one? I always wanted to learn how to shoot." It was what Mika, let alone her mother, would have called *a goddamn lie*, but if it got Liv a weapon ethical considerations were pretty secondary. Her hands were cold, and she tried to look lonely and waifish, scrubbing her fingers together. "You can teach me."

If that wouldn't stroke a guy's ego, she didn't know what would.

"Are you kidding?" At least he looked powerfully tempted for about half a second before moving aside to block her view of the cabinets. He was certainly big enough to eclipse them, and it was eerie how he could just decide to step quietly and even the mat underneath hushed its protest. "Father'd kill me."

That would certainly take care of one of my problems. Liv tried again, this time with even more soft innocence. "I don't want to go back to the room." She was all but cooing at him, and a swift flare of self-disgust was a spot of sour heat behind her breastbone. "Can we go somewhere else?"

"Library?" He took another gliding step, this one toward her. "Kitchen?"

She was backing up, she realized. The man was herding her again. "How about the kitchen?" She could even smell him, a faint thread of healthy, slightly oily maleness, without the chemical tang of aftershave or cologne.

Of course, they probably didn't believe in nice-smelling stuff. Or deodorant. Maybe monster hunting deadened the nose.

Jake took another step forward. He'd driven her almost back to the door, and it didn't look like he was even *conscious* of it. "You just can't wait to get your hands on a weapon, huh."

Damn it. Was it printed all over her face? "I just wanted to . . ." Abruptly, Liv was exhausted. At least now she knew where the guns *were.* Getting to them was a problem that could wait for a little bit. "No, you know what? Fine. Let's go back to my cell."

"The *liraim.*"

"*Liraim,*" she repeated, taking a last longing look at the racks of guns and that metal door. The word wasn't that hard to pronounce, and whatever language it was in, she had a sneaking suspicion it meant *jail.*

Just like everything else here.

Once they reached the suite she didn't politely ask if he wanted to come in, just swept the door shut as she stepped through, wishing hopelessly for a lock on her side. She considered dragging a chair over and bracing it under the knob, but that was useless too since it opened out.

From the other side came a low, satisfied chuckle before a breathless quiet static folded against the heavy wood. Maybe she hadn't fooled him at all.

Still, she knew more than she had this morning. And when Erik came on duty, she might have another shot at getting to the weaponry.

All in all, Liv didn't think she'd done too badly.

Bad Dreams

"WHERE THE HELL were you?" Erik folded his arms, hoping he looked forbidding. Coming around the corner to find the *liraim* door open and both of them gone was a bad shock, but hearing them approach from downstairs was almost worse. They were silent, and when she reached the *liraim* door, she slammed it practically in Jake's smug grin.

She hadn't even noticed Erik in the shadows, his chest a sudden furnace and his knuckles tingling because his hands were fists. Had Jake tried something?

It was ridiculous. You didn't turn against your brothers. But if Jake had tried sealing her . . . she was just a little thing, not bathed in the Flame yet, and she couldn't fight off a Son.

Not yet. There were laments sung of the *liraim* sealed against their will. It was never a happy occasion, but what was done was *done*, as the Fathers always said, and at least they weren't holding gladiatorial bouts to win admittance to a *lirai*'s bed anymore.

Modernity was good for something other than firepower.

"Downstairs." Jake was too busy preening to notice Erik's expression, thankfully. He all but rubbed his callused hands together with glee. "Our *lirai* has now seen the range."

Of all the . . . Words almost failed him, and Erik's throat had turned dry as baked glass. "You took her to the range?" he croaked.

"Yeah, she wants to fire a gun. Can you imagine?" Jake's grin was as wide and sunny as ever. He hooked his thumbs in his belt and shook his golden head. It was a good thing their conversation would only be a formless whisper through the muffling—and the sound of thumping a younger on his silly, stubborn head wouldn't get through, either. "Even asked me when we'd teach her. Monster hunting, she calls it."

"Father'll have your hide." *And if he doesn't, I might take it myself.*

"He'd have to find out." Jake eyed him sidelong, a flash of bright blue. "You gonna tell him?"

"Not sure." It wasn't a threat; Erik just liked to turn things over inside his head before he reached any decision. Hopefully his younger would realize as much. "Did you let her?"

"Hell no." Jake shook his head, looking horrified and baffled at once. "A *lirai* starts shooting, all of a sudden they think they don't need us any more, right? Besides, she'd just as likely empty a clip into me and take off running. She was looking at every damn window like she wanted to throw herself through."

I don't blame her. "It's what potentials are like." They went over the list of potentials' coping mechanisms in training—worst, and most dangerous, was the apathy that ended in suicide attempts.

Hopefully that could be avoided. Twenty-four-seven watch was invasive, and one of them might *have* to seal her, just to keep her from doing herself some harm.

"Like *you* know." But Jake shook his head, robbing the observation of any sting. "You okay? You look a little rough."

"Bad dreams."

"You too?"

Now that he was closer, he could see a touch of pink on Jake's eyelids, faint shadowing under the eyes themselves. He wasn't drooping yet, but if both of them were having a rough time in REM, it meant that a potential's strengthening was affecting them—and the Mad God, in his blind, crawling way, had no doubt taken notice.

Of all the things the Mad God liked, draining potentials dry and snacking on their bones were top of the list. Full *lirai* were slightly more difficult prey—but only slightly. They needed more Sons, not just to keep her safe but also to watch each other.

It would only take a moment of inattention to invite catastrophe. "Listen," he said, softly. "Father's been trying to get hold of other temples. No luck."

Jake froze for a few moments, then his blue gaze swung to lock with Erik's. "No luck?"

"Control isn't responding." It could be a temporary communications outage, since the Mad God would know by now that a potential had been found by frontliners. "I think he's . . . worried."

"Then we should be, too."

"Yeah." Erik's shoulders were relaxing; the *liraim* door was right there, and she was safely inside. With any luck, she wouldn't find out how much danger she was truly in until they had her safely in a real temple with other *lirai* and access to the Flame. "As far as I can tell, he's going to follow orders. Maybe it is better to wait for longer days before we move her." The winter solstice was generally the worst time for the whispers, *and* for the shadowbeasts to come out and play.

"Stationary defense is better defense," Jake quoted, chapter and verse. "A few can hold against many."

"So you were listening in tactics classes."

"Well, yeah. It was just easier to copy your answers." Jake grinned, tilting his head again, scratching at his cheek. It was an attitude of deep thought, and Erik patiently waited for his little brother to get to the same place he had. "I'm packed anyway, but I'll polish everything twice. Should we say something to her?"

"Probably not." Erik didn't want the *lirai* worried. She had more than enough to deal with. "But, listen. Maybe you could pack something for her just in case? Clothes, energy bars, first aid kit, something for her to do in the car."

"Like a toddler." Jake's mouth turned down at both corners; he was used to being the only, albeit heavily armed, child in sight.

"An angry one." When someone didn't understand certain dangers, it was even more important to protect them, right? It didn't help that the girl had a double dose of both smarts *and* bravery. The foolhardy died first in battle, and she wasn't even trained. "Speaking of which, how's she feeling?"

"Feeling?"

"Yeah. Because we should care." Erik kept his own face a wall, but Jake was staring at him like he'd grown another head. "I'm gonna be on guard duty later, all right? I want to know what I'm facing."

"You like her." Jake shook his head, a cat dislodging a few drops of cold water. "You really like her."

"Aren't we supposed to?" It was hard not to admire the Dreamers once you knew what they'd accomplished, even if it was thousands of years ago. The fact that they kept continuing the fight—not to mention the relief they provided from the Mad God's tiny, teasing, tempting whispers—just made the debt deeper. "Plus, she's smart. A lesser woman would've given up by now."

"I don't think *give up* is in this girl's dictionary." Grudging admiration underlined the words, which was a good sign. It was when Jake got dismissive and quiet that you had to look out. "You can finish my guard shift and take yours, then."

"Why, you got a hot date?"

"With my pillow, bro." Jake tipped him a salute, turned, and set off down the hall. He only went a few steps before swinging back around, though. "Listen, Erik . . ."

He waited, but silence filled up the hall like creeping, heavy gas in a mineshaft. *That* wasn't like Jake at all, so Erik made a noncommittal noise. "Hm?"

In other words, *I'm not going to judge you, spit it out.*

"Nothing. Probably just tired." Younger Brother's shoulders dropped and he vanished down the hall, boots light and soundless as dry leaves on the back of a hard wind.

Erik watched that end of the hallway for a few long minutes, trying to decide if he was honestly worried or it was the god whispering in his head, sowing dissent and distrust. He stepped closer to the *liraim* door, but the pressure didn't diminish.

However, an unfamiliar thought struck him. Yule was close. When the tide turned and the days lengthened they'd take her to a proper temple, and it would be Erik shoving her into the Flame until it took. She was going to hate him, but maybe he could get ahead of the curve just a little?

He settled next to the door, his shoulders against the wall, and thought it over.

Oneiros

MAYBE JAKE HAD been yelled at, because there were no more field trips for about two weeks. Instead, Liv was confined to the suite, and her temper rose in direct proportion to the number of days she had to spend looking at the same however-many walls. Outside, the mercury plunged, ice spreading flowery traceries over mullioned windows; the temperature inside never varied. Meals came like clockwork on those silver trays, Ignatius visited every evening for at least a few moments, trying to convince her they weren't so bad but giving no further explanations.

Of the three of them, only the dark-haired guy escaped her ire, mostly because he didn't try to sugarcoat her captivity. He was also the one who would answer the most questions, though that was faint praise. Every time she asked about "sealing" Ignatius all but blushed, and she was getting a very bad feeling about the whole thing.

Especially since she was dreaming again, vivid color-soaked fantasies and nightmares striking almost as soon as she closed her eyes. There was nothing to do *but* sleep; pride wouldn't let her ask for a television so at least she could keep up with daily soap operas.

Her grandmother had called them *my stories, gotta have my stories*; Liv was thinking Gramma Poe, who got her first job at fifty-five because Gramps was retired and hanging around the house all day driving her crazy, had understated what living in a confined space did to your ability to watch ridiculous programming.

She was at the window when Erik tapped at the door; she was even distinguishing between the different styles of knocking now. "You might as well come in," she muttered, staring at the icy quad below—naked, frostbitten trees, slippery stone paths, frozen grass, shivering bushes. It looked like the lowest circle of Dante's hell.

At least they brought her books. She suspected she was going to have a helluva library by the time this finished—if there was, indeed, a finish line in sight. She was getting used to handing Ignatius lists with increasingly rare and recondite legal textbooks; if they couldn't find an edition right away one of them would apologize like a maître d' faced with an irate but very influential food critic.

If this kept up, she might even read a few of the deliveries. Brooding only took her so far, and maybe she could find some sort of legal remedy for after her escape.

That first step's a lulu, Mom would have laughed.

Liv half-turned; it was indeed Erik, in his usual dark T-shirt, dark jacket, jeans, and a gun butt peeking out from under his left armpit. One of his hands was behind his back, and she eyed him warily.

If she could just get out of the room without a chaperone, she might have a chance at getting into one of those gun cabinets. Or maybe there was a back door in the kitchen.

Outside was where those *things* were, sure. But if she had a weapon, maybe that "potential" they were always talking about would wake up and do something supernatural?

It wasn't a bad assumption, but how could she ask?

"Ma'am?" Erik didn't stutter, but it was close. She'd never heard any of them sound so tentative. "I mean, uh, Miz—"

"It's Liv. Just Liv." God, they were all irritating as *fuck*. She had to get out of here somehow. "What do *you* want?"

"I just . . . you know . . ." He produced a small, brightly wrapped box—silver paper, a floppy blue bow which clearly wasn't professionally done. In fact, he thrust it at her as if it contained a bomb. "Happy Yule."

"Yule?" The package went blurry for a moment as her eyes filled with hot water; the box was heavy, resting in her numb fingers. "You mean Christmas?"

"A little before. It's the solstice." He took a catlike half-step back, giving her space. Jake liked moving in on her and seeing if he could herd, while Ignatius kept a certain distance, probably more out of pride than any consideration for her comfort. But Erik paid attention, and she liked that about him. "Longest night of the year."

"Great." She blinked several times, because the salt water in her eyes wouldn't go away. She had to sniff hard, too. "Uh, I didn't get you anything." Not that she could have, trapped in here.

"You don't have to. A *lirai* is a gift all by themselves." It sounded like a quotation; Erik paused. "Well, you can open it. If you want. You don't have to. I just thought—"

"No, it's great. It really is." She rubbed at her right eye with the heel of her free hand, swallowed hard, and tried a smile.

Erik examined her face. It was weird—he was so much bigger, and armed, and inhumanly strong. But right now he looked like an anxious preschooler searching for his teacher's approval. "I didn't mean to upset you."

"It's just that I've been here a while. And I didn't get you anything." Were her friends having Christmas parties? Mika had been talking about flying back to Los Angeles to visit her brother, Jada usually had a "refugee's Christmas" at her apartment in Hana Heights, Lou and his husband would be celebrating an anniversary—God, she missed them all so, so much.

Were any of them thinking about her? That was probably the worst thing about being kidnapped—wondering if you'd ever be found, if anyone was still looking.

"You don't have to," Erik repeated.

The paper crumpled easily. Mika was an inveterate smash-and-tear; Liv preferred to carefully work taped edges free and save ribbons or bows. She never reused them but she kept the nicest ones; the blue bow on this box was kind of childish. Erik took the discarded wrapping paper, carefully avoiding her fingertips, and if he was bored at her slow unveiling of his present, it didn't show.

It was a plain white box; she exhaled in wonder when the top came off. Nestled on white cotton was a necklace—the gem was milky-translucent, the dull grey iron setting like twisted branches, and the chain a little thicker than she usually wore because of the sheer size of the thing. "Oh, wow." She touched the stone with a fingertip and almost dropped it, because vivid colors spread from that single point of contact. Now it looked like a fire opal, so bright it seemed unreal.

"Every *lirai* should have their own *oneiros*."

"Oneiros." It sounded vaguely French, but nothing she'd ever heard before. Would they tell her if she asked? It was always *after the Flame, you'll see*. "Is that what this is?"

"Yeah." Erik's mouth twitched, a tentative smile. "A dreamstone in a meteorite iron setting. Made the old way."

Meteoric iron sounded intense. And she didn't know the difference between an old way and a new way; they probably wouldn't tell her either. "Guess I won't be going through any metal detectors with this on."

"Mostly, when *lirai* travel . . ." He trailed off when she frowned slightly. "Well, anyway, it's a protection. When you meet the Flame it'll become a tool, too."

"It's beautiful." At least she could be polite. The thing looked too heavy to wear, but she should at least try it on. The chain was too short to fit over her head, and there was no clasp. "How do I put it on?"

"I can. Just take it out of the box and hold it to your, um, to your neck. Wherever you want it to rest."

She settled the nestlike setting against her breastbone, over the black sweater. "Like this?"

"Yeah. We can shorten or lengthen the chain. It just takes a second." He reached out, halted, glanced at her face, and let his fingertips hover just over the gem. His eyes narrowed slightly, and a strange warmth slid from her crown to her soles, nailing her in place for a moment. The chain twitched, rose, moved like a snake, and finally fastened around her neck, seamless and whole.

Liv let out a short, garbled blurt of surprise, but Erik didn't move. The necklace settled against black cashmere, warm and oddly familiar, and it wasn't heavy at all.

Light as a feather.

The stone flushed again, colors she knew and others she couldn't quite name moving in lazy swirls under its surface. "Wow," she breathed, tucking her chin, and the idea that she was staring basically at her own tits wasn't as funny as it should have been. "Do they all do that?"

"On a *lirai*, yeah." Erik was busy refolding the wrapping paper into smaller and smaller squares. "Do you like it?"

"It's weird. But beautiful." She could afford to be polite, even if she suspected this was some kind of trap or one of their weird little games. "So how do I take it off?"

"Just tell me, and I'll take it off for you." For once, his anxiety seemed to match hers. "Do you want me to?"

Strangely, she didn't. "No, it's okay." Liv found herself touching the stone's surface, warm and hard, watching the coruscating colors. The gem rested against her breastbone like it belonged there, and the iron setting wasn't scratchy. The chain didn't grab at her hair, either, which was a miracle. "I like it. Thank you."

He nodded. The folded-up paper went back into the box, but he didn't try to take the bow. "My pleasure, *lirai*."

"Liv," she corrected, and his dark gaze flew to hers.

"Liv." Another twitch of his lips, a suppressed smile. "Dinner should be up in a little while. I'll, uh, just be outside."

"Okay." She watched the gem as he left, closing the door with a quiet sound. "*Oneiros*," she said, testing the word. The swirling colors were almost hypnotic; she probably shouldn't have accepted the damn thing.

But it was pretty, and it felt nice against her sweater. If the gift had some hidden cost, she'd find a way to tear it off. And it went without saying that as soon as she found a way to escape, she could take some bolt cutters to the chain.

The icy wasteland outside her window didn't look so forbidding now. Neither did the room—the table with neatly stacked paper and the huge collection of gel pens, the bed neatly made, the bathroom just as painfully clean as when she'd been deposited here. All the sludge of daily living just seemed to disappear.

These guys could hire themselves out to clean houses, I bet. It was a good thought, a strong, sane thought, and she was startled into a laugh.

Liv clapped a hand over her mouth, horrified at herself. It was probably all part of their plan—give the trapped girl a pretty piece of gimcrack jewelry, and watch her be so pathetically grateful. She had to stay strong, watch for her moment . . .

. . . and then what? Fight the monsters by herself?

Liv stared at the frostflowers at the window, wondering if that was a better or worse prospect than being held in these rooms for however much longer.

The sun, having better things to do, slid down from its apex toward the horizon's grim swallowing line.

SHE HID IN THE bathroom, trying not to feel like an errant child while Jake dropped off the usual domed silver tray. She did it again when Ignatius, again as usual, visited, and told herself hunger was a reasonable punishment for accepting anything from them at all. Curling up in the bed was a welcome reprieve, though she probably should have slept in the bathtub or somewhere else uncomfortable just to drive the point home.

The necklace didn't catch in her hair or try to strangle her. It simply lay quietly where it was supposed to, warm and comforting. Was it a tracking device? Some kind of weird ritual?

Was she beginning to bend toward what they wanted, isolation and fear chipping away at her personality? Humans were social creatures, and it was only a matter of time before she lost all sense of reality and started believing whatever crazy shit they could come up with.

It didn't help that she'd seen the monsters. Once your own eyes were on your kidnappers' side, what chance did the rest of you have?

Liv thought she'd have trouble sleeping, but she was out as soon as her head touched the pillow—that is, until past midnight, when the strip of light under the bathroom door dimmed and a sharp icy wind scraped the windows. A formless mutter crossed her lips, her fingers turning into claws at a signal from her dreaming brain, and she tossed restlessly, the *oneiros* glowing against her breastbone. Small, swift-moving shadows dappled the walls.

Skritch-scratch. Another shadow brushed against the window, rubbing like a cat. The light under the bathroom door dimmed further, sputtered out; mullioned glass creaked, an uneasy murmur like her dreaming.

More scratching, and the *oneiros*'s glow was a single dim star in the room's thickening gloom. It flashed once, a bright pale stiletto.

Liv Stellack sat bolt upright amid tangled, sweat-damp blankets, her hair a dark mass, her eyes wide and wild, and screamed.

Part Two: The Flame

Incursion

THE BAFFLE BROKE into shivering pieces; Erik almost took the door off its reinforced hinges. His potential huddled amid rumpled sheets and blankets, her eyes white-ringed and her mouth contorted with a cry of utter terror. That was worrying enough, but the bigger danger was the cracks flowering over the ice-freighted window, rippling and bulging as sorcerous energy wedded to its physical structure sought vainly to keep something inimical out.

Oh, shi—

He launched himself for the bed, hoping he wouldn't break any of her fragile bones, and hit just as the window exploded, broken glass and sorcery-stiffened iron shrapnel peppering walls, furniture, and floor. A burning slice touched his calf right before he hit the ground on the left side of the bed, his arms full of stiff, still-screaming, impossibly small woman. The *oneiros* dug into his chest, a dilating scorch-spot, and he was upright in a trice, wishing he'd been able to roll her to the other side. As it was, he'd be bottled with her in a corner, which wasn't so bad—he could hold out for a long time, if he had to—but it wasn't optimal.

Still, she was unhurt. There was no delicious, wickedly perfumed tinge of *lirai* blood or trauma filling the room; the *oneiros* flashed with an uncoordinated flood of a Dreamer's power, lighting up the battlefield as hairy questing tentacles coalesced through the shattered window. The bulk of the creature was trapped outside by the solidity of the temple's walls, and as soon as he realized as much Erik bent, his fist closing around her right arm, and hauled.

His *lirai*, now fully awake, screamed again and began to struggle. The tentacles, tiny hairs bristling at the sound and sensing a high-value meal within range, snaked for the corner with spooky, fluid speed—

—and retreated, bunching against themselves, as Erik lopped off two sensitive, questing tips with one knifestrike. The *lirai* was a vulnerable softness behind him; he backed her into the corner by the simple expedient of retreating so she was trapped against the wall between the bedside table and the corner; then he exhaled sharply, dropping into the groove of the battle like a record player's needle into a vinyl valley.

Next came getting her over the bed and out into the hall, but he couldn't do that until the thing in the window was at least partly driven away. The wall groaned, the temple's stone structure and massive timber frames tolling like a bell. Something whizzed past his head—it was the pretty stained-glass lamp from the tiny bedside table, the twin to the one on the nightstand. It was a good, accurate throw, and glass shattered against rubbery, squeaking tentacles. Far more damaging was the burst of weak, untutored power wedded to it.

It was nothing more than a gifted civilian might throw under extreme duress, but when focused by the *oneiros,* it must've stung like hell. The thing writhed, its screech spiraling into a diseased, sawing falsetto as its arms curled like salted slugs.

The knot's outside. It'll heave itself through, given enough time. The thought flashed through Erik and away, and something soft hit his back.

It was her fist. She punched him again, with more enthusiasm than skill or force, and Erik turned his head slightly as the tentacled shadowbeast pulled back, ready for another assault upon shattered stone, shards of sorcerous protection attempting to heal the breach. "It's me," he snapped. "Calm down."

His *lirai* went still, but whether it was from fear, shock, or because she'd heard and understood was an open question. Erik inhaled, bracing himself, and when the beast at the window heaved forward again he lunged, knives biting deep in unholy flesh. It lurched back, surprised by the sudden stinging pain—which was exactly what he'd hoped for.

"Now!" he yelled. "*Over the bed!*"

She had far more presence of mind than the usual civilian. Liv scrambled onto the mattress and over, her knee catching in tangled blankets; she spilled down on the other side, freeing him from the need to keep her defended in the corner.

Now he had some space. If she ran for the door . . .

But she probably had forgotten the door even existed, at this point. His *lirai* kept going, scrambling across hardwood on hands and knees with little bruising sounds, and fetched up against the dark wooden wardrobe, making a soft hopeless sound that tightened every string in his body as Erik danced, knocking tentacles aside, lunging, one of his boots landing on a rubbery, ichor-spraying, slippery writhing that threatened to throw him if he hadn't been moving so fast. Superhuman speed was a blessing; he rammed a knife into what he sensed was a direction-finding appendage loaded with dark nerves and was rewarded with a blast of foul air as the thing gave an only partly psychic shriek.

The *oneiros* flashed, and in that transitory glow the thing was exposed in pitiless detail as it tried heaving through the crumbling wall again. It wasn't like a juvenile *shoggoth* to attack a temple, even a minor one without a resident *lirai* and access to the Flame. How the hell had it broken the perimeter? Where was Jake, where was Father? He was making a *lot* of noise, they had to be alerted.

More ichor sprayed, stinking and smoking; he retreated step by step, teaching the thing that the snack it was after had sharp spines and would use them. "Get up," he yelled, hoping she wasn't yet in shock or crazed with fear. "On your feet, *lirai*." Erik almost barked *soldier* instead of *lirai*, as if she were Jake on a training run long ago.

That was when he heard the other noises—terrible slipslithering, tapping, inhuman steps, groan-creaking exhalations—coming from the wrong direction.

From the door he'd busted down in such a hurry, and the hall beyond.

Erik's entire body turned to ice; for a moment he thought he was trapped in one of the Mad God's nightmares. The temple was not just breached but outright invaded, and the larger *liraim* was about to become a deathtrap. He hopped onto the bed, his ichor-filthy boots sinking into its softness, and was at her side a moment later as the tentacles, most of them bleeding as they writhed, turned themselves to the work of busily widening the hole in the wall.

Most shadowbeasts weren't exactly smart, but they were cunning. And robust.

Stone crumbled, and when Erik reached down with his filthy left hand she grabbed on with surprising strength, her fingers biting hard. He hauled her up again, trying to be careful of her fragility; the *oneiros* spoke again, a scintillating gleam describing the thing in pitiless detail. His *lirai* let out a short, wounded cry at the sight of cilia-crusted tentacles slithering forward, some hanging by ropes of wet gristle, others painted with steaming, splattering foulness.

"It's all right," he found himself saying, though this was the very definition of *far from fucking all right, thank you*. "It's okay," he continued. "I'm here, you're okay. Don't look at it."

"H-hard not to," she stammered, and his heart hurt. For a moment he thought the beast had flung a spine-dart at him, never mind that it was the wrong species to do so. It *felt* like it had, and he snapped a quick glance at her, checking for damage.

Her hair was a soft, glorious cloud, her arms and legs were bare. The black tank top and grey boxers she wore to bed clung to her curves, and if he hadn't been full to overflowing with battle-rage he might have stopped for a moment to consider her state of undress with some appreciation.

Instead, he grabbed her arm and edged sideways, keeping an eye on the tentacles. "Door," he said, and they were almost there when the first *jana*-spider scuttled through and he shoved her for cover. His *lirai* screamed, landing with a thump in the corner between the wardrobe and the wall, and he was prepared to die fighting when a solid length of silver blurred down, piercing the thing's fungus-starred carapace. Bulbous red grape-bunch eyes flickered and the spider screeched, mandibles clicking angrily.

Ignatius twisted the broadsword viciously, ripping it free of the floor and tearing unlife from the thing with a muttered, sorcerous word.

Relief was a dirty orange explosion in Erik's chest, but there was no time. Now he heard gunfire echoing in the hall—Jake, mopping up *jana*-spiders and whatever else was scurrying out there. Ignatius stepped over the thing's remains and glanced at the *lirai* huddling behind Erik, her hands clasped to her head and her mouth trembling, her eyes rolling like a maddened horse's. Father nodded fractionally and moved forward, thin purple ichor slithering down the broadsword's shining length.

Erik promptly consigned the thing in the window to the realm of *not my problem* and hauled her for the door. She went almost willingly, and he had a terrifying desire to laugh.

She'd thrown a *lamp*. At a tentacled horror most normals would go gratefully insane upon encountering.

Good job, beautiful. Just stay with me, and it'll be fine. The last part was a lie, but that wasn't why he swallowed the sentence. It tasted like iron going down, probably because his mouth was bleeding.

The hall was a shambles, splattered with purple ichor and scattered with *jana* husks crumble-rotting and sending up streams of nasty ichor. Jake put two bullets in the last one, popping both primary compound eyes before glancing up, his face a feral mask and his blue gaze furiously alight. "Garage," he snapped, and his gaze passed down the *lirai*'s body in a smooth arc, looking for damage. It didn't even halt at her chest or hips, thank the Dreamers. "Let's go."

Their *lirai* stopped, digging her heels in.

"Come on," Erik husked, his voice strange after combat, and the *liraim* shook with a combination of the tentacled thing's keening and

Ignatius's battle-roar, a sound too immense to come from such a narrow, seemingly elderly chest; it had been a long damn time since Erik had heard that particular sound.

He realized she was barefoot and the floor was awash with ichor. *Shit.*

She shook her head, wildly, but he'd already sheathed his remaining knife and bent, scooping her into his arms. Liv let out a short surprised sound, and Jake rolled his eyes.

"Fine, take the easy job," Younger Brother snarled, the fey glee of a good fight still contorting his face. "Let's *go*."

Not Safe

SHE WAS FINALLY, *finally* outside her cage, but Liv couldn't even feel good about it—and forget feeling liberated. Ignatius, his gaunt face masked with drying blood and guck, slumped in the passenger seat of a very expensive, very heavy black SUV. Erik, splashed with fifteen different flavors of goop, gunk, and bright stripes of blood as well, was in the seat next to her. Of the three of them, Jake looked the least wounded, but half his face was puffy with dark bruises and he winced uneasily behind the wheel every time he braked or turned.

The engine hummed quietly; she was not just out of her cage but outside the big stone pile, too. But Liv was shaken with the irrational desire to try to run back into the building because the thought of those things *outside* and chasing them . . . well, now she knew why even abused pets often stayed in familiar spaces rather than risk escape.

She'd been turned into a goddamn hamster.

Liv huddled on the back bench seat, her teeth wanting to chatter. Erik had only put her down once on the mad rush to the garage, at the end of a long hall with suits of armor between regular pillars on either side. It looked just like a movie set, but the armor was all dented and broken in varying, horrifying places, the edges of each rip, gouge, or puncture blackened with age.

Stay here, Erik had said softly, and she had, but not because she wanted to. Oh, no. She'd stayed right where he placed her, tucked behind a pillar, and watched him bolt down the hall, meeting a tide of those horrifying half-spider, half-vegetable things with their bulbous crimson eyes, because she was too scared to move. Jake stayed a few paces in front of Liv and his gun only spoke once, roar-lighting the entire hall with a millisecond flash that made every bristling hair, every slavering tooth, every faceted gleam of those terrifying, bulbous, utterly *wrong* eyes stand out.

He'd shot the one that had somehow gotten past Erik.

Even if she'd wanted to run away, she couldn't have. Her traitorous, cowardly legs had fused into trembling sticks and she simply stared, incapable even of screaming.

Even that wasn't as bad as the half-seen shapes beside the car as they rocketed down the driveway, the necklace on her chest giving a strobe-flash to illuminate them in pitiless detail. Jake had almost run over Ignatius at the great iron front gates, barely slowing the vehicle enough for the older man to pile inside.

Erik had his eyes closed like Ignatius, and the sudden certainty both he and the grey-haired guy were corpses sent a violent shudder down her back. Her hand flashed out, pawing at the door release; the lever rose obediently, but without any click of opening.

Child locks? Seriously? A cold, jagged laugh boiled behind her breastbone, as whipsaw-hysterical as Mika's after the car accident that icy long-ago December, both of them just out of college and looking for jobs. The rancid chuckle rose hot and acid in her throat, sounding suspiciously like a whine.

"Don't," Erik said, harshly. "Please."

Liv stared at him, trying to stop the sound, swallow it, stuff it back inside her chest. Ignatius stirred, a gleaming sliver showing under his eyelids. "Hurt," he husked, and coughed. "Is she? Hurt?"

Oh God. Liv's jaw dropped, and the sound died in her throat. Why in the hell was he asking about *her*?

She couldn't stop thinking about the dry rasping sound the spaghetti-tentacles of the thing in the window made, the hideous smell, the spraying of thin, weird, greasy blood. And then the *spiders*, only they weren't properly arachnoid, not with their bodies studded with horrifying vegetable growths—

"She's fine." Erik turned his head a fraction. They were on a two-lane country road, streetlights passing regularly but further apart than in the suburbs. "Physically, at least."

"The longest night of the year," Jake said grimly. "Of course."

"You . . . both . . . did well." Ignatius shifted slightly, and the lines around his mouth deepened. "Following?"

"Not that I can sense." Erik's hand, loosely cupped in his lap, twitched like he wanted to reach for something. "Liv?" It was the first time he'd really used her name, and her gaze jumped from his dirty fingers to his filthy face, to the window past him, back to his hand. "I know you're scared, but it's okay. Just tell me, do you feel any more of them after us?"

How in the fuck should I know? Irritation stung, a welcome heat through the numbness. And *scared*? Oh, boy howdy, scared was not the word.

Terrified was more like it. She'd read about people's hair standing up from fright, and the sensation was so much like tiny insect feet all over her that a vision of the spiders reared up inside her head again, their legs bending in the wrong directions and their scuttling in random arcs sending a jolt of pain through her heavy skull.

"She in shock?" Jake let the SUV slow, and the idea that maybe he was stopping made a gush of sweat break out all over her.

"Don't slow down," she heard herself gasp, ragged as if she'd been suckerpunched. "For God's sake, don't stop."

"It's all right," Erik grabbed her wrist, and Liv realized she intended to scramble forward, between the seats and into the front, because maybe their doors would unlock and she could wriggle past. "Calm down. Calm *down*, Liv. Stop it!"

She couldn't kick out the back windows with bare feet, but Liv was about to try, pitching violently aside.

"Keep her contained," Ignatius rasped. "And, Erik?"

"Yes—*oof*." Her elbow sank into his midriff, but Erik had her arms trapped in short order, and she found herself smooshed against his chest. His shirt was in tatters, his armored jacket only slightly better, and the drying creature-blood on him stank. "Shhh, Liv. It's okay. Sir?"

It is goddamn well not *okay!* Liv wanted to scream, but she had no air. The panic was back, robbing her of breath and hope, and the stuff on him was *blood*; it was *monster blood.*

And now it was getting smeared all over her, too.

"She has an *oneiros*." Ignatius wasn't breathing right. Every word sounded painful.

Erik paused, but maybe that was only because she was still trying to writhe free of his grip. "Made in the old way, sir. For Yule."

"A traditional gift. Miss Stellack, please . . ." Ignatius coughed, a dry cricket-whisper, and the thought that he was maybe dying filled her with both unsteady glee and howling fear because nobody should be killed by those terrible *things.*

Nobody. Not even one of the names on her very short list of Super-Duper Hated Assholes deserved that.

Besides, he had helped fight the things off. Of course, if it wasn't for these lunatics she wouldn't be here; she would be safe at home, dreaming of Christmas in a few days and wondering how she was going to pay the heating bill.

"Please, be calm," Ignatius said in that choked whisper, and Liv went still, but only because more frantic motion would waste energy.

"I hate you," she whispered. The words came out strange because her cheek was mashed against nylon webbing. Erik had weapons strapped all over him, even at three in the morning. "I hate all of you, and I hate that you kidnapped me, and I hate the fucking *monsters*."

The fact that she'd been dreaming of the hideous things right before her bedroom window was smashed was beside the point. Or at least Liv was going to do her absolute level best to pretend it was.

"That's all right." Erik wasn't fazed in the least. "I expect it. Hating us is safe."

Nothing about this was safe. The necklace was a stone egg between them, digging into her breastbone hard enough to bruise. It still felt warm, somehow reassuring—and the tentacle thing had howled each time it flashed.

That probably meant something. She just couldn't think of what.

She wanted to get out of this goddamn car and run screaming down the gently rising and falling road, coming around on a shallow curve she realized was north of Longpoint, like Erik had said. That meant west of the city proper, out near Statler Farms where she and Mika went each summer to get flats of fruit for Kiki Vannonberg to turn into bespoke preserves. Glimpsing the long billboards painted with dancing fruit threatened to burn her retinas, an iced-over beacon of sanity lost in curtains of falling, whirling flakes.

It was *snowing*. At last. Happy White Christmas, deck the halls with monsters.

"It's all right," Erik repeated. "You're safe. They didn't get you; you're with us. You're safe."

"Let me go," someone moaned, and Liv realized it was her own voice. "Just let me go, for God's sake just let me *gooo*."

Jake piped up. "How far's the nearest active—"

"Three hundred miles, Jacob." Ignatius made a low pained sound. A strange creaking crackle came from the passenger seat, and he sighed, gustily. "That's better." He sounded like his usual dry baritone self now. "Ribs are marvelously designed, but not for that."

Oh, God, please. "Let me go," she whispered. "Please."

"They'd kill you, Liv." Erik's chest rumbled under her cheek. "Just calm down. We've got clothes packed, we'll stop in a bit to clean up."

Oh, sure. Clean up. That'll be great. "I don't want—"

"You were dreaming." His usual diffidence was gone; this Erik was coldly efficient, and the crispness to the words sounded an awful lot like anger.

She tried again to wriggle free, but his arms were immovable. "H-how did you . . .?"

"You screamed. Nightmare, right?" Each word soft and precise. "Only you woke up and it didn't stop."

All the fight drained out of Liv, water down a drain. She flat-out felt it leave, arms and legs turning limp, her heart dropping into her guts with a splash. "Shut up." *I want my life back. I want all this to go away.*

He did shut up, but he didn't let go. Liv shut her eyes, and the thunder of his heart, regular steady *tha-thumps*, filled her ear. He was covered in guck and holding her too tightly and he was one of her jailers—but he'd also fought off those nightmare things twice now, and his heartbeat kept repeating *don't be afraid, someone else is here, don't be afraid, someone else. . . .*

"We'll stop in an hour or so, around Coringtown," Ignatius said, finally. "Control has to be alerted. They'll send backup; they have to. Can you last that long?"

"Yessir." Jake was now hushed and somber. "Sir?"

"Yes, Jacob." Ignatius sounded, for the first time, actually weary. "I know. This rather changes things."

What? What does it change? Liv found out she didn't want to know.

"Doesn't matter," Erik said, quietly. "You're safe, Liv."

Doesn't sound like it. But she just kept her eyes closed, listening to his reassuring, lying heart, and wished it were true.

Other, Fouler, and Smarter

SHE'D RETREATED into civilian numbness by the time they reached the outskirts of Coringtown, and when Jake brought the SUV to a smooth stop in a motel parking lot she didn't try to lunge for the door or the front seats again. Which was great, but Erik didn't like her wan, terrified muteness.

Their *lirai* didn't even demur when she was ushered into a room, or when Ignatius indicated the bathroom and handed her one of the backpacks brought from the go-shelf in the garage. *Please take a warm shower and get dressed,* Father said, courteously enough, and she obeyed with the dreamy slowness of an almost-catatonic.

Which left Father, Jake, and Erik to the work of reloading, making sure their weapons were in good order, cleaning up with sorcery, and changing ripped or unusable clothing. As soon as she was finished—she didn't take long, and peered from the bathroom door as if she expected them to be gone like a normal nightmare—Ignatius and Jake bundled her back into the SUV and Erik took the first running shift.

Wet snow fell in increasing blankets, but when you kept a vehicle in sensing range through an urban area you could leapfrog from roof to roof, a Son's strength and speed playing with physical space and time in a way that would turn a normal person into a howling, vomiting mess.

When you were already halfway to god-fueled insanity, little things like moving faster than a human being should be able to, popping from rooftop to rooftop, or even crouching on the top bar of a streetlamp and watching the traffic whiz by underneath didn't matter so much.

If shadowbeasts took notice of the transport, Erik wasn't trapped in a metal cage; he could arrive from an unexpected quarter to give the *lirai* and close-guard enough time to get away. They should have had several trios performing this duty and at least two other vehicles crammed with backup while moving a potential, let alone a *lirai.*

But Father hadn't been able to get hold of Control. Not from the hotel landline, and not from the prepaid cells either. He'd just dialed and listened to whatever was on the other end with a grim expression.

It wouldn't be the first time communications with a minor frontline temple had somehow been cut. The shadowbeasts were opportunistic predators, but there were other, fouler, and much smarter things in the hierarchy. Generally it was a short-term problem, and modern technology eased it tremendously even while it made avoiding cameras and law enforcement a little trickier.

But being unable to reach a larger temple, or Control itself, meant the entire sector might be interdicted, and that was seriously bad news. Especially with the closest active temple three hundred miles away.

Snowflakes tried to hurt when you smacked through them at high speed; a shell of sorcery slid them aside. The streak Erik cut through their falling was invisible to normals, but another Son or a shadowbeast would see the smear.

The only thing he didn't like about rooftop running was that it gave him too damn much time to think.

It broke the boundary protection without alerting us, and it came straight for her window, Erik. Why would it do that? And the *jana*-spiders—they didn't mass like that unless they had been sent; they weren't separate hunters like *lengs.* Ignatius had been too wounded for a simple clutch of spiders, but he didn't speak of what else had breached the temple's defenses and Jake had, by all appearances, been very busy in his own right.

Not only that, but the incursion had been virtually invisible in its beginning stages. If Liv hadn't screamed in the grip of nightmare . . .

Funny, how thinking about what *could* have happened slowed him, cold fear in his veins and the unsteady, unstable rage under his skin mounting another degree when he thought about how close they'd come to losing their potential. No breath of her should have been discernable outside the *liraim*, that was what the suites with their heavy shielding were *for*, and yet the tentacled horror had expended serious effort and energy poking its snout through a window that should have looked, from the outside, no different than all others.

Erik didn't like what he was thinking.

His jacket snapped as he unfolded in a leap, the SUV below flashing past Coringtown city limits. Now it was freeway game, energy expended on staying almost invisible while he settled on the top of a rattling, wallowing semi carrying a load of consumer goods from one point to the next. If predawn traffic thinned a little more, he'd land light as a leaf on the SUV's roof itself, ready to move in any direction to face a rural attack.

It would be bitterly cold, but that didn't matter with the mark burning on his wrist and wine-dark power flooding him from toes to scalp. The snow thickened, flakes melting as they reached salted roadway—a mild winter so far, but the iron tang to the wind said that was about to change—and Erik danced atop a stream of rumbling commercial traffic, keeping a toy car and its tiny, tempting, tormenting kernel-gleam of a potential inside.

What are you thinking, Erik?

What if, for example, a control liaison had been turned? A full *lirai* checking a liaison's work could sense any hint of corruption, but . . .

The snow thickened, flakes shrinking slightly as the temperature dipped. A storm settling over the area, shadowbeasts breaking a minor temple, communications failures galore—it certainly seemed like someone who shouldn't have knew about their potential and, furthermore, wanted to make sure she never reached the Flame.

That someone might have a little friend in the Sons, a good little half-mad helper. That's what you're thinking, isn't it?

Even though he didn't want to.

Erik's stomach was full of acid, not from any indigestion or hunger. No, it was the rage—and a sinking sensation, much more frigid than the weather, that their problems had only just begun.

Grateful

THIS TIME IGNATIUS drove and Jake was in the back seat with her, which was *not* an improvement even if the smell was gone. Somehow they had magically cleaned up the monster blood, and even though she didn't want to sit in the stuff, the apparent ease of wiping it away didn't help her keep her calm.

None of this did.

Jake's face was still bruised, but it looked yellow-green and old instead of blue-black and utterly fresh with red fringes. Ignatius shifted sometimes as if his chest hurt him, and his dark gaze rested on the rearview mirror more than on the road.

He was watching her. So was Jake, whose apparent lounging relaxation didn't fool her. She'd seen how goddamn fast he was. And Erik, too.

It was Ignatius who broke the tense, humming silence of tires on pavement and the engine forcing them to turn. "I must apologize, Miss Stellack."

Oh, God. For what? Liv's fingers tangled against each other; she pulled hard against them, her knuckles turning white. She said nothing.

"The decision to wait until after the solstice to move you was apparently the wrong one," the older man finally continued, and returned his gaze to the road. That was good—the last thing they needed was an accident right now.

Monsters she could handle. A car wreck was altogether different. Liv strangled a completely inappropriate laugh. She tried to think of what to say, settled for absolute truth. "I want to go home."

"You won't last an hour out in the open," Jake piped up. "Not with that thing on you."

She stopped twisting her hands against each other only because her right fingertips leapt to touch the necklace's hard lump under her fresh grey T-shirt. The backpack had held toiletries, a change of clothes, pajamas—everything she'd need for a few days, assuming she didn't want any of the left-behind books or her lists, or the journal she'd begun to write, stashing it in the cell's mattress.

Now she was hoping someone would find it somehow, and realize she'd been kidnapped.

"It's a traditional gift, Jacob." Now Ignatius sounded even wearier. "Ma'am, did Erik ask you for anything in return?"

None of you have asked *me about single thing.* Liv took a deep breath. "It was a Christmas present. Yule. Whatever." She forced her hand back into her lap. "He didn't ask for anything."

"At least that," Jake muttered, and turned to stare out the window. Why had they left Erik behind? He wasn't as forbidding as Ignatius or as irritating as the blond; of course they'd get rid of the one she halfway liked.

"It couldn't have drawn the unclean; dreamstones are free of corruption." Ignatius changed lanes, sliding around a lumbering semi. Snow whirled, caking at either side of the windshield where the wipers ended their irregular arcs. "That was a very well-planned attack, Miss Stellack, and we're taking you to the closest active temple with a *lirai* and access to the Flame."

"You still won't tell me what that is." Or sealing, or a hundred other little cryptic terms.

"Some things have to be experienced before you grant them reality." Ignatius turned his head slightly as if he wanted to look into the back seat. "Like right now, for example. Erik is outside, keeping pace with us. An additional safety measure."

But that's impossible.

What a ridiculous thought. She'd just seen half-vegetable spiders and a monster land-walking squid with fangs and smoky red eyes studding every tentacle, after being held for weeks in a secluded stone monastery by a trio of sorcerers. Nothing was impossible anymore.

"I want a gun." Maybe, if they wouldn't give her one, she could have a tantrum. Even if she was smaller and weaker, there were ways—toddlers did it all the time, right?

"Absolutely not." Jake's hand shot out as if he would touch her, but Liv shifted, leaning against the door, and he stopped cold.

"Are you trained in firearm safety, then?" Ignatius didn't quite scoff, but it was close. "Close combat? The anatomy of shadowbeasts?"

You don't get to move the goalposts on me, sir. "I'd be trained a lot more if you'd bothered to do it rather than sticking me in a cell."

Jake didn't try to grab her again, but his blue eyes all but glowed with indignation. "The *liraim* isn't a—"

"And you would have taken such training well, then?" Ignatius sighed, returning his attention to the road. "My apologies once more, Miss Stellack." He wasn't as sarcastic as her grandmother could sometimes be—but it was close.

Maybe adrenaline and a change of scenery would shake off any lingering brainwashing these guys had performed on her. Liv shuddered, but pressed gamely on. "I wouldn't need training if you guys hadn't kidnapped me."

"Nah, you'd've been eaten. The thing in the alley . . ." Jake paused, as if he expected Ignatius to shush or interrupt him again. When the older man didn't, he continued. "Erik hit you right out of your shoes to keep you from walking smack-dab into it. When they get hold of a normal it's bad enough, but a potential? They'll suck you dry like an orange slice, babe, and it's not comfortable."

"Your life has been upended, and we have compounded the distress by following protocols you don't understand." Ignatius stared at the road, and in the rearview, tiny blue gleams rotated inside his pupils. "When we reach our destination, all shall be revealed. But for right now we must travel quickly, and it will be easier if you do not fight." He paused. "For all of us."

Yeah, let's save the fighting for the weird spiders made out of smoke and potato shoots, and the big hell-squids. That'll be best, don't you think? Her own sarcasm boiled in her throat now, tasting like acidic smoke. "I'll try to make it as easy as possible on you." *There. That's helpful, right?*

"You should be grateful." Jake didn't think much of her restraint. "Any one of those things could have—"

"Jacob." The single word brooked no argument. Ignatius stared at the road, those tiny glowing blue dots in his pupils moving slightly as his gaze roved over traffic. "Do me the honor of checking our trail for followers. Just because our *lirai* doesn't sense any doesn't mean we're clear."

"Yes, Father." Jake shifted slightly on the bench seat, but he darted her a sharp, very blue glance. "Uh, so you're thinking . . ."

"Yes." Ignatius nodded, unsurprised. "Our *lirai* did not leave the temple; we checked every ingress and egress, and she had no chance to send a message through the shields. We have been cut off from Control. Someone knows she is with us, though, and also knows precisely when to attack. Someone powerful, and quite possibly treacherous."

Wait a second. "Like one of you three?" Liv inquired, almost sweetly. "That's what you're saying, right? Either that, or others in your . . .

organization?" She kept a nervous eye on Jake, whose hands had relaxed against his thighs. His eyes half-closed, and she *felt* his attention move, the way she could sense being stared at on the bus or in a crowded bar. Only this stare wasn't directed at her. It flared behind them like radar, a cloud of intent.

"Yes, Miss Stellack." Ignatius shifted in his seat again, and the blue dots in his pupils winked out. "That is exactly what I'm saying. You will never be left alone with only one of us, and all three of us will require examination once we reach our destination."

"That's great." Liv could only see one problem with the plan. "What if two of you are in cahoots with the monsters?"

"Then we are all lost, and this is yet another exercise in futility." One of his shoulders lifted, his jacket scratching against leather upholstery, then dropped. "The world is full of such things. Something else troubles me, young one."

Well, at least he's not calling me Miss Stellack anymore. "What?"

"A simple potential shouldn't be able to use an *oneiros*. Wear it, certainly—but use it? No." He shook his steel-grey head, a fractional movement, and Liv thought Erik might never know how much he copied the older man. "You must be a very strong Dreamer indeed. And as such, you are very valuable not just to the Sons and the shadowbeasts, but to the Mad God himself."

Well, that's just great. Liv looked out the window. The snow was really coming down, and there was no grey line of dawn on the eastern horizon. "I was afraid you'd say that."

"He won't get you." Jake's attention retracted like an antenna. "We won't let him."

Pardon me for not being very comforted. But saying as much was counterproductive, so Liv just settled on her half of the bench seat and stared out the window. Traffic was thickening, semis rattling and throwing gusts of snow to either side. If Erik was out there, somehow keeping up with them, he was probably very cold.

So was she, as a matter of fact. Her teeth wanted to chatter, and she hugged herself, hoping neither of the men in the SUV's warm, plush cabin would notice.

Not Opportunistic

JUST BEFORE SUNRISE the snow intensified, the flakes growing again as predawn warming touched the clouds. Despite that, Erik was as dry as could be expected, especially since they were inside Grove City limits. The suburb wasn't big enough to have a temple, and Erik wondered why they weren't swinging north and a little east to hit the larger metropolis. But some cities, big as they were, didn't have active temples with Flame access, just minor ones to relieve the pressure from the zones where the shadowbeasts hunted almost at will. *Lirai* were rare, almost lottery-winner rare, but they were also long-lived after the Flame, well-protected once the Sons found them, and he'd thought the clear zone extended further.

If Ignatius thought the best bet of finding an active temple was in this direction, then that's where it was—especially given the trouble getting hold of Control. After all, he was the one in contact with other Fathers, their age and experience providing a steady anchor. It was the Fathers who selected new candidates and chose the territories, who had survived longest with the god's whispering in their heads, who kept the Younger Brothers stable and taught the Elder Brothers how to endure.

Still, Erik's nerves were raw and danger was a piece of cold metal in his mouth, the taste coating his palate. The SUV was slowing, coming off the freeway—maybe their *lirai* needed a bathroom break.

Jake wouldn't take over the running until dawn, which would put Erik in the car with her. She had the *oneiros*, even if she couldn't use it to laser-focus invisible force or spark the Flame in a new well yet. The created gem would call if she was upset or attacked, and he'd *know*. It wasn't what he'd been thinking of while making it, his concentration a white-hot glare as he forced power and stone to his will, but even if she hated him for giving her to the Flame she'd wear the necklace and he could be content.

Even if another Son made a replacement for her, maybe she wouldn't put the first one in a box. Erik could think of her with star-metal resting against her breastbone, the chain touching her nape, the stone—made the old way, a gift only a Son of Ymre could give—singing its soft, almost inaudible lullaby as colors shifted in its pale heart.

Erik pitched forward, falling through space, boots kissing the rooftop several stories below with a jolt he was moving too quickly to really feel. The SUV swayed into a long curve; he reached a good vantage point just as it came to a stop at the end of the exit, left turn signal blinking, and remained there for just a touch too long.

What the hell?

He skidded to a stop, losing momentum, and scanned. Nothing but the usual seashell buzz of people thinking, dreaming, sleeping, eating, shitting—maybe a few lucky ones were having sex, bright spikes of pleasure in a fogged landscape. The snow whirled, a curtain drawn before him, and he took off at a tangent, sorcery-fueled intuition prickling under his skin. When they stopped, his job was to hold the perimeter, then—

WHAM.

The impact was so sudden two of his ribs snapped, and he tumbled sideways, knowing he was going to hit hard, rage rising red under his skin like a *leng*-urchin's spikes. The vast hidden dream-plateau where the half-real servants of the Mad God's elder liches eked out their miserable hungry banishment was riven with deep gullies, cracks, and balkas; sometimes the *leng* creatures slipped through the bottom, finding themselves in low, evil earthly places. Erik realized that was another thing that bothered him—the *jana*-spiders and the nightmare beast at his *lirai*'s window were from different parts of the nightmare lands.

Neither were generally opportunistic, even the juvenile *shoggoth*. They were *sent*.

Erik landed, a roar of pain from broken ribs spiraling through him. The fury tore him out of the soft, strangling grip of the thing, its pale misshapen hands squirming for his throat, its eyes full of diseased blue pinpricks dancing on shoals of black mud. The constellation-gaze was an *igsoth*'s greatest weapon—that and the fact that they were practically invisible until they attacked.

Unless you had an *oneiros*. The dreamstones pierced their veils and could often hold many of the loathsome hatchlings at bay with its glow alone. He had a brief moment of feeling glad he'd finished making his *lirai*'s before the agony wedded to fury poured through him again and he struck, knives biting deep in the thing's guts loosing a flood of foul brackish fluid full of wriggling gutsnakes—the thing was infected, just to add to the fun—and he sensed more than heard the crumple of metal, the tinkle of falling safety glass, and a rush of gasoline-fed flame.

His ribs healed messily, sorcery sparking under his jacket and torn T-shirt, snow crusting his hair because he was rolling, knives unerringly finding the *igsoth*'s throat and ignoring the thing's tiny, diamond-sharp claws swiping his coat sleeve. A single one wasn't going to keep him down for long, but the damage was already done.

Don't let anything happen to her. There was nobody to pray to; the jeering cackle of a mad god inside his skull reached a feedback squeal as he tore the life from the *igsoth* and rolled, coming up caked with more snow, flicking ichor and wriggling parasites off his blades with quick habitual movements. If the *igsoth* hadn't bled out when dawn came the sunshine, however weak, would take care of it—they were creatures of deep night.

There was a stinging rosette of red and gold in the near distance, flickering on the other side of a gas station's bulk. They'd barely gotten off the freeway; his *lirai* was probably hysterical with fear.

Keep her safe for a few seconds longer, guys. He barely noticed the pain, going straight up the side of a brick building, bolting across the roof, and now he could see the fire more clearly. There was another low crumpling sound, oddly distorted by the snow, and he flung himself into empty space, landing with a jolt across the street from a deserted but still fully lit Shell station. Now he heard gunfire, too, dull terrible popping through veils of falling snow, a treacherous wind rising from nowhere and driving frozen-wet stinging into his face.

That's not an igsoth. They can't work windveils.

More gunfire. A battle-cry—Jake's, but weirdly distorted, the snow swirling. Erik was soaked, water drift-streaming from his skin and clothes as he tore through shell after shell of illusion, an arrow flying for its target—

The thing in the snow chuckled and squealed. Dawn was so, so close; if they could just hold out, the longest night of the year would soon be over.

Should've moved her before now. But Control—

For a moment Erik wasn't sure why he'd stopped. Then he looked down.

Thunk. The sound reached him late, cotton-fog shock filling his ears, and he stared at the dirty ivory spear-claw embedded in his chest. It smoked with poison, and its golden chasing, not to mention the gems along its handle, would buy you anything in the waking world you desired.

It would also pay for passage to the dreaming lands, but unless you were careful you'd end up sold for a handful of clotted-blood rubies and taken to the nightmare country, carried in the stinking hold of a black ship with banks of oars like serried teeth along each side, its prow a frozen scream under a pair of staring crimson lamps.

Oh, shit, Erik thought, and the thing in the snow laughed. It loomed before him, its fingers stained by the filthy spear-claw wrenched from an almost unimaginable beast in the lands bordering the fair far shimmering of the deepest dreams. Those rolling green hills and bright shining city were a place the Mad God hated almost as much as this tiny inconsequential planet whose inhabitants, through whatever freak of genetics, magic, or just plain chance, could bleed away his force, betray him, and bar his passage, not to mention impede his plans.

It didn't matter. Even the claw in his chest, digging relentlessly for his heart, didn't matter. Erik closed one bloody, dripping, grimy hand around the spear, spat a mouthful of liquid glittering red in the faint glare of citylight off snow, and yanked it free, not caring if he sliced his fingers down to bone or even lost one or two.

They'll grow back eventually. Kill that thing, Erik. Kill it now.

The creature who could wield that claw came from deep in nightmare, though it might look human enough except for the extra joints on its long, strong fingers and the wasted, terrible almost-beauty of its pale, lipless face.

Sarnaki. One of the Great Liars creeping through the fringes of normal human dreaming, voracious but banished from the waking world—unless they were summoned and sent to inhabit one of the god's fleshly hands. Fast, unpredictable, deadly toxic to *lirai*, utterly committed to its task, they were also very, very difficult to destroy.

For one thing, they regenerated almost as quickly as a Son.

Erik's knees turned to melting snow, and he staggered. The thing laughed again, using the falling flakes as a shield, and if the *sarnaki* wasn't splitting its attention between an Elder Brother and those he was protecting, it could only mean more than one of the Mad God's centurions was lurking in the blizzard.

"*Lirai*," Erik whispered, and the thing halted, snarling. For a single cold, heartstopping moment it was clearly visible; Erik shoved himself forward, the wrenched-free spear in his hand keening and the hole in his chest giving a splattering gout of bright crimson.

Stop the Whispers

ONE MOMENT SHE was looking forward to peeing in a filthy gas station restroom, maybe being able to write a note on some toilet paper—though she might not, the police probably couldn't help her if nightmare creatures and superhuman monster hunters were in the mix—and the next, Liv was blinking, her hair hanging in her face and the *oneiros* tapping at her chin.

It was tapping because she was upside down. Smoke filled her throat and scorched her nose; she tried to make some sense of what was happening.

Dream. It was all a dream, maybe? Her hands hung, fingers twitching as her brain tried to make them move. Her eyes ran with salt water, the back of the driver's seat only indistinctly visible.

A crash and tinkle of falling glass, a hungry roaring. Hands on her, warm and iron-hard. Liv struggled, a drugged kitten batting at a threat too big for comprehension. Someone was dragging her out of an upside-down car.

What the hell? This wasn't the long-ago accident in Mika's sporty little orange coupe—for one thing, this hulk of crumpled metal and crumbling safety glass was a lot bigger. Not to mention she and her bestie hadn't ended upside down, just bruised and shaken with the front end folded around a concrete pole.

Also, it was snowing instead of dry and crystal-clear icy, and Liv hadn't dreamed this accident.

For once.

"*Give it to usss,*" something hissed.

The voice was *wrong*, scraping and burrowing through her head without going through her ears. She convulsed, a weak little whisper-scream sliding past her chapped lips.

Something popped, and whatever had spoken gave a thin glassy howl. It sounded like it hurt, and she was dozily glad for *that*, even if its pain tore at her as well.

"Go fuck yourself," another voice snarled, but the words were blessedly human, male, and totally pissed off. For a moment, she thought it was Erik and her heart gave a weird leap, almost lodging in her smoke-jammed throat.

She was dragged the rest of the way through the window, the shattered, misshapen safety glass grinding against her jeans. Her sneakers dangled as he lifted her, and the necklace settled against her again, a warm, comforting weight.

"It's all right," he said, softly. "Almost dawn, Livvie. Just hang in there."

Don't call me that, asshole. Darkness swallowed her, and just before she passed out, she heard a massive, grinding noise.

The SUV had exploded.

IT WASN'T ERIK. It was Jake, and when she opened her burning eyes he was looming over her, his blue gaze oddly empty and the ivory plastic bedside phone clamped to his ear. He dropped the receiver into the cradle as she inhaled, scrambling away—her neck ached, her back was a solid bar of pain, and both her legs felt like wet noodles.

Whiplash was a bitch, and she was in yet another hotel room.

Her shoulders hit the headboard of a cheap motel bed. He was right after her, his knees sinking into pillows on either side of her hips, and his big, warm, callused hand clapped over her mouth. "*Don't* scream," he said, pleasant and low. "Please. It's . . . distracting."

OhGod, ohChrist someone, anyone, please . . . She stared at him, her shoulders pressed against the headboard—who knows what had been wiped off thin, pale-pink vinyl?

This room wasn't quite seedy but it wasn't entirely nice either, and the mirror on the far wall showed Jake's shoulders, his wild snow-frosted hair, but not his bruised face or the bloody grime on his hands. He looked, quite frankly, like he'd been put through the wringer.

"Good," he said, still in that deceptively quiet, mild tone. It clashed uneasily with the glittering rage in blue eyes and the flush in what little uninjured parts of his face remained. "That's better. Now, I'm gonna take my hand away and you're gonna play nice, or I will gag you. Clear?"

Her chin dropped, rose again. Her eyes were welling with smoke-induced tears. They both reeked of gasoline and the terrible, stomach-churning miasma of monsters. A tear tracked hot down her cheek, touched his fingers.

Jake peeled his palm away from her mouth, ready to clamp down again at any moment. "I'm gonna clean the ichor off both of us. Can you hold still while I do that?"

Liv swallowed, hard. Nodded again.

"Good girl." The soft edge of approval was terrifying, a thin veneer over a deep well of fury. It was very much like being locked in a cage with a hungry tiger—not that she ever had been, but Liv could goddamn well extrapolate. "After that, I suggest a change of clothes. We're gonna move when the sun's high enough. All right?"

Move where? It was a silly question, she decided. She pushed her shoulders back into the headboard. "Okay." Her voice shook, but she managed to produce an almost normal tone.

"*Very* good girl." Jake's right hand dropped to her shoulder, cupping gently. He exhaled, hard, and the sensation was odd—tiny bubbles sliding over her skin, steam-ribbons of monster blood lifting and shredding into nonexistence. A powerful, almost musky smell folded over both of them.

Who knew magic had a scent? Liv certainly hadn't until now. As Lou often intoned while telling stories about his husband's antics, you did indeed learn something new every day on this blessed earth.

"You hurt anywhere?" Jake studied her face. "Bruises, cuts? You've got to tell me. Even a papercut, Livvie. Anywhere at all?"

How the hell should I know? "Whiplash," she managed between dry cracked lips. "My neck, my back. Other than that, I think I'm—"

"All right. Hold still." His hand tensed against her torn, smoke-stained jacket, and a flood of warmth slid down her back, reaching insubstantial fingers to stroke her nape. Her muscles went liquid and she sagged, gasping. "Be easier if you were sealed up, but—"

"When will you tell me what that is?"

"I suppose I should." He retreated inch by inch, but the warmth remained, bathing her from top to toes. It even combed through her hair, and she could have sworn she felt every individual strand trying to twitch and grow some more. "But not if it's going to freak you out."

"Honestly, how much more could . . . no, wait." A nervous toss of her head, her shoulders sliding against pink vinyl. "Don't answer that."

"Smart lady." He retreated, again very slowly. The way he moved, catlike and supple, was both comforting and deeply disturbing. "Go on into the bathroom and change. There's a backpack in there."

"Let me get this straight." If she could just find some sort of handle on the situation, *any* handle, she'd feel a lot better. "You pulled me out of a burning car with monsters attacking and you stopped to get a change of clothes?"

"For you." He slithered off the end of the bed and rose to his full height, dried blood and monster-goo cracking on his skin and jacket. "It's the training, cupcake. Every single thing living on this rock owes the *lirai* everything. Debt's never paid, and gets deeper all the time. So we make it easy on you. But there's something you can give us, when we've been very good boys."

Since there aren't any daughters, only Sons. Ignatius had explained *that*, at least—*lirai* were any gender, but the Sons were all boys. The mark wouldn't stay on a woman; it just burned through the skin and kept eating, and the end result apparently wasn't pretty in any way, shape, or form.

Looked like their mad god did *not* believe in equal-opportunity hiring.

"What's that?" Her eyes still smarted, yes, but the terrible burning was gone, and the deep smoky pain in her lungs had receded. All things considered, she felt all right.

Except for the shaking. Not to mention the urge to howl and bolt for the door, just run flat-out until her heart burst and she saved all the monsters the trouble of killing her.

"You can stop the whispers." He spread his hands and shuddered.

Liv watched, fascinated, as the monster blood slid off him in little steam-threads. The fresh crop of bruising on his face went back to yellow-green, looking weeks instead of bare hours old, and a fluid feline shiver went through him again. He rolled his big shoulders, muscle settling almost audibly, and when his eyes snapped open again she was almost surprised to find them still blue, and very human. No funny sparks or diseased glow, just . . . normal.

"They tell you, before you even start training." For the first time, Jake didn't sound sarcastic or arrogant. Instead, his tone was soft, reflective, and he turned his hands palm-up, studying his fingers like they held a secret. "Then they keep telling you over and over, but it's like the first time you get shot. You really don't know until you get there."

"You've been *shot*?" Liv didn't mean to sound so horrified. Why that should bother her with all the rest of this going on, she couldn't quite say.

"Couple times, yeah. *He* has human hands, too. Just because we turned doesn't mean all his servants did." Another shiver passed through Jake. "Anyway, you get the mark, the *lirai* cauterize it, and if it doesn't kill you the whispers start. The mark makes you stronger, faster, probably smarter too—Erik and I argue about that sometimes." His

Adam's apple bobbed as he swallowed, dryly. "But when you can see the shadows, they can see you. And so can *he*."

Liv's throat ached, but not with smoke. A sarcastic, domineering douchebag she could handle—she could outright fight. But Jake now looked lost, a little hopeless, and incredibly . . .

Well, he looked lonely.

"The nightmares aren't so bad," he continued, still staring at his now-clean palms. His tone dropped even further, confidential and soft. "It's the fucking whispers. You can't be sure if it's your own thoughts, or . . . *his*. That's why we watch each other, all the time."

"It sounds exhausting." *And terrifying*. She didn't want to add that, though—men reacted awfully to any intimation that they might be, of all things, scared.

Maybe it was the right thing to say, because he dropped his hand and gazed fixedly at her. "Yeah, well. A *lirai* can stop the whispers. It's a kind of intense process. It, uh . . ." Was he *blushing*? It mixed uneasily with the bruising all over his face. "Well, you know, it kind of requires a . . ."

Liv waited, but he seemed to have vapor-locked. "What, it requires a virgin sacrifice or something?"

"Not *virgin*." His eyebrows rose meaningfully, and she got the message.

"Oh. Wow. Uh." *Oh, my God, how awkward. We just almost got killed by monsters and now this.* "No wonder Ignatius didn't want to explain."

"Usually the older *lirai* explain to new ones, once they're safe. It's not even really sex, it's just . . . Anyway, Father didn't want to travel with you while the nights were still getting longer." Jake stiffened; his head tilted. He looked a little like a dog hearing a familiar footstep, and his face changed a few millimeters. The cocky, self-assured mask slipped back on and his hands blurred, one reaching for the gun low on his left hip and the other suddenly holding the hilt of a short, wickedly curved knife with a strange, crystalline blade. All three of them carried a set of those, and they were definitely *not* Ginsu. "Get in the bathroom."

"What?" But she was already moving, sliding off the now soot-stained bed. Her sneakers were oddly pristine—of course, this was the first time she'd worn them outside, and Jake had hauled her away from the wreck, carrying her like luggage.

That was happening a lot lately. Where was Erik, and the older man? The SUV had blown up, but—

Oh, God. I'm not handling this very well at all. "Is it the monsters?" she whispered, edging for the bathroom door.

"Don't know," Jake answered just as softly, a sharp half-turn making his sliced jacket flutter. Now he faced the door, and there was no sign of indecision or insecurity. He looked, all things considered, fairly relaxed. "If it is, I'll kill them, so you get in the *bathroom*. If I can bottleneck them—"

A fast, light series of taps on the room door echoed, and Liv jumped, her hand flying to her mouth to catch a tiny, wounded sound. There was a pause, then three distinct, deliberate knocks. Another pause, then two more.

"Great," Jake muttered. He was suddenly at the door, the knife disappearing and the gun held low. He unlocked it and stepped back; the knob turned, and Liv's knees were gelatin. She couldn't have moved even if she wanted to. "Took you long enough."

"Yeah, well." The answer was a harsh growl. "Where is she?"

Wasn't Me

HIS CHEST HURT. *Everything* hurt, and it took more energy than he liked to stay upright. Of course, killing two *sarnaki*—never mind that one of them had been almost shredded by Jake's gunfire, Younger Brother had a distinct gift for projectile mayhem—was an achievement. He should have been overjoyed.

Instead, Erik wanted to sleep for a week, and maybe for another afterward. He might even have tried it, if there wasn't the prospect of dreaming.

And if there wasn't a *lirai* to save.

"Hello to you, too." Jake beckoned him inside, glancing over Erik's shoulder to check the hallway. There wasn't much to see—a rundown motel was no fit place for a *lirai*, but it was right over a tangle of water lines and jammed among high-waisted, frowning apartment buildings providing a variety of psychic cover. It was the sort of place that charged by the hour or the night, but with a marked preference for the more profitable former. "You look like shit."

"Feel like it, too." The instant Erik was fully in the room Jake slammed the door, and the shields—probably placed as soon as they reached this imperfectly safe harbor—folded back into place.

And there, clean and whole, her dark eyes huge and her honeydark hair a wild mess, Liv stood near the bathroom. She was deadly pale, and for a moment Erik thought she might scream. The *oneiros* at her breastbone was alive with deep coruscating colors; he hadn't realized, inside the temple, just how much she hummed with invisible force. Every scrape, puncture, slash, and slice on him drank in that power, the potential, and he understood more than ever why the spiders, the hellbeasts, the shadows, and the Mad God himself wanted to own that wine-bright, intoxicating drink.

To *consume* it.

Erik didn't realize he was bearing down on her until she flinched, throwing up one small, perfect hand as if to ward off a blow. His bloody, filthy boot-toes dug into cheap patterned nylon carpet, and Jake's hand closed around Erik's left arm.

"Easy, bro." Younger Brother sounded only mildly concerned, but the vibrating tension in his grasp said that if Erik shrugged him off and kept going, things would heat up in a hurry. "Let's just all calm down, okay?"

"Hurt," Erik rasped. "Is. She. Hurt?"

Liv's chin rose. "I'm fine." The words trembled, but she wasn't lying. The display of sheer courage was just a little humbling—a civilian, facing horrors that would drive the regular nine-to-fivers into screaming until their throats gave out, and not retreating an inch. Worse, with a potential's sensitivity, she could sense the underworld and its predators—which might be how she was still alive, but probably also soaked her with high-grade anxiety every day of her life, tension she didn't notice because it was so incessant. "You . . . we need to get you to a hospital."

Did she actually sound concerned? Erik bit back a terrible, harsh bray of laughter. "Won't do me any good, but thanks." *You're what I need.* It lingered on the tip of his tongue, but he swallowed it just like he'd taken down the pain, the desperation, and the mounting rage when Jake's trail—and hence, hers—faded and flared maddeningly.

Ignatius couldn't be dead, could he? With *sarnaki* everywhere, the car burning, and a *lirai* to protect, the old man might have taken one too many hits.

Mourn later. Do your job now. Erik could find Jake because he knew all of his little brother's tricks, but the shadowbeasts might not be able to. And now, with both a younger and elder Son alive and in attendance, she was safe.

Or at least, safer.

Now, suddenly, he was aware of just how hurt he was. Erik swayed, and she stepped close, grabbing his other arm. Her bare palm met filthy, blood-streaked skin, the armor patches in his sleeve sliced free. "Come on." Still pale as milk, she was also surprisingly strong, or maybe he just wanted to obey. "You need to sit down."

The touch roared through him, a *lirai* willingly putting her hands on a Son. Without the muffling of sorcery, unconsciousness, or clothing it was a raw, unfiltered jolt, and his chin tipped up as his eyes closed.

"Do we have a first aid kit?" She pushed him into the room's single chair, which creaked alarmingly under his weight but held up. "Band-Aids? Anything?"

"I'll be fine," Erik mumbled, but she wasn't listening.

"He just needs a chance to breathe." Jake's chin had set and his hands were tense. "Go in and get changed, ma'am. We'll move once the sun's up."

It was the best course of action. Erik sagged in the chair, beginning to believe he was still alive—and that she was, too. Jake was a little battered, but he'd had time to bathe in that glow; she was putting out a lot of power for an untriggered potential.

The sooner she met the Flame, the better.

Still, she lingered, her hand still on him. "Wow," she breathed, softly.

She didn't mean it as an invitation, but his body responded anyway. Which gave Erik an entirely new set of problems.

"See?" Jake sounded almost kind, for once. "We heal fast. All he needs is time."

Erik's blood-crusted eyes refused to open. He wanted to surge up out of the chair, find the rest of the creatures hunting her, and murder them with every savagery he could possibly muster. Kill, kill, and kill again until the world was cleansed and she was safe.

But that persistent softness against his arm was a shackle; he didn't dare move for fear of disturbing it. She was probably seeing the bruises fading in fast-forward, rips in skin and muscle closing up from the inside out, bits of glass or tiny rocks from when the *sarnaki* dragged him over pavement forced free. The deep ache in his chest refused to quit, though—it had been close to piercing his heart.

Very close.

"Erik?" she persisted. "It looks like it hurts."

"Fine," he rasped. "I'm fine." *And if you ask again, beautiful, I'm not sure what I'll say.* He could handle getting stabbed with a *sarnaki* claw-spear, but she was about to undo him.

The touch faded but the glow remained. Without the Flame she was so much more vulnerable, sleeping or waking.

The bathroom door shut with a click. The shower chugged to life a few moments later, and he hoped they had decent soap in there. When he could force his eyelids up a fraction, blinking irritated at the blood-crust, he found his little brother halfway between him and the bathroom door, shoulders tense and chin level.

"They knew our route," he said, flatly, as if he expected a challenge. "Or they were watching every possible road."

Which was a sobering realization. If Jake kept thinking like this, he'd make Elder Brother status in no time. "Looks that way." Now Erik could relax a little, so he let himself sag, muscle by muscle. The chair didn't creak again, but if it broke he might just sprawl in the pieces and try for a catnap.

The room was full of the heavy, heady fume of cleansing sorcery. Looked like Jake had been attending to their *lirai* personally. It shouldn't have irked him; Erik should have just been happy to have found them and doubly happy she was cared for.

But Jake was right. This was a lot of effort for the Mad God's underlings to go to, even for such a high-value potential. A temple had been breached, Ignatius was missing, Control wasn't answering, and if Younger Brother wasn't suspecting Elder Brother—and vice versa—then neither of them were doing their job.

The walls here were paper-thin, and other rooms full of activity despite the hour. Faint mortal sounds ran through the building—other showers running, low voices, moving bodies, and the hum of conscious normals. Some of them were due at work before dawn; others were done with a long, hard, cold night. The snow was showing no sign of letting up.

"It's not me," Jake said, harshly. "If it was, you wouldn't have found us."

Which wasn't entirely true, but there was no point in saying as much. "I know," Erik said quietly. *But you have no way of knowing it's not me. And this close to dawn, you'd be smart to wait for dark again. If it was you.*

Jake finally got around to asking one of the more important questions. "Where's Father?"

"I don't know. By the time I reached the wreck you were gone; there wasn't a trail. Except yours." Which meant the tactic of two in the car and one running sweep had worked as intended, even though Erik was lucky to have killed not just a single *sarnaki* but a pair of the fuckers.

"What was it?" Little brother was settling into the work now.

"*Sarnaki.*"

"But they shouldn't have . . ." Jake's face changed, the equivalent of a door slamming.

Erik watched his younger realize that someone would have had to call the *sarnaki* to them instead of just covering routes out of town, and Erik had been out running perimeter with plenty of time to do so. It was no use. He'd known as soon as he'd realized what he was fighting that it would end up like this. "I didn't," he said, harshly. "I don't expect you to believe me. But I *didn't*, Jacob."

The shower shut off. Maybe she'd only rinsed. The thought called up a series of interesting images, ones Erik didn't have any time to pursue. Lucky hot water, getting to touch, to slide over curves and—

"It better not have been you," Jake said, finally. "Look, it's possible they're covering all the routes to the nearest active temple and just got lucky with *sarnaki* and hunting hounds. Father might even have suspected; he knew we were being followed. Maybe he drew the hounds off. I didn't have time to check; there were six or seven goatmen."

Erik nodded; he'd smelled the goat-things through the wet snow. Even that slight movement hurt, which was the surest sign the battle was over.

Or that things were about to get much, much worse. Goatmen were opportunistic, but they were also pursuit predators. The double-horned fuckers could have been chasing the SUV since the temple; their escape route had been semi-rural in patches and the hairy fuckers liked that terrain.

"It's possible," he said. Now his skin began to crawl, another sign that the fight was past and he'd survived again. Once she was done, he'd go in and wash his face. What strength he had left would have to be spent on his weapons and clothes; he was too tired for more sorcery unless they were attacked again.

"So what do we do?" Jake's sandy eyebrows were hiked almost to his hairline. "Just . . . watch each other?"

"And get her to the active temple Father was aiming for." *That's the important thing. We're both going to be dredged to see if we had anything to do with this.*

"They already know where we're going."

"Maybe," Erik said, listening to the *lirai* move in the bathroom—material whisper-shifted; she was changing into fresh clothes, and *that* was a deliciously distracting thought, too. "You know what that means."

"We're all gonna die?" But a tentative, lopsided smile returned to Younger Brother's face.

"Better." To be an elder was to pretend you knew what the hell you were doing; it was Erik's lot in life and might steady both a Younger Brother *and* their exhausted, far-too-brave potential. "We're going to have to be sneaky."

Fight in the Dark

IT WARMED A few fractions and snow stopped briefly mid-morning, but the sky remained an even, depthless grey. Liv hitched the backpack strap higher on her shoulder and tried not to look like a kidnapped woman chased by murderous hell-squid and vegetable spiders.

Maybe it even worked, because a forest-green SUV pulled up to a crumbling curb in the Overlook Motel's parking lot and Jake opened the front passenger door for her without missing a beat, as if he squired women into large cars every day. "Your chariot awaits, Livvie."

God, I hate that. She clambered inside while Jake kept a hand hovering as if she were a child who might bump their tender head. The door slammed, the engine roused, and the SUV pulled smoothly away. The side mirror was empty, and when she craned to see out the heavily tinted windows, there was no sign of the blond man—just a parking lot, the tense, dispirited bulk of the motel, and sleeping cars placed neatly in painted spaces, most bearing a fringe of snow.

Erik had a fresh navy-blue T-shirt, but his jacket was just as torn as Jake's and traces of moisture still clung to his dark hair. Long nose, thin mouth—his profile was severe as a Roman statue's, and Liv's throat was dry.

"So this is what you disappeared to do." She searched for something else to say. "Is it stolen?"

Erik checked the rearview, a quick flicker of dark eyes. "Technically, maybe. We could carry you, but that's not very comfortable." No faint trace of a smile; he was all business. The shy man who had given her the necklace was nowhere in sight.

Was it a relief? She couldn't tell.

"Do I want to know the technicalities?" *Or how fast you can really move?*

"Not really?" Now he glanced at her, obviously gauging her desire for details, and pulled out of the lot proper and into rumbling traffic. "Don't worry, Father's tough. He'll probably meet us there."

I wasn't worried. Ignatius was the least of her concerns right now—after all, *he* had a gun.

But it sounded like Erik was anxious, or just needed a subject change. "I'm sure he will." When had it become her job to comfort him? Jeez. "Are we going to get pulled over if the cops run this license plate?"

"Spoken like a true paralegal." No smile broke his expression; still, a ghost of amusement lingered in his tone. "But no, we won't."

Of course they knew she'd been working for a law office, but she was still irritated. "Why not?"

"Sorcery's useful." A flat, declarative statement. Erik touched the brake, nudged the SUV into a clear spot in the left lane, and his dark eyes narrowed. "They won't even notice us."

"What if they do?" And to think she'd been so focused on escape just a short while ago. Going to the cops looked like a childish fantasy at the moment.

What officer, no matter how determined, could deal with gigantic hell-squid? There wasn't any precedent in all the law books of the world for that one.

"Then I'll handle it." Erik said *handle it* like it meant *kill them*, and maybe it did. "All you have to do is stay near me or Jake, Liv. I'm kind of surprised you didn't try to bolt, though."

"I thought about it." Which was a lie. The only thing she'd been thinking about was screaming and possibly escaping horrible, hellishly *real* monsters, with a heavy side helping of being glad someone else was fighting them off. "Except it doesn't seem too good an idea now, does it."

"Guess not." The SUV rolled to a soft stop at a red light, spatters of tire-thrown slush dewing the windshield. The upholstery didn't smell new; there was only that strange, almost musky fragrance of the shimmering energy Jake had used to clean them both of monster blood.

Magic. Sorcery. Nightmare creatures. All things considered, she was doing pretty well with all this, right? Her hands shook, almost imperceptible tremors. Her body was a tired, hunted animal, and she hadn't washed her hair at the motel. Consequently, she felt greasy and unkempt. She longed for a plain latte, for a giant cranberry walnut muffin, and for a good long bitch session with Mika.

While she was at it, she could wish for Gramma Poe to be alive again, for her father's fatal car accident and her mother's murder to be just a pair of bad dreams, and to top everything off she could ask for a pony, too.

One she didn't have to clean up after.

"So you might have noticed the, uh, the *oneiros* does a few things."

His hands were precisely placed on the wheel, the ten and two o'clock position she remembered from ancient driver's ed. "It's kind of like a tool for *lirai*, and one of the things—"

Oh, God. Panic swelled under Liv's breastbone. "Is this more magic?" If it was, she wasn't sure she wanted to hear it. Not right now.

"Kind of. Well, it's sorcery. If you want to get technical."

Oh, my God, if you start giving me a lecture on proper terminology I really might scream. "Can we get some coffee first?"

"Oh. Yeah, sure." Now he was stealing small glances at her, as if gauging whether she was going to reach for the door and try to dump herself into traffic. "Sorry, *lirai.* I didn't think about it."

"We're on kind of a tight schedule, right?" Now she felt even more ridiculous. If she was putting this into a calendar, how would she name it? *Get up early for monster invasion. Remember breakfast. It's leg day—run away from monsters!* "I mean, if we don't have time, I understand."

"I think we can swing getting some java." His shoulders relaxed—maybe he'd expected her to start screaming or being difficult again.

"Okay." It was going to take a while before she was up to presenting any difficulty at all, Liv realized. All she felt was cold and shaky, with a giant blister of pure grade-A terror simmering underneath. How many people in the cars around them, heading to work or school or errands or whatever, knew about the nightmare things creeping through the dark? How many of them even suspected the creatures were *possible*? Had anyone found the exploded SUV? Were emergency crews scratching their heads, wondering who'd been in the car? "Why doesn't anyone know about this?" Her voice shook. Her tough-girl façade was cracking bigtime.

"Mostly because they don't want to." Erik's calm was maddening; she wished it were infectious instead. His dark stubble was ferocious; sorcery must not be good for shaving. "*He* has his servants, of course, but they keep a low profile."

"Why? You'd think . . ." Her stomach was a ball of hot acid, but she wasn't hungry.

Liv was thinking she'd never eat again.

"Well, if everyone knew, it wouldn't just be us guarding the *lirai.* Everyone else would too." Erik glanced left, visibly considering a small, independent coffee drive-thru. He'd have to turn a few times to get to it, though, and she almost *felt* him discard the idea. "*He* wouldn't be able to get through the cracks as well."

"And you guys don't publicize it because—"

"Because if we did, without unveiling an easy enemy for humanity to band together against, they'd turn on the *lirai* the same way they do on anything different or strange." The light changed, he pressed the accelerator, and Liv's stomach turned over hard. "It's equilibrium—neither of us wants the war to mushroom, but for different reasons. So we fight in the dark."

"Oh." She touched the gem's hard, opalescent dome. It was still vivid, almost glowing in the weak grey light, colors following her fingertip. The clouds were thickening, and even inside the car she could smell the iron tang of more snow. The news would work itself up into a lather about a winter storm watch, and everyone who'd lived in this part of the world more than a few months would roll their eyes. "What does this thing actually do?"

"Acts like a focus for a Dreamer's power, mostly. Some things can't fool you with illusion when you're wearing it; others have to assume their true form when its light hits them." His blunt, callused fingers twitched, one after the other, counting off the possible uses. "And it . . . well, it'll call me, if you need me. Or want me."

Liv crossed her ankles. She didn't even have a purse to put in the footwell—there was just the backpack she had never seen before last night, full of clothes that fit her and tiny trial-sized toiletries she might have liked using if not for the situation. "I could just text you." *Except you took my phone.*

He opened his mouth, shot her a glance, and realized she was joking. "I guess. But an *oneiros* does lots of other useful things." A disbelieving smile crossed Erik's weary face for half a second before swiftly submerging. He hit the blinker, pulling into the right lane—there was a Pilgrim's Coffee dead ahead. "Doesn't send pictures, though."

"Technology wins again." The trembling was getting worse, which was ridiculous. It was during the day, and those things were gone. She stared at the coffee shop's sign, the funny buckled hat and secretive smile on the eponymous Puritan turning into a monstrous grimace. "Erik?"

"Yes?" At least he didn't sound annoyed, or even distracted. He was, in short, just the same as he had been at the stone house, except significantly more unshaven. At least he wasn't covered in monster gunk now. A casual observer might not even notice the rips in his jacket or the faint marks of bruising or scrapes healing in fast-forward. There was barely any evidence left of last night's games.

She meant to ask where precisely they were going, what was going to happen when they got there, and maybe follow it up with *are you sure you won't let me go home?* Instead, what came out was a wistful, completely ridiculous question. "Why am I shaking?"

"It's normal." The SUV took the bump up into the Pilgrim's lot gracefully. The coffee shops were everywhere, and at least they had good scones. Erik shifted, reaching for a back pocket, and a knifehilt peeked out from between two rips in the leather jacket. "Adrenaline crash. Fight-or-flight's hard on the body; you're tired."

"Oh." It made sense. Her head was tender, and her stomach just wouldn't stop rolling. No doubt he'd have an explanation for that too. "Okay."

"We've got you, Liv. Me and Jake, we're good at what we do. Don't worry."

"I'll try not to." But now she was thinking of Ignatius's dry, quiet, precise tone.

You will never be left alone with only one of us, and all three of us will require examination once we reach our destination.

Except here she was, alone with one of them, and she didn't even *know* their destination. Liv stared out the window, wishing the sun would pierce the clouds even for a moment, and Erik said no more beyond asking what kind of coffee she wanted, and if she was hungry.

Liv, far from trying to get the barista's attention and signal her kidnapped status, simply asked for a plain latte and a cranberry scone, letting Erik handle the ordering. He had a wallet, just like any other guy, and no shortage of cash. Which was thought-provoking in its own way—just like the sense she had of being watched while she peered out the passenger window, wondering where Jake was.

Daylight Attack

THE CLOUDS THICKENED as noon approached, a beaten-iron ceiling hung threateningly low. He took the exit with careful braking, his nerves raw and his skin tingling with her nearness, and even the consciousness of Jake running guard wasn't truly comforting.

Not with what he suspected.

"Rochester?" His *lirai*—oh, it was stupid to even think in such possessive terms, but he couldn't help it—stretched catlike, looking around with bright interest. Her honeydark hair was a glorious cloud, obviously glad to be free of confinement, and once he'd handed over the latte she'd relaxed all at once, abruptly, and even smiled at him. "Why am I not surprised?"

"You know the town?" Erik should have been feeling an active temple's pull the instant they got off the freeway. Instead, they rolled to a red-light stop at the end of the onramp and a few large, heavy, feathery flakes whirled down, whisked from the windshield by a quick flick of wipers. He felt nothing but mounting unease. The wind was rising, too, and everything pointed to a blizzard soon.

He wanted her safe in an active temple with other *lirai* explaining everything and other Sons handling his and Jake's debriefing. He'd expected Ignatius to reappear long before now, too; Father's absence was . . . troubling.

If Erik had fought off two *sarnaki*, what had the older man come across once the hounds were led safely away? More goatmen? They could mass like the *leng*-spiders and bring a lone fighter down. Ignatius was old and canny; it would be an undignified return for long years of sacrifice and service.

You didn't get into this line of work without knowing it could end that way, bleeding out alone in the snow while the Mad God's minions snacked on your entrails. If a control liaison had turned, who knew how much damage had been done? If it was one of their trio, though . . .

He was well on the way to even suspecting himself. It wasn't anything new, but it was distinctly uncomfortable.

At least his *lirai* wasn't as anxious now. "We lived on the west side when I was in elementary school, after my dad . . . well, my grandparents lived off Shaffee Road, too. Never thought there would be monsters *here*." Her faint smile widened—good childhood memories, from the look of it—before fleeing, but at least it had been a fact for a few milliseconds.

"An active temple should keep them away." Erik decided left was the correct direction and waited for the light to turn, still uneasy. There should have been a tingle all along his arms and legs, but all he felt was emptiness and a swimming, indefinable dread. *I don't like any of this.*

"Should?" She managed to raise a single eyebrow, a feat Erik had tried once or twice in the mirror when younger and failed dismally at. Of course she would be able to, and of course she'd fasten on the one word in the sentence that said more about his unease than he wanted her to know.

"Well, some of the unclean aren't very bright." Erik sensed familiar, disciplined attention behind them, approaching quickly. Jake would have been riding the giant refrigerated semi Erik had been careful to keep in range, making sure Younger Brother didn't have to jump too often to keep up. Jake might even complain about the bone-slicing windchill, though it rarely bothered a Son.

The same thought returned, swirling through his skull just when he needed clarity and calm the most. *It can't be him.* But if it wasn't Erik, and it wasn't Jake . . . it couldn't be Ignatius either, especially since the older man had drawn the hunting hounds away.

There had to be some other explanation. He *knew* them, both of them; Erik had trusted his life to Jake and his conscience to Ignatius more times than he cared to count. It just wasn't possible.

Still . . .

"Green light," Liv said, and the smile was gone. Instead, she eyed him sidelong, and any small progress he'd made toward soothing her was probably demolished.

"Yeah." He checked, though the intersection was deserted, and the green SUV slid smoothly to the left. A few more flakes whirled down, heralds announcing a dignitary's arrival. "Just waiting for Jake to catch up."

"Is he back there?" She twisted to look, a stray breath of heated air from the car's vents bringing her scent, with a thread of harsh hotel soap and the deep spice of a pretty dark-haired woman, across his nose. "I don't see anything."

"You won't unless he wants you to." Erik's nape crawled, tiny dread-tipped fingernails trailing down his back. "Better luck feeling him, but don't try right now."

"Why not?" The question wasn't a challenge. Another civilian might have been sunk in shocked apathy, but his *lirai* was curious, attempting to gather any information she could.

"Because it's like a searchlight." There was no time to instruct her in the fine and patient art of tracking, even if she'd somehow take the lessons without irritation. "And once you see things, they can also see you. Generally."

"I've seen them all my life." She settled back in her seat, and the worry invading her scent was deep blue. The mark gave him sensory acuity, and she was almost an open book. "Not while awake, though. You probably guessed that."

Actually, I didn't. He would bet her dreams had been vivid, color-saturated, and probably gruesome most of her life. She'd probably considered it no big deal, the way any kid thought their family was absolutely normal until they grew up.

No family was normal. And she didn't really talk about hers.

"You keep things close," he said, noncommittal, and wished he could feel an active temple's welcoming, reassuring calm. "But your potential's pretty high. Which is great. You probably avoided *his* servants by chance and minor precognition."

"Not that it did any good in the end." She shivered, reached for the heater knob, cast a sideways glance at him, and her hand fell back into her lap. The small movement sent a thin, sharp pain through his chest, right where the *sarnaki* had driven the spear-claw.

"You cold?"

"Yeah. It's snowing again." She was pale. The town rose on either side to swallow them, a GasGo station across the street's blue and yellow sign glaring in the thickening dimness, a smattering of fast-food restaurants and a Dewdrop Inn ready to service the concrete artery swinging around the city center. As far as he remembered, the temple was on the northern edge, so he started looking for a major thoroughfare heading that way. "You were right about the dream with the yellow door. I never . . . well, you were right."

She's trusting me. A sudden, suspiciously warm glow in his chest made his discomfort sharper. "I wish we could have moved you earlier." The scattered flakes thickened, and he flicked the windshield wipers to a steady speed instead of just occasional flicks. "Or found you earlier."

"Kidnapped me, you mean." But she didn't sound combative, or even angry. Just sad, and more than a little unnerved. "Erik?"

Let me think. But when a *lirai* spoke, a Son listened. "I'm here, Liv."

"Something's wrong." She hugged herself, palms cupping her elbows, and he realized how drawn and exhausted she looked. The *oneiros* was a plain white eye in its iron setting against her grey sweater, and that wasn't usual either. "I'm not imagining it, something's really not right."

That was when he realized the streets were too quiet. Rochester was a thriving large town or small city, depending on who you asked, and Main Street had pretensions to both culture and commerce. The buildings glowed with electric light, but nobody hurried hunch-shouldered along the storefronts, trying to escape the storm. Parked cars stood sentinel, most of them swiftly vanishing under falling snow, but a silent menace lingered in the alleys between buildings not quite tall enough to scrape the sky. No bicyclists, no public transport moving, no shadows in the lit windows—it looked like a stage set, and his *lirai* was absolutely right.

"I know." *Hoped to give you a few more minutes without worrying, beautiful.* "It's all right, Liv. This close to a temple, we're practically home free."

He was lying, he realized, and it didn't bother him as long as it kept her calm.

She stirred uneasily, her head turning—Jake was on a rooftop high on their right, which wasn't the best, tactically speaking. He should have been on the left, setting himself up for a quick hop across more than one office building and a furniture store.

Which meant either he was the traitor or was sensing a trap, and Erik had to make the right call either way.

Oh, shit. He stamped the accelerator, snow tires chirping as they dug in a scrim of slush and ice; the vehicle leapt to obey just as a cold, snarling, invisible mass hit where they had been a moment before.

"*Ow!*" Liv flinched, though nothing had touched the car, and Erik's jaw set.

"Hold on." He twisted the wheel, and if they expected him to stay bound to the road when there were no pedestrians, they were sorely mistaken. The engine guzzled at fuel, translating it into motion, and both of them were shoved back into their seats by an invisible hand.

A daylight attack. What in the name of—

He didn't have time to finish the thought, because something bulleted from the sky, a streak of gold with a straight, disciplined sword of darkness at its center, and Jake gave battle with a bellow and a spatter of gunfire.

Roulette

FALLING SNOW gathered in wet white clumps on windshield wipers; the SUV swayed dangerously as it lurched halfway onto the sidewalk, narrowly avoiding two parking meters and a fireplug at once. Liv let out a short, blurting scream, her hands flying to her ears as Erik twisted the wheel. The popping noises were gunshots, and the SUV's back window disintegrated as a high, keening cry scraped through her skull, digging in with hideous, misshapen invisible claws.

The sound was *wrong*, and that wrongness burned.

Liv's head bobbled as Erik wrenched the wheel again, taking a sharp left and plunging down a street she remembered walking along with her grandmother, bright shop windows on either side and her hand caught in warm safety. The necklace was a steady spot of heat against her shirt, and that comforting touch made the memory clearer, more tangible, filling Liv with fiery steadiness.

The thing digging in her head screeched, retreating with a last vicious twist. The necklace's soft blazing effect dilated, but she didn't have any time to wonder or worry because Erik sent the SUV into a skidding, looping turn, stamping the gas and exhaling hard as tires bit through slush and fresh snow.

She barely realized she was screaming as Rochester's downtown, snow-choked and eerily empty, revolved around them and cold air poured through the broken back window. More gunfire popped and pinged as the vehicle's hind end lifted and dropped with a sickening thump.

He'd run over something.

That's not good. The sudden grinding sound and lurching turned her stomach over, and the latte she'd had hours ago tried to crawl out her throat. The worst thing was the utter helplessness, trapped in a seat belt while the world went mad around her.

No, that wasn't the worst. The worst was that high keening screech again, trying to dig its way into her skull. Into her *mind*, and Liv's right hand flattened over the lump of the *oneiros*, fingers curling and pressing the carved iron into her palm hard enough to bruise.

It helped. The stone's scorch intensified, and sudden deep silence folded around her with soft heartbeat wings.

She had time to study Erik's profile, his mouth drawn tight and his dark eyes lit with pale specks in the very center of the pupils. It wasn't like Ignatius's gaze with its terrible blue pinpricks; the gleams in Erik's reminded her of stars.

He looks worried, she thought, and the windshield showed a long straight shot up Rochester's Cameron Hill, great sledding this time of year if you didn't mind the prospect of being run over *or* cracking your head open at the bottom. Her hair fell in her face—she was motionless, but the rest of the world was moving forward, albeit at a snail's pace. The dangling curls swayed as the SUV began its lurching for the hill, and she knew exactly what was going to happen.

Paradoxically, there was no time to brace herself. A stunning impact hit the back passenger door, and the vehicle slewed wildly. A stinging snap like a rubber band against an unsuspecting wrist in grade school, weightlessness like the one time she and Mika had done bungee-jumping at the county fair and Jada had chickened out, and the thing that had hit them was scrabbling through silver crumbles of falling safety glass while Erik, in calm, complete defiance of rationality, kept his left hand on the wheel. His right, now full of a very businesslike gun with a squarish barrel and a dull black finish, snaked between the front seats, and he fired out the back window.

A deafening roar, a gush of foulness, and Liv's stomach was a bubble trapped in a splashing stream as the SUV lifted on its two left tires, wavered for a moment, then fell, skidding like a trapped beetle on a greased plate.

The jolt tossed her out of that strange, floating stasis. Iron sky, snowy air, and dirty stained slush all changed places; now she knew what the ball felt like when spun along a roulette wheel.

Another strange sensation, a temporary skip like a song stuttering through headphones, and the car came to rest on all four tires, canted to the right because both rubber donuts on that side were popped. Erik was moving, freeing himself of his seat belt with a quick motion, and freezing, iron-scented air filled the interior.

Well, that's my second car accident in the last twenty-four hours. These guys sure are exciting. Liv found herself clutching the necklace to her chest, afraid to let go, and staring through the cracked windshield as snow fell down in a heavy curtain, Erik a moving shadow sliding across the hood Dukes-of-Hazzard style.

"Look out!" The cry burst from her mouth without any conscious volition just as a hideous, misshapen shadow-shape hit him with a devastating crunch she felt in her own chest.

Kill It Twice

THE BLAST OF untutored power from inside the car was, at least, a sign that she was still alive and conscious; Erik's boots slid through a mix of ice and greasy slush, finding purchase as the rage took him. If there was ever any doubt that someone had betrayed them, it was now gone—and with it, the need to keep things quiet.

If the Mad God's bastards would attack during daylight, Erik was more than happy to teach them the folly of that tactic.

The *ibling*, toadlike and armored against what weak sunshine could penetrate driving snow and heavy cloud, leapt not for him but for the green SUV and its precious, vulnerable inhabitant. He caught it at the apogee, driving down with a jolt, his right-hand knife slipping through leathery skin, probing for the nerve-juncture at the back of the heavy, ungainly head. It hiss-screeched and he popped a single shot into it, a jolt of recoil slamming his left wrist. That was just to distract the thing; the real weapon was the force along his curved crystalline knife blade, burrowing in, seeking, the hot businesslike joy of a fight filling him with silty red wine.

You could just take her, you know. Find a quiet corner, seal her up—

The tip of his blade found the right gap and he shoved it home, withdrawing as soon as the *ibling* went limp, limbs twitching with nerve-death and corruption racing through its tissues. He unfolded in a leap over it, colliding with the half-seen clot of nightmare shadow scratching at the shivering, shattering front passenger window, and Liv's scream was a spur to an already maddened beast.

The snow thickened, a knife-sharp wind directing the blast at him; Erik's eyes, half-closed against the sandblast-scour and the bonesnapping impact, told him the thing couldn't be another *sarnaki.* It wasn't an *ibling* either, and he was frantically trying to figure out what would be out during daylight and capable of this much coherence when the knife, wiser than he was, plunged deep, rose dripping, and plunged again.

Training forced him into a crouch as the thing howled, and training helped him again, pushing the gun to the right angle and squeezing off another single shot, a thundercrack muffled by driving snow and a subtle, slow, creeping illusion-poison.

Well, that answered the question of what he was facing. Erik stabbed again, the blade sinking into half-real resistance like warming gelatin. The *kthul* howled, more snow gusting and spinning—it was using the weather as a cover; they'd had plenty of time to prepare this little set-piece battle.

Maybe they hadn't counted on Jake warning him. Or maybe Jake had been a distraction and the real danger was out there, lurking in veils of falling white.

Kthul could stand weak sunlight, especially if they weakened it still further with their illusion-veils. They were nasty, slip-shifting things, more suited to feeding on unsuspecting and weakly gifted mortals than facing a wary, angry Son.

It tried to retreat as its stubby vestigial wings worked frantically, blundering along the side of the still-rocking vehicle; the SUV's engine was making a high whining sound and there was a sharp stink of gasoline. Liv hadn't stopped screaming; she probably hadn't even run out of breath yet. Things were happening far too quickly for a civilian to comprehend.

Just hold on, beautiful. I'm working on it.

The only problem was *kthul* never hunted alone. He stabbed again, the blade finding one of its blood-bladders deep below the skin; the smell was colossal, titanic. An unclean thing shuddered into death under him and Erik rose, his eyes still half-closed, the gun blurring for its holster. He had to turn, putting his back to the car, and at least the reek of gas was better than the smell of dead, fish-rotting *kthul.*

"Liv," he said, sharp and low to cut through the moan of the wind and the engine's ratcheting. It didn't sound good under that hood, no sir. "Liv, sweetheart, talk to me."

She gasped, a deep terrible coughing sound. Was she hurt? Had the goddamn thing managed to lay a finger on her?

If it did, I'll kill it twice, he decided, and the relief of having a clear course of action was just as dangerous as the whispering.

The door moved, hitting his hip; he took a half-step aside and kept watch on the shifting snow. More gunfire, but he couldn't tell from exactly where.

Jake, for the love of the Dreamers, don't do anything stupid. Erik's priority now was the woman who slithered out of the broken-backed car, clutching at his left elbow with both her soft, pretty hands—and if he had to move to meet another fucking *kthul*, he'd be handicapped.

"Oh, God." A broken almost-sob. "Erik?"

"Hurt?" He coughed to clear his dry throat. "Are you hurt anywhere?"

She was doing her best to keep up; snow kissed her tangled hair. "I don't . . . oh, God, what the *hell* is that?"

"*Kthul*." He had his breath now, and tried to ignore her patting at his elbow. "Dead. Don't worry."

"Don't worry?" A jagged, half-screaming little laugh escaped her, vanishing into the snow. "Don't fucking *worry*?"

That's right, beautiful. They won't even get close enough to smell your perfume.

Except they had. A *kthul* had been within arm's length of her.

Standing and fighting was an option, sure. But he had a *lirai* to protect, and the temple had to be close. It might even be under attack, and another potential to add to the force of the Dreamers inside its walls would be welcome, not to mention another Son to help hold the defenses. Maybe that's why he hadn't felt it once they were off the freeway?

Erik found out he didn't care. The only thing that mattered was the shivering woman next to him, her *oneiros* lighting with deep coruscating colors and her warmth about to be lost in a whirling, unnatural storm. Snow smacked ceaselessly at them both and she shivered again, her eyes wide and wild like a frightened animal's.

That decided him. The knife, flicked free and clean of ichor, slid back into its home; his arm circled her waist. "Stay with me," he said, and gathered himself. "Just stay with me."

It was time to vanish. The SUV stilled its rocking, a spill of gasoline lighting with a soft *wump* lost under the sound of the storm.

Place Is Dark

HER HEAD BOUNCED against Erik's shoulder so hard she almost saw stars. At least he wasn't carrying her over said shoulder like a caveman, but the jolting, bouncing ride with snow spattering a hard invisible shield a few inches in front of them was bad enough.

It was almost like being on horseback, an elastic bunching and leaping, but the world was doing funny things under his feet, sliding away like oil on a hot griddle and turning into a patchwork of bright snow and twisted, shadowed landscape that made her abused stomach consider emptying itself through whatever upward route was handy. It was better when she closed her eyes and pushed her face against Erik; he was warm, comforting, and safe.

Just when he'd become so she had no idea, unless it was the exact moment the window shivered into pieces and the blackened, frostbitten, terribly *wrong* face with its nest of writhing things near the far-too-large mouth had leered at her.

Or maybe it was when Erik moved his chin slightly, rubbing against her hair, his stubble scratching. He didn't have to offer any comfort, but he did and Liv shut her eyes, wishing—not for the first time—that she'd never gone on that stupid date with Neal Whatever-His-Last-Name-Was.

It bothered her that she couldn't remember. Why it did when there was so much else to be worried about, she had no idea.

"Almost there," Erik muttered, and relief made her a limp noodle. He wouldn't say it unless things were going to be all right—and at the moment, she couldn't care less if it was Stockholm syndrome or not, all she cared about was the monsters going away. "Almost . . . huh."

They landed with a wrenching jolt; Liv's cheek mashed so hard against muscle and what felt like an armor plate under his jacket she barely felt the impact. She was clinging to him like a piece of arm candy holding onto an action movie hero, she realized, and couldn't make herself loosen up even a little bit.

The sudden stillness was a blessing. Her heart thundered in her ears;

her breath came in short, jagged little chunks suspiciously like moans. The shaking was back, filtering through her bones, and the idea that she could simply refuse to lift her head, that she could stay there and breathe in the smell of a man used to hard workouts and not a lot of cleaning up, a blessed, healthy, human tang under a screen of fresh air, snow, and the faintest hint of nauseating monster blood, was all but overwhelming.

It sounded like a good plan.

He went utterly still, his arms steel bars—one under her knees, the other holding her close. "Son of a bitch," he muttered, and the venom in it made her feel a little faint.

Or maybe a whole *lot* faint.

Another silence. It probably felt a lot longer than it actually was, mostly because Liv was quite content to just huddle in his arms. There was something to be said for a guy who could pick up a regular girl and carry her without huffing and puffing. Maybe it was all the monster hunting that did it. Helluva workout, and all that.

Liv, you're not doing very well.

She knew. Oh, God, she knew.

"Liv." His chin touched her hair again, stubble scratching snow-damp curls. "Liv, beautiful, we've got a small problem."

I don't like the sound of that. She gulped at air, shook her head slightly. It was cowardice, she was what Mom would have called *a piker*; she had, in Gramps's pungent parlance, a *yaller strip down 'er back*.

She didn't care one single bit as long as she could stay right where she was, her face pressed against Erik's torn coat and her body trembling as if she were a toy trapped in the mouth of a small, vicious animal that killed its prey by shaking.

"Oh, hey." His tone softened. "It's all right, beautiful. I'm not about to let anything happen to you, you can count on that. Just . . . things have gotten a little complex."

What, like they were simple before? But she couldn't spend forever hiding.

Well, she could try. She'd been hiding all her damn life, one way or another—from the dreams, from the creeping dread, from the déjà vu, from her mother's murder, from everything else.

She couldn't very well continue. That bus, as Mika might drawl, had done passed the stop.

So Liv dragged in the deepest, shakiest breath she was capable of and lifted her head an inch. Two inches. "What?" Her voice was a harsh croak. "What *now*?" she amended.

"Well, we're here." He didn't move; his arms were still steel bars and the frigid wind beginning to raise its voice and get really serious. "But nobody's home."

That doesn't sound good. "You can put me down now," she lied.

He did, slowly, with exquisite care. She slid down his body, found out her legs would hold her up—barely, and only under protest, but good enough—and tipped her chin back, staring at him.

A stripe of drying blood painted one of his stubbled cheeks, and his dark eyes were hot coals—charcoal getting ready for grilling, before a protective coat of ash hid the deep black burning. No trace of monster goo remained, but she could get a faint whiff of that awful smell if she tried. Much closer, and much nicer, was the heat-haze hanging on him, snow melting before it could reach his skin but touching his hair with frozen little caresses.

He was looking over her head. A muscle in his cheek flickered, and his jaw was set. Liv gathered every bit of her nonexistent courage and turned very carefully, very slowly, afraid her knees would fold if she moved the wrong way.

"Oh." It was Saffron Hill instead of Cameron; it was impossible that they'd come so far from downtown Rochester in such a short while, especially on foot. Before them, a lone driveway crumbling at the edges was already drifting with wet-packed, driving snow; at its end a stone bulk loomed, an honest-to-God round tower at its eastern edge. It looked a little like the other stone "temple," but this one was obviously bigger and the curtaining wall at the end of a long driveway was just visible, along with a pair of spike-topped wrought-iron gates.

She recognized those gates; Gramma Poe had often driven past them. Liv had always wondered where that long, barely glimpsed ribbon of paving went, but trees and the hill itself had screened the house from view. "It was here the whole time," she said, wonderingly.

Erik shifted slightly, as if embarrassed. "Yeah, the walls have stuff on them to keep curious people out. But the trouble is, the place is dark, Liv."

He was right. No smoke rose from the chimneys, and no golden electric light glowed through shuttered windows.

"So what does that mean?" The words shook a little, and Liv was past caring. "And it's daytime," she realized, blankly. "I thought you said the monsters didn't come out in daytime."

"They don't *like* to. Some of them can." Erik shook his head. If he was tired from fighting off those things, a car accident, and carting her around, it didn't show. "I don't understand. Control said this place was active."

"Control?" She had a better question, though, and hurried to add it. "Wait. Active?"

"Had a *lirai.* More than one. There's bound to be access to the Flame. It'll be blocked off, but I can . . ." He trailed off and finally looked down at her, his eyebrows drawing together. "Liv, look. Do you trust me?"

How the hell am I supposed to answer that? "I guess?" she hazarded. "Provisionally."

He opened his mouth, but Liv never found out what he was about to say. A thin, high, cruel cry sounded behind him, piercing the wind's screech like a sharp bone needle, and the snow thickened. It was so *dark*, it didn't seem like daytime at all. Even the snow seemed greyish instead of white.

The cry sawed through her head, and now she understood why people in earlier centuries bolted their doors when dusk arrived. Living with electricity, you forgot just how terrifying it was to hear something in the darkness baying for your blood.

Something you couldn't *see.*

"Come on." Erik offered his hand, palm up, a curiously old-fashioned movement. "We have one chance, Liv. I'm sorry about it, I'll fight as long as I can, but I'm going to need your help."

Oh, hell no. "What do I have to do?" she whispered.

"I think I can unblock access to the Flame, since this place was once active." He didn't move, snow gathering in his hair despite the invisible shimmer keeping it off his skin and shoulders. "We don't have a lot of time. They're on our trail."

Oh, the Flame. That thing none of you would ever tell me about. Like sealing. "Fine." She didn't move. "Let's go, then."

Still, he stood motionless, his hand hanging in midair, until she reluctantly laid her fingers in his palm. His skin was so warm, and there was a traitorous little lurch in the pit of her stomach.

"I will fight as long as I can," he repeated, staring down at her like it was a promise she should understand. He clasped her hand in both of his, oddly gentle for a man who could kill monsters. "They won't get you while I'm alive."

It was ridiculous, how much she believed him. How could she not? And yet, the unspoken codicil—*as long as I'm alive, for however long that is*—hung between them, heavy as the unnatural gloom.

He didn't wait, just dropped her hand, scooped her into his arms again, and raced uphill for the massive, four-story stone block.

First Ever

EVERY OBSCENITY he knew beat time inside his head. What the *fucking hell* was going on?

You know what this is. Control fed Father wrong information, or—

Erik could figure the treachery out later, if they were both still alive to do it. The good thing about their situation was that he knew the layout of most temples and could break a window on the first floor, carefully laying his sliced, battered coat over the glass before giving her a boost through. It was child's play to hop through himself, but he heard the hunting cry again behind him, much closer than before—and the silvery wrong notes of a horn winding through a deep, diseased descant.

Shit. A lun'nyie*, out during the day?* Though the solstice was officially past it was still the dark time of the year, and the blizzard, helped along by the unclean, was a lid over the sun's cleansing eye.

This temple had indeed been active once; a faint feeling of welcome clung to the dusty, shuttered rooms. No stick of furniture left over, not a scrap of cloth—nothing of whatever *lirai* had sheltered here remained, except that slight lingering warmth.

"Big place," Liv whispered. Her dark eyes were huge, deep circles underneath. Terror wore on the body like lack of sleep. She wasn't bruised, though she moved a little stiffly—car accidents weren't good for anyone, even with healing sorcery.

Those weren't accidents, Erik. "There were probably two or three *lirai* here once." If Jake was still alive, he'd work along their path, clearing stragglers and attempting to reinforce his Elder Brother. Unless he was dead, or part of the treachery—but Erik couldn't afford to think about that at the moment. "The Flame'll be below."

It wasn't hard to figure out which of them was braver. Liv let out a soft, strained sound trying to be a laugh. "Great. You going to tell me what it is?"

"It's kind of . . ." He paused as the hunting horn cried again outside, a glassy trill blunted by the solid walls but still nerve scraping.

"What's that?" she whispered.

Hunters, beautiful. They rode big leng*-spiders back in the day—among other things.* "Bad news." He checked the hall, ghosting through half-open doors. That hallway would lead to the main armory; there would be smaller ones on each floor for convenience and in case of siege. Nothing would be left in them, of course.

It was a pity. More weaponry was always better.

"I can tell that much." Sarcasm, shaky but definite, tinted her tone.

"I know." The whispers rose inside his skull for a moment, and his temper almost snapped. It wasn't like him, he *knew* it wasn't like him, and the thought that the god might be taking a personal interest in chasing down this very powerful and practically unattended potential was enough to make him sweat. "Just don't want to scare you. More than you already are, I mean."

"That's awful nice of you." Her voice broke, and she did something strange.

Liv's slender, chilled fingers found his, threaded through, and squeezed. She was actually *holding his hand*, and a soft haze of power poured up his arm, took a break in his aching shoulder, and flooded the rest of him with warm honey.

The whispers stopped. Their sudden cessation was a balm he didn't deserve, and Erik found himself stock-still in a hall leading to a low archway, bare blocks of blue stone fitted carefully together without mortar. His head was down, his chin almost touching his chest, and a thin tremor ran through him, much like the shaking in her own small, vulnerable hand.

"Sorry." Now Liv just sounded sad. "I thought it would help." She attempted to tug her fingers free, but his clamped down. Not hard enough to hurt, just enough to contain.

You mean, just enough to trap. "It does," he said. "You can't know how much. Come on, this way." He gave a gentle, experimental tug and she followed as if she did trust him, and more than just provisionally. "Nothing can really prepare you for the Flame. If the planet has a soul, that's kind of what it is. Or a pulse, maybe." He was chattering; any information he gave her now would be hopelessly mangled.

"Oh." She absorbed this, following him almost fearlessly. She hadn't been taught to step only where he did, or to send sonar-rings of numinous force through him to scan their surroundings. There was so much other *lirai* had to teach her, but first they both had to survive this.

If they managed that miracle, finding another temple would be easy.

Past the archway was another short hall of undressed stone leading to yet another black, blank archway. If the place was active, there would be Sons on both sides, standing and sweeping guard, and a full *lirai* with Liv, keeping her calm. The air would sing with pleasant tension, and maybe Erik would be drifting behind his potential, haunting her steps.

Literally. And waiting for the moment when he'd have to do the unforgivable.

She flinched a bare moment before the entire main structure shuddered, mutely protesting an invasion. The fucking unclean had made it to the temple, and while its residual blessing would be uncomfortable for them, it wouldn't slow them down.

Not with valuable prey so close.

"I can't see anything," she whispered, and the fear in her voice was almost enough to break him.

He'd forgotten to hold some corpselight since she couldn't see in the dark, and of course the *oneiros* would be mute—she was only potential, not *lirai*, and the danger wasn't close enough to make it flash. "There's stairs," he said, and decided he wouldn't use the light. Blindness was terrifying, but seeing what he was about to do would be even worse. "A spiral, going down. Just keep holding my hand."

"Sure." Her tiny, jagged laugh held more panic than amusement. "This is a weird first date, Erik. Even for you."

The pain in his chest wasn't from the claw-spear; that was well-healed. It was all *her*. "Yeah, well, it'd be my first ever, so I'll take your word for it."

"Ever?"

"The Sons are taken young. Generally, straight from the orphanage." His voice bounced off stone, fell into a deep well of overlapping echoes. "Stairs. There's the first one . . . good. I know you can't see, just hold onto me. Don't let go."

"Oh, no fear of that." She flinched again as the entire temple shuddered, even its wings and outbuildings noticing the incursion. "They're here."

"Don't worry." The words were ashes against his tongue. "I can hold a door for a long time."

Her hand tensed. He moved carefully so she didn't stumble even in this absolute blackness. The Flame would give her a type of dark-vision; a full *lirai* could use the eyes of the Sons around them as well as the corpselight.

But right now, she was blind. And he could only see because of the filthy mark on his wrist, the doorway he drew strength through—and the god behind it, writhing with fury, would eat her alive if he could.

The end of the stairs came sooner than he expected; he would have liked a few more seconds with her hand caught in his. Her fingers had warmed; a moment's worth of simple sorcery flushed her with heat and she exhaled sharply. The shadowbeasts and nightmares were tearing through the temple above; they wouldn't expect Erik and his all-but-helpless charge to go *down*.

"The Flame'll come." Was he trying to convince her, or himself? "It, ah, might not be very pleasant."

"Neither will getting eaten by those things." She swayed slightly on the last step, and he was glad she couldn't see the great circular stone lid in the middle of this chamber, its surface crawling with glyphs in a language long dead. No *lirai* would see such carvings without a shudder. "Erik?"

"Yeah?" He got her to the edge, and his fingers slipped reluctantly free. "Stand very still. I have to open it up."

"Great." She froze, and for a long moment he examined her face. Pupils swollen in what was total darkness for her, her chin lifted, her hair a mess and her shoulders dusted with gemlike drops of melted snow, she was utterly beautiful. "I'm sorry I was mean to you." It came out of her in a rush, as if she could feel his gaze. "It's just . . . this is all so much."

She was apologizing to *him*? His chest hurt even worse. "It's fine," Erik mumbled, crouching. His hand found the space it wanted between the lines of blocky carved symbols telling the story of the Breaking, when *lirai* and Sons made their final stand with their backs to a blood-red sea deep in the nighttime lands the *lirai* ruled, their gleaming lost city amid its green fields burning and the greatest of ancient Dreamers sacrificing blood, life, and their very souls to lock the Mad God away. "Just stand very still."

"I can hear them." It was the whisper of a child alone in the dark. "They're about to find us. Whatever we're going to do, please let's just make it quick."

The stone lid shuddered; a slow, deep grinding began. The hieroglyphs twitched into motion as stone separated with clockwork precision, and if she'd been able to see it, the wrongness of the lid's crumbling in defiance of earthly physics might have made her apprehensive.

Erik looked into the black hole. Of course, the Flame had retreated when it was blocked off.

He just hoped it would sense her need and come back in a hurry, or could be sparked by the *oneiros*. "All right." He straightened. "Liv—"

"Oh, God," she whispered. "They're on the stairs."

Shit. There was nothing else he could do. Erik's right hand found a knifehilt, and for the first time since his initial week in the Sons' training dormitory, his palms were damp with fear.

Now came the betrayal.

Forgive Me

IT WAS PITCH BLACK, and if not for the sense of Erik breathing right next to her, the tiny sounds as he shifted, and the absolute calm confidence in his voice, she might have done something embarrassing. Like screaming, or worse—her bladder was full, her back teeth all but floating. It was probably terror doing something to her kidneys, or the morning's latte looking for escape.

It was bad enough being chased by monsters. But to pee her pants was downright *undignified*, and she loathed even the possibility. She hated everything about this, except maybe Erik.

Hadn't he been able to produce some kind of light before, when Jake let her out of her cell for the object lesson in monster reality? Now, deep in a stone cellar, there wasn't a single photon. Just that blackness, pressing against her eyes like a blindfold. It was so dark she couldn't even feel her fingers, and the thought that her body had been swallowed and she was simply a naked, shivering consciousness in a cold black well was terrifying.

Still, it was hard not to feel charitable and a little less frightened when someone had carried you away from both a car wreck and hideous things screaming in the snow, their voices full of hard brassy hatred. Even the thought that she wouldn't have needed rescuing if they'd just left her alone was threadbare, the kind of justification that would keep you sane but wasn't exactly, well, truthful.

It was hardly time for a reckoning, but Liv might as well. She'd dreamed about the things chasing them, of course, almost every night since she could remember. Her sleeping head was tuned to whatever bizarre station Erik and his friends lived on, and had been all her life. Now the insanity had spilled into the daylight world, and she was stuck in it.

She might as well deal with it, in whatever time remained. Except she couldn't quite figure out how, unless it was simply keeping herself from fear-based urination.

There was a deep grating grinding noise. Over it, the footsteps on the stone stairs beat an insistent tattoo, and the sounds were just plain *wrong*—some too light, some too heavy, some with a strange metal ringing and others with a clicking like dog nails on hard flooring.

There were a lot of them, and a cold draft touched her cheeks.

It felt like there was an opening nearby. A big one. The fine hairs all over her body rose, sensing danger in the absolutely impenetrable darkness, and she wished, with a sudden vengeance, that Erik was still holding her hand.

"Jesus." It just slipped out. "They're on the stairs."

"I know." His voice was close. The draft intensified, stirring her hair, fingering her shoulders. Was there a tunnel? If there was, it felt like something was coming through, pushing a wall of tepid air as it accelerated, and Liv was doing her absolute best not to scream, pee, cry, or throw up. Her stomach was a seesawing fist. "Liv . . ."

"What?" *For God's sake, whatever you're going to do, now would be a great time.* "Please don't let them eat me," she continued, aware she was babbling. "Shoot me before they get a chance to eat me. Please."

"It's all right," he said, heavily, and he'd straightened. She felt him, very close, and his fingertips skated over her cheek. It was a soft touch, and she almost flinched. "Forgive me, *lirai*."

What the fuck for? But he had her arm now, his fingers sinking in, and she knew what he was going to do a bare moment before it happened.

Erik took a single step to the side, half-turned, and shoved her into the abyss.

Battle-Roar

SHE SCREAMED as she went in, a hopeless trailing cry yanking on his every nerve. The mouth swallowed her without a murmur, and Erik turned back to the door, his free hand blurring for a gun. He'd bottle them, and wait for the Flame to spark in the *oneiros*, answering his *lirai*'s need.

You stupid asshole. She's going to die.

He met the first creature at the opening with a shattering jolt, sweeping the knife under its strike. The blade bit deep, unseaming the *lun'nyie*'s guts, and its wounded cry was a brazen trumpet stripping his filthy hair back, digging into his staring eyes, striping his cheeks and shoulders with tiny razor cuts.

You killed her. She'll fall, she'll hit, the Flame won't come, you have failed. A gleeful, lipless voice caroled inside his skull, and now Erik understood why his training had been so unforgiving. His body knew what to do even if his mind was cracking under a separate assault, clawed fingers sinking into his head like a metal pick digging the meat out of a walnut's shell, a fraction of attention from an old, foul, insanely powerful *thing* draped in ancient jeweled cerements and howling with glee. *Just give in. Let go. All you have to do is pause, just for a moment.*

He was not the only one the Mad God was focusing on, but even a microscopic sliver of that being's notice was more than mortal sanity could stand.

Good thing I'm crazy then, huh? The gun spoke; he batted aside the first *lun'nyie*'s dying-weak strike and found out he was growling, a low buzzing in his chest and another of the tall, pale four-armed things with their wide, horribly beautiful blue eyes looming on the stairs above, its slender body taut-bent backward as it held thin leashes of golden leather in each six-fingered, extra-knuckled hand.

The moon-runners weren't the biggest danger. It was the hounds, bigger than the *sarnaki*'s fellow hunters. These were hulking, slavering, dirty ivory-colored things with their golden collars, rubies dripping from their harnesses and their serrated teeth foaming with disease. The spiral staircase rang with activity; these were just the quickest pursuers.

Spray, before the wave broke.

They had the high ground, but he could stack the dead in the doorway and buy himself a little more time. A *lirai* was only partially immune to the moon-dogs' bite; the viral venom would drive a Son into killing rage.

Good. Come on, bite me. The growl caged in his ribs spiraled up; he popped two shots into the leash-holder. If he could get it down and tangle the dogs up, he'd have a chance.

Until the next wave came.

The battle-roar filled his throat, but he throttled it. Better he should choke, better that more spear-claws should pincushion his body and the hounds splinter-chew his bones while he denied them the pleasure of screaming. Better he should die than give voice to that massive, world-wrecking scream.

After all, he had no right to speak her name. Not now.

Erik lunged, his right-hand knife finding unclean flesh, and was too busy to prepare himself for the inevitable.

Equally Cliché

WEIGHTLESS, HER hair combed by a shrieking wind, Liv tumbled through darkness. The hole was *big*; she was in freefall with no sense of the walls. It was so damn dark she wouldn't know they were there until she hit, and her stuttering scream trailed into nothingness.

Later, she wondered just how far she fell. She wondered what she thought, if her life flashed before her eyes, or something else equally cliché. The necklace tapped her chin, bumped against her chest as she somersaulted, *up* and *down* changing places in the womblike darkness so quickly she felt, for a bare moment, as if she were flying.

She didn't remember dreaming of this.

The only thing she could remember later was a burst of ecstatic fear so huge it was painless, and a single thought.

How do I know I'm not dead already?

She had always been falling, she would *always* fall, trapped in this darkness.

Then . . .

. . . a spark.

Rising, Inexorable

THERE WAS NO time to wish Jake was providing fire while Erik and Ignatius took the brunt of the attack, retreating only when forced. There was no time for anything other than stabbing the double-lobed eye of the nearest hound—the guns just couldn't put them down fast enough, knifework was his only hope—wrenching the blade free, kicking another one in the snout as it lunged for him, a quick sharp curse turning into a blood-glittering dart on his lips, splattering on yet another hound's face and making the monstrous thing squeal. Its falsetto, pain and rage mixed, scraped through his skull, but he didn't care.

Sanity was overrated, anyway. It was an investment with no return, especially when you'd just thrown a woman into a hole leading to the very veins of the planet without preparation and without warning, betraying her trust and killing her outright.

He'd killed a lot since becoming a Son. It was inevitable, it was almost nightly, and it was just a job.

But today, in the bowels of a sanctuary, he'd committed *murder.* Even if he'd had no choice, even if it was a cleaner death than these things would grant her if the Flame chose this one time to not answer a *lirai*'s need, it was unspeakable, inexcusable, and he was doomed.

He always had been. The paper-whisper laughter in his head was proof. The Mad God was pleased, and now it only remained to take slow, painful vengeance upon an errant Son.

More hounds crowded behind the leash-holder, scuttling and keening. Erik spat defiance, ignoring the blood coursing down his thigh and the burning of hound venom. The slices on his shoulders and cheeks, barely missing his eyes because he had time to snap counter-curses, bled freely as well, and the smell of claret would madden them. The last hound died as he wrenched the knife back and forth in the eye socket, grinding against bone, and he knew that the *leng*-spider crouching above the screeching *lun'nyie* would spring and he would have to take the hit.

He was going to go down, and they were going to feast on his guts.

His left knee buckled; he folded just as the thing leapt and when it reached apogee, its eyes glowing with hellfire and the dying leash-holder hissing yet another curse, Erik's shoulder hit stone wall with bruising force and his eyes stung.

Stung? No, they were scoured, a nuclear flash burrowing inward through tender, bleeding sockets, and at first he thought one of the unclean filling the stairs' throat had managed to spit acid at him, a rugose horror like the *taik* flowers or a wingéd ghoul-cat.

But those were creatures of deep darkness and the *taik* weren't ambulatory enough to chase; they simply lay in musty corners, waiting.

Erik staggered, almost going down in a graceless heap, but a vast painless wind was at his back, holding him upright. The sensation was welcome, warm, and familiar, for all he'd rarely felt it before receiving his posting and arriving at a frontline temple with Ignatius in the lead and Jake in tow, both Sons nervous at being sent to an inactive temple and hoping the assignment wouldn't last long.

But it had. It had lasted *forever*, and he'd never asked Ignatius if he, like his boys, longed for a chance at something else.

What the hell?

It poured through him, a delicate, immensely powerful touch closing the worst of the wounds and filling him from toe to scalp with brimming pleasure. A soft inhalation drew him away from the doorway he was supposed to die guarding, but he couldn't struggle. He couldn't even twitch; the invisible force dragged him free of the aperture before surging through him and away, stone creaking as it sought to contain an immensity more than physical.

The sharp, evil laughter inside his skull cut off with the feedback scratch of a needle dragging across a record's valleys, gouging and splintering. Erik's arms jerked wide, dripping knives running with brilliance, and that was the pain in his eyes.

It was *light*.

Rainbow coruscations edged with dappled gold flooded the stairs, rising inexorably, and a mad god's hunters died under its lash. Erik was held ruthlessly in place, a lens focusing a laser to killing intensity and paradoxically spreading its force wide to catch every beetle in a killing jar. A low thrum, every church organ in the world all giving out the same chord at once, passed through him and receded like a tide along a rocky shore.

He dropped, a discarded doll. Knives clattered on stone, a sweet chiming. Blood crackled, dried on his skin by an immense warm draft smelling of golden spice, warm bread, and everything good in the world.

Erik's eyelids fluttered. Illumination flicker-strobed, clean glorious golden light reaching into his brain and shutting the basement door with a bang, leaving the Mad God howling outside. The mark on his wrist gave a painless twitch; he spilled onto his side and lay, exhausted.

And behind him, light as a leaf, he heard a pair of sneakers kiss stone.

Off-Key Lullabies

HER KNEES WEREN'T quite reliable; Liv staggered drunkenly away from the hole with her head full of a strange ringing, echoing chord.

Gramma Poe had taken little Liv to the orchestra a few times, and if the great swell of tuning, instruments suddenly in sync and becoming part of a chorus instead of a babble of disparate voices, was ever dropped into a bathtub full of champagne it might have felt like this. A deep wash of incredible warm wellbeing she hadn't felt even in childhood tingled in her arms and legs, filled her head, and made each swaying footstep a joy.

Still, she didn't ever want to do that again. Erik lay on his side, curled up like a snail. His fallen knives glittered sharply; there were shapeless mounds of scented ash clogging the doorway.

It was dead silent, and she could see because the necklace was glowing. So were her hands, gold-edged rainbow light like a living glove moving between her fingers, pooling in her palms, dappling her knuckles and casting strange underwater reflections against the ribbed walls and dome of this stupid, cold, hellish vault.

She suspected the rest of her skin was glowing under her clothes, too, and dropped to her knees next to Erik with a jolt. "Hey." Her voice sounded thin and piping after all that deep immensity. "Oh, God. Please don't be dead."

It was a ridiculous thing to say, but what else was there when you'd just been thrown in a deep hole, and somehow . . .

. . . what the hell had happened? She couldn't quite remember beyond a sudden burst of golden light and that deep, inescapable feeling that everything was going to be all right, as if Mom had come in her room again after a bad dream bringing warm milk and a soft voice, stroking a fevered forehead and singing one of her off-key lullabies.

How do I know I'm not already dead? Well, it was simple—she was breathing, she was glowing like a light bulb at a drugged-out rave, and she still had to pee.

A *lot.*

"Hey." She touched his shoulder with two fingers, then clutched at his shredded jacket. "Hey. Erik. Come on, Erik. Don't . . ." *Don't be dead,* she was going to repeat, but it wasn't necessary.

His eyes snapped open, he inhaled so sharply the sound was like a cough, and he sat up so fast they almost cracked foreheads. She sank back, her ass meeting the floor with a tooth-clicking *thump*, and thank God she didn't piss herself right there, because his dark eyes were wide, haunted, and she had the odd feeling nobody was home behind them.

He stared at her, in fact, like she'd just shaken him out of the mother of all nightmares.

For Something Bigger

IT DIDN'T TAKE much to re-block the well. Erik triggered the release and the stone lid clockwork-crawled over the black eye; he shot a quick glance at his new *lirai* to see how she would handle the sight.

She didn't even seem to notice. Familiar light crawled over her hands, veined her face, and filled the *oneiros* with a deep, satisfied gleam. The earth's secret pulse had risen to answer her need, bathing a potential in its glory, and the Dreamer was awake. Liv cupped her palms and stared at the slow, hypnotic swirls. The pulse had reached through him, destroying the unclean on the stairs, and all that was left was that same feeling of blessing and warmth. Grey grit on the stairs, some piles still sending up incense-coils of perfumed smoke—and Erik's wounds closed right up, not even scars remaining. His knives, their crystalline blades drinking the illumination, were clean.

His clothes were a mess, though. He pushed himself upright, wincing a little as tender muscles twitched. A more skilled *lirai*, a Dreamer with more control, would have filled him with vital force almost as an afterthought, attending all hurts no matter how minor. But as things stood, he was grateful.

He was, in fact, ready to drop to his knees, slice his wrists, and beg her forgiveness. It was useless, of course—once the shock wore off, she'd hate him all the more. She'd been taken for her own protection, held in isolation, terrified out of her wits, and chased through a blizzard and two car accidents.

To top it off, he'd betrayed any nascent trust she might have felt in his direction.

You could return a potential to the Flame until it took, dread replacing unexpected terror. Some theories said the fear of death triggered the release, others held that the earth's pulse simply cleaned away the accretion of daily life and habits, a sort of cosmic coffee jolt. Maybe that gunk was too thick to be scraped away on the first try for some, so the process was repeated in a few cases.

It didn't *hurt* them, but most potentials didn't take kindly to being shoved into a dark hole by their guardians. Even with another *lirai* calling the Flame and holding it steady, even *expecting* the great gout of earthblood from deep within the secret chambers of the rock humanity called home, it was a terrifying thing.

To fall like that, into absolute blackness—Erik was dead certain he wouldn't have the guts to endure it, even if the unfiltered power wouldn't consume him in a single agonizing instant, not just cauterizing the Mad God's corrupting mark that gave him strength, power, and resilience but eating him whole.

But she was *lirai*, a potential fully awakened and now slightly more durable. Dreamers and Sons, working together, could take on the mightiest of the god's minions, not to mention the incidental predators of night and fear. But she still needed the peaceful hum of an active temple—and at least two trios standing guard over her every breath—before she was even close to safe.

His job wasn't over yet. The stone glyphs crawl-trickled into place; the lid was complete again, the words of an ancient, completely dead language moving uneasily before settling.

Now he had to face her. It was cowardice to hope that maybe she'd be too stunned to really understand what he'd done.

Erik let out a harsh breath, rose, and turned with military precision.

Liv still stared at her hands. The Flame coated them, working into her skin. It would vanish until she fought again—or until her emotions reached a certain pitch. One more reason for the deep guard and seclusion of the *liraim*.

"I thought it would hurt." Her great dark eyes rose, wide and dazed, and the look threatened to stagger him. "But it didn't."

"Good." *If it had . . .* He couldn't afford to think about that, not even briefly. "We need to get going."

He expected a protest, no matter how shaken and exhausted she was. Instead, Liv simply stared at him, deadly pale under the light, her hair a mad tangle, and the Flame shining from her so brightly his eyes smarted.

Sure, Erik. Blame it on the light.

"You shouldn't be alone with just me," he continued, hating the necessity but compelled.

"Ignatius." A little more sense filtered into her wide dark eyes. "He . . . he obviously thought one of you was telling them where to find me."

"It happens." *No other explanation, beautiful.* It could be a control liaison, but wouldn't a full *lirai* sense treachery, especially since liaisons were scanned regularly? It couldn't be Jake—but a Younger Brother wasn't quite steady even at the best of times, and the Mad God's voice dug in through the cracks. It couldn't be Ignatius either, but Fathers lived with the whispers a long while. Endurance was their game, but sometimes it was finite.

There was simply no way to tell when the Son next to you reached his limit.

Liv shuddered, and the rainbow coruscations over her hands and face intensified briefly. "It's not you," she said, quietly. "If it was, you'd let them take me."

"Not if I was saving you for something bigger." It had to be said. "You're just a little less vulnerable now, Liv."

"Good thing you're here." Another shiver—a stone cellar in winter was not the best place for a *lirai.* "I can see why you didn't explain." The shudders weren't quite from the temperature, though. Her gaze moved past him, wandering in a way he wasn't quite sure he liked. "You can't explain something like this to someone."

I should've found a way. "I'm sorry." Two pale, stupid little words, staggering under the weight of his guilt. "Go ahead and hate me. But I'm going to get you to an active temple, Liv. I'm *going* to."

"Okay." The light was sinking rapidly into her skin now, her slim shoulders dropping, and as its last gleam was swallowed—oh, she still shone, just not to normal eyes—her warm, tender fingers touched his aching left hand. "Do we have time to find a bathroom?"

Huh? "Uh, the water's shut off." He aimed them for the stairs, wondering how in the hell she could touch him when he'd just done . . . what he'd done.

"I don't need to flush, I guess. Ew." She gripped him with surprising strength. "I can sort of see now. Is that part of it?"

"Kind of, yeah." Now she had a Dreamer's uncanny night vision, and if she wanted to, she could use his eyes as well. The thought of her inside his skin, unexpectedly intimate, made his throat dry up and his palms damp.

Outside, far away, another high, glassy hunting-note sounded.

Normal Business

FLYING, DRIVING, bunching snow swirled around them. It was goddamn unsettling to have snowflakes melt before they even touched you, pushed aside by a hard invisible shell. It was even worse to bury her face in Erik's shoulder and *feel* the invisible force propelling them along, his footsteps dropping into the thick muffling of falling flakes. He didn't so much contact the ground as glide over at high speed, a toe or heel occasionally touching down to propel them in a slightly different direction.

Maybe he just stayed still and let the planet whirl away underneath him. Which was another horrifying thought, and Liv curled up tighter. Once you got over the indignity of being hauled around like a sack of potatoes, it was sort of nice being carried.

Except it gave her too much time to think about monsters, about falling into dark holes, about golden-rainbow fire shading through every color in the spectrum and a few she was sure weren't, and the hard lump of the *oneiros* digging into her breastbone when Erik shifted.

The world stopped spinning. He was still for a long moment, head upflung, and if it bothered him to cart her around like this, he made no sign. Liv pried her eyes open and peered at his profile, trying to ignore how she was clinging to his shoulder, one arm around his nape like a dopey illustration on the cover of a romance novel.

Her grandmother had loved those. Especially the bite-sized read-in-one-afternoon numbers with the implausible titles, farfetched wish-fulfillment plots, and airbrushed couples clinching on the covers.

Liv didn't blame Gramma Poe one bit. Fantasies were sometimes the only comfort available in the huge pile of bullshit that was adult life.

Snow somehow avoided Erik's damp dark hair, and there were pinpricks of that strange bluish light in his pupils. It was paler than the glow in Ignatius's eyes, and somehow comforting. Sort of.

Not really.

Liv turned her head, peering into the driving snow and failing afternoon light. Erik stood on a rooftop amid a collection of buildings clinging to the interstate and huddling under the lash of a white wind. They were atop a four-story building, in fact, and she didn't recognize this town.

We're not even in Rochester anymore. How in the hell . . .?

Except she knew how. Magic, or something like it. If they could move this fast, why had they bothered driving?

Another high, trilling bugle call lifted in the distance, stuttering uncertainly through the storm. She should have been freezing her ass off, but the invisible shell over them both kept their heat trapped. It was a welcome luxury, and one she didn't want to think too deeply about since it might be related to the little trick they did with her meals in the other stone house.

"They're still looking for us," she whispered, aware that she was stupidly stating the fucking obvious, but after being thrown down a mineshaft she didn't quite mind being a little off her game.

"And it'll be dark soon." Erik didn't look at her, too busy scanning below. "We need transport. I could carry you the whole way, but . . ."

"I'm too heavy?" It was a pale attempt at a joke, and he barely noticed, giving her a short, distracted, sideways glance.

"Hardly." Those pinpricks in his pupils swelled for a moment, and a strange warm breeze, like a just-started heating unit, ruffled her hair. "I could run for weeks with you."

Let's do it, then. Let's just keep going. It wasn't the sort of thing you could say to a guy who'd just fought off a bunch of monsters before *something happened* and they turned into monster dust. "But?"

You know what happened, Liv. That was you.

"But you're safer in a car. So I'm looking for one."

"Oh." If she focused on grand theft auto, maybe she could get through the next few minutes without bursting into tears or screaming. It was a mercy her bladder was empty. "We're going to steal a car?"

"Probably. But not *we*, beautiful."

"I see." *That's not the first time he's called me that.* Liv decided it wasn't a bad nickname, even if it was wildly inaccurate. At least he didn't call her *cupcake*, like Jake did. Or *honey*, like Sal Kinnock; her boss probably had a brand-new paralegal to harass by now. "I was looking forward to committing a felony, though." It was another pale attempt at a joke, and this time, it got her a long considering stare.

With his ferocious stubble and dark circles under gleaming dark eyes, he looked raffish and exhausted at once, and one corner of his mouth twitched slightly. "I expected you to be screaming by now. Or passed out."

"Tried that. Didn't work." Nevertheless, she was pretty glad he was still cradling her. Standing on her own seemed damn near an impossibility. "So, we're not stealing a car?"

"*You're* not. All you've gotta do is stand still and look pretty."

I don't feel pretty. Liv's eyelids were heavy. They drifted down, and the last thing she heard was Erik's voice, soft and reflective.

"Don't worry, beautiful. I'm on the job."

IT WAS LIKE A CD being jostled, or a momentary loss in coverage causing your streaming music to hiccup. One moment she was curled in Erik's arms in a snowstorm, the next her eyes flew open and she stared uncomprehending at a windshield, snow-choked wipers moving in leisurely arcs and a cone of headlight glare dancing off whirling flakes.

It was still coming down. *Storm of the century, folks.* She blinked and turned her head, hoping the disconnected feeling filling her skull didn't mean a nightmare.

"You passed out from overload." Erik was in the driver's seat. It was yet another SUV, white, jacked up high, and with snow tires biting through a slippery soft blanket of killing white. A faint ghost of cigarette smoke clung to the interior under the screen of that funny, musky cleaning-magic; this vehicle wasn't nearly as nice as the others.

Is that what happened? Liv couldn't find a single blessed thing to say.

"It's normal after a fight like that," he continued softly. "But good news, we're almost there. You feel it?"

She felt something, all right. At least it wasn't the miserable need to pee, thank goodness. "Weird," she managed, her tongue a little too big for her mouth.

The road in front of them looked freshly plowed. Buildings pressed close on either side, and there was a rising seashell murmur slipping directly into her skull if she looked out the window and concentrated, so she didn't. Instead, she studied the dashboard, the cigarette lighter—God knew you couldn't leave *that* out of an American car, and this one was probably well-loved—and her jean-clad knees sitting obediently side by side.

She was dry, she was warm, but the strange sea-noise was getting louder. Was she hearing their mad god? "I can hear things." Her hands turned into fists, well-bitten nails digging into her palms. The childhood habit of chewing on her fingertips had returned with a vengeance. "All sorts of things."

"I know." It was either deeply comforting or completely irritating that he sounded so calm and certain; she couldn't decide. "It'll be better inside the temple, but for right now just close your eyes and think about walls."

"Is it *him*?" Funny, how she was laying the same stress on the word the three of them did.

"What? Oh, no, Dreamers are immune. It's probably just telepathy."

Oh, is that all? "Where are we?" Her empty stomach lurched again, informing her it was definitely not impressed with any of this bullshit.

"Just outside St. Cloud. Don't worry, I can *feel* the temple here. They chased us almost to the city limits; good thing you were out cold."

Yeah. Super. "It's getting louder." The urge to clap her hands over her ears rose, but it wouldn't do any good. The call, as Jada would intone during Movie Night, was coming from inside the house.

"I don't doubt it." Erik hit the blinker, swinging them into a wallowing left turn. "Keep your eyes shut and think about walls, Liv."

What the fuck? "Why walls?"

"It'll help you keep them out."

"Them?" How strange; she'd thought her fear-maker was busted under recent strain, but apparently it was still capable of cranking out the high-octane stuff. "What's *them*?"

"People, beautiful. Just normal people going about their business." Erik sucked in a harsh breath, but he didn't hit the brakes. The vehicle wallowed a bit before chains bit again and they crept forward. "It's natural, and it'll be okay. I was betting you'd show some secondary talents as soon as you met the Flame, too. Just relax. They can get loud, but they can't hurt you. It's just like a turned-up radio."

"It's in my head." Unsteady, oozing panic began to beat behind her breastbone. "Oh God, Erik, it's in my *head*—"

"Yes." A single short, sharp word. "Once we get inside the walls, it'll be better. I need you to hold on, Liv."

Oh, sure. Hold on. That'll do it. But it helped to know what was happening, and helped some more that he sounded crisp, authoritative, and absolutely in charge of the situation.

Her throat was dry as the Sahara. "Is this ever going to stop?" The darkness behind her eyelids wasn't comforting, but it did help turn the volume down a little. It was like hearing your neighbor play music so loud the words were gone and your dishes chattered a little bit in the cupboards.

She was never going to see her condo's tidy, sunflower-themed kitchen again. There were people who cleaned up houses and apartments after violent crimes; there had to be ones who took care of the disappeared. How many of the statistics were people like her?

How many had been eaten by monsters? Liv laced her shaking fingers together and tried not to think about it, squeezing hard.

"Temple walls are shielded," Erik continued. "It'll be nice and quiet there. They'll get you looked at, get you fed, get you settled in a *liraim* and—"

"Another cell?" She shivered, though the vents in the dashboard were giving out plenty of heat.

"It's safe, Liv." Quiet and patient. The car rocked a little as chained tires dug into ice; the temperature was falling rapidly.

"And you'll be there?" She hated the edge of whine in her own voice.

"Once they make sure I'm not a threat."

That doesn't sound good. "Can't we just—"

"It'll get worse. You had a lot of potential, and it's fully activated now. You're sensitive. A whole city full of people screaming through your skull isn't fun, and I can't block them all." There was a faint clicking—he'd hit the turn signal again. "They'll take care of you, and they won't let me near you again until they're sure I'm not a threat."

"That's ridiculous. Why would you be taking me there if—"

"You're not gonna be the only *lirai* there."

Oh, isn't that a relief. The voices swirled closer, a crowd in a nearby stadium instead of a seashell-trapped mutter. The car slowed further, took another wallowing left turn, and there were tiny dazzles in the darkness behind her squeezing lids. The stars winked out, one by one, as Erik negotiated another slow, slippery turn, this time to the right.

The release of pressure was instant, and she almost choked. Her eyes flew open, and for a moment nothing she saw made sense.

A long, sealed-black and snow-free driveway ran, ruler-straight, toward a bulky stone building with a giant main center and raked-back wings—all these guys had the same architect, and he apparently liked Gothic bullshit. The central structure had three squat, round, point-topped towers, snow whirling between them and coming down in sheets. Erik let out a probably unconscious sigh, the tension inside the vehicle spilling away. The necklace's reflection against the windshield swirled with deep, impossibly vital colors.

"It looks like a fucking theme park," she muttered, glancing guiltily at him.

Erik's mouth twitched again, the barest hint of a smile.

The grounds were probably pretty, but they were buried under a thick white blanket. Still, Liv's shoulders relaxed, and the sudden, blessed quiet was welcome.

Except she could still feel the noise outside, pressing against whatever thin boundary they'd crossed.

Erik took a deep breath. "They're going to ask you if we were respectful. Tell them everything honestly, even how much we fucked up, okay? Don't hold back." Did he actually sound nervous now?

That was a first.

"Oh, I won't," she muttered. "I won't hold back at all."

"Good." His knuckles were white; the steering wheel made a soft, stressed groan. "If they find out I've been turned, they'll take the *oneiros*. Let them, okay?"

Fuck that noise. "You gave it to me." Her chin set, stubbornly. "You're taking it back?"

"Not while I'm breathing. But if I'm a danger to you, I *want* them to take it. Just to make sure."

Oh, for the love of . . . Her irritation, once more, was a tonic. If she was pissy, things couldn't be that bad, right? At least, that's what Jada would say.

God. None of her friends would understand this bullshit. And just thinking about the monsters getting near any of them, especially Mika, sent a chill down her back.

She hated all of this, but she hated most of all that her captors were turning out to be right.

The building drew closer, a lot larger than it seemed from the end of the drive. For a moment the damp grey walls glowed with rainbow traceries, as if they had one of those funky holes in the basement and the strange variegated fire had decided to crawl up and around in questing tendril-veins. "There's a word for taking back a present, Erik. It's not a nice one."

The driveway widened into a circular area with a round, snow-choked garden space trapped in its center; the SUV banked, rolling to a gentle halt in front of a flight of sharp-edged granite stairs. That was when she noticed no snow clung to the driveway or the steps, despite the heavy white curtains robing the rest of the structure.

Snow shoveling by magic. A wild, inconsequential, braying laugh died in her throat.

"I'm gonna get out," Erik said softly, staring out the windshield. "They'll treat me like a threat, and they're right to do so. Just wait for them to get you out of the car."

Like hell I will. Still, what were her options? "What if it's the monsters?" She sounded five years old and scared of the dark.

What a coincidence, Liv realized. *That's exactly what I am.*

"It's not." Erik reached for the door handle, hesitated. "Liv?"

"Don't get out." She couldn't make her fists loosen. "Let's just leave. Keep going. Get *away.*"

"This is the safest place for you." He popped the release, a burst of cold mineral-scented air filled the cab, and he slid free of the driver's seat, rising with agonizing slowness and keeping both his hands visible.

He left the door open and stepped away. The invisible shell over him was gone, snow gathering swiftly on his tousled dark hair and the shredded jacket's shoulders. Both his big, capable hands were up and empty, the classic *I surrender* stance.

The snow swirled. The SUV's door-chime dinged softly, over and over.

A voice—hard, deep baritone, a tone used to command—came out of the snow. "*Somniorum serve.*"

"*In omni re.*" Erik put his chin down, keeping his hands high. Liv gasped.

They melted out of the snow, men in dark jackets with short haircuts and muscular shoulders, all moving with that same eerie, predatory grace. Liv huddled in the car and watched them surround Erik. Several had guns, they all had the strange crystalline-bladed knives he and Jake carried, and the older ones had swords and gleaming signet rings like Ignatius's. They didn't all look the same, but that strange fluidity and air of danger made them seem related.

She found out she could move after all, and hit her seat belt's release. Had he buckled her in?

It would be just like him.

"Wait," she said, a tiny cricket-whisper. Her arms and legs didn't quite want to work. She scrambled across the console and spilled out the driver's side behind Erik, ignoring the constant dinging. *Door open, door open, door open.* "Wait. Don't hurt him. Don't *hurt* him."

They didn't, but they also weren't very gentle, pushing so he went down to his knees in the snow.

"Stop it." Liv's hands were fists; she stepped forward. They all outweighed her, they were probably all super-strong, but she considered throwing herself at the closest one—grey-haired, his eyes a piercing blue, the snow avoiding him even as it clumped on Erik's shoulders.

One of the older men produced strange, oversized matte silver handcuffs. Liv tried to heave away when two of the older men, their swords vanishing into scabbards fastened to their backs—neatest trick of the week—took her arms and began practically carrying her for the slowly opening front doors. Golden light widened, a crack in the whirling white, and they dragged her, gently but irresistibly, into the stone building.

She screamed Erik's name the entire way.

Part Three: The Dreamer

Bait on the Hook

THE WORST PART wasn't being cuffed with Flame-blessed metal. It was hearing her cry his name, over and over, as she was carried into safety. Everything in him wanted to surge from his knees, snap the irritating metal bracelets like the fictions they were, and kill them—kill them *all*, if that was what it took.

If that would keep her safe.

Instead, he stood right where he was, shivering and sweating like a horse run too hard, and glared, nose down but eyes up, at the Son in front of him.

Blue-eyed, toffee-haired, the guy was built wide instead of with Jake's leanness, and had the faraway, listening look of an Elder Brother. "Name?"

"Erik," he said, crisply, and added the long string of his numerator as if he wasn't longing to leap on this fellow and put him down quick-like. That was only the first step; he would have to take out the two Younger Brothers on the other side of the stolen white Suburban next. "My *lirai*—"

"Yours?" Wheat-colored eyebrows rose, and his fellow Son examined Erik in a long, leisurely sweep, from Erik's stained boots to his torn jacket and the ribbons of his T-shirt. At least his jeans were mostly whole, except for the long tear on the inside of his left thigh.

One of the spiders had been going for his femoral artery.

"She's new," Erik managed. "She's terrified. I have to report."

"He's clearly one of us, or was." This Father, his iron-colored hair combed back from a ferocious widow's peak, clapped the blond on the shoulder. "Take him to the Chamber. We'll debrief you there, Elder Brother. Where were you trained?"

"Erik," he said again. *Chapter and verse.* "528-Alpha-X Ray-3840. My Father is Ignatius, my Younger Brother is Jacob. I was trained at Nightshade House of Belmont Temple, '28 to '33. Sent to Islington to satellite in '74, and stayed there since. We found a potential a few weeks ago, but we were chased—"

"Erik?" Another voice, this one vaguely familiar, came from his left. The Younger Brother there was slim and coal-eyed, his woolly hair cropped close and his guns vanishing into their holsters. "By the Dreamers. It *is* you."

"Someone you know, Stan?" The Father nodded, slightly, and the brothers' hands weren't rough, but they weren't overly gentle either.

Stan? He vaguely remembered the boy, lean and smiling before his mark, somber and big-eyed afterward, just prior to Erik and Jake's departure. "Stan. You took your mark in September. We went out drinking afterward." *Slipping the leash.* It wasn't a good thing to admit, and the alcohol didn't do anything to a Son's enhanced metabolism, but it was kind of expected—and it was something nobody else would know, except Stan, Jake, and the other Elder Brother present that night. What was that asshole's name?

I can't remember. That's a bad sign.

"It's him," Stan said, grimly. "But, Father Grigori . . ."

"Spit it out," an Elder Brother in braces, jeans, and a natty dark leather jacket said, softly. "We still have patrols to run tonight."

"All in good time, Tannis." Grigori gazed at Stan, but it would be foolish in the extreme to think he wasn't fully aware of—and prepared to handle—Erik's capacity for violence. "What is it, Stanley?"

"It's him, without a doubt." There was a time when Stan would have rolled his eyes at being called *Stanley*, but now he just shook his head slightly. "But he and his entire trio—they were reported dead over a decade ago, Father."

What the hell? Erik might have said something, but another Father, this one with a deep, ugly scar down the left side of his face, stepped closed. "Peace," the man breathed, the collective sorcerous force of the Sons with him channeled for a bare, stinging moment.

The world fell away on a tide of thick darkness, and the only mercy was that there were no dreams.

HE SURFACED briefly when they clipped him, naked and shivering uncontrollably with need, in the restraints. The Truth Chamber wasn't a place any Son liked to visit; the light was bright, the stainless steel tables along one wall were chilly, and the apparatus in its center was a confection of spun metal and whipped-cream glass, dreamstones—each one made in the old way—glowing along its spines, a mosaic of beauty.

There was a *lirai* there, too, but not the one he wanted. There was something very important Erik had to remember, as he was carried—

not violently, but not with the care they'd handle a Dreamer—to the apparatus and buckled in.

They would never subject a Dreamer to this.

The *lirai* was a slim dark young man with bright hazel eyes and a shock of floppy chestnut hair, his hands—a little too big for his wrists, he hadn't finished growing when he'd met the Flame—clasped before him. He wore a blue T-shirt with a red and white shield on the front, the star in its center bright but wavering as cloth moved, and his own *oneiros* wasn't as bulky as the one Erik had made. It was finer, more delicate, probably a younger's work.

That was what he'd forgotten, and Erik began to struggle, knowing he shouldn't but helpless not to. *Where is she? Is she hurt?*

"It's all right," the *lirai* said, in a soft, easy tenor. The peace flowing from the words enfolded him, but Erik continued to twist and jerk, the table's dreamstones lighting with a rill of bright, undeniable power. "Everything's fine, I'm just going to take a look, all right? You're okay."

"My lord?" Grigori plainly wanted to tell him to get on with it, but you didn't hurry a *lirai*.

"I know," the Dreamer said, his gentle tone never altering. "I just wish this wasn't so hard on you guys." He stepped forward, and the shadows around him did too. He had two full trios, but it was the Younger Brother on the right who touched the Dreamer's shoulder with two fingers, silently offering comfort.

Probably sealed. *Where is she? Is she all right? Traitor could be anywhere. What had Stan said?*

Declared dead over a decade ago. But they still received gear and funding, they still ran patrols, and Ignatius was still in contact with a control liaison.

The *lirai* nodded, stepped forward once more. His gaze turned distant, and other shadows against that warm, forgiving light were Sons closing in to protect him if Erik had been stuffed full of venom and sent by an old, foul intelligence.

Bait on the hook.

"*Lirai*," he gasped. "My *lirai*."

The Dreamer glanced at Grigori. "Is he . . .?"

"Unlikely." The Father shrugged, spreading his hands. "The young lady is active, she has an *oneiros*—fine work, really—and Lady Sara says she's recently been in the Flame. They're caring for her now, but she's a little—"

Erik surged against the restraints. The whole room rattled and the

Sons tensed, ripples running through preternaturally strong flesh. The light didn't dim, electric glow taking on a depth like a honeyed summer afternoon. "*Lirai*," he heard himself moan, helplessly.

"Erik?" The Dreamer's voice took on sonorous depth. The stones along the arms and studding the base of the table would add to his force, channel and filter it—and filter anything Erik might throw at him, too. Or anything that had been set inside his flesh and bone and breath, snuck through a temple's protections to strike at those the Mad God hated most.

It didn't matter that Erik was innocent—or that he thought he was. He had to endure, before he could rest.

Always. First came the endurance, and afterward a breather if you were lucky.

If you weren't, well . . .

The pain came then, a wave tearing and digging through his skull. It wasn't as bad as the mark, his essential self torn free of his body and hung upside down, the sleeping world vibrating underneath him as the cities—some of them transient, lasting only a mortal night while a normal slept in the grip of humanity's most ancient magic, others eternal, full of cathedrals and avenues added to by generations of Dreamers—spun and slid fast as wet ink upon a greased plate.

It certainly wasn't as bad as the glimpses of the Mad God's home, cyclopean blocks of stone quarried from unspeakable cliffs and hauled with much suffering before being lifted by invisible, bleeding fingers and rammed together to make a whole of geometry no mortal mind could stand, with the black tower in its middle and the yellow gleam at its top—

"Just a little more," the Dreamer crooned, invisible fingers stroking the inside of a Son's skull.

Fighting to keep the god out meant you reflexively battled any breach in your mental borders, even a Dreamer's soft, skilled touch. It meant that the amount of force necessary to dig through a Son's head and find innocence was extreme.

And very painful.

"He's coding," someone said. There were other callused, ungentle hands on him now and invisible force humming through his bones, shocking his heart, forcing the dumb meat to squeeze its cargo of blood. The scar on his chest, pink and shiny, flushed a deep angry red. So did the other imperfectly healed wounds from the last forty-eight hours. "Look at that. Is that a—"

"*Sarnaki*," the Dreamer hissed, his head tipping back. "And others. All of them. Sent, not summoned."

"Is he clear?"

The *lirai* shuddered, his hair rising and eyes widening. His hands darted for his face but both youngers of his trios intervened, grabbing his arms. The Dreamer clawed at empty air, his throat swelling with a terrible, rising cry.

There were things in a Son's head no *lirai* would deal comfortably with.

The young man stiffened. Invisible force swelled and crackled in the room. One of the dreamstones on the table popped, shards flying, and a wall of Sons closed before the vulnerable, bow-arched *lirai*. His feet, in glittering red high-top sneakers, drummed the tile floor, and his trios grabbed whatever they could reach of him—Fathers, elders, and youngers all seeking to bleed off the excess force, to comfort and restrain.

The Dreamer's cries were white birds above a golden shore, ringing like crystal bells. Erik's spine curved, crackling as a convulsion hit, and he began to scream as well, a low, husky guttural cry rising behind the Dreamer's, both repeating over and over in strange, disjointed tandem.

"Liv! Liv! Liiiiiiiiiiv!"

Value of Normal

THIS PLACE BORE as much resemblance to the other stone houses as the Louvre did to a roadside tourist trap. The lights were bright, the sconces expensive, the carpets were plush, the hardwood drenched with beeswax and polish, and it was full of quiet activity, grim-faced men hurrying back and forth on booted, whisper-quiet feet. Even the empty halls they carried her through—like she couldn't walk on her own—somehow managed to give an impression of being full, though you could have heard a pin drop in the hush while she babbled on and on.

When she was finally carried through a sitting room, into a bedroom, and deposited on a solid wooden chair with high carved finials as well as an entirely inadequate horsehair cushion, she was beginning to think Erik had, after all, made a mistake. And it only got worse when the questioning started.

"It wasn't him," Liv insisted, knowing she sounded like the poster girl for Stockholm syndrome and not caring a single bit. "He *saved* me. If it was him, he would have given me to the monsters. Christ knew he had . . ." She rubbed the heel of her hand against her forehead, scrubbing hard as if it would give her the right words to make them see. "He had enough chances," she finished, lamely. "They all did, I suppose."

This suite was much larger than the ones at the old place, and the curtained, rumpled bed was draped with wine-red velvet. The sitting room looked very Louis Quatorze, a walk-in closet the size of a small apartment was stuffed to the brim, and there were *two* bathrooms, one with the door half-open showing the edge of a clawfoot tub that looked older than Liv and her mother combined. The windows were the same as the other stone houses, though, mullioned to within an inch of their lives, and she could *see* the shimmer over them clear as day.

Protection. Had the other place been crawling with that shimmer too, and she just hadn't noticed it? Her skin shrank from the air, the light stung her eyes, and even though everything was different here, the man questioning her looked a little like Ignatius.

It was around the eyes, mostly, and the way he moved, upright and efficient, no motion wasted and his signet giving a bloody gleam every once in a while. He paced in front of the empty fireplace—bare, scraped clean, and big enough for Liv to crawl into—until the woman glanced at him. Then he stopped dead, even though she didn't say a word.

And the woman. . . . She was tall, with a mass of long dark hair flowing in soft glossy ripples down her back. She'd obviously been shaken awake in a hurry, because her eyelids were sleepy as a tired child's and that amazing hair was mussed. She was wrapped in an honest-to-God blue and gold patterned kimono over silk pajamas, and not the cheap kind, either. Both kimono and pajamas looked handmade, and her light-brown skin had the kind of sheen you only got with incredibly expensive skincare *and* good genetics. Her *oneiros* was heavy, its sharply geometric setting almost barbaric, but it probably didn't scratch her soft skin either.

It was enough to make Liv, rumpled and dirty and monster-chased, want to scream. If there hadn't already been so much to scream about, that was.

"Nevertheless." The greying man stood to attention, his hands now clasped behind his back like Ignatius—was Liv actually *missing* the old man? And cocky, self-assured Jake, too?

She wasn't exactly sad about making them fetch her books and other listed items, or about trying to escape. But she hoped like hell they were okay.

"What Albert's trying to say is that we're not ruling anything out." The woman—Sara—settled in the chair across from Liv's. It was warm enough in here to melt the snow in Liv's hair and any residual chill out of her bones as well; Sara's bare feet had some great pedicure action going on. Her toenail polish matched the couth pink on her fingernails, and both were buffed to a high gloss. "They believe in being careful, when it comes to *lirai*."

Yeah, I noticed. "Look." Liv gripped the arms of her own highly carved, not very comfortable chair. If the table wasn't rosewood she'd eat her nonexistent hat, and the chairs looked like antiques, too, with their wine-red horsehair cushions. If they were going to keep her in here, maybe she could use the furniture for firewood. Send up smoke signals. Something, *anything*. "They kidnapped me, all right? I'm really mad about that. But there are the goddamn monsters, right? There was the squid thing coming through the window and the spiders in the hall, and they all got beat up *really* bad getting us out of there. Then the car blew up, and then the *other* car blew up, and it was just Erik and me. He took me to the place Ignatius said, but it was closed up—"

Sara glanced at the older man, who stirred. "Rochester, my lady."

"Shuttered for twelve years." Sara looked at the door to the sitting room. There was an overstuffed fainting couch in there, embroidered with *pineapples*, of all things. "Or is it thirteen?"

"Eighteen, my lady." It should have been funny, but the way Albert said the last two words was deadly serious and utterly respectful. Liv had hung out with a few Renaissance Faire types in college, but they'd always sounded self-conscious saying *my lady*.

This guy definitely didn't.

"Time gets strange in here," Sara murmured, and shook her head. "But if this Ignatius was working from old information, it could make sense."

Albert didn't scoff, but his nostrils twitched slightly like he smelled something bad. "When he could simply call in and have transport at a satellite temple within hours?"

"Perhaps communications were cut off? Do we know who his Control is?" Sara now studied Liv, who tried not to fidget. Much.

"Where's Erik?" She couldn't help herself. He was the only familiar thing in all this insanity, and they'd handcuffed him. "I want to see him."

"Did he make that?" Sara leaned forward, one of her hands freeing itself to gracefully indicate the necklace.

"Yule gift." *And I'll bet someone made yours, too. But he probably wasn't as nice*. "Erik's all right, okay? I didn't like any of them, but they didn't deserve . . . that."

"Fostering dependence. Not moving her *or* calling in immediately." Albert wasn't ticking them off on his fingers, but he gave a good impression of wanting to.

Liv had an answer for that one, but she was beginning to suspect it wouldn't satisfy them. "Ignatius said they were supposed to wait until the days were longer."

The man's eyes flashed, those blue pinpricks like Erik's showing for a moment before being swallowed. "Standard procedure for the last decade is to bring the potential *immediately*—"

"Albert," Sara said, softly. "Not helpful."

Amazingly, he dropped his gaze, staring somewhere between the two women. "Forgive me, my lady."

"Of course. We'll approach the questions of the control liaison and Islington being shuttered as soon as our new sister has been settled." Sara's smile looked unforced, unfeigned, and completely forgiving. What would it be like, to be this calm? She returned her attention to Liv, tapping thoughtfully at her pretty mouth with one finger. "So, Erik gave you an *oneiros*. And he brought you to the Flame?"

"Well, he pushed me into the, uh, the hole." Liv's entire body ached, and she couldn't help but shudder. "I get it, you know? It's not the sort of thing you can explain, and if he'd tried, I probably would've fought."

Probably? No, she would have tried to claw his eyes out and escape—and run right up the stairs into the monsters, if she could have gotten past him. Which was a very big *if* indeed.

They might both have died down there, if she'd tried. In the dark. And all this talk about "*Control*" and "*being shuttered*" didn't sound good at all.

"Well, you're taking it more gracefully than I did." Sara's slight smile held an edge of pain. "It took me a long time to forgive my betrayer."

"Betrayer?" Man, these people had a whole new language, even if they were using English for the spare parts.

"That's what they call it. *Betrayed to the Flame*." Sara exhaled, harshly, and for a moment something like pain flashed in her great dark eyes. "A potential can still live a normal life, or some value of *normal*. A *lirai*? Not so much."

He didn't tell me about that. Still, it made sense. "So he dunked me in it yesterday—I think it was yesterday, at least. Something happened. We drove most of the night to get here, and now I can't turn off the radio in my head and—"

"Radio in the head," Sara murmured. "That's a good way to put it."

Liv couldn't help herself. She looked at the door to the sitting room, invitingly open. Maybe she could reach it before the older guy caught her, maybe not.

Should she try?

"The rest of my Flight are in that room." Sara's gaze was disconcertingly direct. "Except the youngers; they're probably in the hall past it, first line of defense. It took fifty mortal years for the blind urge to run stopped tormenting me."

Fifty years? And there was that other little word too.

Mortal. "You don't look a day over twenty-eight," Liv said, numbly.

"My, you're polite. I would have said mid-thirties. We tend to stop when the Flame hits, but I've been around a while. Experience shows in the eyes, I think." For a moment the other woman's mouth turned down, and Albert made a restless movement near the fireplace.

A snowy night like this pretty much called for a nice crackling fire, but maybe the chimney was blocked so something couldn't get down it. The image of a monster Santa Claus was horrifyingly detailed inside Liv's head, and she flinched. Outside the windows, the snow was still steady.

It wasn't the individual flakes. It was the accumulation that caused problems. It piled up on you, and Liv was already exhausted from carrying so much.

"Fifty years." Liv's voice was a dry husk. "*Mortal* years."

Sara's slight grimace didn't alter her beauty one whit. "You'll have some trouble with the notion. It's natural."

"None of this is natural, ma'am." Was she taking refuge in sarcasm? Maybe. "I want Erik. I don't trust you."

"That's wise. I think it's quite possible he'll be cleared and will build your trios, but we have to make sure. Will you at least agree to take quarters here, and learn what you've landed in?" Sara leaned forward slightly, and she was right—there was something around her dark eyes that said *I've seen it all, and disliked most of it.* Not lines, and not dark circles, though the rumpled velvet-choked bed had to be hers.

"Like I could go anywhere else." At least Ignatius had respected Liv's intelligence, or it felt like he had. Even if he didn't like her much personally—but to be fair, that feeling had been overwhelmingly mutual. "Like you'd *let* me go anywhere else."

"That's fair." Sara smiled, and extended her hand again over the table. "It's not a bad life, all things considered. You've had a rather . . . nonstandard introduction to it, and for that I'm sorry. But we're not the enemy, Ms. Stellack."

"We are a lesser evil, my lady." Albert dropped his gaze to the floor when the women both looked at him.

"Funny." Liv reached across the table, clasped Sara's hand. A strange, champagne-fizzing sensation slid down her back; Sara's necklace brightened, the white stone filling with vivid colors. Her own was probably doing the same. "That's what Ignatius said."

"If he's alive, we'll find him. And the Younger Brother, too." Sara shook hands the way women used to a lot of men did—quickly, with an almost apologetic half-smile, taking her touch away as soon as possible. "You seem in remarkably good shape for a *lirai* who has endured what you have, which speaks well of this Erik. Daniel—he's one of us—is checking him now, and if the elder's cleared you'll see him again soon. In the meantime, perhaps something to eat? Your *liraim* is being readied, and you'll have at least two temporary trios while we sort this out."

That means absolutely nothing to me, thanks. "I'm fine. I just want Erik." She sounded like a dippy teenager, Liv realized, and dropped her hands into her lap. At least the surf-sound of the city outside didn't penetrate this place, but she didn't trust the quiet, either. "But I suppose you'd like to go back to bed."

Sara shook her head again, a slight, graceful movement. "I doubt there will be any more sleep for me tonight. Or for you, just yet. Shall I order some coffee?"

Oh, for God's sake. "Sure. Knock yourself out."

"We'll be civilized, then." Sara paused. "It will be nice to have another woman here," she added, finally. "Daniel's *lirai*, of course. But I miss girl talk."

I don't feel really friendly right now. "Girl talk is my specialty," Liv lied.

It would, after all, be good to have an ally. And she couldn't help but wonder what else Ignatius—and even Erik—hadn't told her.

Trust Us or Yourself

THE STORM TAPERED off in the early morning hours while Erik lay in a deathly doze, stretched motionless on a narrow cot in the dormitory. He felt the weather system shift, a malevolent claw easing its grasp and natural forces reasserting their primacy.

It had been a long time since he'd been in an active temple. When full consciousness returned he lay very still, his breathing keeping its sleep-pattern, every inch of his skin alive with attention and anticipation.

Where is she? The thought was quite natural, and it was time for him to admit a few things to himself.

First, though, he listened.

Footsteps. A subaudible hum. Cloth moving, soft breathing very much like his own. The dormitory was usually dim even on a summer afternoon, a restful cave for those who were, after all, night creatures. Further away, there was chiming, slipslither of metal against metal, exhalations of effort.

That would be the sparring halls; this place probably had more than one. He hadn't realized how much he missed the reminder of community, of collective endeavor. Many Sons meant many eyes, and also meant a better chance of staying on the rails.

A shifting, unbearably sweet whisper far beneath this room was the Flame. This place would have unfettered access. At least one *lirai* here, probably more if the warmth teasing and tickling along his skin was any indication. Above, in the shifting grey where his unphysical senses turned into insubstantial fringe, there were breathless-crackling accumulations of force, shielding hard and durable around glowing pearls.

That's where she'll be, then.

The relief was indescribable. He wasn't in a cell, chained to stone walls while the god ran rampant through his head. If he was in the dormitory, he was clear, and even if they didn't let him near her, even if she hated the one who had betrayed her to the Flame, she was safe.

Unless Control was a traitor. This is the closest active temple. Is it one of them? Or . . .

There was a spot of suspicious silence to his right. Erik kept his breathing to the rhythm of deep sleep, and thought about things.

"You can stop pretending," his fellow Son said, softly.

Erik's eyes drifted open. He examined the man in the chair pulled to the cot's side; this was a regular Sons' dormitory, one he'd seen versions of for decades. High stone walls, ribbed and vaulted ceilings, the light fixtures glowing electric globes—it used to be gaslight, Ignatius always said, and Erik felt his age for a few moments before studying the Father at his bedside.

"Grigori." He found the man's name, let it slide between cracked lips. He needed hydration, and some plain old calories wouldn't go amiss even if he'd had enough bloodshed lately to keep him charged for a long while. "Right?"

"Indeed." The Father's widow's peak was just as pointedly pristine as it had been yesterday. He sat ramrod-straight but with his legs stretched out, probably weary after a long night of excitement and quite possibly patrol. "And you are Erik. Very spry for a dead man."

"So I gathered." No, Erik decided, this guy probably hadn't been on patrol. They had more than enough Sons here to run both city sweeps and guard duty, not to mention easily hold some in reserve for events like last night as well. An active temple had resources a frontier one couldn't dream of. "Is she all right? Liv, is she—"

"Our lady Stellack is being settled in the third primary *liraim*, she has two temporary trios and our other *lirai* are doing their best to welcome her. She asks after you constantly, I am told. I would suspect a fostered dependency, but this appears a most irregular situation so we are reserving judgment for the moment."

Mighty decent of you, sir. Erik swallowed the sarcasm. It was something Liv might have said, her chin lifted and that fire in her dark eyes. Of course, she could say whatever she wanted here, and probably would. At length, and with all her arguments arranged neatly like anyone who spent any time around attorneys learned to in sheer self-defense.

Erik, however, was forced to different measures. He cleared his dry throat, winced, and pushed himself upright, swinging his legs off the cot. It even *smelled* like a Sons' dormitory—stone, heatless power, the tang of men living together, working a dirty job and cleaning up as best they could. "Am I clear?"

"Yes." Grigori nodded sharply but otherwise didn't move. "The vehicle you used has been attended to, new gear has been issued you, and as soon as you finish debriefing I will be taking you to our new *lirai*."

He hadn't expected that. "She might not want to see me."

"If so, she's chosen a very strange way of expressing the preference." Grigori gathered his long legs and rose with a Father's restrained, eerie grace. It looked like he favored black linen button-downs, crisply ironed, jeans also ironed, and engineer boots, which wasn't quite standard for Fathers but well within limits. His signet gleamed reassuringly. "What is it you fear, my Son?"

The traditional question, an invitation to absolution. Ignatius hadn't asked him in a long damn time, probably because the old man knew what Erik feared, and vice versa.

Or did he? Now that he thought about it, there were some troubling things swirling in Erik's skull where the Dreamer had gone looking, invisible fingers stroking a brain's cargo of impressions and memories. "Failure," he said, heavily, as he had every other time.

Except now, the fear was crystallized into a single form. He almost wished they *had* found more than the usual garden-variety corruption in him. It would be better than suspecting a control liaison of treachery, and far more comfortable than suspecting men he'd fought with, trusted his life to, and lived with for so long.

"What manner of failure?" Grigori was ruthless, but then again, you wanted that in a Father. No quarter given to others or himself made a Father, just as hair-trigger temper and self-assurance made a Younger Brother.

Erik didn't want to answer. He perched on the edge of the cot, his gaze dropping to his hands. Big, callus-hardened palms, blunt fingers of surprising dexterity, no healing scrapes across his knuckles because the Dreamer had flushed him with vital force at the end of the questioning. Soon Liv would do the same as a matter of course after any engagement, and the thought sent a hot spear through his guts.

He was still in last night's shredded T-shirt and dirty jeans. His socks were filthy with blood and grit, and his boots were probably past repair. His skin crawled.

But when asked, a Son gave an answer. Otherwise, the slim chance of absolution whittled down to zero. "I should have sensed something." He exhaled sharply. "I should have known. I failed my *lirai*."

"Your *lirai*." Grigori paused. "Are you sealed, then?"

So that was why he was still here. He could lie, of course. If ever he was tempted, now was the time. "No," he admitted. If he had a useless mortal scruple or two, well, it was better than the alternative. Another Son might think differently, but Erik's own line in the sand was clear.

"There has been no consent."

"I see." No commendation, but no pity either. "The *lirai* judged you clean, my son. Nevertheless, we will be watching."

"Good." Erik made his legs stiffen, forced himself upright. It was harder than he liked. The problem wasn't physical—he was in fighting shape, ready to take on the worst. Rest and a *lirai* worked wonders, especially for a Son. "I made her a dreamstone, Father. If I . . ." *If it turns out I'm not clean after all.* The *lirai* had cleared him, but he had to make sure. "Well, it'll need to be destroyed, if the worst happens. Will you do that?"

"Of course." The Father's tone plainly said he considered the promise superfluous, but who cared? He'd given his word, that was the thing.

"She might fight it." *She's a stubborn one,* he almost added, but that was a step too far. Judging a *lirai* was simply not done.

"They generally do." A shadow of the man's true age crept into his tone, and he rose several notches in Erik's estimation. "You do not trust us or yourself, do you."

Of course not. "No, Father."

"*Very* good." Grigori nodded. "In your case, I would not either. Come, let's get you clothed. You'll feel better with weapons."

THE MACHINERY of the Sons was working at peak here, a welcome change. T-shirt, jeans, new jacket with the collar shape he favored, boots of the same make as his old ones. The weaponry was fine if a little heavy, and his familiar knives were burnished to a high gloss, handed over in a new harness that would creak until he broke it in.

The crystalline knives were utterly personal; you didn't draw a new one unless the old broke. Erik flicked them out in turn, tested the heft, scanned each blade from tip to pommel, nodded, and eyed the .45s. *Thought they shifted to 9mms.* "Haven't carried those for about five years."

"Your last requisitions sheet before Islington went dark had .45s," Grigori said. "You would prefer something else?"

"No, thanks. They'll do." He rolled his shoulders, the harness buckling the way it was supposed to—looked like they'd made a couple changes to the design, but those were all to the good. The Younger Brother behind the requisitions counter exchanged glances with the Father, and bright curiosity burned in the redheaded youth's eyes.

Erik shrugged into the jacket, and tensed. "So my last few req-and-pref sheets haven't come through?" When, precisely, had their temple been written off—and why hadn't Ignatius known?

"Not since it went dark. Normally we would have sent a team to look for wreckage, but that was a bad year. We lost a *lirai* here, New York lost two, and Boston was under siege for six months. Chicago held out, but their *lirai* both unraveled a little from the strain; they're still recovering even now. There was a traitor in Charleston, another in Des Moines, and a full-blown incursion in Dallas. We pulled several *lirai* back in a hurry, including the one holding Rochester. Several other fringe temples went dark; Islington seemed a likewise casualty." Grigori paused, his mouth tightening and pain flashing briefly in his gaze. "We mourned."

"All in one year?" Erik's tone hit *what-the-fuck* levels it hadn't since training. "We didn't hear any of that. I mean, our younger and I didn't." Jake would have said something—unless he was better at keeping secrets than Erik ever dreamed.

Which was possible. But Ignatius should have briefed them both, and they should have been pulled back for active defense.

It boggled the mind. Where was Control? Just who had Erik's Father been talking to?

"So it seems." Grigori indicated the hallway and Erik fell into step beside him with a nod of thanks to the younger behind the counter. It was like keeping up with Ignatius, only far less comforting. "However, there is some good news. There's been a spike in the number of potentials found recently."

"Good news that might not be," Erik muttered. Humanity tended to produce those capable of becoming *lirai* in waves, usually in response to stressful events—like any species, struggling to evolve and survive.

Striding through the halls, other Sons glancing curiously at him but going about their business, a Father leading the way up several flights of stairs—it was like rain on a thirsty desert, and he hadn't realized how much he missed it. Bright snowy sunlight pierced windows broad and narrow, and the entire stone fabric of the temple hummed, happy to hold *lirai*. The counterpoint of thrumming basso power from the Sons only served to make that bright depth more marked, more vivid, more *real*.

His internal map told him they were heading for the eastern tower, and his palms grew damp. He was going to see her soon.

"Indeed." Grigori's pace, an even glide, was inalterable as fate. "Now I have something else to tell you, Erik."

"Proceed." It was a fairly good Ignatius impression. Maybe he'd shift to Father in a while, if his hair started going grey.

A few months ago, he might have been pleased at the notion. Now he wasn't so sure.

"Would you be surprised to know your Younger Brother Jacob called a very old dropline the evening before last, asking for teams to bring himself and a potential to Rochester?"

The relief was instant, and total. "No, I wouldn't. He must've called right before I found them, after the *sarnaki* attack."

"Yes." Grigori nodded. "My lord Daniel says you held off two of the spear-wielders. An accomplishment."

Erik's throat had gone dry. There was nothing to say, and they reached the top of a long sweeping spiral, another hall studded with shafts of winter sunlight stretching before them. At the end, a pair of iron doors etched with a dreaming-tree stood, and two Elder Brothers on guard duty bookmarked it on either side. They eyed him curiously as well, and Erik set his chin.

"Courage, my son." Grigori's pace didn't slacken; he obviously felt some things were best done quickly, like ripping a facehugger off a drained corpse.

Yeah, I think I'll need it. He waited for the Father to knock, and an irritable noise from inside managed to filter through the waterfall of baffling over the door.

She sounded just the same.

The right leaf of the door opened a crack. A Younger Brother— sienna skin, short red-black hair, and a proud high prow of a nose—peered through, and his expression went through several small changes before settling on profound relief. "Is it him?" he asked, sweeping the door wide and beckoning Grigori.

"In the flesh," the Father replied, somewhat sardonically, and Erik followed, helpless not to.

"Thank the Dreamers. This one's a handful." The younger stuck out his hand in Erik's general direction. "Dakshi, brother. Well met."

"Erik." They clasped forearms, a greeting old when Rome was a collection of mud huts on a riverbank. "Let me guess. She's making lists."

"You *do* know her." Dakshi's rueful grin was far more expressive than Jake's, but he felt a little older. "Come in. Let's not keep our lady waiting."

The *liraim* was beautiful, the kind he would have wanted for her to begin with. The floors were stripped pine, and the furniture was spare and more modern than he'd expected. A dove-grey linen sectional couch, comfortable wide overstuffed chairs, a coffee table's sinuous pale ashwood curve—maybe she wouldn't like it, but he thought it suited her perfectly.

And there, her arms crossed, a wide-necked black sweater slipping to one side to show a slice of her collarbone and the hollow before her shoulder, her dark hair damp and braided back tightly, Liv Stellack regarded him over acres of sunny *liraim* air that suddenly wouldn't fill his lungs. The *oneiros* gleamed against her breastbone, the jeans made her legs look longer than ever, and she had a pair of sneakers he remembered packing for her a few days ago.

It felt like a lifetime.

"Oh, thank God," she said, and the *oneiros* lit with a warm pulse that flashed through him and away, rattling all the sitting-room furniture. "Erik."

"Liv." There was something in his throat. She wasn't looking at him like she hated him. In fact, she dropped her hands and took two steps forward. Three. Straight for him, and he braced himself for a slap, for a screaming woman, for a *lirai* to be pried off him as she pummeled her betrayer and he stood absolutely still, because he deserved it.

Liv flew across the remaining distance, threw her arms around him, buried her face in his chest, and hugged with surprising strength. "You *asshole*," she hissed against his T-shirt. "Took you long enough."

A Live Snake

IT WAS DISCONCERTING to be surrounded by a blob of heavy-shouldered men moving with catlike grace through sunlit, stone-floored halls. She was never, ever going to get used to it, even if Erik was always in the same place just behind her right shoulder, his jaw set and his dark gaze flickering everywhere.

At least they let her out of her cell daily, and said cell had way more walls than the last one. Sitting room, two bathrooms, walk-in closet she would never be able to fill, bedroom—did the closet count as a room? Depending on whether it did, there were sixteen or twenty, and she wasn't sure if a wall counted if it had a door.

She spent a lot of time thinking about it in the wide navy-blue bed, which was curtained kind of like Sara's, but not nearly as heavily. She didn't like the grey linen furniture in the sitting room, but when they asked, she enthused about it until Erik shot her a perplexed look.

Which was gratifying.

"Cheer up." Daniel spread his arms and danced sideways down the stairs, his shiny red and white high-tops tapping like a Fred Astaire re-mix. Today he wore a Batman T-shirt, the yellow logo well-washed and glowing sunnily. "We're not going to throw you in the Flame again; that part's done."

"Color me excited." What Liv really wanted was to break out of the shell, run down the stairs, lose herself in the crisscrossing passages, and maybe find a way outside.

Not that it would do much good. The temperature had dropped and the snow was covered with a slippery, murderous layer of freezing rain. It was beautiful, certainly—the view from the mullioned windows sparkled enough to blind her when she stared at the hillocks and humps of white that might be green in a few months but were merely featureless and sterile now.

Even if she did manage to get to the wall skirting the grounds, stepping outside was another proposition entirely.

You had earplugs, Daniel had said gravely. *Now they're out and they won't go back in. You'll need a trio, probably two, to keep everyone around you from shouting their most intimate secrets through a bullhorn, straight into your skull. Scrambles your brain, that does.*

It was a relief to get some questions answered, even if the answers were complete nutbar.

"It takes a while to settle." Not much sobered Daniel for long. If Sara was depressive, he was almost manic, and the aggressive cheerfulness was almost as bad as Sara's eternal, glassy calm and slow, somnolent movements. Despite wanting girl talk, the female *lirai* didn't seem too inclined to reach out to get some. "Be gentle with yourself, Liv."

Like there's any other choice. "If I wasn't, they'd stop me, right?"

"A *lirai*'s too precious to be risked. I tried suicide four separate times my first year." Daniel's expression didn't change, as if killing yourself was a natural, unavoidable consequence of learning there were monsters and monster-fighters hanging around most large cities at night, not to mention being dunked in rainbow fire from the bowels of the earth.

Liv couldn't really disagree. She wished she could grab the banister, but Dakshi was in the way. He was a lot quieter than Jake, but smiled all the time like him. The old guy, Robert, looked a little like Ignatius, and had a habit of wearing suspenders. That comprised her "regular trio," and there was a rotating cast of other brawny guys filtering through daily on "guard duty."

She couldn't possibly remember all their goddamn faces. All told, there were rarely less than a half-dozen men hanging around her. She could barely visit the bathroom alone, and consequently she'd taken to long hot baths.

It was the only time she got any peace at all.

"Then I sealed Eddie, and River." Daniel sobered, but only partly. He still danced sideways down the curving staircase, and Liv thought it was possible he'd practiced a lot, a prancing extra in a Depression-era musical extravaganza.

Maybe he knew he wouldn't fall, or that they wouldn't let him.

"Another thing they wouldn't tell me about." Liv preferred watching her own feet—she'd remarked that she liked Erik's boots, and within a few hours a pair in her size, with cushier insoles, had showed up in a plain white box.

The Sons apparently had all sorts of money, though she was pretty hazy on where it came from and there wasn't a good way to ask with everyone listening. With all that cash, why did they still have all these stairs? The place could have used an elevator or two.

Maybe the steps were to keep everyone in shape. God knew her glutes were getting a workout.

"It's not polite dinner conversation, that's for sure." Daniel finally stopped soft-shoeing and turned to descend backwards. "It's very personal. Even Sara doesn't talk about it much, and she sealed her entire flight. She can't stand to see them suffer."

Maybe he was showing off? Liv's stomach lurched; Erik's hand closed around her elbow. The touch, warm and unsettlingly familiar, steadied her.

Daniel was watching her when she glanced up, his young face solemn for once. It was eerie to see him moving backward, weight transferred with easy regularity, dropping from stair to stair with barely a sound. He'd probably been taking lessons from the Sons.

When he was sure he had her attention, he continued. "Some *lirai* do that, you know, seal their entire flights—a flight's a group of trios, naturally."

"Naturally." *I got that,* she wanted to say, irritably, but there was no use in it. When a man wanted to lecture, he'd do it despite any impediment.

"It makes it easier on them, sort of inoculates—that's a great word, *inoculate*—it makes 'em immune to *him*." Daniel didn't shudder, but his expression soured for a moment. "They don't say *his* name, ever."

"Then how do they know it?" At least she could ask all the questions she wanted, and they were getting a lot better about actually answering. At least, the *lirai* did.

The Sons barely spoke, except for Erik. And even he wasn't a championship chatter.

"Oh, they know. Same way you know how to breathe, or how to pulse through a trio and flambé the shadow-fucks." His lips pursed slightly as his eyes danced too, a little boy caught making swears. The end of the staircase arrived; Daniel did a tolerable Motown-esque twirl, grinned at her, and set off at an angle across parquet flooring, his trios closing around him.

Liv stopped on the last stair, her head down, her throat suddenly a pinhole. Erik's hand was still on her elbow, a steady, anchoring pressure. "It's all right," he said, quietly, his breath brushing her ear. "Just breathe, Liv. Everything's fine."

Panic attack. She was dismally aware it was a reasonable response to the whole deal, but with her heart hammering and no air in the entire stone pile, sweat tracing down her spine and gathering behind her knees, slicking her underarms despite powdery antiperspirant—oh, no wonder Sara gleamed, the toiletries here were magic as the rest of the deal—there was no escape from the dumb animal her body had become, hiding in a corner and shivering.

"Easy, beautiful." The murmur in her ear didn't change. "She's cycling. Dakshi?"

Another hand laid itself on her opposite shoulder. Liv shuddered, but the panic retreated, draining away down some collection of subconscious pipes.

Maybe there was a mad god crouching down there. Why not?

When she could open her eyes again, Daniel had stopped by a pair of glass double doors, observing a safe distance with his own trios gathered around him. Even with all the variations in skin tone and bone structure, the Sons looked vaguely alike.

Family resemblance, maybe. I wonder who they take after? Probably that god of theirs.

"Don't think about it," Erik continued. "It's all right, Liv. We're here."

She pushed her shoulders back. She hadn't had panic attacks since the terrible six months or so after Gramma Poe died and the nightmares intensified, replaying with feverish intensity each time she closed her eyes.

Don't think about it. Right. Easier said than done.

"Should we take her back to the *liraim*?" Dakshi didn't quite sound nervous, but it might have been close, if he hadn't been a Son.

She was learning, wasn't she? Learning a *lot.*

"No," Liv heard herself say, sharply, decisively. "I don't want to go back. I'm okay." She shook their hands away and set off across parquet, heading straight for Daniel.

The young man smiled, a small, pained grin. "Better," he said. "You really are determined."

"What good would I be as a monster hunter if I wasn't? You promised to train me." She could feel her chin settling in what her grandmother always called *decided fashion.*

"That I did, and you've done wonderfully with the preliminaries." Daniel's teeth gleamed white, and she wondered blankly who did his dental work. Were you still afraid of tooth-scrapings when you knew about monsters? "Come on. Today we're going to have some fun."

A GIANT EXPANSE of hardwood held a crowd of Sons, the vastness lit by snow-dazzled sunshafts falling from piercing skylights and heavy golden electric lights caged in thick white glass and wire. Racks along each long wall held a fantastical array of implements—wooden quarterstaffs fit for Robin Hood and Little John to start dueling, polished iron ones to match, honest-to-goshkies swords of every size and description, neatly lined-up knives, chains, things she was sure were flails or maces, and other wicked-looking weapons very capable of puncturing, bludgeoning, slicing, and dicing not just monsters but human beings as well. A galvanic movement ran through the entire space when Daniel appeared, and it was disconcerting to see the place clear out in fast-forward, even the guys in workout gear boxing or clanging at each other with those clattering iron sticks halting between one movement and the next. No few of them streamed past Liv on their way out, each bowing their heads and making a strange gesture—the left hand touching the heart, the lips, then the forehead.

"We interrupted them." Liv tried an apologetic smile, but none of them really looked at her, their gazes sliding away.

"There are other sparring rooms." Dakshi—the name meant *competent*, he'd told her with a slight smile—was close enough she could feel the heat coming off him. Erik was warm too, but it didn't make her uneasy when he crowded close.

Or at least, not *very* uneasy.

"Believe it or not, this is polite." Erik didn't touch her, but the imprint of his hand on her elbow still burned. "If one of you pulsed through everyone here, you'd blow out all the lights and probably the walls too."

You say that like it's a bad thing. Still, it was food for thought. They talked about how it was instinctive, how the force coming through Dreamers was amplified and channeled by Sons, but it was all so much weird incomprehensible mishmash.

Still, you couldn't understand some things about, say, driving a car until you actually *did* it. A lot of life was like that, and at least they were going to take a whack at training her.

It was a giant goddamn relief. Maybe sometime soon she'd stop feeling so helpless.

Daniel's voice echoed, bouncing from hardwood, stone, and the mirrors on the short walls of the rectangle. "Liv? If you'd stand right over there, please. Gentlemen, we'll just be doing flux today, so no real weapons. Just knives."

"I don't know what I'm doing," Liv said. "Shouldn't I start out with a punching bag or something?"

"If anything gets close enough for you to punch, we haven't done our job." Robert didn't speak much, but when he did, the dry crisp edges of each word sounded vaguely British.

"But shouldn't I know how to do some kung fu or something, and then, you know, work up to this?" Liv eyed the rows of swords, and wondered if the thought of swinging one was supposed to be a comfort or a fresh terror. "Whatever this is?"

"Relax." Dakshi stepped away, fading behind her. "It's instinctive, my lady Liv."

Oh, Lord, the 'my lady' bullshit. Sara and Daniel considered that normal—or they seemed to. "Just Liv," she muttered, and stood right where the other *lirai* had pointed. "Okay."

Erik moved just slightly in front of her, and Robert stepped neatly to her left. A faint sound was oiled sharpness leaving a sheath; Erik held one of their strange crystalline knives in his right hand, the blade along his forearm. Robert followed suit, and a fluttering queasiness filled Liv's belly.

Daniel straightened. "Are you ready?" All trace of levity was gone, and he looked at least ten years older now. His two trios had taken their places, like well-oiled machines, and a few of them drew knives as well.

Does it matter? "No." Might as well be honest.

"Good," the other *lirai* said.

It happened all at once. Daniel leaned forward slightly, feet planted, and only his torso slightly inclined. His dark eyes widened, his floppy hair moving as if brushed by invisible fingers.

A solid wall of invisible force thundered across the space between them, smacking against Liv's entire body. Her hair blew back, her eyes watered, her black sweater flapped, but her shoes were stuck fast. Her hands jumped free, palms out, and the invisible *whoosh* snapped neatly aside, cracking against a wooden rack bolted to the wall. It was full of long sheathed broadswords, and the wood groaned, an unhappy, stressed sound. A metallic ringing lingered, filling her ears until she thought she'd gone temporarily deaf, but something inside her stretched.

That was the only way to describe it, a peculiar internal elastic *shift.* The invisible draft swirled behind her, gaining force as it whipped in a perfect semicircle and bulleted back toward Daniel, some of its strength bled away by smacking into the wall but the rest caught, conserved—and added to, a rumble like a freight train at midnight filling Liv's internal spaces.

It hit both Daniel's trio-Fathers with a crunch, driving them back, their boots squeaking against hardwood. The other *lirai*'s eyes widened, he spread his arms, and the Elder Brothers in front of him were driven back too, both youngers stepping forward in synchronized motion.

Daniel's hands spread, hanging loosely at his sides. His eyes glowed, and Liv almost-saw what he was doing to bleed the excess power off.

Oh, no you don't. A flood of hot, almost embarrassing anger broke loose, rushed up her spinal column, and poured out of her. Liv's mouth opened; she screamed, a long trailing cry forcing Daniel and his trios back still further; one of the Fathers' boots left a single dark dragging streak on the flooring, matching several older marks.

Daniel parried, his grasp on the power sure and impossibly, sinuously strong. It was like holding a live snake, and now she could sense the force moving through Erik and Robert, amplified by strange echoing cathedral-spaces inside them.

Oh, so that's what—

It hit her sideways; a weightless sensation bleeding out through her fingers and toes as her feet rose from the floor, hovering a good four or five inches in empty air. She hung for what seemed a very long time, surprised and pinned, before she was tossed into Dakshi's arms and crumpled, her head ringing, a coppery taste on her tongue, and her eyes refusing to work quite right. The world was a bright, indistinct smear, but she heard their voices from very far away.

"My, she's a pistol." Daniel didn't sound upset in the least. In fact, he was audibly his usual cheerful self, and it was irritating as all fuck. "Nothing to worry about, I should say. All she needs is practice."

A significant pause. "My lord." Robert, every consonant precisely enunciated. "Are you considering—"

"Of course I am." Daniel, again. "She and I can do the sweeps, it'll be fun. We've needed a third for a long time. With her and me keeping the streets clean, Sara can handle trainees and find other potentials instead of engaging, because . . . well, you know. It's the answer to our prayers."

"She's been targeted, *lirai*." Erik didn't sound happy. It was only because she knew him that she could hear the faint breath of . . . what? "Stepping foot outside the temple might not be wise."

"She can't hide any more than Sara or I can, Elder." Warm fingertips brushed Liv's cold, damp forehead, and a different warmth spilled through her from the touch. "Take her back and put her to bed. Make sure she gets dinner, please. We'll run a few more trials tomorrow and the day after, and then—showtime."

I'm right here, Liv wanted to say. *Don't talk about me like I'm not.*

She was lifted. Her eyes still wouldn't work, though nothing hurt and nothing seemed wrong. It reminded her of anesthesia side effects when she'd had her wisdom teeth taken out, the winter just before Gramma Poe died and the nightmares came back with double-decker intensity.

God, don't think about that, either.

"Elder?" Daniel said.

Erik's response was immediate. "Yes, *lirai*?"

"There's some power there. She'd better be sealed, and quickly."

". . . yes, *lirai*."

Best of Bad Options

THERE WAS NO thaw in sight, though the weather forecast—and the male *lirai*—said more snow was coming. The freezing rain had made the normals miserable, and running patrol in the cold wasn't anything Erik would have looked forward to even if the temperature made little difference once you had a mark. Outside in the hall another trio was on duty, in case of incursion or if Liv took it into her head to go for a walk.

Which didn't seem likely, even if she was handling this far better than Erik ever dreamed possible.

"He's right, you know." Dakshi stretched, a long lithe movement, and dropped across the grey linen couch their *lirai* said she liked so much.

Erik didn't think she was being quite honest, but if it pleased her to try a little misdirection, so be it. "Hm?" He leaned against the bedroom door, his shoulders warm against the baffle, and hoped little brother wasn't about to start making good sense.

"She should be sealed." Robert, standing at ease near the fireplace, was paging through a glossy magazine. His weapons harness, old-fashioned but evidently nothing he felt the need to update, was soundless as he rolled one shoulder, then the other, settling himself for an article. He kept asking Liv about her clothing preferences, obviously used to more fashionable *lirai*. "To at least one of her primary trio. As a bare minimum." The fire, eating well-seasoned wood, sang its soft, popping, crackling song.

At least she seemed to like that, so they made sure there was always a blaze going. Flame was mortal, but it could still drive away the shadowbeasts.

"When she settles in, she'll choose." Erik glanced at the windows. No help there, only the failing light of a winter afternoon. If there was something to fight, he could have put an end to the whole conversation.

"It's dangerous." Dakshi might look like a lounging feline, but he was tense and ready. Both of them were. They were solid soldiers, and even if Robert didn't quite have Ignatius's dry humor and Dak didn't have Jake's fey battle-rage, they were at least both Sons, very good at mayhem and ready to defend his *lirai* to the death.

She needed another permanent trio. She made absolutely no move to select them, though Erik had begun sounding her out for preferences. Liv needed time, and he would give it to her.

As much as she needed. As much as was possible.

"Everything's dangerous." The conversation was getting old, fast, and the fact that it happened just about every time Liv went to bed wore on his nerves. "Especially for *lirai*."

"You're trying to protect her." Robert turned a page. The fire added counterpoint, a soft pop and a shower of sparks.

"Aren't we supposed to?" *And I'm getting tired of chewing this same old meat. Either find a different subject or shut the fuck up.*

He couldn't say it, but they could probably tell his temper was wearing thin. Not that it mattered; nobody cared what *he* thought.

"She's safer sealed." One dark eye peered past the edge of the magazine, and Erik realized Robert was pushing, ever so gently. Ever so delicately, as if Erik himself was a *lirai*.

His shoulders were full of iron sparring rods; the muscles along his spine had transformed as well. "It's not enough that we're criminals and marked by *him*, but we have to be rapists as well?"

For a moment, even he couldn't quite believe he'd said it so baldly. It wasn't like the familiar corralling of Jake's enthusiasm; this was a *Father.*

"It's not like that," Dakshi said, but he'd paled a few shades. He rubbed at his left wrist; the more active the temple, the more active the mark, and the brief moments of respite from a *lirai*'s presence sometimes made its throbbing worse by contrast. It did no good to wonder what form the whispers took for another man, but sometimes it was impossible not to. "It really isn't."

No, it wasn't. But for Erik, it was close enough. Maybe he was old-fashioned, or more modern—given male behavior through the ages, he couldn't decide.

There was so little a Son could take a stand on. He was just fine with this one.

"You've been out of touch for a decade at least." Robert's tone couldn't possibly be any drier or more academic, but Erik got the sense the tall, spare, iron-haired man was choosing his words with care—and the spaces between them, too. "For whatever reason. Things have changed, Elder."

"Our lord Daniel's the oldest *lirai* on this continent." Dakshi kept

Erik in his peripheral vision, dropping his hands onto his chest and interlacing his fingers. "If he says—"

"She needs time," Erik said, softly, but each word held an edge. They were having trouble pinpointing just who Islington's control liaison had been; records were damaged and the sudden coordinated attacks ten years ago had kept everyone too busy.

There were no records of Islington's funding requests, requisition shipments, or anything else—even the recent purchases for their found potential. The money had to come from *somewhere*, but . . .

"My son." Robert matched Erik's quiet—a good strategy. "Every *lirai* we've lost in the last eight years was unsealed. We don't know if *he* is responsible for it, or if it's simply chance."

Erik was very still. "Every one?"

"I thought you knew." Dakshi sighed, settling back into feline stillness. "I hate to say it, but maybe communications to your temple weren't simply cut, big bro. In any case, you're clean, and the best thing you can do is seal her. Just in case."

Don't you think I've considered as much? Erik's jaw had turned to iron too, his teeth aching. All of him was metal, cold and brittle. "How many times am I going to have to betray her?"

The answer, of course, was *as many times as necessary, to keep her safe*. Thankfully, neither of them said it aloud.

"Your dedication isn't in question, Elder." Robert turned another page. Ignatius had never sounded this kindly, even in the first few days at Islington. "Neither is your capability."

At least a few sessions in the sparring room had taught his fellow Sons to respect Erik's professionalism, not to mention his reflexes. They didn't quite look at him sidelong—if a *lirai* said you were clear, you were clear—but a man was an unknown quantity until you fought him.

Always.

Another bad idea occurred to Erik, tiptoeing velvet-shod through his head. Islington was a smallish city, yes—but he and Jake hadn't come across any potentials before Liv Stellack. Not a single one, on endless nights of patrol.

Ten years was a long time for treachery to ripen, but the Mad God was immortal and his Sons, unless they met a horrifically violent end in battle, shared a measure of that longevity.

Dakshi was still eyeing him. "Can we at least consider another full trio for her? If she won't choose, why can't we just nominate?"

"It's an excellent idea," Robert weighed in. "She's uncomfortable with her own power, but every *lirai* begins there. More amplifiers, more force, but . . ."

"But she's safer that way," Erik said heavily, and knew he wasn't just agreeing to selecting another trio. They were deferring to his primacy because he'd found her first and known her longest, but that wouldn't last forever.

Especially if one of the others caught her eye. Lonely and vulnerable, in freefall with normality snatched from underfoot and thrust into high-danger situations, Liv would naturally look for some comfort.

It would be . . . easy, to take advantage. He could even tell himself it was the right, the safest thing to do. But the tiny voice of his conscience, the only part of his mental landscape the Mad God hadn't managed to crack, was still speaking loud and clear.

Would it be better if it stopped? Or worse?

"That is the goal," Robert said. "Our overarching, our only goal."

Dakshi's dark eyes hooded, sleepy and thoughtful. "I thought it was fighting *him*."

"Try doing that without the Dreamers." Erik tipped his head, rested the back of his skull against the door, the baffling-sorcery tingling pleasantly on his slowly relaxing shoulders.

Once a man decided, all that remained was to perform. And Erik found, with some relief, that he was still going to stick with his conscience, come what may.

HER SCREAM ENDED on a throat-cut gurgle, and if there was anything that put a cold knife in his guts, it was the thought that something had breached this temple too, slithered through a window, and found its way to her.

The bedroom was dark except for a soft edge of pale gold from the bathroom nightlight, and he ripped aside navy velvet curtains as Dakshi headed for the window, guns drawn. Robert, his sword a glimmering bar, halted near the door, ready to move in any direction.

Liv fought—clawing, kicking, biting—and managed to elbow him on the cheek before he could pin her, grab her wrists, and immobilize her slight frame. The resident chefs apparently couldn't tempt her with haute cuisine, and she'd lost some weight since arrival.

It was a bad sign, and this was another one. Every night, in the dim dead reaches of deep darkness, the nightmares came.

By the time he had her wrestled into stillness she was awake, tears slicking her cheeks and her ribs heaving with deep, hopeless moans. She shuddered like a trapped animal, and he heard his own voice, soft and soothing—or as soothing as a growl from a Son could be.

"Shhh, beautiful. It's all right, I'm here. *We're* here. It's a nightmare, just a bad dream."

Liv went limp. He gathered her up, glanced at the window. Dakshi's guns were gone; he was reinforcing the invisible shimmer of sorcerous protection on glass, metal, and stone. Soft orange snowlight, the ground reflecting the city's electric stain, feathered his dark hair, and his back was wide open, exposed to the room while he concentrated.

It was an unintentional compliment.

Robert was still in the door, a sticklike figure with his signet giving a single harsh glitter, his sword dipping slightly as he decided, increment by increment, there was nothing to fight.

"The door," she whimpered. "The fucking *door*, my God, my God, *make it stop!*"

"It's stopped." Robert, with the snap of command that made a Father polishing the edge of both words. "It is done, *lirai*."

Silk moved. She liked the pajamas; they'd arrived in a plain white box with a small, exquisitely painted card from Sara. *Lirai* knew what others of their kind would need, it was axiomatic. Erik moved, getting his legs underneath him, and finally Liv settled against his chest, pushing a knifehilt out of the way so it didn't dig into her cheek. He propped his back against the headboard, wishing he could get his boots off the bed, and stroked her hair—but he didn't loosen his grasp otherwise, just in case the fear returned.

She couldn't hurt him, but she might do herself some damage.

Liv trembled, and Erik stroked her back with his fingertips. Low, soothing nonsense slid past his lips—*it's over, it was just a dream, it's fine, shhh, I'm here.*

He should have said *we're here*. He was part of a trio, he wasn't sealed, and yet he couldn't do it. "Just a dream," he repeated. "It can't hurt you. I'm here."

"What if it's . . ." She shuddered again. Her ribs stood out starkly under thin silk.

"*He* can't touch you, Liv. You're a Dreamer, you're immune. It's all right."

"You hear him all the time." She quieted, but the trembling didn't stop. "How do you fucking *stand* it?"

"Stubbornness, I suppose." Erik glanced up. Dakshi had turned from the window, regarding the bed with bright interest. Robert's sword vanished and he stepped inside, sweeping the door half-closed. It was standard procedure, but Erik wished they were both gone.

Oh, he could certainly do what they wanted. The persistent whispers would stop and he could settle into his work, a new lodestar glimmering on his horizon. She'd be safer.

And yet, he was even more selfish. He could dress it up like conscience or honor, but truth be told, he wanted her to agree because she *wanted* to, as if he was somehow special, as if he had somehow earned as much.

He was risking a *lirai* for some stupid, silly schoolboy idea.

"I'm all right." She pushed at his chest, and he could have kept her.

He could have done a lot more. But Erik slid aside, set his boots, and stood. He tucked her in, but when he would have drawn the bed's curtains, she shook her head. "It's too dark that way. You guys can go. Except . . ."

He waited.

"Erik can stay. If you want." She huddled against snowy pillows, her dark hair a river.

Dakshi nodded, shot Erik a triumphant glance, and retreated. Robert didn't linger, just shook his grey head and closed the door with a soft click.

Erik stood, his head down, at the bedside. His eyes closed, and the god whispered. This time the sibilants took on a sharper edge, singing of putting his hands around a slim throat and *squeezing*, and the welcome granted him by the Mad God's servants once he accomplished such a task.

I can give you much, the whispers said. *You know I can.*

Sons owned nothing but their knives. Everything else was a gift from the *lirai*, and the interest on that debt mounted daily. To those who pleased him a mad god could grant luxury, power, conquest.

He could give them the world.

"It's not like I haven't noticed," Liv said, finally. She swallowed, an audible click in a dry throat. "Jake told me about it, and Daniel, too. I know what you want."

Do you? If I told you, it might surprise you. "It's not that, Liv. It's what *you* want that matters."

"Daniel said they've been losing unsealed *lirai*." One of her arms slid from under the covers. He heard her fingers brush across Egyptian cotton, down comforter, heavy velvet. "For a long time. And I was dreaming about my mother. I think one of the monsters got her, Erik."

She needed sleep, not old traumas reopened. Erik settled himself a little more comfortably. "You should get some rest."

"What if they're right? I mean, I'd rather it was you than a . . . a stranger."

"They won't without your consent." Stubbornly, to make her understand. "I won't let them. You've already had enough, Liv." *It was for your protection, and I'm not sorry. But I'm not going to add to it.*

Not until I have to.

"But it'll stop the whispers." Her hand lay, outstretched and cupped. Was she hoping he'd reach for it? "For you."

"Yes." No point in lying. "That it would."

"Do you not like me?" She sounded wistful, now.

"That's not the problem."

"What is, then?" Just like a *lirai*, asking a question that sliced to the bone. The Fathers were ruthless, but the Dreamers were gentle.

Which only made the cut that much deeper.

I want to believe I'd have a shot if I wasn't just the best of a bunch of bad options. There it was, silly and selfish and stupid. Not to mention he could pretend to have a clean conscience, despite the god's tempting, taunting teasing inside his skull. "Maybe I like you too much, beautiful."

"That'd be a first." She snuggled back into the blankets and he could feel the relaxation, a pleasant bath of champagne bubbles over his skin.

His *lirai*. Sealed or not, whether she knew it or not, it didn't get much simpler. "When you're ready, Liv. When you're *sure*, not before. And if you choose someone else, fine. But I'm not going to let them force you. Not this way." *Not if I have a choice, all right? Let me be as good as I can.*

"Okay." She inhaled as if she wanted to say more, but let the breath out with a sigh.

He waited; she said nothing else. If she moved, or made another sound . . .

Her breathing deepened. She fell back into sleep's arms, that gentle solace denied Sons even if they achieved a simulacrum of it in frontier temples. With active *lirai* and an open Flame-mouth around, they didn't need a lot of rest.

It was a relief in some ways, but not in others.

He folded down, rested his elbows on the bed and his knees on pale hardwood. His fingers creaked as he clasped his hands tightly, rested his sweating forehead on them. It was almost like prayer, except he counted her breaths, one after another, and forced himself into utter stillness.

The others would be disappointed. The other *lirai* might be, too, and they'd be at Liv to do something, to choose. But for this night, he could give her a gift, like an *oneiros* made in the old way, wrenched jagged and bleeding from a terrible dry shore past the borders of the waking world and polished until it glowed.

His *lirai* slept, and if she dreamed again, it did not wake her.

Never Gets Old

LIKE EVERYTHING else, the armory here was a lot bigger than in the other temple. Liv looked longingly at the racks of guns, pretty much of every shape and size, and her palms were damp. "I don't see why we don't go armed."

"Earthly weapons are just distractions." Daniel's usual cheerfulness was muted, and his floppy hair was combed back and slicked down. He was all business, and instead of his usual superhero T-shirt and jeans, he was in unrelieved black. The effect was startling, and made him look a lot older. "We don't fight with physical force, that's for Sons. It's why this marriage works."

Oh, it's a marriage now? Outside, a crimson sunset throbbed on the western horizon and there was a dark line of cloud in the north, creeping closer by increments. Everyone was saying more snow was on the way, but so far the sky was clear and the nights were deep-frozen. "I'd feel a lot better if I had a gun," Liv muttered. "A knife. A spork. *Something.*"

"You don't need it." Daniel rolled his shoulders under a hip-length leather jacket very much like the ones the Sons wore, and glanced around the armory's beehive activity. Heavily muscled, quiet-stepping men signing out enough weaponry to start an insurrection, drawing ammunition, making short cryptic comments to each other and the guys behind the long, mirror-polished counter running the length of the room—everyone knew exactly what to do here except her. "Listen, Liv . . ."

"Hm?" *Wear something that makes you feel pretty,* Daniel had said, but Liv was damn sure a dress wasn't going to cut it for monster-fighting in subzero temperatures. She'd decided on practicality instead—the boots Erik got her, jeans, black long-sleeve thermal shirt, black merino sweater, a black woolen peacoat with gloves and a knit hat stuffed deep in the pockets.

"You're going to overheat in that. They'll keep you warm."

I'm sure they'd like to. She shrugged, trying not to think about Erik in the dark, holding her while the nightmares vibrated inside her skull. "You can always take layers off, you know."

"I guess." He glanced at the far end of the armory as if expecting another arrival. "Listen, we have to talk."

Oh, for God's sake. "Now?"

"Now's a good time." His hand made a small movement, like he wanted to brush her arm; it dropped back to his side. *Lirai* didn't like to be touched, they said, and Liv could understand; the hideous overwhelming noise of a city full of strangers *thinking* at high volume was absent in here, but she could well imagine physical contact with a normal person producing something like an internal feedback squeal. "You're still unsealed."

Liv contented herself with a neutral noise. Halfway down the room Erik was conferring with Robert, their heads together as Dakshi made various weapons disappear into his harness, the Younger Brother's coat over the counter—ready to be pressed into service as soon as its wearer was fully loaded.

"I'm told the elder you came in with is resistant to the idea. You've got to let go of . . . well, of the idea that it's something shameful." Daniel took a step closer, leaning in confidentially. Everything in his expression shouted *serious business.* "It's self-defense, and—"

"Do I get to talk about your love life if you get to talk about mine? Does it work like that?" Liv restrained the urge to fold her arms, sink her weight in one hip, and pin the guy with her mother's patented *Do Not Push It, Young Man* stare. She wished Mika was here to help her deal with this asshole, but then again . . . she didn't.

Thinking about any of her friends running across some of these monsters—the fungal-scarred spiders, the thin pale four-armed houndmasters, the tentacled horrors—made her stomach turn over hard and send sour heat crawling up her esophagus.

"It's not love, Liv. It's not even really sex, even if it replicates the mechanics. It's just something that has to be done, like going to the dentist or paying car insurance." Daniel sighed. "Erik's not doing you any favors by putting it off."

So you say. Liv's hands tingled. The urge to throw a punch was well-nigh irresistible; she'd never been a violent person, but dear God, she was beginning to see the attraction. Lou would have already been brawling at this point, Jada would have already verbally flayed someone, and what Mika would do didn't bear thinking about. "If I fucked him, would you leave me alone?"

"Liv." Now it was Daniel's patented patient tone, the one he took while Sara only got quieter and more withdrawn. "I understand. I held out against it for a long time, but then I lost two Sons to the whispers. I never want to lose another, and I don't want to see you lose one either."

Her irritation snuffed out, leaving only cold ashes. "What does that mean, *lost them to the whispers*?"

"It's not pretty." Daniel looked past her shoulder, probably at ebon-skinned River with his cornrow braids and rare, beautiful smile. "Both of them chose to . . . well, they did it to themselves, rather than hurt me like *he* wanted."

For a moment, perpetually cheerful Daniel looked almost haunted, the color draining from his coppery cheeks and his eyes widening.

Liv wanted to touch his shoulder now—just a soft brush, to let him know someone was listening—but if *she* didn't want to be handled, she couldn't inflict it on someone else. "I'm sorry." That put a different shine on things altogether.

Would Erik do that? Something to himself, rather than hurt her? Was that what the whispers wanted?

Funny, they talked about the Mad God all the time, but nobody mentioned Jesus. Her grandmother would have some thoughts about that; Gramma Poe had been Baptist through and through. Mom marrying a Catholic had been a Big Deal.

Not that it mattered in the end, with Dad dead in a car crash and Mom . . .

Unless he came in through the chimney, the detective told Gramma, while young Liv huddled on a carpeted staircase, watching solemnly despite all attempts to insulate her from the news while a victim's advocate tried to interest her in a stuffed toy.

There was no insulation—or distraction—from finding your mother torn to pieces in the living room. Ever.

"Me too." For a moment there was a shadow of deep age around Daniel's dark eyes. "It isn't fair and it isn't right, but it's what we have. And we make people safer every night." He stepped back, ran a critical eye down her outfit. "Are you sure that's what you're wearing? Sara goes in heels."

"I don't fight in heels." As if she'd ever fought at all, beyond a few playground tussles in elementary school. *Use your words*, everyone said. Girls weren't supposed to punch, kick, scream.

"They won't let your feet touch the ground much anyway." Daniel was clearly not in the mood for further emotional sharing. He rolled his shoulders again, stretched one side of his neck, then the other. "Sara's dealing with a new batch of trainees; it's good to have another *lirai* here so we can keep the city swept too."

"Trainees?" It was nice to have a chance at answers, even if she suspected her questions were amateur-silly. You had to start somewhere.

"Sons aren't born." Daniel brightened, glancing over her shoulder. "They're made."

"My lord." It was River, armed to the teeth and observing a careful distance from Liv. "We're almost ready. My lady." A single nod in her direction.

"Thank you, River." Daniel took a single step sideways, examining Liv's face. "Just remember, it's instinctive. You know what to do. Trust your Sons."

Except the ones who might want to hurt me, right? Liv nodded. Daniel looked like he might say more, but simply gave a tight smile, probably meant to be encouraging, and was whisked away on a stream of heavily armed men.

Liv found she was hugging herself, staring at the end of the armory where barred windows glowered, baleful crimson eyes.

The sun had almost set.

AN ICED-OVER city at night was beautiful, twinkling freeze-jewels clinging to concrete, glass, road, and window. Unfortunately, Daniel was right—she was too warm. Each Son was a living heater, invisible force passing through her in steampipe-lines from their proximity, and he was right about something else, too.

They barely let her boots touch the ground.

She started out liking it. In fact, for the first half hour or so it was flat-out *amazing*, a superhero dream of flying between lit-up spires, her hair barely stirred by cold, questing air. The Sons moved with the eerie flowing speed of travel in flying dreams; Erik carried her for a while, then Dakshi while others spread out in looping patterns, leaping from rooftops, streaking through alleys, running and jumping with graceful, incredible, unnatural authority. She was the middle of a moving flower, its petals dark streaks of Sons tearing through reality inside hard, invisible personal shells, and the strange thing wasn't how fast they were going, the sudden changes in direction, or the deep undeniable warmth.

No, the strangeness was how *natural* it felt. She remembered the nightmares, but her pleasanter dreams tiptoed back into memory as the Sons poured through downtown, a tide of unseen motion. Nobody looked up to see them on rooftops, silhouetted against the swiftly clouding sky; nobody peered into the dark throats of alleys, and even when they streaked alongside cars with jewel-glowing headlights, Liv felt invisible.

Best of all was spiraling up a tall granite-sided building, alternately squeezing her eyes shut against vertigo and staring in disbelief until Dakshi set her gently down on a shuttered observation deck, carefully tucked away from a security camera's glassy eye. She wouldn't have even noticed the camera if he hadn't pointed at it with a quick smile before turning to gaze at the glimmering city as Erik hopped blithely over the railing and skidded to a stop next to her.

"My God," Liv whispered.

It spread beneath them, a wonderland of snow, headlights, taillights, streetlights, golden windows behind which human lives were proceeding at their usual pace. Even at this hour there was plenty of activity; an ambulance's mournful cry echoed through concrete canyons somewhere in the middle distance.

"Yeah." Dakshi gazed over the railing, his short dark hair teased by a strong cold breeze which died before it could reach her. "Never gets old."

Erik drifted closer. "Everyone's in position." His shoulders were tense. "See if you can feel anything wrong down there, Liv. Just close your eyes and reach out."

All you have to do is let it happen, Daniel said in the sparring room. Normally when a man said that Liv wasn't inclined to go along.

At all.

But Erik was looking at her, and he obviously believed she could do this, even if the hideous roaring pressure of so many normal, thinking people lurked just outside a small sphere of silent peace. The sound retreated all the way inside the temple, but out here she could feel it just beyond the fence of Sons, their net keeping her from drowning in an abyss of lives crowded together, a paved warren crammed to the brim.

So Liv closed her eyes and gasped again, because the lights didn't go away. They simply changed color and location. A thick, dense field of stars surrounded her, the bright ones trembling with voiceless cries.

It's people. Every one of those is a person. Except those, they're . . . other things? Maybe?

A swift, painless internal tug, a sensation of dream-falling arrested just before striking the ground by lunging into wakefulness, and Liv stiffened. Erik's arm was an iron bar around her waist, and they were moving again. Overlapping rings of force poured through the Sons, and she felt Daniel in the distance like thunder on the plains during a road trip the summer after her senior year in high school, outracing a storm on arrow-straight roads reaching for the horizon.

How did the other *lirai* stand it? Her inner vision expanded with breathtaking force, sonar rings meeting and melding, dead spots where the Sons fell upon pieces of pulsating, clawed *wrongness.* She felt the spots of bloodthirsty foul corruption, the breath in the Sons' lungs, foxfire edging their crystalline knives and the broadswords Fathers carried, the Younger Brothers choosing their shots carefully while a cloak of silence ate the sounds of bullets exploding free.

More than knife, sword, or firearm, warm golden power with rain-bow-dappled edges raced through the Sons, multiplying as it leapt from man to man, striking a nest of tentacled horrors in the basement of an apartment building, falling on the backs of lean pale hounds with their rows of sharkteeth dripping rank diseased foam, blaze-blinding the crimson-bunched eyes of scuttling horrors bearing only the vaguest relation to arachnids despite their jointed legs and pinch-waisted thor-axes. Those eyes popped and oozed under the light's assault while the things screeched and the Sons fell upon them, wading through thin stinking ichor, cleaning nest after nest.

There's so many, she thought, and the consciousness of being in so many different places at once, pulled and pushed in a thousand directions, would have been terrifying if she'd had any way of struggling against it.

It went on and on. Battles fought in corners, in blind trash-choked alleys, under deserted highway bridges, on quiet streets between trim, closed-up homes, on the roofs of apartment buildings.

All that time, not a single mortal gaze was attracted. A knife-cold wind poured through concrete gulches, stinging Liv's cheeks, and she sagged in Erik's arms.

She hadn't even realized he was holding her; the motion was jarring, disrupting her trance. For a moment the giant, pounding-surf roar of the city's mortal minds poured through her, a butterfly transfixed on a pin.

Liv bent in half, retching. Erik's hand was flat on her back, warm and sure. The cold vanished, and so did the terrifying sensation of fragmenting, her *self* splintered into thousands of blinking, breathing, fighting pieces.

"Easy," Erik said. There was an odd chiming sound, a muffled thumping. "Easy, beautiful. Just breathe."

The thumping was her pulse, high and wild. The chiming was metal against something sharp, and they were moving again, acceleration pressing against her midsection. Someone yelled—it was Robert, a short coughing cry she shouldn't have been able to recognize except she'd been *in* him a few moments before, a stringed instrument's long tone passing through an amplifier's dry throat.

More sounds—crunching, wet gristle-snapping, liquid spraying. The sense of absolute, sickmaking *wrongness* crested; the monsters were close.

And it was pretty likely they were pissed, too.

"They're behind us," Dakshi snapped. "Call everyone back!"

"She might not be able to." Robert gasped at the end of the sentence. "But they're on their way, they'll feel her distress. Well?"

Yeah, distress isn't the word for this. Liv struggled to breathe, shuddering. The monsters had found them, and everything in her screamed *get out of here, get away*, the blind imperative to run denied by the arms trapping her.

"They're closing in," Erik said. "Move. Move *now.*"

The world turned over, wind rushing past her ears. The thumping receded, her heart finally deciding to go about its business without alerting her to each squeeze. Liv coughed, her own throat scorch-hot as Robert's, the rest of her pulled apart and jammed back together wrong.

There you are. A cold lipless voice squirmed under the skin of the world, reaching for the small struggling spark that was her invisible, barely conscious self. ***Little thief. Did you think to take my Sons from me?***

She had wondered how they knew the Mad God's name. Now Liv Stellack knew it too, and she began to scream like a small animal in an iron trap, bleeding to death while the hunter watched.

And while he stared, he *laughed.*

The Infinite Wisdom

"THEY WENT RIGHT for her." Dakshi hissed as his fingers probed a bloody slice on his upper arm. Normally a Son's flesh expelled anything foreign—gravel, toxins, bullets, fragments—but you could help it along with a squeeze or two, especially if you didn't want the thick tarry venom from hair-thin *ghola* darts to eat at skin and muscle until it was neutralized. "I hate those bristly little fucks."

Robert's eyes were half-closed, and his ribs made small creaking sounds as they popped back into place, slivers of bone easing back together. The Father sucked in a harsh breath, blinked, and the faraway quality of his gaze told how much it hurt. The pain didn't come from the bone itself, but the sleeve of richly vascularized tissue around it; Erik hated having his ribs broken.

It was oddly familiar—a Younger Brother bitching, a Father too pained and wary to let more than a sigh escape, and an Elder Brother caught in the middle, the fulcrum that made the whole thing stable. "The *ghola* were riding the *leng*-spiders." He shook his head, almost shivering as cleansing sorcery crackled down his arms and legs. "Never seen that before." *At least, not in this world.*

"They come from the same place." Dakshi glanced at the bedroom door. Liv was sedated; she hadn't stopped screaming until Sara pushed the plunger of a hypodermic down, a few cc's of welcome oblivion a *lirai*'s body wouldn't burn off as a matter of course entering dark venuous hallways. "But I haven't seen them do this before either."

"It's as if they can tell she's unsealed." Robert finally straightened, and his blood-stiffened shirt flapped. "I wouldn't care to do that again."

That makes you sane. Or at least, close to it. Erik made a noncommittal noise; the bedroom door opened and Sara stepped out, the edge of her long multicolored broomstick skirt fluttering on a purely personal breeze. Two elders from her personal trios flanked her, the brunet tall and lean, the blond almost Erik's size.

"She's resting," the *lirai* said, and every Son in the room snapped to attention. "You're the elder she came in with?"

"Yes, ma—my lady." He corrected himself midway, since this was an older temple and the traditional ways were absolutely clinging to life. Erik was about to add his name and numerator, too, since he didn't know what the hell else to do when a *lirai* addressed him directly.

Unless, of course, it was Liv.

"This may be a silly question." The *lirai* halted, her skirt swirling and one of the tight leather bodices she favored, laced over a linen shirt that could have been made from a Renaissance pattern given its sleeves, alive with subtle stampwork. "But was there any indication before you left your previous temple that *he* has any significant interest in her personally?"

"No, my lady." Erik forced his shoulders back, settling into parade rest with something close to relief. At least this Dreamer knew how to handle his kind. "We found her by accident during city sweeps, my younger and I."

"A frontline temple marked dead but somehow still surviving, speaking to a Control somewhere, receiving directions not to move her. And your younger called in after the attack, but has not appeared since." Sara folded her arms and tapped a well-manicured finger thoughtfully against her linen sleeve. "It's all very odd."

If that were all, I'd call it good. Not really *good* since losing Jake was an unpleasant thought, but if a Younger Brother had arrived at another temple with a story to tell, the Sons there—not to mention the *lirai*—should have been all over the airwaves asking questions and looking for a lost potential. "It was odd before that, ma—I mean, my lady. We just didn't know it."

"*We* being . . .?"

"My younger and me, my lady." Erik found his hands clasped behind his back, his chin level but his gaze down. "We ran sweeps while our Father stayed in the temple. It was just easier that way. He hadn't left the walls for a long while, and the night we brought her home . . ." He was starting the story in the middle, and mucking up any chance he had to be truly heard. What could he offer but a mass of inchoate suspicions? "It was the first time either of us had seen a potential since training at Belmont. And Control didn't want to move her until after the solstice. We figured, you know, orders. And Father knew what he was doing."

"You didn't see a single potential all that time?" Sara spoke slowly, but he was willing to bet not a lot escaped her methodical calm. "And you were in Islington for how long?"

"Since '74, my lady."

"You're right. That *is* strange." Sara studied him from top to toe, a thorough but benevolent inspection. "Daniel's told you about unsealed *lirai* being at risk?"

"Yes, my lady." Erik debated tacking on the fact that other Sons had, too, and decided that if the *lirai* wanted to know, she'd ask.

Keeping his mouth from running was always an elder's best strategy.

"And you haven't . . ." Delicately, she trailed off.

"No, my lady."

Sara clasped her hands. "Why not?"

"I was trained that consent matters, my lady. Especially in modern times." Erik's cheeks were hot. You couldn't be angry at a *lirai*. Maybe he was just embarrassed. "Any order to the contrary didn't reach us in Islington."

"Commendable, if not very effective." Sara's gaze was very much a *lirai*'s, dark with thoughts you could only guess at moving behind a screen, sad and well aware of the price of her gifts. Soon Liv would look like that, too, though she probably wouldn't dress like the other woman. He almost wished she would make another list of things for the Sons to run and fetch. It would be better than her fierce, fragile determination to fight. "Do you need a direct order?"

Erik's lungs ached. He inhaled, and the fire in his cheeks was almost nuclear-hot. "Is that an order you'd give?" A heartbeat's pause. "My lady?" he added, an afterthought.

"God's wounds," the Dreamer said, softly. "I hope not."

The blond elder was staring daggers at Erik; the dark one's hand was on his *lirai*'s shoulder, offering comfort—if there was any to be found. One of them probably had the hypo, and the queasy sensation that went through Erik when he thought of a needle piercing his own *lirai*'s skin mixed with the heat suffusing his face and the tension in his shoulders.

There wasn't a scratch on him from the night's games, because he'd been carrying Liv. And it was lucky that there had been other trios relatively close to the Pangborn building clearing out a nest of *taik* flowers in the depths of a parking garage. They'd dropped their work and streaked back for the *lirai* as soon as they realized something was amiss, arriving just as Dak and Robert were almost overwhelmed.

It did indeed seem like the Mad God had it in for Liv personally. Maybe he—or one of his subordinates—had figured out something that made potentials and unsealed *lirai* even more vulnerable? Innovation wasn't confined solely to mortals.

It was a chilling thought.

Finally, Sara shook her head. "This will not end well," she said, quietly. "I gave up the hope of being better than what we fight long ago. I've settled for being fractionally less malignant, and it's worked. Sort of. But I'm telling you, Elder, *this will not end well.*"

Don't you think I know? Either he disobeyed his conscience or he was responsible for endangering his *lirai.* It was a no-win situation, as usual. "I'm doing all I can, my lady."

"I know. We all are." Her sigh, soft and impatient, brushed every surface in the *liraim.* "All right, you three. Hold still."

Sara's eyes half-lidded. The pulse ran through them all, its touch far lighter than Liv's, and though you weren't supposed to, Erik thought he preferred his *lirai*'s directness to this one's flowery, ornate curlicues. Nevertheless, the heat was welcome and his weariness vanished; both Dakshi and Robert regained their color and stood a little straighter, all bruises gone, scrapes sealed, and all bones whole again.

"There." She set off for the door, her elders flanking her, and paused, her profile from some ancient Mediterranean coin. "Erik, is it?"

"Yes, my lady."

"If you had to guess, which would you suspect?" Her mouth turned down slightly, bitterly; she didn't like asking this question any more than he would enjoy answering it. "Your Father, or your Younger Brother?"

"I'd suspect myself before either of them, my lady."

"Charitable of you," she murmured. "And short-sighted. Considering that you've been cleared and your Younger Brother called what was no doubt the last dropline he had a number for."

"Which I'm told was more than a decade old. My lady." It couldn't irk him that she would presume to judge either Ignatius *or* Jake. He'd done so himself, and arrived at a few unpalatable conclusions. "And our Father was in touch with Control, or something acting like Control, for a long time."

Still, Erik was a stupid Elder, not the sharpest knife in the drawer, the dim bulb on the marquee sign. Jake would have a few other terms to add, too, and he'd be at Erik's shoulder, solidly behind his big brother.

Or would he?

"That's true, I suppose. But not a single potential in Islington, all that while?" Her head turned slightly; she met his gaze, and he read exactly the thought he'd arrived at his first night here, lying semiconscious in the dormitory and waiting for the echoes of Daniel's examination riffling through his brain like a card index to stop ricocheting.

"Not one my Younger Brother and I found, my lady." In other words, there was nothing else for him to say. The implications were plain as paint; it didn't help that Ignatius was probably dead under a tide of goatmen and unable to answer questions. This *lirai* was checking all control liaisons in the Truth Chamber, but it was slow work along with examining trainees and candidates. Daniel was occupied with sweeps, and Liv soon would be too.

Sara nodded before fluttering from the sitting room, no doubt eager for the comfort of her own *liraim*. How long would it be before Liv felt the same way? Before she understood, more than intellectually, the meaning of *refuge*?

Dakshi let out a long low sibilant sound that wasn't quite a whistle. He was looking at Robert, who shrugged slightly as the door closed. Both of them would have to visit their cells along the hallway for fresh clothes. And maybe to rinse themselves; cleansing sorcery got the grime off, sure, but sometimes a man liked scrubbing.

Especially as an antidote to thinking.

"What do you make of that?" Dakshi persisted, since Robert was Father-silent, clearly considering verbal analysis superfluous.

"I think she can guess who the traitor in my temple was. *If* that's where the treachery lies and it's not with a control liaison burrowed in like a tick somewhere, possibly doing a decade's worth of damage." Erik stared at the bedroom door, its semipermanent, invisible baffle folded aside and the *lirai* behind it deep in the grasp of chemical sleep. "And she agrees with you and Father, so don't repeat yourself. I don't want to hear it."

"Yessir," Dakshi mumbled, and a knock on the sitting-room door was a replacement trio, stepping in so the primaries could all change and clean up.

Erik, however, strode for the bedroom. Dakshi, thankfully, said nothing. Robert merely shook his head and shooed the younger man out. Maybe both of them were thinking he intended to seal her while she was out cold.

It was enough to make a man want to smash a few windows. But Erik had some thinking to do, and he'd never have a better time.

Besides, he didn't think it would take very long for the treachery to be revealed in all its fetid glory. Especially now that Daniel, in the infinite wisdom of a *lirai*, had waved Liv before the Mad God like a sequined cape in front of a very angry bull.

SHE SLEPT THROUGH dawn, past noon, and into the short dusk of yet another winter night. The sky dropped, turned depthless, and flakes began to whirl down as the sun, busybody that it was, went westward to pursue other business. Erik stayed at her bedside, counting her breaths and thinking things through.

By the time she stirred, restless and with an edge of metallic burning to her scent as her body metabolized the last of whatever Sara had administered, he was nowhere nearer a plan.

But he still knew what was going to happen.

A True Lirai

HER MOUTH WAS full of cotton. So was her head. But the hideous laughter was gone, and so was the cold, and everything except the need to pee—of course—and a deep emptiness in her midsection.

It had been a while since she'd been actually hungry.

Liv pushed herself up on her elbows. There was a dark shadow near the window, and she might have been frightened—or, at the very least, unnerved—if she didn't immediately know what it was.

Or, more precisely, *who*. The *oneiros* gleamed; Liv managed to prop herself semi-upright, her head a bowling ball balanced on a dried cornstalk, and rubbed at her eyes as soon as her hands were free. "Ugh." Her voice had been dragged through a gravel pit, and the rest of her felt the same. "Do you usually get a hangover after a night like that?"

"It was your first." Erik, his arms folded, barely moved. He just turned his head slightly so she knew he was listening. "Most *lirai* scream and throw up after theirs. You got the full package."

"Is that what it's called? Lucky me." She tested her arms, her legs. Everything seemed in working order, and she supposed her bladder was working too because it hadn't opened the floodgates, so to speak. "God. I never felt this bad even in college, and that's saying something."

"Sara had to come. She gave you a sedative." Erik's tone was dead level. "They were waiting for us to bring you out, you know."

Was that what happened? She didn't want to ask. Liv slid her feet free of blankets, dangled them off the bed. Next came standing up. She'd been doing it since she was a toddler; it should be no damn problem at all. "Lucky me."

He let her stagger to the bathroom under her own power, thank God. She even took the time to brush her teeth, since her mouth tasted like something dead. Several pounds lighter and much more clear-headed, she swept open the door to the bedroom again and almost couldn't see him in the deep shadows despite the necklace's soft glow.

Maybe it was camouflage, or that eerie stillness. Sorcery.

Or maybe he was just part of the furniture now. An appliance, an appurtenance like the rest of this luxurious, pamper-soft deathtrap. "I don't like it very much here." She didn't even have to ask who'd put her in pajamas. Getting dressed while knocked out was kind of par for the course nowadays. "But I suppose you'd say it doesn't matter."

"I'd say *at least you're safe here.*" Erik still didn't move. "But . . ."

The pause brought Liv up short. She didn't need breakfast—or maybe it was dinner, an unanswerable question like how many walls really made a prison cell—for her brain to work, really.

Although she would have liked it. Still, her stomach did a slow roll as well as gurgled, and good luck eating anything now. "But you don't think so."

"They came right for you, Liv. Even Dakshi noticed. And you were screaming." Now he moved, shoulders rolling as if settling his weapons, stretching his neck to one side, then the other. "About *him.*"

Is that what happened? She shuddered. "Is that usual?"

"No." He all but bit the end of the word off.

She'd never seen him truly angry before. It was partly gratifying, partly terrifying, and all new. She didn't need those new senses—ESP or whatever crap the weird rainbow fire had done to her—to feel it. No, his rage circled the room like a restless panther, just looking for something to sink tooth or claw into.

New wasn't the word for those senses, though. The longer this went on, the more inevitable getting knocked unconscious and carried off by monster hunters seemed. It had all been there from the beginning; even Gramma Poe wouldn't be surprised.

You got a bit of intuition to you, just like your mama.

"My mother was killed by a monster," Liv heard herself say, dully. "My father died in a car accident when I was six, and when I was ten my mother . . . well, I spent the night at my grandmother's. I shouldn't have, it was a school night. But Mom said yes when I asked, and I've always thought she maybe . . ." She shuddered. "Anyway, everything was locked up. All the security dowels in the windows and the patio door were there. It should have been impossible. Unless the . . . the killer had a key, they said, or unless he came down the chimney." Liv didn't want to say the next part; it curdled in her throat, hot and bitter. "She was torn apart."

She wasn't telling the story right, but she didn't need to, and in any case, she suspected she wasn't able to explain it rationally. Who could explain finding their mother in bite-size bloody bits spread over a living room of to-order furniture you'd helped her put together? *My little mechanic*, Mom used to call her. *Make a list, check it twice, huh, Livvie?*

The pajamas did nothing against the cold. Oh, it was nice and toasty in here, and so warm she really didn't need the blankets. Still, Liv shivered. "I lived with my grandparents after that," she continued, inadequately. "Mom was . . . it tore her into *pieces,* Erik. You know of anything that does that?"

He turned, slow and fluid. His eyes were mere gleams in the dimness, answering the *oneiros*'s glow, and the window behind him was full of falling snow.

She was beginning to hate winter.

"Some things," Erik said, quietly. "Let me guess. Your mom was special."

"Oh yeah." Every little girl's mother was special, though. "She knew things before they happened, sometimes. She could tell where lost things had ended up most of the time. Gramma joked about it until she was killed, then all she ever said was *don't let anyone know what you know.* Words to live by, right?"

"And you had bad dreams. All your life." He didn't sound surprised. The tone of quiet, flat confirmation was either comforting as all get-out or terrifying as hell.

"Yeah. So did Mom." Liv found she was hugging herself again, cupping her elbows in her palms, tense as a violin string. "*Nightmares like your mother*, Gramma said."

"She might've been a potential, Liv. Or not. Sometimes psychics aren't *lirai*, they're just tuned in."

"That makes it even worse." In fact, it made Liv guilty as fuck, because she'd asked to go to Gramma Poe's. *I hate school,* she'd moaned. *Don't make me.*

A therapist would call it the result of trauma, and adult Liv—not to mention her psych degree—*knew* no eight-year-old was responsible for a parent's murder. Irrational as it was, though, the guilt wouldn't go away.

Ever.

"I know." And the way he said it made it seem like Erik did, in fact, know. "Because you can't help but wonder if the thing was after you."

Oh, God. He understood far more than she gave him credit for. It was an uncomfortable feeling, to say the least. "Maybe you should just let them have me, Erik."

Tiny blue lights flashed deep in his pupils, clearly visible in the gloom. "That's not an option."

"Who are you really trying to save?" It felt eerily inevitable to be standing in a dark bedroom having this lunatic conversation with an armed monster hunter twice her size, too.

Go figure.

"Spoken like a true *lirai*." At least the tight, taut misery was gone from his voice. He even sounded a little amused, if you listened closely.

If you knew him.

"I mean it, Erik," she persisted. "Who? Me or yourself? Or maybe Jake. You knew him a lot longer."

"Jake's probably dead."

"Great." They kept bugging her to eat, but with conversations like this, no wonder she couldn't even choke down dry toast for breakfast. "Another corpse I'm responsible for."

"Not you, Liv." A quiet, patient correction. "*Him*."

"I used to think it was funny. The way you say *him* and it's immediately . . . like, I know you're not talking about the mailman. So to speak." She was doing the nervous-babbling thing; it didn't help that she . . . well, she *liked* Erik. It might have just been trauma bonding, but as long as Liv was telling some truths tonight, she might as well admit a few to herself. "Jake said it the same way. So did Ignatius."

"Looks like *he*'s very interested in you, beautiful." Erik went still again, but the fury returned, teasing at her skin with wirebrush strokes. Not enough to hurt, just . . . prickly. "I don't have to tell you that's a bad sign."

"And I'm supposed to fall into bed with one of you strapping young lads to get it all sorted out?" The *oneiros* flashed; Liv squeezed herself even more tightly. Mika would have heard the sarcasm in her tone and known to duck for cover.

Was Mika all right? Were her friends going about their lives, blissfully unaware of mad gods and monsters in the dark?

Christ, I hope so.

"I told you, not until you want to." Erik made a single restless movement, more sensed than seen. "But they're right, Liv. Lady Sara is taking care of trainees and examinations; that's work you'd like even less than city sweeps."

Lady Sara. "Great." It seemed impossible that either of the other *lirai* had ever been this scared, or this uncertain. Liv knew it was possible, true, but her overworked imagination just couldn't serve up a mental image, for once. "Tossing me right out the window is sounding better all the time."

"Please don't joke about that."

Who's joking? "Humor helps me get a handle on things, you know."

"I know." The tiny blue glimmers in his eyes had vanished, and now he was just a patch of deeper shadow. "But please, Liv, *don't.*"

The way he said it threatened to make her hands shake even more, so Liv hugged herself tighter, like a penitent schoolgirl in the principal's office. "Okay. I'm sorry."

"You don't have to be."

"What do I have to do, then, Erik?" She was a half-step away from unloading on him, she realized, just because she was scared. "Because I've gotta tell you, I'm fresh out of ideas. Not that I had too many to begin with ever since I got kidnapped."

No. This feeling wasn't simply *scared.* It was flat-out *terrified.*

"I don't have ideas, Liv. My job's to keep you alive. Or die in your place, if need be. That's all."

"Well, that's a shitty job description." Her voice rose; she couldn't help herself.

There was a faint creak of leather. Maybe he'd shrugged, spreading his hands, maybe it was just an uneasy shifting of his weight. "It's all I've got."

"So what do we do? I mean me-and-you, Erik, because I have to say I don't trust anyone here."

"You should trust them more than me."

"Don't say shit like that, all right? Just . . . oh, for *God's* sake." She groped for patience, found none. She was either petrified out of her head or boiling with irritation for weeks now, with no middle ground. The whipsawing back and forth could give you ulcers—or give an otherwise reasonable person a complete goddamn nervous breakdown.

There was no telling what she might have said next if a sudden chill hadn't slid down her back, icy claws trailing over shrinking, goose-pimpled skin.

Erik's chin rose. He cocked his head, listening.

"You feel that too?" she whispered, stupidly.

"Of course." And he nodded, as if he'd expected it. Maybe he even had. "Do you really trust me, Liv?"

I swear to God . . . No threat or obscenity seemed even halfway strong enough. "If you tell me not to *one more time—*"

For once, he interrupted her. "No, not that. I just don't want you where anyone can find you, and it'll be easier if you're not fighting me."

"Would it matter? If I fought, I mean."

"I'm trying, Liv."

He didn't say for what, but she knew—he was trying, in his own way, to be decent.

"I know." And, because she was silly and stupid and Stockholm-syndromed to the max, Liv exhaled, hard, and dropped her trembling hands. She forced her chin up, and tried her best Mika-on-a-mission impression. "Well, where are we going?"

It came again, that shiver, and a sharp pain lanced between her temples. But Liv was saved the trouble of crying out or flinching, because Erik blurred across the dark emptiness between them and she was scooped up, once more, as if she weighed nothing.

"The last place anyone'll look for a *lirai* during an attack," he said. "Hold tight."

Bastard Tactics

"Are you sure this is a good idea?" Dakshi was clearly unconvinced, but he still covered Erik's six. It was Robert he worried about, but the Father simply nodded and followed, probably because Liv had put the problem to him with her characteristic pizazz.

Lead, follow, or get the hell out of the way, sir. Pick one in the next two seconds, and I'm telling you, you're not leading, because Erik's in charge.

Maybe it was her psychology degree.

The only problem came when he handed her over to Dakshi, who accepted a *lirai*'s slight weight with alacrity but a bit of confusion. "We just . . . wait?"

"Until I come to get you. No one else."

"Who precisely in this temple do you suspect, Erik?" Robert wanted to know. "You think that a control liaison—"

"Wait a second." Liv began to wriggle. "I didn't sign up for—"

"Nobody," Erik said. "It's someone outside, and he'll know where a *lirai*'s likely to be." *We're going to have to be sneaky*, he'd told Jake.

Just because Erik was an Elder Brother, that didn't mean he'd given up on misdirection, or what the Father who trained them in third-year advanced close combat called *bastard tactics.*

As in, the trick to being effective is being a right bloody bastard about it.

Sometimes Erik wondered what happened to old Marcus. He'd been harsh, true—but his students usually survived their marks.

"*And waiting in the tower he shall find only death.*" Robert's smile, like Ignatius's, was dry, precise, and though infrequent, quite warm. "Go. We shall do very well here."

"Wait. Wait just a minute. *Erik*!" Liv was still struggling when Dakshi carried her through the massive ironbound doors.

Past those slabs of metal were stone spiral stairs and bright variegated golden light playing gently over every edge, shading into rainbows as it moved. This Flame-mouth was active and open, providing strength to any full *lirai* within range, and with Dak and Robert nearby she was as safe as it was possible to be.

Erik heard the bar settle into its brackets on the other side of the door. He whirled and took off, streaking through hallways now full of running feet and crisp, half-heard orders, information passed along in short bursts.

And the snarling, as creatures from dreaming's more toxic corners poured through a hole somewhere in the defenses and tried to run riot. The temple shivered again, and its towers lit with the vibrating attention of alerted *lirai* and their Flights.

Incursions weren't daily occurrences—it took a lot of energy and trouble to break a temple's defenses—but they certainly happened, and this one would serve several of a traitor's purposes.

It wasn't until he reached the third tower, climbed all the way to the top, and found it echoingly empty that Erik realized perhaps, as sneaky as he was, someone else had the edge in age. And treachery.

Not to mention a deep understanding of just how a certain Elder Son's brain worked.

Sane Thoughts

SHE WAS GETTING tired of being hauled around like a sack of potatoes. Erik and Dakshi were respectful about it—as deferential as you could be, really—but being tossed over someone else's shoulder and carried into a dark hole wasn't really respectful *at all.*

It didn't help that the creatures swirling at knee height behind her new kidnapper were snap-snarling, their smokeglass teeth champing and splashes of yellow foam from their misshapen muzzles wriggling briefly against the floor. The *oneiros* was torn from her throat with bruising force and Liv heard Dakshi yelling her name before a squeal trilling up into falsetto was cut short with a wet, distant crunch.

The man carrying her rounded a corner, her head bouncing like a doll's. He was lean, tall, and made out of iron, his fingers biting cruelly. Her pajamas fluttered, and she forced herself to go limp, turning into deadweight. With any luck he'd think she'd passed out, but she was thinking furiously, trying to count the turns and straightaways of these strange, tangled tunnels.

What the hell just happened?

Erik had shut the big metal door and Robert had dropped a bar into brackets, effectively blocking it. The older man had led the way downstairs before stopping dead, his greying head held high like a prairie dog sensing danger, and Liv had only the confused idea that the jagged yawning hole in the side of what Dakshi called *the Flame-vault* wasn't usual—the other one hadn't had it—before the *things* boiled out through it and surrounded him.

She hadn't even had time to cry out, which was a mixed blessing because when she could get a breath in, her midsection cruelly thumped at every step by her kidnapper's muscle-stiff shoulder, it reeked something awful.

These rocky, rough-edged passages were roughly oval, their walls gleaming with slick phosphorescence and the bottoms swimming with strange sticky stuff looking for all the world like slug-slime. It made her suspect the tunnel hadn't been dug but somehow *chewed*, and the resultant flood of mental images was sickening enough to empty her stomach if she'd had anything in it.

And if she hadn't already been nauseated from the smell.

She timed her movement between steps, waiting for that critical moment when weight shifted from one foot to another, and surged aside, trying to roll out of his grasp.

It would plop her down among the tentacle-backed creatures, doglike except for the nest of rubbery arms sticking stiffly up from their spines, but she'd cross that bridge when she burned it, as Mika was always saying.

Pain roared through her. There was a snap like a lightbulb wrapped in a balloon breaking, and a furious, buzzing noise ran through her skull, a feedback whine fit to purée her brains.

It felt like he'd just taken her off the temple grounds. Without Erik or another Son around to help keep the voices out, a wave of unfiltered thought crashed through her shivering, unprotected psyche. Liv cried out, miserably, and the creatures running at her carrier's knees, somehow not tripping him, answered with a cacophony of howls, squeaks, barks, and rubbery noises.

His fingers bit afresh, and she stopped trying to struggle. Her eyes ran with tears, she was breathless from the muscled shoulder she was folded over, and to top it off, she was still in a tank top and loose silky pants.

She didn't even have her *socks* on. Dakshi had been carrying her; maybe this asshole had killed him.

God, I hope not. It was a good thought, a sane thought, *her* thought instead of the howling traffic-noise roaring past her inner ears. Maybe he'd just knocked the Younger Brother over.

Another thought, hard on the heels of the first. *Erik will come get me.*

But Erik was heading upstairs. He had some idea what was going on, and it didn't look like a pleasant one. No, Liv was, as usual, on her own to deal with this bullshit.

The man carrying her wore a harness like the Sons, oiled leather straps lying flat against a thermal shirt but no jacket. Her hands realized this before she did, and hanging upside down bouncing in the dark wasn't the best of conditions, but if she stretched, her fingertips could just brush the butt of a nasty-looking, matte-black firearm.

Screw the whole "no physical weapons" shit. She began wriggling with more purpose as the tunnels sloped down, crossings and turns taken with what felt like nightmarish randomness. If she could just get her hand on the gun, things might turn out all right.

At least I can save one bullet for last, she thought, quite naturally, and writhed with fresh strength as the feedback noise inside her skull mounted. It wasn't so different than ignoring a hangover while working a pole to pay for college tuition, the lights strobing and the music a migraine attack. She was doing pretty good, she actually had a chance of grabbing the weapon—

Until, that was, one of the tentacle-infested hounds leapt for her, jaws snapping shut with the heavy sound of a good clean break on a pool table and catching a hank of her hair instead of her dangling arm, which it was probably aiming for in the first place.

Liv screamed, her lungs burning, and the man carrying her snapped something definitely not in English, a short curt word that burned her ears worse than the massive cicada-scream of the city overhead.

Was the accumulated rock and dirt keeping the rest of that hideous mental noise from swallowing her? Liv devoutly hoped so, and choked back another scream when the dog-thing thumped back to earth, slavering over a mouthful of her hair. A few others trotted alongside, snaking their muzzles in as if trying to get a nip or two; the snarling turned into a brawl among the pack. They fell behind as her kidnapper put on a burst of speed. The indistinct silvery glow from the slug-slime coating had intensified, and the carrier's boots splashed in a good two inches of muck.

Oh, gross. Another sane thought, and she twisted again, trying to lunge for the gun so temptingly near. There was a small leather strap holding it in the holster, but if she yanked hard enough—

It was too late. The walls and ceiling leapt away as Liv's kidnapper veered into a large echoing space. A vast susurration filled a giant cavern, stalactites festooning its vault and stalagmites its floor. The stone spears looked wrong, twisted and tortured, and the temperature shot up—which would have been welcome if the heat wasn't sick, moist, and clinging, like the inside of an indifferently brushed mouth. The noises doubled over, lapped at the walls, broke into fragments, and splintered among what sounded like a crowd.

It was indeed a gathering, but Liv, hanging half upside-down, didn't think it was a concert or even a rally. Tiny impressions in her peripheral vision made her even more glad her stomach was empty, because the shapes pressing forward weren't anything close to human.

Or even earthly.

The monsters had her, and her carrier heaved her up a flight of slick stairs coated with a fly-buzzing crust. Clouds of the lethargic insects, their dark bluish carapaces glittering with pale diseased fungal light, rose and swirled at knee height. Her nerveless fingers brushed the gun again, and she made one last gasping, strenuous effort.

It failed, and he tossed her with a heave onto a rectangle of black, glossy, glassy stone, its edges vanishing under the same rancid crust as the stairs. The smell—rank copper, decay, vegetable rot—filled her nose, and she was lightheaded from the sudden stop as well as being turned right-side up, however temporarily. There were pale bipedal creatures at each corner of the altar stone, and they leered as they grabbed her wrists and ankles with sweating, tepid hands. It was like almost-cold pasta wrapping around her limbs, but the strength in each flabby appendage was apparent and every hand had six fingers instead of the usual, normal four-and-a-thumb.

Oh, God, Liv thought, pointlessly. There was no god here, unless it was the cackling, leering thing in her nightmares, cavorting behind a merciful, smudging screen of unreality in its heavy golden robes, its grey skin sagging and its cherry-red tongue flickering as it screeched and capered, each footstep grinding through the dust of centuries.

Her kidnapper rolled his shoulders, stretched his neck—first one side, then the other, of course it was hard work carrying a struggling woman—and leveled his chin, gazing remotely down on Liv as her back met the altar and the pale things hauled on arm and leg to keep her trapped. The echo of Erik made bile whip at the back of her throat; familiarity did not, in this case, breed comfort.

"Miss Stellack," Ignatius said, with his usual dry politeness. "I see your temperament has not improved."

No Dying Allowed Tonight

"IT WASN'T A bad plan," Robert husked.

"Stay still." Sara's hands plunged into the bleeding mess of his abdomen and she exhaled hard; Daniel, his hand on her shoulder, closed his eyes and swayed, the bandage around his head glaring. Looked like he'd been hit with flying debris, but he was grimly determined to stay upright.

Not only had the adult *shoggoth* chewed through bedrock with something prodding it from behind, but another of the foul things had taken wormshape and drilled up onto the temple grounds, a ragged icy hole belching the main body of the attack. The one down here had groped blindly for the Flame-mouth, and the sucking sounds as it roasted to death while attempting that nourishment—as well as the gusts of caustic black smoke and thin nauseating steam—weren't good for the *lirai.*

Still, none of the Sons made a move to drag them to safety. There were larger matters afoot. "Who was it?" Daniel murmured. "Tell us, Father."

Robert coughed. Erik, temporarily frozen with Liv's *oneiros* cupped in one nerveless hand, stared at the dead savaged mess of the slime-drenched *shoggoth*, not to mention the *nthlei* hounds with their crop of parasitic tendrils, had made of a fellow Son.

Casualties weren't heavy, but that was no comfort. Especially to this poor bastard, or the ones up top.

The gem in his fist sang unhappily, a low note of strain. Of course the traitor could break the chain; it was a Son's sorcery, after all.

Dakshi staggered, leaning heavily on another Younger Brother's shoulder—the one with the short braids and the slow sweet smile, sealed to Daniel. "The entire wall," he repeated. "Just . . . the entire *wall*."

Erik didn't blame the younger. Seeing a fucking *shoggoth* up close was enough to put a dent in anyone's evening. The rushing in his ears wouldn't go away, and the sick sensation under his ribcage wouldn't either.

He eyed the hole—nice and oval, big enough to heave a giant snout through—on one side of the vaulted room. The breach outside was a feint, but a good one. They'd been so busy responding to it nobody had thought about down here until Erik, hoping he was wrong, had battered down the door he'd insisted Robert and Dakshi bar behind him.

He'd delivered her right into the traitor's hands.

The body of the *shoggoth* slumped further in the throat of the Flamewell, and the golden light, burning away corruption, spilled through rents in its protoplasm. The last of the *nthlei* dogs squealed as it died upon a Father's blade, the lean man in a scorched jacket leaning hard to drive steel completely through, killing the tentacled parasite as well as the canine host.

Both were equally dangerous.

"It was . . . one of us," Robert said. His eyelids drooped, and that was a bad sign. As long as he was conscious the *lirai* could work wonders, but when a Son gave up, very little could be done. "Grey hair. Far gone. Corpse-eyes."

A Father, then. A fresh shiver passed through Erik from crown to sole, and he tucked the dreamstone absently in his jacket pocket while he edged soundlessly for the hole in the wall. The *shoggoth*'s sludge at the bottom, opalescent when there was something to eat through, was blackening in wisps as the Flame's influence spread, soft and inexorable. *Someone who guessed I'd bring her down here, knowing the usual places wouldn't be safe.*

Put that way, it was academic, wasn't it? Like one of Liv's lists, the shape of her thoughts lying under a neat vertical row, one item attached to the next, a daisy chain of coping mechanism.

The only question was whether or not he had help.

"Stay with me," Sara murmured. "I'm not going to lose anyone else tonight, Robert. *Stay* with me."

"My . . . lady . . ." Robert's eyelids fluttered. The *lirai* swore, softly, and her fingers tensed. She pulled the last sharp, glassy *nthlei* tooth out of the mess of guts and tossed it into a small pile of similar obsidian triangles. Then her bloody fingers descended again and the Flame responded, bubbling to the lip of its enclosure, eating fully through the *shoggoth*'s corpse, and sending tiny rainbow tendrils up through the smoke, valiantly trying to consume and purify that pollution as well.

The pulse—*lirai* calling upon the cleansing fire and the heartbeat of the planet itself responding—passed through every Son crowding into the vault, the ones in the halls, even those out sweeping the temple grounds and using sorcery to close the great black gash in snowy earth where the other *shoggoth* had breached.

Robert gave a barking, agonized cry. Gut wounds hurt like a sonofabitch, but at least with a *lirai* arriving so quickly the Father had a fighting chance.

Dakshi was debriefing at high speed as he swayed, a knot of Fathers around him. Grigori, though, fell into step next to Erik. This Father wasted no words. "Can you track her?"

Meaning, are you sealed?

"No," Erik said, heavily. *How long ago did he turn?* There was no time to think about it; the only *how long* that mattered was the one leading to his *lirai*. "And they stripped her dreamstone. But I can track *him*."

"Right into an ambush." Grigori glanced around the Flame-vault, and one eyebrow raised a fraction. "This was a good plan, though. It would have worked."

Except he knows me. Knows how I think. Well, it cut two ways. Of course, Ignatius only had to mention Control often enough to keep suspicion pacified, and there were ways of acquiring money—nothing was easier, especially with the Mad God's help.

Erik had fallen for it, of course. Just going along dumb and happy, too busy running patrols in an infested frontline city to really think, hoodwinked and misled for *years*.

Then they'd found a potential, and it had all unraveled. Had the traitor been waiting for it, or had he been hunting different prey each night while his Sons were busy patrolling? How often had Liv eluded his grasp, and had he sensed a prize temptingly out of reach? How fucking long had Ignatius expected it to go on?

It didn't matter. Not now. "We have no time." Erik had been hoping to get to the hole before anyone noticed he was moving; backup would follow as long as there was a chance a *lirai* was still alive. "He won't have struck without a plan, and a place to do his dirty work."

"Probably deep, and the trail laid with traps." Grigori didn't quite hesitate, but he did ask again, as if he couldn't quite credit what he was seeing. "Are you *sure* you can track him?"

"I can." Erik plunged into the ragged, chewed oval opening, its bottom fringing as the *shoggoth*'s slime-trail ate at rock. Cleaning and closing it up was going to be a bitch, too.

If she's alive, I'll do it myself. And I'll sing while I work. "I can," he repeated. The *oneiros* was a heavy weight in his pocket, crying out with tongueless distress. "And when I find him, the god himself won't recognize that traitor." *Not to mention whoever's helping him—maybe Jake, maybe really a control liaison gone bad, maybe all the Mad God's minions at once.*

I will kill them all.

"Careful, Elder." Grigori nodded at another knot of Fathers, who didn't waste time questioning, simply began working their way through the crowd for the breach. "The *lirai* is of primary importance. Not wounded pride."

She's probably already dead. He won't want to waste time. But Erik couldn't make himself say it.

Instead, Erik lengthened his stride, and as he hopped into the aperture, his boots sinking into decaying sludge, another pulse of strong, soft, undeniable power roaring through him.

"That's right," Sara said, crisply. "No dying allowed tonight, Father. Come on, fight. For me. *Fight* for me."

When a woman put it like that, there was nothing else a man could do.

Erik's stride lengthened, Grigori at his shoulder. The last thing he heard was Dakshi's raised voice.

"I don't care, dammit! My *lirai*'s down there, my Elder's going to go get her, and I am too."

"Younger brothers," Grigori muttered, but very quickly there was no more breath for commentary.

They were moving too fast.

Appealing to Vanity

"SSSTAY *SSSTILL*," ONE of the six-fingered strangling things said as Liv heaved from side to side. "Thisss won't hurt, preciousss little thing." Its voice, whistling and wrong, was forced through a throat not even remotely close to human, and the reptilian sibilants proved it, lingering under each word.

Ignatius reappeared, looming over her. His pupils held those strange blue smears, different than the star-prickling shine on Jake's or Erik's eyes when they got excited. The pair of misshapen glowing dots, a bright diseased blue, made the rest of the grey-haired man's face look like a mask.

Like someone—or some*thing*—else was peering through. The effect was nauseating, and helped along by the sagging under his skin, flesh twitching or caving with no rhyme or reason. His hair was wildly disarranged and his mouth worked slowly at a cargo of dry air, his lips shining with saliva.

And in his right hand, a short, vicious-looking, curved knife glinted, a mockery of the Sons' crystalline blades. Its flat was smeared with something viscous, a slick black gleam halfway between used motor oil and hot, soft tar.

Liv froze, staring at the knife, and Ignatius's lips stretched, rubbery and obscene. "That's right," he crooned. "Look at it, you little bitch. Not so high and mighty now, are we?"

She could barely think, could barely *breathe*. Not only was the city, however many miles of earth and rock above, screaming in several different flavors of crowd-noise, but the entire massive stone cathedral was full of half-seen shapes and skittering whispers, tall moon-pale blue-eyed things with multiple arms and others with twitching, waving tentacles, gaunt dark humanoid shapes with tumorous excrescences crawling on their torsos, small grey darting things with big black eyes, fungus-starred spiders crowding against the snap-slavering tentacle-hounds. Bigger things loomed in the back, exhaling a collective cold *wrongness* that threatened to turn her into jelly or send her howlingly, gratefully insane.

You're immune, beautiful, Erik would have said, but he wasn't here. Ignatius probably had some sort of plan to kill *him*, too, and the thought snapped Liv out of hypnosis as the Father lifted the knife and the things holding her down hummed, one of them snatching a hand back and shaking its fingers as if Liv's bare skin burned. It didn't matter—it clasped her wrist firmly again with both flabby appendages, but the quick, almost unseen motion gave her an idea.

"You're a Father," she said, desperately. A susurration went through the unholy crowd at her voice, just like a bunch of lions at the watering hole scenting a wounded zebra. "You're better than this. You *know* you're better than this, Ignatius."

"Do I?" His teeth, strong and white, snapped together with a startling click. "Do you have any idea what it's like, you little bitch? *Him* in your head all the time, no rest and no reward, nothing but endless suffering? And little bitches like you running around, wasting your lives on television and fast food—you and your kind are a plague, Miss Stellack, and *he* is the cure."

I think you've got that the wrong way around, mister. Still, the knife had paused, and she had a fighting chance. If she could keep him occupied, maybe she could think up a decent plan that didn't end up with her carved like a Christmas turkey on whatever the fuck kind of altar this was.

However immune she was to a mad god's mumblings, she was *not* immune to stabbing.

Wait. Wait just a minute. "He needs you," she said, desperately. "Needs your hands, because he can't do this himself. He's weak, Ignatius. You're stronger."

He was a male, so appealing to vanity might conceivably work. She surged against the things holding her limbs, and one of them hissed again as something invisible shifted. Her necklace was gone and she had no big brawny amplifiers around, but if the goddamn city overhead would just stop screaming maybe she could use that hidden force to—

The monsters holding her arms yanked cruelly, and she was so tired. Kidnapped, dragged on a two-accident road trip, forced to fight monsters, nightmares whenever she tried to sleep—oh, it was bullshit, all of it, complete and hopeless *bullshit*.

"Oh, I am strong," Ignatius said. "You're right about that. *He* has need of a strong right hand, and is ready to welcome me back into service."

Keep talking, keep him *talking*. "You're stronger than *him*," she repeated, words cracking as she struggled to think of something, anything to keep him engaged just a few more seconds. "How many years did you hold out? A long time, right?" *Just not long enough.*

"Enough," the thing gripping her left wrist hissed, as steam rose between its clutching fingers. A terrible, sickening smell of rotten, burning meat wafted up. "Do what you promisssed, *traitor*."

Ignatius's chin dipped toward his chest as the knife rose another inch, quivering in his hands. He was striped with monster blood, eyes glimmering with that faint blue foxfire between his lashes, and his teeth snapped again.

Like the thing inside his skin was hungry.

Tiny black plague-dots clustered his hand, massing and crawling up from the knife's hilt, invading his skin. Liv swallowed more bile and stopped struggling, her own eyes half-lidding, and the smell of burning intensified.

Instinctive, they all said. She hoped like hell it was true, but without amplifiers, she was close to a sitting duck.

"You're stronger." She tried to sound certain, and also tried to sound admiring. The deep drugging languor from whatever Sara had injected her with had worn almost completely away. "Way stronger than any two-bit demigod who can't even keep his own followers under control. Stronger than all the rest of the Sons, too. You're far more intelligent than them, right? Be smart, Ignatius. Be *smart*."

Metal clashed, and she realized they were holding her only until they could get the chains ready. Cold hard metal slithered around her right ankle, and Liv couldn't help it—she cried out, the invisible *something* the Flame had freed inside her rippling in concentric waves.

The six-fingered bastards screeched, their fingers bursting into pale flame refracting through the spectrum, blessedly normal colors alongside those there were no names for because human eyes usually couldn't see them. Liv scooted sideways, hips wiggling and shoulders scraping glassy stone.

Ignatius lunged, with a Son's eerie, flickering speed.

The knife blurred as he drove it down, crying out the old, foul word the Sons never said because it could draw *his* attention. The god's name scorched his lips, poured a gobbet of blood-blackened foam down his chest, and scraped through Liv's head like a hot edge through frozen butter, fracturing what it couldn't melt. A thin lick of fire along her hip, and her cry became a spiraling scream because it *hurt*, the blade's coating burning through flannel and into her skin.

She writhed away, another pulse blooming through her and knocking the six-fingered things back like dolls. The monsters began to screech, howl, slitherclack, yap, moan, stamp, and groan in return, their voices swallowing hers, a vast dark collective pressure dropping like a bell jar, pinning her in place.

Ignatius crawled onto the altar, his knees smacking shatter-hard and his face a mask of gibbering hatred. He had no pupils left, just that soulless, devouring flame dancing in his collapsing eyeballs, and that terrible *something else* looked out of his flesh for a moment as his right hand reared up, his entire body taut against the invisible force from Liv trying to batter him away. He looked like a man leaning into a heavy wind, and she concentrated desperately because as soon as her strength failed the knife would descend and she couldn't slide out of the way. Her body was held fast in sticky, terrifying invisible hands even if they hadn't managed to chain her, obscene invisible spiderfingers crawling over her like the tiny black things making a living glove down Ignatius's stick-thin but steel-strong arm.

He strained against the power, and Liv's hold slipped a fraction.

The knife dipped.

Critical Window

FOR ONE VERTIGINOUS moment he thought he was wrong, that they'd taken a bad turn back in the tangle of tunnels, that the strong, certain, but inarticulate imperative beating behind his breastbone and filling his arms and legs with wine-dark strength had failed him.

Failed them *all.*

Then he realized he'd outdistanced the others, even Grigori—the Father was quick and ruthless, dealing with scattered rearguards in the tunnels with maximum efficiency, freeing an Elder Brother to forge ahead. Consequently, Erik burst into a knot of scuttling hellspiders and was almost past the rancid bulk of yet another *shoggoth* when the pulse came, spilling through him from crown to sole, filling him with strength and lighting up the battlefield.

The cavern was a temple-deep, of course, the stalactites dripping from the ceiling corkscrewed by foul, ancient exhalations as underside creatures gathered to worship the god promising them food and power. That terrifying, insane intelligence spun and twisted the creatures of the dreaming land's healthier corners, whispering promises and rewarding their service when it did not consume them. Some, like the stranglers, had probably evolved in terrestrial spaces; others, like the *sarnaki* with no need to clothe themselves in flying snow now because no sunlight could reach them, were of a different order entirely.

But they were still largely loyal—or, barring that, still *hungry.* The slow torture and eventual death of a *lirai* would strengthen them immeasurably, and give them a feast long spoken of afterward in hellish, chattering tongues no human mouth could pronounce.

None of it mattered, because he could see the stairs at the far end, a dais rising at sickening, nonhuman angles, its fly-covered steps crusted with blood both old and fresh. The shadowbeasts and nightmare creatures preferred *lirai*, of course—but potentials would do handily, and the lingering death of normal humans would give them a short-term boost as well.

This place had seen many such banquets.

The altar reared, a stone like obsidian warping and shimmering as the sacrifice fought. A sticklike figure stood silhouetted against that glow with one arm raised, and the creatures around Erik began to notice his presence, the chance of sating murderous hunger blunting their response.

A critical window, Ignatius would call it, and Erik understood the entire charade now, didn't he? Elder and Younger Brothers out running sweeps at night, leaving a Father to his own devices. When had Ignatius murdered his first potential? Had it been an accident? Had the god been whispering, prodding, poking, enticing?

Oh, yes, Erik knew. Because he'd heard the same promises and blandishments from that terrible lipless mouth, and still did. Thrumming in his chest, creeping through his subconscious, claw-tipped nails scraping lightly at the folds of his mortal brain.

Let it happen, the god whispered. *She deserves it, the little bitch. Look at what she's done—look at how she's treated you.*

It would have been easy for Ignatius to give him and Jake the right sectors of Islington to clear, safely away from noticing a potential. Most of them moved a lot, anyway, minor precognition keeping them one bare step ahead of the monsters.

And if Erik and Jake returned early to find empty halls, Ignatius could always say he'd sensed something outside the temple and pursued it. After all, they were a small frontline outpost, forgotten in a corner. Which meant he'd probably murdered his first potential well over a decade ago, before the war heated up and the frontier posts were ordered to fall back. Maybe there was even a treacherous control liaison somewhere, but at the moment that wasn't Erik's problem.

This was, now that he saw the whole pattern, very much what Ignatius would do. Waiting with unholy dry patience, year upon year, biding his time and clearing potentials—or, even worse, simply tagging them for the shadowbeasts, standing back, and letting the inevitable happen.

And Erik and Jake had suspected *nothing*, even though Sons were to watch a Father carefully—and he was supposed to return the favor.

Had Ignatius thought he might actually be able to bring Liv in and escape examination, somehow redeem himself? Erik hoped that was the case and that the entire charade back in Islington hadn't just been the spider humming softly to himself as he readied the web, knowing a stronger potential was a better, more pleasing meal to the god.

A full *lirai* was best of all, of course, a ticket straight to the Mad God's forgiveness and high esteem.

Erik drove forward, slipping between nightmarish unclean, clearing a surprise-clicking patch of *jana*-spiders with a single leap, extending again to spring between two musk-rotten goatmen already baying with excitement, a group of *dagoi* suddenly realizing danger had found them and raising a thin warning scream.

His *lirai*'s pulse came again, but it was fading, as if she were wounded. The god gibbered inside Erik's head, trying to slow him down, distract him.

No, fuck no, just let me get there, just let me get to her—

Both knives out, rising like a hawk and a deep coughing sound of effort escaping his chapped lips, Erik *soared* . . .

. . . and a *sarnaki*, with more presence of mind than its fellows, hit him from behind with a shattering crunch.

My Favorite Son

THE WORLD NARROWED to a knife hanging above her, its claw-sharp point swelling with a pregnant drop of tarry black. The slice on Liv's hip burned, poison eating at silk and flesh both, and the metal cuff clasping one of her ankles hurt too, a deep drilling pain.

They'd managed to get at least one chain on her, somehow. But she had Ignatius pinned too, and a lifetime of stubbornness rose inside her, holding the invisible force strong and secure. He strained against it, the thing in his flesh shoving at her control with clumsy, flaccid fingers that sent hot spears of loathing through her.

The other monsters were muttering, a rising growl, and if they all decided to walk up the steps and help themselves buffet-style she was looking at a very short, very messy end to her entire existence.

She didn't think these guys only ate the meat, so to speak. Especially since she could *see*, in some strange way, how the god had cored Ignatius like a fruit, pouring into the empty places and yanking at muscle-strings to move a puppet. Seen with that strange inner vision, Liv was a smear of rainbow flame guttering but not dead yet, the monsters a swirling hungry darkness with occasional sickening flashes showing under a glare of punky low foxfire—

Corpselight, that's what they call it, and that's why.

—and Ignatius was a creaking, swelling tumor of vile, violent yellow, a single crimson eye at its crest as he strained against the ropes of light holding him prisoner.

Was that what the ancient Dreamers had done? Chained a god in some forgotten hole or just banished him from the physical world? Either way, no wonder the Mad God was pissed.

How much longer can I keep this up? Liv's hold slipped another fraction; the knife jerked, driving downward. Once it plunged into her chest, she suspected she'd lose the ability to hold him off—but she didn't think she'd die right away.

No, she was miserably certain it might take a very long time, and she'd scream through the whole process. The thing, this mad god, would *eat* her screams.

Several things happened at once.

There was a high metallic ringing and a crunching noise like a stack of potato chips smashed all at once and the sound run through huge speakers until it could break bones. The monsters, their famished cries halted for a brief moment, hung in a bubble hollowed out under a human city, the tangled passages around it meant to confuse any pursuit or penetration but well known to all things creeping in darkness, hiding from the sun's glare. The knife quivered again and sank a handspan; Liv's throat burned because she was making a low guttural noise of effort as well, her gaze locked with Ignatius's.

Or maybe it wasn't Ignatius anymore. The thing inside him swelled, swallowing any remaining vestiges of humanity, and it leered at her, its lips moving rubbery as more foam dripped.

I killed your mother, little bitch. I ate her right . . . the fuck . . . UP.

The attack came out of nowhere, those filthy claws burrowing into her own head despite the cringing pain of touching something inimical.

Immune didn't mean *invulnerable*, after all.

It leered, it gibbered, it whispered, it keened, and Liv Stellack almost, *almost* lost her hold, her mental fingers growing clumsy. Kidnapped, dragged around like a sack of produce, sedated, dumped in a hole, terrorized beyond belief, she stared at the thing that wanted so badly to kill her, and a strange peace folded through her bones.

You think you're so bad. It was laughable, how scared everyone was of this . . . this *thing*. It was strong, yes.

But only if you gave it an opening. Temperament, genetics, or simply blind chance—not to mention the deep soft warmth of the earth's very heartbeat—meant Liv didn't have one.

I'm not dead yet, she realized, and the thing howled. Fresh strength poured into her, and there was a popping clatter she realized was gunfire. There was another familiar sound, someone yelling her name over and over as the monsters realized they were not about to have a leisurely picnic.

A dripping point protruded from Ignatius's chest. It was from a razor-edged, crystalline blade, and its tip gleamed starlike as thick, blackened blood welled around it.

The Father's head turned, an eerie, lizardlike movement. "*My Son*," he crooned. "*You were my favorite. Help me now.* He *will forgive us.*"

Erik's bloody face rose over his Father's shoulder, almost close enough to kiss. His eyes blazed, the blue sparkle-points in his pupils gathering strength. Tiny cracks and veins of black began at the corners of Ignatius's eyelids, spreading in horrifying fast-forward.

"There is," Erik said, softly, "no forgiveness for us, *Father*." He shoved the knife deeper, and Ignatius's body stiffened. The older man's arm jerked, still trying to drive the black blade down through stiff, resisting air.

Liv willed Erik to look at her, willed the invisible force inside her to fill him, to close the shredded flesh on the left half of his face, the other injuries she could *feel* burning in him. There was something sharp stuck in his back, and for a dizzying moment, she was inside her own familiar body and somehow inside his at the same time, marveling at the pain he apparently didn't notice as it crashed through nerve endings, cut and twisted muscles in his back twitching as a blue-eyed nightmare monster drove a slender spear more firmly into it. The thing stabbing him howled as warm invisible power rayed out from a *lirai*, and the splitting of her focus gave Ignatius the opening he needed.

The curved, tarry-bladed knife flashed down.

A Gift

IT WAS A GIFT, given with open hands as the *lirai* were shown in ancient codices and mosaics. A Dreamer's force poured into him like hot cocoa into a thick china mug, warmth flooding his skin and running through the marrow-canals of his bones. Liv lay, small and glowing and terribly vulnerable, her dark eyes alive with far more than a mere echo of the Flame. She stared at him; he longed to meet her gaze, longed to glance down and mouth *you're all right*, longed to let her know that her touch was welcome, filling all the broken and battered places in his body with light and the scorched wasteland of his mind with deep calm.

But he had the bastard pinned, and even the *sarnaki* digging its little toy into his back could wait. He stabbed once more, driving a second crystalline blade deep. It writhed, the thing inside his teacher, his friend, his Father attempting to worm-twist away. He denied it—the rest of the beasts might descend upon him and tear him to pieces, but dispensing with this threat would give the *lirai* time to slide free of the altar into a jumble of bones and husks rotting on the other side where the scavengers would return between sacrifices to crunch and lick.

And maybe, just possibly, his death would give her the slimmest chance of getting away.

He felt her attention shift for a tiny gap in time, a slice of a mortal second.

It was enough. The thing that had been Ignatius howled with glee and brought the knife down.

So the elder Son did the only thing he could. He drove himself backward onto the *sarnaki*'s spear, dragging Ignatius with him, and the black-bladed knife sank into the glassy stone altar's surface as the spear-point shivered, sank deeper, and found Erik's heart.

Never Missed

IGNATIUS'S DAGGER sank hilt-deep into glassy stone, cracks cringe-radiating in every direction, and Liv surged upright—or tried to; her arms wouldn't work quite right and the cuff on her left ankle hurt atrociously, something smeared on the cold blackened metal eating through her skin.

The Ignatius-thing, dragged backward, clawed for her with empty hands. Liv stared at it, and that warm, soft, invisible force filled her again. The metal on her ankle chimed, shattering and sending jagged slivers flying; Ignatius howled, still scrabbling.

But she had him now, and the force roared through her, amplified by dark, disciplined whirlpools at the far end of the giant cavern. Monster-noises bounced against the ceiling, shivered the stalactites into free air, and smacked the stone walls. Mental noise from the city overhead turned jagged and discordant as nightmares filtered into dreaming heads, slipped for a brief moment over the border into reality—and faded, snow blowing through their tattered reflections.

Ignatius let out a single wrecked, massive sound, more a train's siren than a scream. The thing inside him, stung, retreated like oil slipping down a drain, a choked gurgle at the end. Black cracks veined through the Father, a statue made of ancient discolored porcelain, and his boots drummed as he was held, spitted, upon a pair of knives. The hair-thin spreading crevices became streamlets, the streamlets rivers, and a rag of rotting bone and zombie-putrid flesh still kept trying to force itself onto the altar and toward Liv.

The noise, both physical and mental, was overwhelming. Gunfire boomed, and *that* meant the Sons had found her. Liv jerked her knees up, ignoring a flare of red pain from her abused ankle, and as the dead, rotting thing slid from Erik's knives her heart gave a giant singing leap. She didn't care she was in the middle of a pitched battle, didn't care that her ankle was bleeding and her hair full of crap from the altar's crusted surface, didn't care that she was trembling-weak as a kitten and her neck ached after the jolting, jouncing ride down here.

All she cared about was Erik, who stood with his chin slightly tucked as he gazed down at a man he probably loved turning into a twitching mass of rot. Erik's face was healing in fast-forward, but just as she was about to slide off the altar and fling herself at him, he swayed.

The thing behind him had blue eyes, a wide wound of a mouth locked in a rictus, and it held a long, frail-looking spear with glittering red gems dripping from its gold-chained haft.

It had stabbed him right through the heart, and as Erik folded down, going to one knee with a jolt Liv felt in her own body, it leered and lifted the dripping spear, staring right at her.

No. Everything inside Liv stilled, came to a single hot point.

No, you son of a bitch. You can't have him.

The thing pitched forward, and the next item on its agenda was clearly to stab her. She sensed its weight shift, dropping slightly before extension of a lunge, and the point of brilliance inside her expanded, sensing amplifiers close—but not close enough.

This one was hers.

You cannot have him, she thought again, and flung both hands out like playing dodgeball back in high school. In those days they played with basketballs, and the teachers turned a blind eye as long as the kids didn't smack each other in the face *too* often.

Teenage Liv thought they were definitely trying to teach cruelty; adult Liv, if she thought about it at all, pretty much assumed it was to prepare kids for an uncaring world. Now, Liv realized that in all those years, she'd never missed.

This time she didn't either. The thing with its spear went flying, trailing a long scarf of thin black blood hanging in the air as it was torn into pieces like it had swallowed one hell of a lit firecracker.

Liv tumbled off the altar and landed in a clattering, fly-buzzing pile of bones at its foot. She retched—the rotting smell was even worse, if that were possible—and made it to hands and knees, then to her knees proper just in time to catch Erik as he collapsed.

Or she tried to. He crashed into her, not even trying to soften the fall, and that was a very bad sign. A bubble of bright red burst on his lips, and they both rolled down the stairs in a confusion of arms, legs, and whatever rancid dried guck was smear-crusted on the edges biting Liv's bruised arms and shaking legs.

It didn't matter. When they reached the bottom she moved frantically, untangling herself as death and combat bayed all around them, and got her arm under his shoulders.

"Don't leave," she whispered. "*Don't* leave, Erik. Hold on. Hold on."

She wasn't even aware of speaking, and the explosion of force had drained her. The power was coming back, but slowly. The bottom of her barrel was well and truly scraped, as Mika would say.

Still, Erik curled into her with a heavy, weary sigh. Liv cradled the muscle-heavy, deadweight bulk of the only sanity she had left in the cluttered rot and refuse, and kept willing, hoping, pleading for him to *hold on, hold on, hold on.*

Really Something Else

IT HURT, ALL OVER. Even the slight movement of breathing hurt despite the softness wrapped around him, the familiar warm pulsing at regular intervals stealing into the black void he had become, sinking a little deeper each time despite his fretful turning away.

I've done enough. Let me rest.

Unfortunately, life seemed to have some sort of hold on his corpse. And that meant the Mad God did, too. Even in the floating darkness, the whispers rose. They were only temporarily muted by defeat and a Son's physical weakness—tiny wisps of thought, nothing more.

He'd often wondered if the god rested between neurons, waiting to hijack the spark of a thought. Or if *he* was somewhere in electricity itself, riding the most intimate of tiny lightnings. Of course, Father said . . .

Ignatius. Soupy, half-conscious alarm flowered next to the aching in his chest. He was aware of movement, cloth shifting.

"Easy," someone said. "*Easy*, brother. All's well, battle's over."

Except it never was. Not while you were breathing, and the sough of air into his abused lungs hurt too. It was cold, and knifed tender tissues.

"He's breathing on his own now, at least." Another voice, male as the first but essentially different somehow, the Flame's warmth threading through it. The pulse of the earth didn't make Dreamers anew, it simply uncovered what was there from the beginning, burnishing it to beauty. "A determined fellow."

That was why the uncontrolled Flame turned Sons into barbecued hulks past a *lirai*'s miraculous abilities to heal, even with the obedience of a Son's flesh to the Dreamers. The glow just showed what lay under a mask of humanity.

The fury, the twisting, and the corruption.

"I don't think lack of determination has ever been this man's problem." Dry and cool, a Father's voice. "We'll wait outside. Call if he starts to thrash."

No. Ignatius . . . something about him . . .

Erik was all but useless. He'd fucked up every way possible, from the very *beginning*, and now they wouldn't let him close enough to—

The reminder hit him squarely, flooding his aching muscles with urgency. He thrashed, his left fist hitting something solid before he was trapped, intangible bindings folding into place.

"Erik." Calm, sure, and certain, a *lirai*'s command in a familiar, sweet, husky voice. "Calm down."

It was *her*.

Consciousness flooded him as he went paradoxically limp. Was it relief or blood, the copper against his tongue? Maybe both, and it would hurt twice as much when they told him he was being posted elsewhere. A Father would shake his head, a younger would simply look solemn—*don't make a scene, brother. Spare her that, at least.*

"Liv . . ." A cracked, choked moan.

"I'm here." The healing pulse came again, startling in its intensity, burrowing past layers of grey shock and into closing, regenerating flesh. It settled on his back, high up on the left, sinking through the angry red mark that would show where he'd been stabbed yet again, the tip of the spear sliding between ribs to pierce pericardium. "Lie still, will you? The poison's out, you're healing, but the scar'll tear if you keep moving."

He froze, his lungs burning, and there was a soft sound of almost-annoyance. Sweet and low, for all its irritation, it still pulled every string in his body taut.

Especially the aching ones.

"I didn't say to stop breathing, Erik."

Air filtered back into his chest. It wasn't cold anymore, and he didn't hurt as much. A thin crescent of glare appeared before him, and he was trying to figure out how the god was attacking now when he realized it was his eyelids rising, slowly and painfully.

Liv's face swam into view. She was still too thin, and shadows of yellow-green bruising were retreating rapidly on her cheek, up into her hair—pulled back and braided tightly, for once, instead of a wild mess.

He found he liked it both ways.

Erik further found out he wasn't in the dormitory. Instead, he was in a *lirai*'s navy-curtained bed, and shame boiled through him when he realized as much. Still, Liv leaned anxiously over him, her soft mouth turned down, and he lost his breath for an entirely different set of reasons.

The *oneiros* glittered against her blue scoop-neck sweater. Another Son must have knitted the chain together for her; Erik's heart gave a funny twitch as if the spear-tip had found it again.

"It's all right," she said, finally. The room was utterly silent except for the soundless static of Sons standing guard beyond the baffle. "Daniel says the hole downstairs is patched up and they won't be able to get through again. Ignatius is dead; they're still trying to figure out if he did have a Control or was working alone. Oh, and they're looking for Jake. They *also* say you're going to wake up worried, so I should reassure you." She paused, and looked thoughtful. "Not sure how reassuring I am, really, but there it is."

He found his voice, cracked and disused. "Safe," he rasped. "You? Safe?"

"I'm fine, you big lug." There was a suspicious glitter to her dark eyes, and she scrubbed at them with her fingertips, irritably. "Dakshi's up and moving around. Robert's still in bed, but I visit him every afternoon. He keeps apologizing; I keep telling him not to. The Fathers are really upset it was one of them."

She said it like she didn't consider the most immense betrayal possible a big deal. A *lirai*'s forgiveness, extended without thought.

"Debt's deep," Erik said. "Gets deeper all the time."

"You're going to have to explain that." She sank back onto a chair pulled close to the bed. "They think I'm crazy sleeping on the couch. Well, except Sara, she says she'd do the same thing. I'm running sweeps with Daniel—*don't* try to get up, you'll break all that repair work open, okay? Things are awful quiet now."

It just means he's planning something else.

"You've got that look," she continued.

"What look?" The more he used his voice, the easier it got. Pretty soon he'd be able to sing again, if they didn't mind glass breaking every time he tried.

But if it expressed his gratitude, he'd give it a try.

"Like you're getting ready to do something dumb and dangerous again." She outright glared at him, hovering anxiously at the bedside. "Give it a rest, will you? I want you to recover."

Then I will, beautiful. "Okay." It was that simple. Sealed or not, he was going to do his best for her. It wouldn't make up for anything, wouldn't put a dent in the debt.

But he was used to losing battles.

"Okay?" She eyed him nervously, sinking down on a handy chair dragged from the sitting room, resting her elbows on her knees with her head cocked and her braid dangling over her shoulder. Icy winter sunshine filled the window. "Is that all you have to say?"

What else is there? "I'm sorry," he managed, dismally aware it didn't matter. "I should have thought Ignatius . . . I should have caught on. I didn't."

"Oh, for the love of . . ." She shook her head, her braid bobbing. Obviously dissatisfied with his thickheadedness, next she'd order them to get the useless lump out of her bed and take him somewhere to recover.

Instead, she fixed him with yet another dark-eyed glare that was immensely cheering to see. "You are really something else, Erik."

"Is that a compliment?" He was feeling more alert by the moment, and in a little while, he'd be able to stand. When that was accomplished, he could fight again.

Still, he was hoping for a few minutes before the next crisis. Both of them needed some rest.

"Don't sound so surprised." Liv sighed, and the tension drained from her slender shoulders. She stretched—hovering over a sickbed was probably hard on the back—and rubbed her hands together. "We're going to have to have a talk about this whole sealing thing, you know." A faint edge of pink crept into her cheeks, and she was suddenly very interested in the blanket over his chest.

Another pulse went through him; a *lirai*'s gift, given again. It worked in a little deeper, and the cold sweat on him was realizing just how close the *sarnaki* had been to ridding the world of one more Son of Ymre—and one precious, irreplaceable *lirai*. "Uh," Erik said, logic and coherence both fleeing him. "Um . . ."

"Unless you don't want to, in which case I'll just be embarrassed but that never killed anyone, right?" Was she actually *nervous*? His *lirai* smoothed the edge of the indigo coverlet, velvet rasping sensitive fingertips. "I mean, I figure it's best if it's you, and besides, being held down on an altar and almost stabbed makes a girl think, you know? It's probably trauma bonding but there's a lot of that in this place. Sara really needs a therapist, and my certification's rusty but . . ." She snuck a tiny glance at his face, and it struck him that, ridiculous as it might sound, his impossible, stubborn, beautiful *lirai* somehow thought he'd turn her down.

"Um," he repeated. "It's, ah, up to you. But I . . . I like you, Liv." What did civilian males say in this situation? Of course, a normal wouldn't find himself in a *lirai*'s bed after being stabbed with a *sarnaki* spear. "I mean, I like *you*. As . . . as a person."

The flush mounted in her cheeks, and Erik was kicking himself for saying the absolute worst, most banal thing possible. She cleared her throat, softly.

"It's not just that I'm, you know, a *lirai*? Because if it's just that—"

"Is that what you think?" Erik sagged into the bed's comfort. He wouldn't mind getting out of it eventually; the damn thing was too soft. But at the moment, it cradled him nicely. "*I* think I was a goner the moment I knocked you out of your shoes, Liv."

She searched his expression for a long, excruciating while, while the hot blush in her cheeks faded. Finally, she nodded, and the *oneiros* flashed, a signal fire atop a faraway hill. The silence between them turned almost companionable, and for the first time he caught a glimpse of what she might look like when she truly relaxed.

It almost robbed him of breath yet again. Erik stared, memorizing her face, the slim column of her throat, the tender hollow at her temple and vulnerable notch between her collarbones, the curve of her wrist when she brushed at her forehead even though her hair was strictly confined.

"Well. Glad that's sorted out. Oh, I have a question." His *lirai* straightened, her chin lifting, and her smile held all the forgiveness in the world. "Can you get them not to haul me around like a sack of groceries? My ankle's a lot better, but the youngers keep trying to carry me everywhere. That's partly why I want you to get better. I might be able to argue you into letting me *walk*."

"You can try." Erik's mouth answered independently of the rest of him, but it didn't look like she minded. In fact, she grinned at him, dark eyes sparkling, and the pounding of his almost-cracked heart was both terrifying and achingly sweet. "I'm surprised you don't have a list of reasons why I should, and another list of demands."

She didn't glare or snap at him. Instead, his *lirai* looked relieved. "*There* you are," she said, softly. "Good to have you back. Also, can I please go for a bit without being kidnapped again? Like, say, a whole week?"

He wondered how long he'd been out, decided that was a question better left for later along with all the others he didn't have the energy for at the moment. "Depends on how much you like getting kidnapped, beautiful."

Then he was afraid he'd said the wrong thing, because she sobered again, watching him carefully. "I don't mind if it's you." Quiet and matter-of-fact. "How funny is that?"

"Hilarious." *I don't deserve to be anywhere near you, Liv. But I'm glad you disagree.* His eyelids decided he'd had enough and began to creep downward. "Give me a couple hours to get back up to speed." The god's venomous whisper retreated, probably because Erik's *lirai* sent another tidal flood of power, this one reaching all the way down to his skeleton and surging outward again.

Reshaping him, he hoped. Making him somehow, in some way, a little better. A little less damned.

"Take it slow." The chair creaked slightly as she moved, and her fingers threaded warm and soft between his bigger, callus-rasping ones. "We've got all the time in the world."

If it was a lie, it was a kind one. The whispers retreated, certainty taking their place as Erik's eyes closed.

He was probably already planning, and his hatred for all Dreamers would be sharpened afresh. The god would return, creeping through cracks, sending his minions, corrupting and claiming.

When it did, Erik would be ready.

"After all," she continued, "we still have to go on a real date. Getting tied up and stabbed doesn't count."

"Glad to hear it." His eyes simply wouldn't stay open any longer, so he closed them and settled a little deeper in the mattress, willing his body to heal. "How about dinner instead?"

Finis

About the Author

LILITH SAINTCROW lives in Vancouver, Washington, with her children, dogs, cat, a library for wayward texts, and assorted other strays.

Made in the USA
Las Vegas, NV
21 February 2022

44327301R00166